A SOCIALITE'S CHRISTMAS WISH

BY
LUCY CLARK

REDEEMING DR RICCARDI

BY
LEAH MARTYN

MILLS
BOON

D1143018

Lucy Clark is actually a husband-and-wife writing team. They enjoy taking holidays with their children, during which they discuss and develop new ideas for their books using the fantastic Australian scenery. They use their daily walks to talk over characterisation and fine details of the wonderful stories they produce, and are avid movie buffs. They live on the edge of a popular wine district in South Australia with their two children, and enjoy spending family time together at weekends.

Leah Martyn loves to create warm, believable characters for the Medical Romance™ series. She is grounded firmly in rural Australia, and the special qualities of the bush are reflected in her stories. For plots and possibilities, she bounces ideas off her husband on their early-morning walks. Browsing in bookshops and buying an armful of new releases is high on her list of enjoyable things to do.

A SOCIALITE'S CHRISTMAS WISH

BY
LUCY CLARK

To Brandon & Clover—
congratulations on finding your happily-ever-after!
Ps 93:4

All the characters in this book have no existence outside the imagination of the author, and have no relation whatsoever to anyone bearing the same name or names. They are not even distantly inspired by any individual known or unknown to the author, and all the incidents are pure invention.

First published in Great Britain 2012
by Mills & Boon, an imprint of Harlequin (UK) Limited.
Harlequin (UK) Limited, Eton House, 18-24 Paradise Road,
Richmond, Surrey TW9 1SR

© Anne Clark & Peter Clark 2012

ISBN: 978 0 263 89200 0

Harlequin (UK) policy is to use papers that are natural, renewable and recyclable products and made from wood grown in sustainable forests. The logging and manufacturing process conform to the legal environmental regulations of the country of origin.

Printed and bound in Spain
by Blackprint CPI, Barcelona

Dear Reader

We always love revisiting towns we've created and enjoying a cuppa and a chat with secondary characters who have appeared in other books. Lewisville, a fictitious town set somewhere near Broken Hill in New South Wales, was no exception.

In this story we get to meet Brandon and, while he's not originally one of the main Goldmark brothers, he is every inch a Goldmark. Having fled his home town of Lewisville in order to recover from a broken heart, he returns home in time for his sister's wedding. And into town comes Clover Farraday, a woman who makes Brandon rethink and re-evaluate everything he's always known.

Clover finds that, like so many other women before her, she is not at all immune to the charms of those dashingly handsome Goldmark men, with their tall stature, their dark good looks and hypnotic blue eyes. Never has she met anyone like Brandon, and before she knows which way is up she realises she's fallen madly in love with him.

It was great fun to spend time with Viola, who is always baking and helping out her friends and neighbours, and also to see Geoffrey and his wife, Joan. We love all the characters—from Ned and May Finnegan to Marissa Mandocicelli. It's secondary characters like these that help bring to life the town of Lewisville, providing a colourful and romantic backdrop for Brandon and Clover to find their own happily-ever-after.

We hope you enjoy their story.

Warmest regards

Lucy

Recent titles by Lucy Clark:

FALLING FOR DR FEARLESS
DIAMOND RING FOR THE ICE QUEEN
THE BOSS SHE CAN'T RESIST
WEDDING ON THE BABY WARD
SPECIAL CARE BABY MIRACLE
DOCTOR DIAMOND IN THE ROUGH

**These books are also available in eBook format
from www.millsandboon.co.uk**

CHAPTER ONE

CLOVER FARRADAY turned up the volume on the car stereo and sang along with the song at the top of her lungs. Laughing, she couldn't remember when she'd ever felt this free. Being born into a privileged family, with a business mogul for a father, who was a constant source of media attention, and a caring, down-to-earth mother who had passed away when she'd been twelve years old, had left Clover feeling as though her life straddled two worlds. One was her father's world, where she spent so much energy and devotion trying to get his attention. The other was the world of medicine, which she adored.

Now, though, Clover felt free, vibrant, not bound by the rules of society or the gruelling expectations heaped upon her by both her father and her now ex-boyfriend, Xavier. Looking back on the past, she realised both he and her father had expected far more from her than she had been willing to give. Although she'd initially agreed to date Xavier, the one man who had been 'approved' by her father, Xavier's recent proposal for them to 'merge' both in business and in their personal lives had been too much.

'It's a sensible arrangement, Clover,' he'd said only

last week. 'My company is merging with your father's. The deal is pure genius.'

'Deal?' Clover had looked at him as though he'd lost his marbles. She'd sighed. 'Look, Xavier, I don't have time to even think about any sort of…merger right now. I have a lot going on at work. I've just finished at the Blue Mountains maternity care centre and soon I'll be heading to Tathra for at least four months to help set up and train the staff of their new maternity care cent—'

He hadn't listened, interrupting her only to make his point, one she hadn't been expected to contest.

'Once we're married, you won't be working, Clover. Your time will be filled with the social duties my late mother used to perform. It's expected that my wife will take over where she left off. Just think, you'll be patron of several very important and influential causes.'

'I'm not giving up my job, Xavier. Not for you. Not for my father. I don't care what's expected of me.'

Xavier had looked at her as though she were a recalcitrant child, then, taking a polishing cloth from his trouser pocket, had removed his glasses and given them a thorough cleaning, as though wanting to wipe away her words. 'I fear you're not yet ready to discuss this properly. Very well. We shall continue ever onwards and upwards for now.'

When he'd replaced his glasses, he'd smiled at her in that indulgent way she'd become used to, and asked if she'd wanted to order dessert.

Annoyed with his placatory and belittling attitude, Clover had declined the offer of dessert, excused herself from the table and made her own way back to the hotel where they had been staying in Port Douglas, trying to hold on to her temper.

After storming around her room for ten minutes,

feeling completely stifled by the two men intent on controlling her life, she decided enough was enough. Packing her bag, she arranged her check-out and the hire of a car. She left a note for Xavier with the concierge, telling him she was taking some time out and would see him when she eventually returned to Sydney. There was no way she was going to let him ruin the rest of her much-needed two-week vacation with added pressure about what was essentially a marriage of convenience.

Instead, Clover found herself taking an impromptu driving holiday from Queensland's north coast, detouring through some Outback towns and then eventually making her way leisurely back to Sydney.

Everywhere she'd visited, complete strangers had welcomed her warmly and she'd enjoyed her time, making new friends and seeing the sights of the Outback, especially the amazing Uluru. As she continued to drive down the long, flat roads, the sinking of the sun making it cool enough for her to wind down a window, the music blaring out and fading away behind her, she couldn't remember feeling such a defining sense of freedom since before her mother had passed away.

Oh, how her mother would have loved this. To be free from oppression, free from rules and regulations, free from the expectations their upper-class living had imposed upon them.

A few minutes later, though, Clover was turning the music down and peering out the front windscreen, slowing the vehicle down.

'A road block? Out here?' She continued to decrease speed, astonished to note that the entire main road appeared to be blocked off. 'Where else am I supposed to go?' she asked, looking around the flat, barren landscape. She checked the car's GPS and realised that not too far ahead was a small town called Lewisville. She'd planned on stopping there for something to eat and to stretch her legs until the sun had set. She'd learned early on that driving just before dawn or dusk increased her chances of hitting wildlife that might be around the road—namely kangaroos.

As she neared the road-block signs, the houses of Lewisville in the background, she noticed a small tent pitched on the side of the road. As she brought the car to a complete halt, a man, dressed in denim jeans that had long ago forgotten any shape but his own and an old faded green T-shirt, which seemed almost sculpted to his firm torso, came out of the tent and walked towards her, a broad smile on his face.

'G'day!'

'Er...hello.' He was wearing a wide-brimmed hat, the kind she'd seen in television commercials when strong, strapping men were riding around on horses, cracking stock whips in the air above their heads. His sunglasses were the mirrored kind and as he bent down to talk to her through her open car window, she could see her own reflection in them.

Good heavens! Was that what her hair looked like? Self-consciously, Clover quickly brushed the wisps of dark brown hair which had escaped her ponytail back behind her ears.

'Sorry about the road being closed. Do you need to get through urgently?'

His tone was rich, deep and for some strange reason was washing over her like a welcome, warm blanket on a freezing cold day.

'Er...' She closed her mouth and tried to get her thoughts together but all she could focus on was the well-muscled arm he was leaning on her car. When he lifted his sunglasses from his face she almost swallowed her tongue as deep blue eyes seemed to pierce her soul. Clover gulped, never before having been so instantly or incredibly attracted to a stranger in such a way.

She told herself he was just some Outback road-worker, who more than likely had women chasing after him, or, better yet, was comfortably married with a gaggle of children. As a child, she'd been taught how to speak to strangers, how to put them at ease, a skill she often called upon during birth deliveries when she was trying to get her patients to breathe and relax while she assisted their precious babies into the world.

He was still waiting for an answer and as her vocal cords didn't appear to be working, she did the only thing she could think of and shook her head.

'Excellent,' he announced, his smile beaming. 'Besides, it's probably better you're off the roads for a while, what with the roos and everything.'

'Yes,' she managed, quite proud of herself for producing a one-syllable word.

'So you'll be staying for the celebrations, then. Beauty, mate. I'm sure we'll be able to find a bed for you for the night but when there's a wedding in town, especially as tonight it's my little sister's wedding, there usually isn't a spare piece of floor space. Fear not, though, for Outback hospitality has never failed us yet. We'll get you sorted.'

'Uh…right.' She was having difficult processing his words but thought it easier to agree.

'Once you're through the barricade, keep on driving…' he straightened his arm out in front of him, the sleeve of the T-shirt pulling across his firm biceps '…going straight until you get to the hay bales. That's where you'll need to park because the wedding reception is set up in the middle of the street. Then just grab your stuff, walk past the pub and the medical clinic until you get to a house with a large sign that reads The Bride Lives Here across the front of the veranda, and you'll be sweet. Head on in, introduce yourself to Viola and she'll get you all sorted. OK?'

'Uh… O…K.' Clover's brain was still sluggishly trying to understand what he was saying. She wasn't sure whether it was due to the man's dazzling smile and good looks or if it was because there was a wedding being held in the middle of a town! 'Are you really sure it's OK for me to join in?' she asked, trying to clarify exactly what he was saying.

'Absolutely,' he agreed with a nod.

'Excellent.' She shrugged and smiled.

'I'll shift the barricade for you.' The man gave her a brief nod then strode purposefully towards the barricades and shifted them out of the way, waving his arm like a windmill for her to drive past. 'See ya later,' he called as she headed towards the town, continually peering in her rear-vision mirror as the handsome stranger disappeared from view.

Her attention, however, was quickly brought back into focus when a flash of blue caught her eye and a voice yelled out 'Hey! Watch it!'

It was only then she noticed two men, carrying a large blue sound amplifier and hurrying to the side of the road so she wouldn't hit them, that she immediately slowed the car to an absolute crawl.

'I'm so sorry,' she called out the window.

'S'all right, love,' one of the men called back.

Clover decided to pay more attention to her surroundings rather than think about the easygoing man

she'd met who—as far as she could see—had just invited her to his sister's wedding. She remembered what
he'd said about where to park her car and when she
reached the wall of high-stacked hay bales, she looked
around for somewhere safe to park, but the only place
appeared to be right in the centre of the road, as other
cars, trucks and SUVs were parked around the area,
forming an impromptu car park.

'When in Rome,' she muttered to herself as she
switched the ignition off and looked about. Everywhere
appeared to be a hive of activity, from people up ladders, hammering in nails and stringing decorative little
lights here and there, to other people setting up tables
and chairs. Some people were already dressed in their
finest clothes, others were still in their work gear. As
she climbed from the car, she could hear a band going
through a sound check to make sure everything was in
working order.

Clover glanced down the street where the two men
who had been carrying the amplifier were now hooking
cables and plugs into the back of the unit. She retrieved
her suitcase from the boot and pulled it along behind
her like an overgrown dog as she made her way down
the street. When she passed the pub, which appeared to
be overflowing with people having a well-earned drink
after all their hard work, she was astonished to receive
a few appreciative whistles. She smiled shyly and gave
a little wave to the men, who waved back vigorously.

As she continued down the street, people greeted her
warmly, making her wonder if they weren't mistaking
her for someone else. She went past the medical centre
and even though there was a sign up indicating it was
closed for the day, she couldn't help but stop and peer

inside, interested to see what an Outback medical centre might look like.

'Can I help you?' a male voice said from behind her, and when Clover turned she found herself coming face to face with a police officer.

'Uh…yes. Sorry. I was looking for…' She closed her eyes for a moment, remembering what the handsome man at the road block had told her. 'Viola? Apparently there's a big sign out the front of the house.'

'Yep. Right this way.' The cop pointed to her suitcase. 'I'm Geoffrey, by the way. Are you just getting into town, eh? Cutting it fine. Would be a shame to miss it as the wedding's due to start in an hour or so.' Geoffrey walked alongside her as they continued down the street. 'So you must be from the Goldmark side of the family. Such a huge bunch they are but all of them are good value.'

Before Clover could correct him, he stopped outside an old weatherboard house with a wide veranda, ringed with a rail. The house looked as though it had been lovingly restored and seemed to stretch back quite a way, making it look small from the front but it was obviously bigger on the inside.

'Here we are! Just head on in. The rest of the clan is inside.' As he spoke the words, there was the sound of a glass being smashed coming from inside the house. Geoffrey chuckled. 'I'll leave you to it.' He tipped his wide-brimmed hat, then turned and headed off back the way they'd come.

Feeling completely out of her depth and as though she were trespassing, Clover climbed the five stairs leading up to the veranda and tentatively knocked on the screen door. There was no answer.

'Hello?' she called, and wondered what she should do next.

'Hello,' a little voice returned and Clover peered through the screen door. 'Can you help me? I broke da glass.' The owner of the voice pushed open the screen door and Clover came face to face with a boy of about three years old, his lower lip quivering. 'It's a accident.'

'I'm sure it was,' she soothed, and, leaving her suit-case on the veranda, went inside to help out. There was a lot of noise coming from the other end of the house, children laughing and playing, women talking and someone asking everyone if they'd seen a pair of black patent shoes.

Clover followed the little boy into the kitchen, where she discovered a stool pushed up to an open cupboard and a glass smashed on the floor beneath the stool. 'It's a accident,' he said again, his lip still wobbling as he looked up at her with big blue eyes, blue eyes that were the exact colour as those of the handsome man she'd met at the road block. Perhaps this was his son? Clover swallowed over the disappointment that the man was already married with a family of his own and focused on the problem at hand.

'We need a dustpan and brush,' she told the little boy, who immediately turned and ran towards a tall cupboard beside the refrigerator.

'In here,' he said, and swung open the door with vigour. Within another minute Clover had the little boy sitting on the stool she'd moved to the other side of the kitchen to keep him safe and was sweeping up the bro-ken glass.

'I see they've set you to work straight away,' a deep voice said from the doorway into the kitchen, and

Clover looked up to find her handsome road-block man staring down at her.

'It's a accident, Uncle Brandon,' the little boy told him in earnest.

Uncle? Clover's interest was once more piqued. Brandon? She watched as he walked towards the boy. The name suited him.

'I'm sure it was, scallywag.' Brandon scooped the boy off the stool and swung him into his arms. 'What about using the tumblers Aunty Vi keeps nice and low for you, eh?' With the boy still in his arms, he located a green tumbler from a low cupboard then retrieved a jug of cold water from the fridge.

Clover stood, all the shards of glass swept into the dustpan. 'Where should I dispose of the evidence?'

Brandon chuckled, such a nice, warm sound that washed calmly over her, and set the thirsty three-year-old down, taking the dustpan from her. 'Leave it with me.' With that he winked at her and headed out the front door. Clover looked at the boy, who was drinking as though he'd just crawled through a desert. When he was finished, he stood on tiptoe and dropped the green tumbler into the sink then turned to look at her, no longer any sign of worried eyes or a wobbling lip.

'I'm Cameron. I'm free and a *half*,' he told her, holding up three fingers as proof. 'What's *your* name?'

'Excellent question,' his uncle said as he re-entered the kitchen.

'Er…' Clover looked from child to man. 'I'm Clover.' She held out her hand.

The man slid his hand into hers, all firm and warm. 'Brandon.'

Clover's eyes widened imperceptibly at the touch and she swallowed over her suddenly dry throat. Why on earth were her fingers tingling? Why was her arm getting warm? Why did one simple touch from this man…a man she didn't even know…make her body react in such a way? She'd come to Lewisville to get away from men, hadn't she? Brandon's hands were smooth, not at all calloused as she'd expected given he'd been in a utility tent on the side of the road when they'd first crossed paths.

He looked from her eyes down to their hands, held in a firm grip, neither of them adding any movement to the action but seemingly content to just touch. It was the oddest of sensations and one she'd never received from a mere introductory handshake before. When he met her gaze again, she smiled and quickly withdrew her hand.

'Shake my hand, too,' Cameron demanded, and Clover dutifully obeyed.

'Pleased to meet you, too, Cameron.' She straightened and looked at Brandon once more. 'Er…are you sure it's all right for me to intrude on what is so obviously a family occasion? I mean, weddings are usually very personal and—'

'Brandon! There you are, and about time.' A woman rushed into the kitchen wearing a lovely light purple dress with an apron over the top, her grey hair pulled back into a soft bun and a pair of fluffy pink slippers on her feet. 'I'm glad someone relieved you from your road-block duty because as the man giving the bride away, you need to go and get ready.' The woman turned and looked at Clover.

'Hello? Are you a friend of Brandon's?'

'Mum, this is Clover. She's passing through town and so I—'

'Invited her.' She nodded knowingly. 'I'll sort things out. Now go. Get cleaned up and changed. Honestly!'

Clover smiled at the way Brandon allowed himself to

be bossed around by his mother. He grinned at Clover, shrugged his shoulders as though to say *Why bother arguing?* and headed out the kitchen. He stopped in the doorway and looked over his shoulder at Clover. 'Promise to save me a dance?'

Clover was a little surprised at the request but found herself nodding as his mother shooed him out of the kitchen. Then she turned to look at little Cameron, who was watching the adults with great interest. 'Off you go, Cam. Time for you to get dressed, too. Your mum's in the last room down the corridor.' With that, Cameron headed off and Clover found herself face to face with the woman who was obviously the matriarch of the family. Was she going to ask her to leave?

'Hi. I'm Viola,' the woman said, coming forward and extending her hand. 'We're all a bit crazy today.'

'Understandable. Listen, if I'm in the way, I can lea—'

'Nonsense. The more the merrier, right? Now, tell me, Clover, do you know anything about applying make-up?'

'Er…a bit, yes.' It was the last thing she'd expected to be asked and nodded as though to confirm it. What with all the balls and parties and functions she'd been forced to attend from a young age, having her hair and make-up attended to, she'd picked up a few things here and there. 'Excellent. Marissa, my friend, was going to do Ruby's make-up but burnt her hand earlier this morning.'

And before Clover knew what was happening, she was whisked away, being introduced not only to the bride but to a plethora of other women and children who all seemed to be a part of this big, crazy family. It was the type of family Clover had always yearned for when she'd been younger and now, seeing and being absorbed into the haphazardness of the Goldmark clan, that secret desire she'd pushed away so long ago came flooding back.

After that, time seemed to disappear as she not only fixed the bride's make-up but showed the other women how to highlight their naturally beautiful features.

'Oh, do you have something to wear?' Viola asked as an afterthought as they all started on final preparations. 'It doesn't matter if you don't. We're all very informal but it's nice to dress up once in a while.'

Clover did a quick mental inventory of her suitcase and nodded as most of the clothes she'd packed had been suitable for a five-star resort. 'I think I can find something.'

'Good. Just change in any room,' Viola called as she headed off in search of the person who was now calling her name.

Clover stood there for a moment, temporarily alone in a strange bedroom in a strange house in a strange town, yet she'd never felt so comfortable in her life.

CHAPTER TWO

'Don't you scrub up nice?' Brandon remarked with deep appreciation a few hours later. The reception was in full swing, the bush band playing their hearts out, the bride and groom dancing close on the makeshift dance floor as though they were lost in their own private world. Clover was sitting quietly at a table near the back of the festivities, just watching and enjoying being a privileged interloper on such an incredible event. She was also giving her tired feet a rest, having been asked to dance almost every dance since the partying had begun!

Attending an Outback wedding had been the last thing on her mind when her impromptu adventure had begun. She also hadn't thought she'd find herself drawn to a man who was, to all intents and purposes, a complete stranger. Quite often as she'd danced, she'd found herself searching the crowd for Brandon, remembering she'd promised him a dance and not wanting the night to end until she'd followed through on it. Yet most times when she'd spotted him, he had been busy chatting or laughing or dancing with someone else. Clover had worked hard to ignore the thread of disappointment starting to curl around her heart at possibly not being able to dance with her handsome stranger after all.

But now here he was, lowering his tall six-foot-four-inch frame into the chair nearly opposite her. Clover tried to tell herself that her increased heartbeat was due to all the dancing rather than the nearness of the suit-clad Brandon. She'd thought he'd looked good in old denims and a tight-fitting T-shirt but seeing him in a black suit, white shirt and red bow tie as he'd walked his sister down the aisle, Clover had been hard pressed not to swallow her tongue.

Now, though, the picture he made was even more sensually disturbing as he shrugged out of his suit jacket and draped it over the back of the chair. Next he undid his bow tie and rolled up the sleeves of his white dress shirt. His hair, which had been neatly combed earlier on, was now tousled, making him look incredibly sexy… and dangerous.

'I could say the same of you,' Clover remarked, her voice a little husky as her gaze drank him in. She sat up a little straighter in her chair and tentatively touched her long brown hair to tuck a tendril behind her ear. It was a habit she had whenever she was nervous and as a child she'd often found herself in trouble for ruining the style that had taken the hairstylists hours to create.

Tonight, especially, given she'd had next to no time to get ready, she'd simply wound her hair back in a lose twist before securing it with a diamond-studded clip at the nape of her neck, little wispy tendrils curling around her ears.

'Do you often drive around the Outback with the latest fashions in your suitcase?' Brandon asked, unable to hide his intrigue with the woman before him. Her dress seemed to be a sort of black-and-silver colour, slim, fitted and yet incredibly flowing and feminine. It looked as though she'd been attended by a swathe of make-up artists and hairdressers yet his mother had told him that it had been Clover who had helped out with the bridal make-up, thereby saving the day.

'I don't often travel by car,' she replied, then bit her lip, wishing she hadn't said that. It would be best if the good folk of Lewisville had no idea of her true identity. The Sampson name was well-known throughout the world and usually when people discovered who her father was, they tended to treat her like a visiting celebrity. She didn't want that, especially with Brandon. She wanted to continue being treated as though she was just Clover, a woman passing through town.

'Really? So how *do* you usually travel?'

She shrugged and looked towards the happy newlyweds, dancing in each other's arms, oblivious to everyone else. 'I don't travel much,' she said, hoping that would put an end to the conversation.

They sat in silence for a moment, both of them watching as Hamilton, the groom, who she'd discovered was Brandon's distant cousin, held his new wife as close as possible, looking as though he had no intention of ever letting her go. Clover tried not to sigh wistfully as the need to have someone hold her in such a way, pulsed through her. She also realised she'd been rather brisk with Brandon just now and should probably apologise. She took a breath to do just that but Brandon spoke first.

'I was away when they fell in love.' He gestured to his sister and her new husband. 'Couldn't be happier, though. Ruby deserves so much happiness after everything she's been through.' He shifted a little in his seat to face her. 'She came to live with us when she was fifteen, after her parents died. My mother used to run a teen shelter—'

'Ah, yes. Viola did mention the teen shelter at one

point. So Ruby came to town and stayed?' There was a wistful tone in Clover's voice. Through tragedy, Ruby had been fortunate enough to find happiness. It gave her hope. Perhaps one day *she* might find true happiness, too.

'She did, and now Hamilton is going to carry her away, overseas to Tarparnii, where they'll be helping out with an organisation called Pacific Medical Aid.'

'I've heard of them. They do good work.'

'I spent the first six months of this year working with them,' he added, and Clover's eyebrows hit her hairline. 'I only arrived back in town two, almost three weeks ago now.'

'You're a doctor, as well?'

Brandon regarded her with a hint of concern. 'Yes.'

'You're the doctor who runs the medical practice in town?'

Brandon smiled. 'Yes. Why, you're not feeling unwell, are you?'

She waved his words away. 'I'm fine. I didn't realise, that's all.'

The two of them sat there at the table, silence temporarily falling over them. Brandon couldn't help but be captivated by this woman. He had no idea where she'd come from, no idea where she was going, and yet for some strange reason he felt compelled to ask her to stay in town, which was utterly ridiculous.

Hadn't he learned anything as far as women were concerned? He'd jumped too fast into a relationship with Lynn and look how that had turned out. He had to slow down, to be more cautious, think things through, and yet the lovely Clover was absolutely tempting. What did it matter if he had a little flirtation with a complete stranger at his sister's wedding? Clover would stay the

night, leave tomorrow and he'd never see her again, so
why shouldn't he flirt and enjoy himself?

The silence stretched on as they watched several people take to the dance floor as the band played a faster-
paced song. The bride and groom, however, continued
to sway from side to side, oblivious to the beat or to
anyone else. Clover sighed. Now, *that* was what true
love was all about—dancing to your own tune.

'That's a big sigh,' Brandon remarked.

'I've had a big day and one I didn't anticipate would
end with a wedding. I mean, with me attending a wedding…not that I'm…'

Brandon chuckled and the warm sound washed over
her, bringing a shy smile to her lips. 'I know what you
mean. I'm glad you stayed, though. Apart from the fact
that it would have been nigh impossible to get your car
past all of this…' he waved a hand at the paraphernalia
presently blocking the main street of Lewisville '…I'm
glad you decided to chance it and stay.'

'Well, thank you for inviting me.'

Silence fell across them once more but this time
Clover was more highly aware of the handsome man
beside her. His firm physique, his hypnotic, spicy scent
and the way he seemed to move with such fluidity as
he stood and walked around so he was soon beside her,
holding out his hand. 'You did promise to save me a
dance.'

Clover shrugged and shook her head. 'It's all right,
Brandon. You don't have to feel obliged to entertain me.'

'I'm not. I'm entertaining myself—and you *did*
promise. Don't disillusion me by going back on your
word. I can't abide untruths. Besides the bride and my
dear mother, you're clearly the most remarkable and

stunningly beautiful woman here. Why *wouldn't* I want
to dance with you?'

Clover swallowed over her suddenly dry throat. He
thought she was beautiful? 'Oh.' She raised a hand to
her chest, slightly overcome at his words. 'Well…er…'
She smiled, nodded and placed her hand in his, unable
to believe the slight tremble passing through her body
at the contact. 'Thank you. I'd love to dance…with you.'

'Excellent.' With a wide smile he led the way towards the dance area, navigating their way around several chairs and tables. Once there and without a word
he pulled Clover closer, resting one hand at her waist
and holding her hand with his other. Her skin was soft,
her scent was like wild flowers on a summery day, and
Brandon found it difficult to ignore the strong pull of
attraction he felt towards this woman who was only
passing through his town.

Again, the logical side of his brain warned him to be
careful. The other side—the non-logical one that had
often led him astray in the past—suggested he throw
caution to the wind. Clover would be back on the road,
leaving Lewisville to continue with her adventures.
Their paths weren't likely to cross again, so shouldn't he
simply let go of his expectations and enjoy dancing with
a beautiful woman at his surrogate sister's wedding?

He breathed in again, somehow knowing he'd never
forget her delightful scent, or the way she felt in his
arms. Perhaps it was the fact that they were two strangers, enjoying each other's company, that made this moment so different. Or perhaps it was the alluring way
she moved her body in time to the music that was drawing him in. She was certainly an experienced dancer.

Even though it was dark, the street was lit with twinkle lights adorning every building, other small lights

placed here and there making the entire area feel as though it had come from the pages of a fairytale book. The music changed and a more upbeat song blared from the amplifying speakers. Clover began to loosen up and soon she and Brandon were zigging and zagging and laughing as they threw themselves into the rhythm. When the song ended, she edged back ready to go and sit down again, a little surprised when Brandon kept a firm hold on her.

'We're on a roll. Let's dance again.'

She smiled and nodded, readily agreeing as that was what she wanted, too. For so long she'd always done as she was told, putting other people's needs before her own, but not this time. This time she wanted to keep on dancing with Brandon and was pleased he wanted it, too. The next song was slower than the others and as they moved at a more sedate pace, Brandon leaned closer so they could talk.

'Thanks again for helping out with the make-up and getting Ruby ready. My little sister looks incredibly stunning this evening.'

'She's naturally very pretty but I was happy to be able to help out. It made me feel as though I had more of a right to be here rather than just some stranger passing through—which is exactly what I am,' she returned with a laugh, her words close to his ear.

She tried her best to ignore the natural, earthy scent mixed with a hint of hypnotic spice Brandon was wearing. How was it he smelled utterly alluring? How was it they seemed to be able to pre-empt each other's dance moves as though they'd been dancing together all their lives? It was an uncanny sensation, to be with someone she'd just met and yet feel like she'd known him for far longer than just a few hours.

'Are you a beautician?' he asked. Clover swallowed, knowing she'd never forget his enticing scent. Did the man have any idea just how he was making her feel? Probably not. He was no doubt used to having this effect over women he met and yet she couldn't picture him as a 'player', a man who went from one woman to the next without so much as an afterthought. 'Mum said you were very natural when you were doing everyone's make-up.'

'No.' She shook her head for emphasis. 'I'm not a beautician but it was nice of her to pass that information along.'

'So…not a beautician. Um…how about a dancer? You dance exceptionally well.'

She smiled and shook her head. 'Not a dancer but I've taken more than a few dance lessons in my time.' Mainly because it was required of all young teenage girls in her social circles to know how to ballroom dance. 'Care to take another guess?'

'Um…' He thought for a moment. 'Professional traveller?'

Clover laughed. 'Far from it.'

'Then I'm afraid I give up.'

'I'm a doctor. Obstetrician, actually.'

Brandon pulled back and looked into her eyes. 'Seriously?'

She smiled. 'I give you the truth and yet you don't completely believe me.' She shook her head, a teasing glint in her eyes. She'd never had this much fun with a man before. 'This isn't a great beginning, Brandon. I suppose to you I look more like a beautician than an OB/GYN?'

'No. I'm just surprised, that's all.' He shook his head as though bemused. 'You're a doctor.'

'Snap!'

'Brains as well as beauty. That's a lethal combination.'

'Thank you…I think.'

'Oh, that was definitely a compliment. So, are you travelling around the Outback delivering babies here and there?'

Clover shook her head. 'Nothing so organised or so exciting. I'm just a doctor on annual leave.'

'Where did you start this annual leave?'

'At my apartment.'

He chuckled. 'That's not what I meant and you know it. Did you seriously plan to drive around the Outback alone?'

'Actually, it was more of an impromptu trip,' she answered, thinking of how angry Xavier had made her.

'Which originated…where?'

'Uh…Port Douglas. I'm heading to Sydney.'

He whistled. 'That's a long way.'

'And I've enjoyed every moment of it.' She shrugged, not wanting to talk about her life, not wanting to spoil the glorious memories she was making with him. 'I have noticed, though, that there are quite a few women here tonight at various stages in their pregnancies. Where do they go to have their babies?'

'Trying to drum up business?'

'Not at all. Just…curious.'

'At the moment, they travel to Broken Hill.'

'That's about two hours from here, right?'

'Yes.'

'So they leave their families and go and sit in unfamiliar surroundings just waiting for labour to begin?'

'Something like that. It's not ideal but out here sacrifice and change are part of the equation. A few women opt to have home births, which either I or Ruby try to attend if we're able to get there in time, but the majority of women head to Broken Hill and wait it out.'

'And if they *do* have a home birth and require hospitalisation? What happens then?'

'Then we call in the emergency helicopter. Of course, there's also the Royal Flying Doctor Service.'

'Still, it must be so disjointing for the women.'

'It can be.' Brandon paused and angled his head to the side, considering her words. 'Why? Do you have some thoughts on the subject?'

Clover beamed brightly as they continued to move around the dance floor. 'And I thought you'd never ask!' With that, she told him about the maternity care centre she'd spent the better part of last year setting up. 'Women who live there can now choose between the hospital or the maternity centre. It's attended by trained specialists and not only gives them a place to deliver their babies but also provides much-needed support for those first few months postnatal. See, that's where this model of maternity care is different from all others.'

Brandon smiled, listening with great interest to what Clover was saying but also appreciating her passion. It was clear that setting up this centre had meant a great deal to her. He admired people who not only had a real passion for a cause but also followed through and did something about it, trying hard to make the lives of their patients that much easier.

A woman with passion—he could see it in her eyes as she spoke. Lynn hadn't really had a passion, not as far as other people went. She'd only cared about herself, about what she could get from others, that much had been crystal clear and as Brandon felt the anger of his ex-girlfriend's deception begin to return, he quickly shoved it aside, instead focusing on dancing and listening to his new friend Clover.

'So many women, especially first-time mothers, feel lonely and isolated and completely unsure of what to do with a newborn baby, and with this new working model, the maternity care centre is there to provide them with support and strategies to help them cope.'

'It sounds as though it would also help decrease the effects of postnatal distress and depression for the mothers.'

'Well, that is one of the proposed outcomes. However, the clinic in the Blue Mountains hasn't been running long enough for us to have any conclusive data on the matter but there is a team in place monitoring it closely.'

'It sounds as though you'd like to be in the Blue Mountains, running the centre yourself.'

Clover sighed so heavily Brandon was a little surprised. 'It would be nice but due to its success a medical centre in Tathra, on the East coast, has also indicated its willingness to open one, which means I'm headed there to help set programmes in place and train the staff.'

'Sounds like an interesting job. And where to after Tathra?'

Clover shrugged. 'Not sure yet. Might just be back to the hospital.'

'When you're not setting up clinics, where do you usually work?'

'Small private hospital in Sydney—St. Aloysius.'

He raised an eyebrow. 'I've heard of it. Prestigious.'

'So some say.' She would say it was full of snobby specialists who overcharged for everything. Both her father and Xavier were on the board of directors of the hospital, which meant they'd managed to infiltrate almost every aspect of her life.

When she'd first told her father she wanted to study medicine, he'd given her a lecture about her duty as a Sampson and how being patron of different organisations was a better way to help people rather than literally cleaning up their messes. However, the next day a message had been passed on through her father's personal assistant, saying he'd approve her choice of career but only if she achieved top marks.

'No daughter of mine is going to just scrape through with average grades,' he'd reiterated when she'd thanked him for his approval. 'You're a Sampson, Clover. Never forget that.'

And so Clover had worked exceedingly hard during medical school in an effort to make her father proud, in an effort to garner attention from him, the same attention she'd been trying to gain since she'd been twelve years old and her mother had passed away.

The poor, bereft child had thought she'd be able to grieve with her father, that their combined loss might, in some small way, bridge the gap that had existed between them her whole life. It hadn't. Instead, she'd become another commodity for her father to manage and the only time he ever gave her real attention was when she achieved the goals they'd agreed upon.

He no doubt wouldn't be too proud that she'd rejected Xavier's ridiculous proposal and that she'd also taken off, daring to do her own thing for once in her life. She shook her head. She didn't want to think about her father and Xavier right now. She was at a wedding, dancing with a handsome stranger, but when she glanced up to look at Brandon she was astonished to find him watching her closely.

Dancing with a man, chatting easily with someone she found incredibly attractive, was something she'd never really been good at. Sure, she'd been taught how to make small talk, how to put people at ease, and she could do that…but not with someone she was attracted to.

It was one of the reasons why she'd agreed to date Xavier in the first place. He was nice, pleasant, safe and gave her a bit more of an opportunity to see her father. Now, with his ridiculous proposal, Xavier had changed all that and he most certainly did not set her heart racing with one simple look, the way Brandon was doing right now.

The song ended but neither Clover nor Brandon seemed to notice, both of them still moving around the dance floor, not caring that the band had once more picked up the tempo. 'I'm really liking the sound of this care centre,' Brandon remarked a moment later, breaking the strange and exciting awareness surrounding them. 'To have a centre like that here in Lewisville would certainly solve the immediate problem of women heading to Broken Hill for a few weeks but would also assist with postnatal care. There are so many women in the town, women who have already raised their families, who would be able to provide not only support but advice, as well.'

'Exactly.'

Brandon steered her towards an empty table, away from the loudness of the dance floor so they could talk more freely without having to shout…and without having to lean in close to direct their words into each other's ears. Whatever scent Clover was wearing was beginning to drive him to distraction and for a while there, as they'd danced, all he'd been able to focus on was the way she would angle her body closer to his, the way her luscious mouth moved, her eyes captivating his soul and…yes, it was time to get off the dance floor and put some much-needed distance between him and his beautiful stranger.

Besides, her clinic idea did sound perfect for Lewisville and as such he needed to concentrate more effectively.

He held the chair for her as she sat, then came to sit beside her, angling his chair so they were facing each other. 'I could apply for government funding, get a grant to set up a care centre here.' His thoughts continued to bubble. 'It could be set up in the empty house next door to my mother's place, as it's been vacant for the past two years.' Excitement filled his tone and Clover found it infectious. She nodded encouragingly.

'I was thinking of expanding the clinic in town anyway as Ruby's going to begin studying again, wanting to specialise in paediatrics, and then after they return from Tarparnii there will be three of us in town available to provide care. And if you're happy to send me the information on the Blue Mountains clinic, it'll make applying for funding that much easier.'

'I'd be more than happy to do that for you.'

Brandon looked at her and slowly shook his head in bemusement. 'You're like an angel sent from above, Clover…' He stopped. 'I don't even know your last name.'

She shrugged. 'It's not important.' She didn't want to talk about anything to do with her life. Instead, she just wanted to live in this bubble world, this fairytale in the middle of the Outback. 'The important thing is to help these women.'

'Yes.' He was slightly curious why she didn't want to tell him her last name but brushed it aside. What did it matter? She'd be leaving in the morning after providing him with just the project he'd been searching for. He leaned forward and pressed a spontaneous kiss to her cheek.

Clover's eyes widened in surprise and she raised a hand to her cheek, covering the spot where his warm lips had left their delightful imprint. 'What did you do that for?' she asked, her words barely above a whisper, and she was surprised that given the music surrounding them he'd actually heard.

'To thank you.' He paused, intrigued by the way the simple action of touching his lips to her soft, smooth cheek had caused a fire to begin burning in his gut. 'Don't people in Sydney do that?'

Clover slowly shook her head. 'No. No, they don't.'

'Then I'm sorry if it made you feel uncomfortable.' Although he was having a difficult time reconciling the way he'd felt a sharp jolt of desire shoot through him the instant his lips had touched her skin. That had never happened to him before.

'Oh, no,' she quickly added, dropping her hand back into her lap. 'It didn't. You just…surprised me. A good surprise. I liked it. It's a nice way of saying thank you.' She was babbling now and closed her eyes for a moment in order to try and desperately gain control over her emotions, but the severe shock of tingles caused by Brandon's sweet kiss on her cheek was still affecting her equilibrium.

'Good.' His wide smile, one that made his blue eyes twinkle, did nothing at all to help her nerves settle down. 'So…' He shifted back in his chair and stretched his long legs out in front of him, leaning an elbow on the table and giving her his undivided attention. 'Tell me more about the care centre.'

Clover couldn't believe how incredibly comfortable she felt with Brandon. When she'd woken up that morning she hadn't even known of his existence and yet now she somehow felt as though she'd known him all her life. It was odd and relaxing and fantastic all at the same time.

The two of them chatted for quite a while, Clover excited to discuss her pet project with someone who was genuinely interested. They could have easily spent the rest of the night deep in conversation but were interrupted as the music came to a stop and the PA system squealed. Hamilton's oldest brother, Edward, who was the MC for the event, took to the microphone.

'All right, all you Jacks and Jillaroos, it's time for that ridiculous yet time-honoured tradition of the garter and bridal-bouquet toss.'

There was a combined cheer and groan but one stern look from Ruby made *everyone* cheer. This was her wedding and things were going to happen her way. Clover couldn't help but admire Brandon's surrogate sister. She sure had gumption. Both the bride and the groom stepped up to the microphone.

'We'll do the men first,' Ruby announced, Hamilton's arm firmly around her waist. Then she lifted her leg and put it on a chair. With the roar of the crowd, some good-natured ribbing and clapping, Hamilton lifted up the skirt on the bride's dress until he'd revealed her leg. A few of the men whistled but almost choked on their tongues when Hamilton glared them down for ogling his wife. It was all in good fun and soon he was twirling the garter around on his index finger.

'Who's going to be the next victim…er…lucky man to get hitched?' Hamilton asked as Ruby held the microphone to his mouth. 'Hey—Bart.' Hamilton laughed as he caught sight of his older, and only single, brother, trying to slink away into the distance. 'Get over there with

the rest of the single blokes.' Hamilton looked around
the crowd. 'You too, Brandon,' he called to his cousin.

'That's your cue,' Clover remarked sweetly, and
couldn't help but smile as Brandon moaned.

'Do I have to?'

'Your sister seems quite insistent,' Clover added,
giggling as he reluctantly rose to his feet. He'd taken
only one step towards the crowd before he turned and
held out his hand.

'I'll do the garter-toss thing only if you agree to do
the bridal-bouquet thing.'

Clover leaned back in her chair, not at all sure that
was a good idea. 'But I don't know anyone here. I'm an
interloper.' She looked around and realised that quite
a few people were watching them, Ruby now insisting
into the microphone that the garter toss wasn't going
to take place until Brandon took his rightful position
amongst the crowd of single men.

'Brandon! Brandon!' a few of the other blokes
began to chant, and even more people looked their way.
Clover started to squirm uncomfortably in her chair but
Brandon only stepped closer, holding his hand out to
her and shaking his head a little.

'I'm not going until you agree, Clover. As a new-
comer to the town, it's imperative you partake in all
the silly traditions we uphold, no matter how outdated
they might be by today's standards.'

She looked around, more people joining in the chant,
more people watching the two of them. Then she looked
into Brandon's eyes and saw that he was one hundred
per cent serious. He wasn't going to move until she
agreed.

'I'm happy to wait but I don't think the crowd will.'

There was a teasing glint to his eyes mixed with a healthy dose of stubbornness.

'Oh…all right, then,' she said, and put her hand in his, once more feeling the tingles of anticipation flooding through her. 'You're certifiably nuts, Brandon Goldmark,' she muttered, but his answer was only to laugh and lead them into the cheering throng.

Clover watched from the sidelines as Brandon took his place with the other single men at this crazy Outback wedding. She'd been to plenty of weddings throughout her life, all of them run with the strictest decorum and pomp and ceremony, where no bride had ever tossed her bouquet, let alone the groom tossing a garter removed from his wife's leg!

She found herself laughing and clapping and cheering along with everyone else as a countdown began, the atmosphere completely infectious. Hamilton turned his back to the group and tossed the garter into the air and down, down, down it came. Some of the men jostled, pretending it was a football heading their way and in their jostling, the white silky garter landed slap-bang in Brandon's hand.

'What? But I wasn't even trying!' he instantly protested, but all he received in reply was loud raucous laughter and a round of applause.

'Hey, Vi,' Hamilton called. 'Looks like you'll be planning another wedding soon!'

'Fine by me,' Viola called back and then to Clover's surprise Viola's gaze rested on her. What was *that* supposed to mean? she wondered.

'And now for the ladies,' Ruby said, wanting to keep the festivities rolling. 'All right—all eligible women front and centre.'

'Your turn,' Brandon remarked as he sauntered towards her, twirling the garter around on his index finger. 'A deal's a deal, Clover.'

'Come on.' Ruby was encouraging.

'And I expect you to really put a bit of effort into it,' Brandon couldn't help but tease.

Clover levelled him with a look. 'I'll put as much effort into it as you did.' With a slight shake of her head and rolling her eyes, she headed into the middle of the dance floor with the other single women.

Ruby turned her back to the women and then on the count of three she tossed the beautiful bouquet of red, pink, purples and blue Outback wildflowers into the air.

Clover kept her eye on the bouquet the entire time and while the flowers seemed to be sailing in slow motion, and even though she didn't believe in this silly tradition whatsoever, she silently wished that perhaps one day she might find the right man for her. It was only after seeing Ruby and Hamilton, so desperately happy, uncaring what others thought of them as they danced to their own tune, that she'd realised just how much she *wanted* that level of happiness—true happiness.

The flowers twirled over once, twice, slowly descending towards the group of women. Hands went up in the air and Clover was astonished to find hers was one of them. In the next instant a cheer went up and she blinked hard, astonished at feeling the bouquet securely in her hand.

'I knew it would be you,' Viola said from beside her, and Clover turned to find Brandon's mother standing there.

'But…' Clover shook her head as she looked around at all the smiling faces, searching for that one particular person she needed to see, needed to witness his reaction, and when her gaze finally settled on Brandon, it was to find him looking at her in stunned amazement.

He'd caught the garter. She'd caught the bouquet.

'You're going to be perfect for each other,' Viola whispered, sighing with maternal pride.

'You and Brandon seemed to be very chatty last night,' Viola remarked as Clover sat at the large wooden family table, drinking a cup of coffee. She'd managed to get a few hours' sleep but knew if she wanted to make it back to Sydney by tonight so she could make her rostered shift tomorrow, she'd have to leave early. She'd managed to find a bed for the night at Viola's and had planned on packing and quietly leaving, putting a small thank-you card against the lovely vase that held Ruby's bridal bouquet.

Instead, she'd found Viola in the kitchen at five-thirty in the morning, fixing a bottle for a five-month-old baby. Clover had no idea which member of the large Goldmark clan the child belonged to but it didn't matter.

'We were discussing ideas for a new medical centre in town.'

'Yes, he mentioned you were a doctor. How fortuitous. Would you like to come and fill in for Ruby while she's overseas for six months? I'd certainly love to have you here.' Viola sighed and looked down at the baby in her arms, who was sucking greedily at the bottle. 'It's going to be so quiet when they all leave.'

Viola's words were soft and low, holding a hint of sadness. Clover wished she could come and fill in for Ruby.

'I'd love to stay but I'm rostered on call at the hospital tomorrow, then next week I leave for Tathra for at least the next four and a half months.'

Clover sighed and glanced out the windows. All the wedding paraphernalia had been packed up after the bride and groom had driven away in a Jaguar sports car just after midnight. Apparently, they'd been heading to a secluded cabin an hour's drive from Lewisville for a romantic evening. Once they'd left, everyone had pitched in, tidying the town and clearing the street so that by two o'clock the road was cleared and ready for use again.

She sipped her coffee and looked at Viola. 'It is beautiful here and I feel so…' she sighed, wondering how best to express the way Lewisville and its accepting people made her feel '… content.'

'Then you'll have to come back again. Even if it's just for a quick holiday. You're more than welcome to stay here any time and we'd love to see you again.'

'We?'

'Yes,' a male voice said from behind her, and she turned to see Brandon walking in the front door of his mother's house. 'We. I thought you might head off early and didn't want you to leave without getting a chance to say goodbye and to thank you once again for sharing your brilliance.'

Clover smiled brightly at his words. He thought she was brilliant? Beautiful *and* brilliant? No one had ever said those things to her before and a warm glow flowed through her at his praise. 'You're most welcome.'

She finished her coffee and stood, not wanting to notice the way that even in his casual attire of runners and tracksuit, his hair all tousled as though he'd just raked his hands through it rather than using a comb, he looked devastatingly handsome. After rinsing her cup at the kitchen sink, she walked back to the front door, where she realised Brandon was holding her suitcase.

'I'll put it in the car for you,' he ventured, and she quickly pressed the button on the car-key remote to unlock the boot.

'Thank you.' She watched him walk out the door and the sensor light came on, highlighting the firm muscles in his broad shoulders and back. She tried not to sigh at the sight and quickly turned her attention back to Viola, who was coming towards her, babe still in arms.

'Promise you'll come back?' she asked as she hugged Clover as close as possible without squashing the baby.

'I promise,' Clover replied, knowing in her heart it was true. Lewisville and its residents had somehow managed to infiltrate her defences and fix themselves firmly into her heart.

'And stay in touch. I'm an excellent email correspondent.'

Clover smiled. 'Will do. Thank you again for your hospitality.'

With a small nod Clover opened the door and stepped out onto the old veranda, watching as Brandon closed the boot of the car and walked towards her, shoving his hands into the pockets of his denim jeans. He wore another tight-fitting T-shirt, this one a pale blue, which only made the colour of his eyes more vibrantly hypnotic. What on earth was it about this man that she was attracted to? Instant attractions weren't a part of her well-ordered, well-structured world.

'Remember now,' he said, as he watched her walk down the steps towards the car, 'if you're ever in need of a change, just come on back to Lewisville and help me get this maternity care centre up and going.'

Clover smiled and nodded, knowing he wasn't serious. 'If I wasn't heading to Tathra, I might seriously consider it.' She looked up at him, unable to understand the way her handsome stranger had the ability to make her feel as though she really was the most important person in the world. Did Brandon Goldmark believe in instant attraction? Giving her head a little shake to clear it from her wayward thoughts, she headed around to the driver's side of her car and opened the door. Brandon followed.

'Anyway, it was great to meet you and I'll email you the specifics and protocols regarding the maternity centre as soon as I'm back in Sydney.'

'Sounds like a plan,' he agreed, as she climbed into the the car. Brandon closed the door and waited for her to put down her window. When she did, he leaned forward and smiled. 'I think this is where we came in.'

Clover returned his smile. 'I think you're right.' Desperately trying to ignore the tingles of awareness zooming around her body at his nearness, she almost jumped out of her skin when he reached into the car and tucked a stray strand of hair behind her ear.

'You take care, Clover.' His voice was deep, sweet, and held an intimacy that only fanned the flames of the fire already lit in her belly. He stared at her for such a long moment she wasn't sure what he was going to do next, which was why he took her completely by surprise when he leaned in closer and pressed a long and lingering kiss to her lips.

'Nice,' he murmured, drawing back a touch, unable to believe the tantalising and incredible sensations buzzing through him.

He'd wanted to kiss her last night but his logical side had won out, telling him he was once again moving too fast. Yet throughout the night he hadn't been able to think of anyone or anything else except his beautiful stranger. Kissing her, especially as he'd never see her again, had seemed the right thing to do.

The only problem he faced now was that he didn't think it possible to stop at just one kiss, his entire body urging him for more, and who was he to argue? Within the next moment he'd pressed his lips to hers once more, purely in the name of scientific research to see whether he'd have the same sensations the second time around. He did.

'Very nice,' he murmured.

'Yes,' Clover whispered in return, her entire body tingling with absolute delight. She'd just been kissed by a stranger and she had definitely liked it…probably far too much as she wanted him to repeat it again and again. With a sexy smile that melted her insides, he eased back, watching as she unconsciously licked her lips.

Her skin was glowing, her body was tingling, and now she was expected to drive? It took another split second for her to force her mind to focus on the task at hand and turned the key in the ignition. He moved away from the car and shoved his hands back into his pockets. As she reversed into the now quiet and sleepy town of Lewisville, Clover couldn't help but wonder at the sense of regret she felt in leaving.

Giving Brandon a final wave, she put the window up and set off down the long, straight, flat road—unable to stop glancing in her rear-vision mirror at the man who stood in the middle of the road, watching her leave.

CHAPTER THREE

Five months later...

WITH the car windows up, the air-conditioning pumping out cooled air at the highest setting, Clover slowed the car she'd purchased only yesterday as she came to the outskirts of Lewisville. She'd done it! The boot and the back seat of the car were packed with her clothes, books and photographs of her mother. She'd written a message to her father, letting him know she'd be out of town for the next few months, but no doubt it would be one of his personal assistants who would read it, note it and file it.

She'd contemplated letting Xavier know but had decided against it. On her return to Sydney after her impromptu trip from Port Douglas, she'd done her best to make him understand she wasn't going to marry him and she would never want to marry him.

'But your father has approved the match.' Xavier hadn't been able to compute what she was saying. Clover had shrugged.

'Then marry him instead.'

She knew it was rare for her father to actually give his blessing, especially to a man Clover dated. Back in medical school, Oswald Sampson had managed to successfully chase away—in his own unique way—boys she'd become serious about.

'Everyone has their price, Clover,' was all he'd remarked when she'd confronted him, asking him if he'd had anything to do with the sudden breakdown of a relationship. The first guy, Pierce, had been at medical school with her and one day, out of the blue, he'd broken it off, telling her they could never see each other again. After her 'chat' with her father, Clover had tracked Pierce down and asked him straight out whether her father had paid him off.

'It was a lot of money, Clover. Too good to pass up. I've got university loans to pay.'

In her last year of medical school, the same thing had happened, the one guy she'd become serious with had accepted her father's most generous offer and broken her heart. After that Clover had decided that enough was enough and refused to be a target for other men who wanted to make a quick buck simply by breaking her heart and discarding her like yesterday's leftovers. Why couldn't anyone like her…for her?

She guessed that was what she was hoping for by coming to work in Lewisville for the next three months. The last time she'd been here everyone had just accepted her as Clover—the woman who had been passing through and who had helped with a few hairstyles and a bit of make-up. Nothing more. Just Clover. It had been refreshing.

On her return from setting up the maternity care centre in Tathra, Clover had been astonished to find an email from Brandon waiting on her computer.

'I've advertised for an OB/GYN to come to Lewisville to set up and run the maternity centre. At this stage I only have initial funding for three months and have yet to receive any applicants for the position. I don't suppose you know anyone who would like to come to the Outback for three months…do you?'

Clover had quickly replied, telling Brandon she was back from Tathra, wasn't due to set up another clinic until March and, if he would have her, she would be delighted to apply for the position herself. Not only was she more than happy to lend her expertise to setting up the clinic but she was very intrigued to once again see the man who had been constantly in her thoughts, especially at night. She still wasn't sure why he'd kissed her and in some ways she wished he hadn't because the action had only made her want more.

It was one of the reasons she'd been eager to accept the job. Would the instant attraction she'd experienced last time with Brandon still be there? Had it been a fluke? A figment of her imagination? She hoped not. Seeing Brandon again, working alongside him, getting to know him much better were all valid reasons for her wanting to return to Lewisville. No man had ever affected her in such a way before and it definitely warranted further investigation.

Thankfully, Brandon had emailed her back almost immediately, accepting her offer of help. Viola had been ecstatic at the news and had declared that Clover *must* stay at her home for the duration of her stay. Clover had managed to take leave without pay from the hospital and then all that had been left to do was to pack everything up and drive here.

As Clover drove into Lewisville, smiling at the large red ribbons tied in bows around the trees and light poles in the town, she noticed a plethora of utes and other dusty vehicles parked near the Lewisville pub, the antennae and bullbars decorated with faded tinsel. Several houses, including the clinic down the street, seemed to be decked with twinkle lights, which would come on once the sun finally decided to disappear around nine o'clock in the evening. It was clear that Christmas had come to town and it only added to Clover's own excitement.

She still couldn't believe she was doing this—leaving Sydney to come to the middle of nowhere on the off chance that the man who had made her go weak at the knees with just one sensual look was interested in seeing her again.

After parking the car outside Viola's home, noticing that the house next door was busy being painted, Clover switched off the ignition and climbed from the car, delighted to stretch her tired body.

She was standing with the car door open, arms stretched up, head tipped back, sunglasses still in place, when he saw her. Brandon stopped in the middle of the road and stared. Clover! The woman who had caused him plenty of sleepless nights during the past few months was now standing three metres away from him. He blinked one long blink, as though needing to clear his vision, before he could accept that she was really back in Lewisville.

It had been desperation that had caused him to email her, wanting to ask if she knew of any colleagues who might be interested in setting up a maternity care centre in the Outback. Secretly he'd wanted her to accept the position but on the other hand he hadn't, preferring to let whatever had existed between the two of them at Ruby's wedding to remain in the past. He had no room or time for any sort of personal relationship.

Since Ruby had left first to go on her honeymoon and then to head over to Tarparnii with Hamilton to volunteer with Pacific Medical Aid, he'd been left holding the fort single-handed. Combine that with trying to set up the maternity care centre and he'd been rushed off his feet.

At night, he'd often dropped into his bed and fallen asleep instantly, waking in the morning with thoughts of Clover fresh in his mind and her name on his lips. It was odd. It was strange because he'd never experienced prolonged dreams about anyone before, not even Lynn. During his waking hours he was master of his own mind. While he slept, his subconscious appeared to have a completely different agenda.

Now, she was here. Back in Lewisville. Ready to help set up the maternity care centre, as well as give him a hand in the day-to-day general practice. He watched as she closed the door to her car and shifted her sunglasses to her head, before running up the front steps of his mother's house, where she'd be staying while she was in town.

He'd been on his way to check on the internal construction progress of the maternity centre, wanting it to look as completed as possible before Clover's arrival, but now that he'd seen her, he couldn't stop himself from heading towards his mother's house, delighted to hear the sound of female laughter as he bounded up the five steps towards the front door.

'Look who's back!' Viola announced to her son a moment later as he stepped inside the cool, air-conditioned house.

'So I see.' Brandon forced himself to keep his distance, not to cross the room and shake her hand, and he especially didn't want to embrace her in a friendly hug. Even being in the same room as her, that sweet, sensual perfume of summertime flowers she wore was already starting to wind its way around his senses. Why did the woman have to smell so good?

It was clear after thirty seconds in her presence that there was still a strong awareness between them. That was bad. At the wedding she'd been a ring-in, someone he'd thought he'd never see again and hence why he'd justified the way he'd behaved, especially when he'd given in to the urge to kiss her. Now, though, things were different. They were professional colleagues—and nothing more.

'Good to see you again, Brandon.' She wasn't at all sure how to play this meeting, feeling highly self-conscious beneath his gaze. Her heart was hammering wildly against her ribs and her knees felt as though they were about to buckle. She reached out a hand to the table for support. Ever since she'd left after Ruby's wedding, Clover hadn't been able to get this man out of her mind and now, standing in front of him, she realised he was far more handsome than she'd recalled. She liked the way his dark brown hair was all messed up, little bits sticking up here and there as though he'd been pushing his fingers through it in a haphazard manner. She liked his deep blue eyes and the way that with just one single glance at her body they'd managed to make her tremble all over. She especially liked his mouth. Her gaze dipped to his lips as she recalled with perfect clarity the way his mouth had felt on hers.

Brandon opened his mouth to say something then closed it again, the action causing Clover to raise her gaze back to meet his eyes, belatedly realising she'd been caught staring. She swallowed and quickly looked away, feeling highly self-conscious.

Although she'd initially accepted the position here, wanting to help with the maternity centre, she had also wanted an answer to the burning question that had been running around in her mind ever since she'd watched Brandon's reflection disappear in her rear-vision mirror last July. Had their time together been just a passing fancy or had there been something more to it?

After just a few minutes in his presence she had her answer—at least, from her point of view. Brandon might only see her as another colleague and nothing more.

Viola pulled out a chair at the dining-room table. 'Sit, sit and I'll get you a nice cool drink. You must be parched after such a long drive from Sydney. Brandon? Drink?'

'Yes, thanks, Mum.' And within the next instant he found himself alone with the woman who, if at all possible, seemed to be more beautiful than when he'd last seen her. Today, as she'd obviously been driving, her hair was plaited down her back, swishing between her shoulders. She wore flat shoes, denim shorts and a loose white cotton top—comfortable driving attire.

'Do you mind if I don't sit? I've been sitting for so long now, it's nice to stand and just stretch out my muscles.'

Brandon shrugged a shoulder, remaining by the front door and not moving towards the table. She started to walk around the room, looking at all the knick-knacks and photographs scattered throughout his mother's open dining and lounge room.

He swallowed, knowing he should probably say something, but at the moment his mind didn't seem to be cooperating too well. What was it about this woman? Even her mere presence had the ability to tongue-tie him. He watched the way she moved, so full of grace, her movements fluid, almost gliding.

'Er...no problem with the drive? Car went well?' he

finally forced himself to ask after the silence between them seemed to stretch to breaking point. Where was his mother when they needed her?

'Yes, thanks. Everything went fine. No problems at all.' Clover picked up a snow globe of Mount Kosciuszko and gave it a little shake before replacing it. 'How about you? I hear you've been burning the candle at both ends, overseeing the renovations for the care centre and running your busy medical practice all by yourself.'

'Hear?'

She indicated the kitchen where Viola was still fixing drinks. 'Your mother's been emailing me, keeping me up to date on the Lewisville shenanigans.'

'Has she, now?' And why hadn't his mother mentioned to him that she'd been in contact with Clover during the past five months? He and Clover had exchanged a few emails when she'd first returned to Sydney but that had been purely professional when she'd forwarded the information about the care centre. After that he'd worked hard to put her out of his mind as best he could but the dreams had continued to happen and in the end he'd given up, deciding to accept the time he'd spent with Clover was nothing more than a fond memory.

Then, in the end, he'd had to contact her about the care centre, asking if she could recommend anyone to help. That had been the extent of their emails and really, the only personal information he'd learned from it had been Clover's surname—Farraday. Clover Farraday. The name suited her. He glanced down at his feet, trying to figure out what to do or say next because nothing made sense at the moment. 'Well…' He jerked a thumb over his shoulder. 'I'd better head next door to check on the care centre.'

'Oh? Can I come, too?'

'Well…er…' Brandon didn't really want to be alone with her, not so soon and not when he was still trying to get control over his senses. 'The painters are in there today. How about tomorrow?'

'Oh, OK.' She'd nodded and forced a small smile but he could see the disappointment in her eyes. He remembered those big brown eyes all too well. He remembered how it would be very easy for a man to lose himself in them and now that he'd rejected her request, he felt instant remorse, wanting to change his mind and take her next door so she could admire all the work that had been done.

He realised he only wanted to do that so he could see her smile—properly smile, which obviously meant he needed to get out of his mother's house as fast as possible if he was going to have any chance of keeping his wits about him. Good heavens. The woman was more tantalising than his sluggish memory recalled. No wonder he'd had a difficult time keeping his lips off her.

With a nod, she turned and looked at a few of the wedding pictures hanging on the wall. There were several of the Goldmark men, Hamilton and his brothers as well as a few others. Clover pointed to one taken many decades ago. 'Is this your parents?'

'Yes.'

'Your father's very handsome.' Clover looked from the photo to Brandon. 'You look identical.'

Had she just implied he was handsome? Brandon blinked one long blink.

'Oh, my Bill was a wonderful man,' Viola remarked as she came towards Clover, carrying three long, cool drinks on a tray. 'Good looking but cheeky and fun loving.'

Clover smiled, delighted at the way Viola just opened up to her. Throughout her upbringing there had always been so many subjects that had been taboo and talking about the past, especially family, had been one of them. In the mansion where she'd been raised, there were no family photographs, no wedding pictures or memorabilia of times gone by. Instead, the walls were decorated with the latest in fashionable art chosen by an interior designer with, as far as Clover was concerned, horrible taste.

At Christmastime she'd never been allowed to help with any of the decorating. She'd never been able to string up some tinsel or hang an ornament on the tree. Everything had been organised by strangers. It was clear Viola was still in the process of putting her decorations up, a large box in the corner with brightly coloured tinsel spilling out of it. She wondered if she'd be allowed to help.

'He sounds wonderful.' There was a wistfulness in her tone, envying Brandon for being raised in such a loving and caring family. She looked from the photograph of a young and excited Viola to the woman beside her. The excitement was still evident in her eyes but the face now held years' worth of experience. 'You must miss him.' Her words were quiet, respectful, caring.

'Every day, my dear.' Viola looked at the photograph of her husband. 'But life is life and you cope with the hand you've been dealt in the best way you can so as to promote happiness, not only to yourself but to those around you.'

'Wise words.'

Brandon stepped forward and put his arm around his mother's shoulders. 'From a wise woman.' He kissed her head.

'Oh, get away with you.' She smiled up at her boy, then turned to face Clover. 'I've made up your room so it's all ready. Brandon, go and help Clover bring her things in from the car.'

'It's all right,' Clover replied, before Brandon could move. 'I can cope. I know you have work to do and I wouldn't want to interfere.'

'Don't be silly. It won't take Brandon lo—'

'No, Viola,' Clover interrupted. 'I'm here to make Brandon's life easier, not more difficult or complex.' She waved both hands in a shooing motion towards the door. 'You go and take care of things at the maternity centre. Don't you worry about me.'

Brandon frowned for a moment before deciding it was best not to stand there and argue but instead to gulp down the drink his mother had made and get out of there as fast as possible. 'OK. I guess I'll see you around.'

'I guess you will.'

With that, Brandon turned on his heel and headed to the door, a frown of puzzlement furrowing his brow as he made his way down the stairs. Had his new temporary colleague, the woman who was only here for the next three months, just ordered him around? Had he just been dismissed?

Perhaps working alongside her was going to be far more difficult than he'd initially realised, not only from a personal perspective but from a professional one as well!

CHAPTER FOUR

CLOVER sat on the porch swing later that evening after the sun had set, her legs tucked under her as she allowed herself to relax. A shower of rain had swept through the town at around seven o'clock, helping the temperature to drop a few degrees, but even now, at almost a quarter to ten, she could read on Viola's outdoor gauge that it was still twenty-seven degrees Celsius. The Christmas twinkle lights on the town buildings were all shining brightly, blending with the stars up above to make a magical sight.

'We're all up later of an evening, wanting to make the most of our summer light,' Viola had mentioned after the two of them had eaten and stacked the dishwasher. 'Early mornings, late nights and naps in the middle of the day when the sun is at its hottest. That's the way to do it.'

Clover had smiled, listening to what Viola had to say but all the while glancing at the front door hoping that Brandon would stop by. When she'd tried to enquire innocently as to whether Brandon would be joining them for dinner, Viola had shrugged.

'We usually eat together a few times a week—probably more since Ruby left. He worries about me being alone but, honestly, on the evenings he's not here, I'm often spending time with Marissa or May or one of my other friends. I'm a busy woman,' she'd told Clover with a smile. 'And now I have you to keep me company, as well.'

When Brandon hadn't turned up for dinner, Clover had tried not to be disappointed. Perhaps that crazy awareness, that thrill of excitement, that powerful tug of attraction she'd felt at Ruby's wedding had been all one-sided. Perhaps after Brandon had kissed her goodbye, he hadn't thought about her since…or at least until he'd needed her help finding an OB/GYN for the clinic. Perhaps he saw her now as nothing more than a colleague and as such hadn't thought it necessary to drop by for dinner on her first evening in town.

When Viola had asked if she'd like to come across to Marissa's for a cup of late-night herbal tea, Clover had declined. 'I'm a little tired, what with the drive and all.'

'Of course you are, dear. How silly of me.' Viola had swiped a cloth over the now clean kitchen and picked up an old tattered book of recipes. 'OK, well I'll head off to see Marissa on my own. She's just developed a new recipe for shortbread cookies. Just sit yourself on the porch, pour yourself a cool drink and relax.' Viola had touched Clover's cheek with her free hand in such a comforting maternal way. 'Tomorrow's another day.'

Clover's eyes had widened at the words, tears beginning to gather. 'That's what my mother used to say.'

'Then she was a wise woman.' With a deep smile Viola had headed off to her friend's house situated not too far away. And so Clover sat on the porch swing, cool drink in hand, and absorbed the serenity of Lewisville. She tipped her head back, looking up at the plethora of stars and breathing in the fresh air, unable to believe how incredibly beautiful it was out here. Her mother would have loved it.

'Hi.'

At the rich, deep voice, Clover immediately sat up straighter, uncurling her legs and almost spilling the remaining contents of her glass.

'I didn't mean to startle you,' Brandon remarked as he walked up the steps and came to stand opposite her, leaning against the railing that ringed the porch. She'd changed her clothes and was now wearing a pair of three-quarter-length jeans and a comfortable T-shirt, her glorious long brown hair flowing freely down her back. He shoved his hands deeper into the pockets of his jeans, resisting the urge to touch it, to feel if it really was as silky as it looked.

'Brandon. What a nice surprise.' Her gaze instantly blended with his and she worked hard to ignore the increased pounding of her heart against her chest.

'Sorry I didn't make dinner,' he offered. 'I had planned to, given this was your first night in town, but I had an impromptu meeting with Geoffrey in the pub, where he needed to discuss the logistics for the up-and-coming billy-cart race.'

'Fair enough. Not that I was…you know…expecting you to be there. Of course you have things to attend to and…' She stopped, realising she was babbling, and quickly took a sip of her drink, hoping the cool liquid would help bring a bit of order to her jumbled thoughts. She was still perplexed about how Brandon could make her feel like an inexperienced schoolgirl by aiming one of his gorgeous smiles in her direction.

Neither of them spoke for a moment, the seconds ticking by and the atmosphere around them starting to thicken. Quickly, she cleared her throat and motioned to the town spread before them. 'I had no idea it would be so pretty here at Christmas,' she ventured. 'There are definitely more twinkle lights than at Ruby's wedding.'

He smiled at her comment and looked at the lights before them. 'It does look good, even though hanging the darn things takes for ever. Still, we're a town that really gets into the festive season.'

'You helped hang the lights?' Clover was astonished.

'Yes. Why wouldn't I?' Brandon was surprised at her question.

'I know plenty of medics who would think such a thing was beneath them.'

'Perhaps you haven't been hanging out with the right people.'

Clover smiled. 'I don't think I've done much…hanging out, as you call it, at all.'

'Why?' He turned and faced her directly. 'Are you a complete workaholic?'

'Maybe. I guess what I mean is I don't tend to socialise all that much.'

'And here I thought Lewisville wouldn't be able to compete with Sydney when it came to the social life.' He was watching her so intently, as though he was desperate to try and understand her. 'You didn't spend time with your colleagues?' He paused just for a moment, his tone deepening, his words softer, more intimately concerned. 'All work and no play isn't good for the soul, Clover.'

She tried not to squirm beneath his inquisitive gaze, rising from the porch swing and walking to the other side of the rail, needing to put some distance between them. 'I prefer to keep to myself.' She shrugged. 'I guess…you could say I'm a very private person.' Especially when her father was clearly in the public eye.

Well, that was fine for him but it wasn't the life she had chosen. 'I don't particularly like to talk about my past.'

Brandon nodded once, as though accepting her words, yet she could feel him still watching her. 'Didn't you have a happy childhood?'

'I had a…' She thought about the nursery in the mansion, about how she'd been provided with every new toy any little girl could desire. Clothes, electronic games, new phones, computers, books, cameras, anything and everything as her father decreed it. No child of Oswald Sampson would want for a single thing except perhaps the love of a father. 'Different childhood.'

Brandon wasn't quite sure what that meant but could see that if he pushed her for answers she would no doubt clam right up. Still, he wanted to know more about what made Clover tick and after his easy acceptance of Lynn when she'd first arrived in town and the way she had left him feeling bitter and hurt, his trust had been broken.

If he was going to work successfully with Clover over the next few months, surely he had a right to get to know her a little better—purely for professional reasons. He'd learned the hard way that where stunning, unknown females were concerned, especially when it was clear things simply didn't add up, he reserved the right to question, to dig beneath the surface and discover the truth. Perhaps he could push just a little bit more for tonight.

'A different childhood, eh? Did your parents divorce? That can always be difficult to deal with.'

'They didn't divorce, no. My mother passed away when I was twelve. My father and I aren't close. Anyway, I forgot to tell you, a pregnant woman called Lacey Millar stopped me in the street just before dinner, desperate for an update on the maternity centre because she really wants to have her baby delivered there.'

The words, both personal and professional, tumbled from her mouth and Brandon realised it was doubtful he'd get more than that from her tonight. He knew he needed to respect that but he couldn't help admitting that even those few words about her parents had only piqued his interest even further.

Discovering more about this alluring and enigmatic woman was definitely becoming a high priority, especially as the sensations he'd felt at the wedding hadn't seemed to have disappeared during the past five months. Seeing her today had only served as a reminder of just how incredible she'd felt in his arms, the way her scent had drugged his senses, the way her mouth had tasted so incredible when he'd given in to the urge to kiss her goodbye.

Brandon forced himself to look away from that delectable mouth of hers and kick-start his brain back into gear. What had she asked him? That's right. The maternity centre. 'Parker, one of the guys working on the project, told me the outside will be finished by tomorrow. There's still more work to be done here and there and a lot of the equipment hasn't arrived but we're getting there.'

'So will I be able to start running the courses straight away? I was talking to your mother about it at dinner tonight and she mentioned that she and Marissa Mandoc—' She paused, trying to recall Marissa's surname.

'Mandocicelli,' he supplied.

'Yes, thank you. Apparently the two of them are desperate to get the courses up and running. They're looking forward to teaching new mums-to-be how to practise putting nappies onto teddy bears and how to bath a large doll.'

Brandon saw the light come back into her brown eyes and couldn't believe how beautiful she looked. The lilt in her voice washed over him and he started to feel the stress in his trapezius muscle begin to ease. What was it about Clover that both relaxed and intrigued him?

'I do have a few queries, though,' she continued. 'Mainly pertaining to the delivery suites at the rear. Is it OK now if we go and take a look?'

Brandon shrugged and led the way, Clover following him down the steps to the house next door where he took out a set of keys, located the one he needed and unlocked the door. As they headed inside he flicked on the light switch, excited when the lights came on.

'I haven't been here at night since the renovations first began.'

'You've done an amazing job,' she said to Brandon. 'I know this used to be an old house but the decision to keep the front room as a lounge room was a stroke of brilliance. That way, when the women come in for sessions, they're nice and relaxed and comfortable and it really does promote the atmosphere that you're just popping over to a friend's place for a cup of tea or a chat about how to cope with sore nipples when breast-feeding.'

Brandon chuckled and Clover allowed the sound to wash over her. With the way he was smiling at her, it instantly brought back memories of the hours they'd spent together in July. Here was the man who had made her heartbeat increase, had made her knees weaken with just one look, who had pressed his mouth to hers in the most tantalising and promising kiss she'd ever had. He was the man who had filled both her dreams and her daydreams when she'd been in Tathra, setting up the other maternity centre.

He was the man who had influenced her decision to return to Lewisville, to see whether or not the attraction had been a figment of her imagination. It wasn't and she couldn't help but wonder that if a simple, straightforward kiss they'd shared had rocked her world that much, what on earth was going to happen if she ever got the chance to *really* kiss him?

'Anyway, from the schematics I've seen...' She turned away from his alluring smile, knowing it was best to focus on what she needed to talk to him about. Professional. She had to be professional. He was her colleague now, not a stranger inviting her to a wedding. 'I have a query regarding fitting the examination couch plus a humidi-crib—when they arrive—and a crash cart into the room.'

They headed down the corridor and studied the delivery rooms at the rear of the centre. The other seven rooms they passed were set aside for those mothers who needed to stay overnight. There was also a family room available for parents who might need to bring older children with them. There would also be courses held for expectant fathers, teaching them not only how to give a bottle and to bath the baby but also how to settle the baby in the middle of the night.

In the end, Clover suggested they shift the position of the examination bed and then everything should fit quite easily.

'We'll know more once all the rest of the equipment arrives,' Brandon said as they headed back to the reception area.

'Any idea when?'

'Still just after Christmas. That's the earliest we can get them.'

'Then we'll have to make do until then.' She stopped at the front desk and nodded. 'I really like what you've done here, that you've managed to adapt the schematics I provided you with for the needs of Lewisville.'

'It's a model to be proud of, Clover, and as its designer and creator you should definitely take credit for it. Naming rights. Proper recognition for everything you've done. It's a stroke of genius and garnering a lot of interest from my colleagues in other Outback towns.'

'Really?' She was completely surprised at this news. 'I just wanted to provide pregnant women who lived in remote areas with the means not only of delivering their babies as close to their homes as possible but also to provide a way for them to *learn* how to be mothers.' She looked down at her hands.

'I know my own mother struggled with it. She used to tell me how she was expected to know what to do, how to change a nappy, what to do if your baby had a fever, how to settle a child that simply wouldn't sleep.'

'You wouldn't sleep?'

'Apparently I was a very colicky baby.' Clover grinned then shrugged her shoulders. 'I remember her saying there should be more places where women could go to teach them *how* to be mothers, to have someone more experienced *show* them what to do.'

Her own mother had been provided with a nanny because no wife of Oswald Sampson should have to wipe a baby's bottom, but nine times out of ten Clover's mother had prided herself on looking after her daughter rather than handing on that responsibility. 'Mum wanted to *do* something but she wasn't sure exactly where to start.'

'Was she a medic, too?' Brandon couldn't resist asking the question and hoped that it didn't cause Clover to clam up again. The fact that she'd even mentioned her mother was wonderful and it was clear through the brightness in her tone that the two of them had been extremely close.

'No, but she would often tell me that I could do anything in the world if I set my mind to it. She'd also mentioned, on more than one occasion, that I was definitely smart enough to go to medical school and become a doctor.'

Clover shrugged and shook her head, realising she'd probably said too much but unable to stop herself. Brandon was very easy to talk to and that was another thing she hadn't experienced before—a man who actually *listened* to what she had to say.

'I guess she's had a bigger influence in my life than I've realised until now but she was always adamant about help for young mothers. There's still so much focus on the actual pregnancy and the delivery, and that's all well and good and still necessary, but what happens next? Keep them in hospital for a day or two and then send them home with a list of suggestions or a book that they feel they have to live up to!'

Brandon leaned against the doorjamb, attracted to the passion burning through the woman before him. Her eyes were alive, her words filled with power, her hands straight and often slicing through the air as she made her points. There was a healthy glow about her and even though he'd seen her dressed up all fancy-like at Ruby's wedding, there was no denying the beauty shining through her right now.

'A book only sets up ridiculous expectations, making the poor young mother feel as though she's failed, rather than catering to the individual needs of both mother and child. What's right for one child is not right for another. Every child is different and from my completed research, it was shown that even mothers with more than one child often had difficulty coping.

'*That's* what my hope for the maternity care centre is all about. Not just a closer place to give birth but a place where the more experienced women of this community, such as your mother and Marissa Mandocicelli, can offer their practical help and guidance for as long as it's necessary.

'If that type of working model is accepted and embraced by other townships, all the better, but as far as giving me naming rights and recognition for implementing a scheme that has been a part of other cultures for hundreds of years, forget it. I need no such recognition. It's the mothers, babies and volunteer women who are the ones that deserve the praise. I'm just doing my job.'

As she finished talking and let out a breath, Brandon couldn't help but applaud. She was surprised and looked rather sheepish, not used to attracting attention like this. 'Sorry. I do tend to rattle on a bit.' She tucked her hair behind her ear, feeling highly self-conscious as he smiled at her. She shrugged one shoulder shyly and gave him a lopsided grin. 'You should have stopped me.'

'And miss seeing you all fired up and passionate like that! Not a chance.'

'Oh.' She wasn't sure whether that was a compliment or not but decided it was probably best not to dwell on it.

'In fact, now that I've seen that fire burning deep down in your belly...' Even as he started to say the words out loud, Brandon wasn't sure it was a good idea but he didn't seem able to stop himself. 'Would you like to be my partner for the billy-cart race? It's held four days before Christmas. We close off the street again and have a big community Christmas party.'

Clover blinked once then frowned a little. 'A street party? I've never been to one before. Apart from that, I really have no idea what you're talking about, or what my rambling on about a maternity centre has to do with billy-carting. Your mother did mention something about it at dinner but I wasn't really sure what she meant.'

'Yes. That's the race I'm talking about. It's a Christmas tradition in Lewisville, where teams have to build a two-person billy-cart from scraps of wood and metal and rope and things like that, then race them down Main Street.'

'Build?'

'Sure. We'll have time after clinic to design and build a billy-cart.'

'Build?' She was looking at him with utter incredulity. 'I've never built anything in my life.'

Brandon spread his arms wide. 'You built a clinic!'

'Not with my bare hands,' she pointed out. 'I don't know the first thing about how to build a billy-cart.'

'Well, chillax, Clover, because I do. I've been taking part in this race for as long as I can remember. You need to be twelve years or over to enter and I waited *so* long to be old enough.'

'Who did you compete with in your first year?'

'My dad.' Brandon smiled at the memory. 'He was the one who taught me how to build a functioning billy-cart. The wheels, the steering column. Geoffrey and Parker and some of the other guys think that style is the biggest criteria. The flashiest machine. The best paint design.' Brandon shook his head. 'I can clearly remember my father telling me, "Son, straightforward and simple is the best design to have. Everything else is just gravy.'"

'How many years have you won?'

His grin grew wider. 'None.'

'None! Then why would I want to be on your team? I thought this race was about a little healthy competition.'

'Ah, see, now, there's that fiery spirit I'm coming to know. Keep that. Harness that as we build our simple but effective *machine of glory*.' Brandon waved his hand in front of him as though announcing a headline. Clover's only answer was to raise an eyebrow.

'So long as you don't call it that.'

He straightened. 'What's wrong with "machine of glory"?'

Clover wrinkled her nose. 'I think we'd better get you out of here. The smell of raw wood and building materials is obviously going to your head.'

Brandon chuckled as they left the maternity centre and headed back next door to Viola's house, Clover gasping once more at the pretty twinkling lights up and down the street. It really was so gorgeously festive, unlike her father's place. Every year a crew came in to erect the four-metre-high Christmas tree exactly one week prior to Christmas and then remove it the day after. Direct. Formal. Clinical.

She shook her head, not wanting to dwell on it. She was having a different sort of Christmas this year and she was going to enjoy it. 'So, has anyone ever been hurt during this race?'

'Oh sure. Last year, we had to forfeit the race because Kurt Shepherd came a cropper and needed medical attention. Broke his right wrist and dislocated his shoulder.'

'Who was your partner last year?' Had he been dating anyone? A girlfriend perhaps? If so, Clover wasn't sure she wanted to hear about it, although she had no idea why.

'Ruby. It was always Dad and I until Ruby joined our family and then Dad would help us build it but Ruby and I would race it.'

'So how do we go about this building thing? Do we need to look at schematics or do some research?' Clover turned to look at him as she spoke and missed her footing on the step, stumbling a little and reaching for the handrail, but it was just out of reach. Crying out in surprise, her hands flailed around for a moment before they connected with something firm and hard—Brandon's arm.

'Whoa! Careful, now,' he remarked as he slid one hand around her waist to steady her, the other reaching for her flailing hands. He caught her in time, hauling her a little closer to him, but at the same time she twisted around and before he realised what was happening, Clover was standing in his arms, facing him, her mouth so incredibly close to his own.

'Sorry. Very clumsy of me,' she remarked.

'Yep.' He smiled.

Disbelief flared momentarily in her eyes. 'You're not supposed to agree with me, Brandon.'

His smile widened into a grin. 'I'm not?'

'No. You're supposed to be gallant and chivalrous.'

'I thought that was what I was doing.' His smile increased. 'But if you want absolute proof...' Before Clover could utter another word, he'd scooped her up off her feet and into his arms. 'How's this?'

'What are you doing?' she protested, heat instantly infusing her entire body at the close contact. 'I'm fine. It was just a little twist. You can put me down.'

'But, you see, chivalry is not dead,' he murmured near her ear as she automatically wound her arms about his neck more for fear that she would fall rather than anything else.

But now that she *was* here, close to his body, the power of his earthy scent teasing its way through her senses, she was going to make the most of it. No man had ever treated her this way before, teasing her yet exciting her all at the same time.

He carried her to the porch swing and set her down gently. Then, kneeling down, he slipped her shoe off the injured foot and with a tenderness that stunned her gently rotated her ankle. 'Does that hurt?' he asked, his tone smooth yet a little deeper than usual.

Could he feel that electrified humming between them? Was he as aware of her as she was of him? How on earth was she supposed to think straight when he was so near, when he was touching her, caring for her? How was it this man could make her forget everything, wiping her mind completely blank, simply by being nice to her?

'Clover?' he asked, when she didn't say anything, and she quickly shook her head, unsure whether she was actually capable of forming words.

She stayed still, noticing he didn't appear to be in any hurry to release her foot. In fact, every time they'd touched in the past, at the wedding when they'd been dancing, afterwards when he'd kissed her cheek or tucked her hair behind her ear; each and every time, he'd been reluctant to break the contact. A small spark of excitement spread throughout her at this knowledge. Brandon was attracted to her. *Really* attracted to her. The knowledge made her bold.

She tipped her head to the side, her hair sliding off

her shoulder as she considered him. She swallowed once, twice before deciding to chance her vocal cords, hoping they worked. 'Are you this heroic with every woman you meet?'

A small smile tugged at his lips as his gaze took in the sight of her exposed neck. 'Are you flirting with me, Ms Farraday?'

'That's *Dr* Farraday, if you please, and what if I am?'

Brandon's smile increased and carefully he placed her foot down as though it were the most precious thing in the world. Then, still on bended knee, he leaned forward, angling his words towards her ear, his breath fanning her neck causing goose-bumps to ripple their way down her arm and spine.

'That's a dangerous game to play, *Dr* Farraday, but I'm willing, if you are.'

When he raised his head, there was a challenge in his eyes and Clover's smile increased. 'A game of flirting,' she breathed. 'Something I've never really done before.'

'I find that hard to believe.' His gaze dipped to her lips, lingering there for a moment before meeting her eyes once more. She had to try hard not to gasp or bite her lip as a wave of heat flooded her being. 'Someone as…gorgeous as you?'

'Contrary to what you might believe, Brandon, I've led a very sheltered life.'

'Does that give me an unfair advantage?' Had he edged closer somehow? Because now when she looked at him, she was positive that if she leaned forward a touch, and if he leaned forward a touch, their lips could finally meet. Was that what she wanted? To be kissed by Brandon? She'd certainly dreamed about it far too many times to count but the fact was she was used to keeping dreams and reality completely separate, not used to her worlds colliding.

'I may,' she breathed softly, 'not know exactly what I'm doing but I'm sure it's hard-wired into my…' she ran her tongue slowly across her bottom lip and was rewarded as a shudder ripped through Brandon, who was now obviously having difficulty swallowing '…system.' The word was barely audible yet it seemed to hang in the air between them.

Neither of them moved. Caught in a bubble in time. What had started out as a simple bit of teasing fun had somehow morphed into something more personal, more intimate. The longer they stayed still, the more she became aware of him.

She wanted to swallow, to breathe, to move, and yet her brain didn't seem to be receiving any signals other than the fact that perhaps, where Brandon was concerned, she'd bitten off more than she could chew.

The man was handsome and sexy, there was no doubt about that, but the way his blue eyes seemed to stare down into her soul, the way his strong arms made her feel more safe and secure than she'd ever felt in her life, the way her heart seemed to beat in time to the rhythm pulsing through him… There was a connection between them, a pure and powerful connection, and she wasn't at all sure she'd be able to resist making that connection physical.

If she angled towards him…just a fraction…

'Brandon!'

At the sound of Viola's voice calling his name, both of them sprang apart, quickly scrambling to their feet. Clover's ankle felt fine as she put weight on it.

'Brandon!' A second later, a breathless Viola came

bounding up the steps to the porch, concern and worry etched on her face. 'There you are. And you, too, Clover. Good. There's been an accident.'

CHAPTER FIVE

VIOLA bent forward from the waist, trying to catch her breath. For a split second neither Brandon nor Clover moved, their minds slowly beginning to lift from the sensual fog and return to the real world. She tried hard to ignore the fact that Brandon had been about to kiss her—again. That meant that what she'd felt at the wedding, what she'd spent months dreaming about, wasn't one-sided at all. Brandon was interested in her...but what would his price be?

Two men had come into her life and two men had hurt her when her father had paid them to leave. Would Brandon be so easily bought? Or was he made of sterner stuff? She hoped so. She *really* hoped so. It was a major reason why she needed to keep her Sydney life separate from her time spent in Lewisville.

Brandon led Viola inside and Clover quickly pulled out a chair from the dining-room table. 'Here. Sit down,' she urged, and helped the woman to sit.

'Take a breath, Mum, then tell us what's happened,' Brandon suggested as he walked to the cupboard in the hall where he knew his sister kept an emergency medical bag packed and ready to go.

He couldn't believe he'd been about to *kiss* Clover! *Again!* What had started out as a harmless bit of teasing, a harmless bit of flirting, had suddenly turned into an awareness so intense he was still nervous deep inside. No woman, not even Lynn, had rocked his world so completely and so easily. He focused his thoughts on whatever had his mother in a tizz.

'I was at Marissa's when she received a call from her niece's cousin, Pamela, saying that two teenage boys in the next-door paddock were playing with the tractors and that they've smashed them and are both hurt. Thankfully they managed to somehow reach one of the UHF radios in the tractors to call for help and this, of course, sent their mother, Susannah, into an absolute tailspin. She couldn't remember what to do and Pamela had just arrived at Susannah's for dinner and couldn't find where the emergency numbers were kept. Anyway, Pamela called Marissa, who lives in town, and then Marissa called Geoffrey, and I said I'd come over here and alert the two of you,' Viola panted.

'Good heavens!' Clover looked from Viola to Brandon. 'What were they doing out on the tractors at this time of night? It's dark!'

'All the more reason to be out as you can see exactly where you're going, especially if you're mucking about.' Brandon shook his head.

Clover shook her head. 'Madness. Total madness.' She patted Viola on the shoulder. 'Breathe, now. We don't need you hyperventilating.'

'Oh, tush. I'm fine. Go and put on a pair of sturdy shoes, girl. Geoffrey and Joan will be here to pick you both up in next to no time.'

'Yes, you're right. As far as police officers go, I have to say he's the most prompt and attentive one I've ever met, and how lucky that he married the town's paramedic.' Clover nodded and headed off to her room. If they were going to be traipsing through paddocks in the dark, socks and lace-up boots were definitely the way to go. She changed out of her three-quarter-length jeans and pulled on a pair of full-length denim ones, nice and comfortable yet sturdy.

She returned and found Brandon talking on the phone, Viola in the kitchen opening drawers and pulling out containers.

'Susannah…Susannah…calm down.' Brandon shook his head, trying to focus on calming down the distraught mother on the other end of the phone, rather than watching Clover as she gathered up her gloriously long hair and tied it back out of the way. He closed his eyes, blocking out the sight of the gorgeous woman. 'OK. Put Pamela on and go and lie down. We're all on our way.'

Clover headed into the kitchen. 'Is he trying to get more information?'

'Yes. Susannah sent the farm manager out to the paddock to be with the boys and to see what's going on. He's just arrived and is relaying messages over the radio and then Pamela's repeating that information to Brandon.'

Clover shook her head in bemusement. 'Another world.' She met Viola's gaze and smiled. 'But a good world, nevertheless.'

Viola nodded, her hands continually busy. 'I knew what you meant, dear.'

'What are you doing?' Clover asked as Viola tipped boiling water into a Thermos.

'Making you and Brandon a relief package. I often do it when he heads out to emergencies like this. Some sandwiches and a flask of coffee. If you don't want them, someone out there will.'

Clover couldn't believe the extent to which this woman continued to give and quickly bent to kiss her cheek. 'You're amazing, Viola. A true mothering kind.'

Viola didn't get a chance to say anything in return as there was the sound of a large vehicle outside and a moment later a deep car horn sounded.

'That's Geoffrey.' Brandon quickly finished his phone call, telling Pamela they were on their way, picked up his medical bag and motioned for Clover to follow him. She held out her hand for the bag Viola had just finished packing, thanked her, then followed Brandon outside.

He opened the front passenger door to Geoffrey's four-wheel-drive, ignoring the way her alluring scent seemed to linger around him. Once she was seated, he closed the door and headed towards Joan, who was driving the ambulance parked behind Geoffrey's police vehicle.

'You're not coming with us in here?' Clover asked through the open window, turning her head to look at him.

'I'll go with Joan. See you there,' he replied, and climbed into the ambulance, a little relieved to have a small reprieve from Clover's enigmatic presence. He was attracted to her. He'd enjoyed flirting with her— far too much—and he knew it was something he could quite easily become addicted to. Having a breather, even if it was only for the twenty minutes it would take to get out to Susannah's property, would be enough time to pull himself together so he could work alongside his alluring colleague.

At least, he hoped it would be enough time.

When they arrived at Susannah's property, they were

met by Pamela, who came out to the cars to give them directions to the paddock.

'I'll stay with Susannah. Keep her calm,' Pamela said.

'Does she need medical attention?' Brandon asked. 'Because Joan could pop in now—'

Pamela shook her head. 'No. She's anxious and worried but nothing that requires medical attention. Seeing to her boys will put her mind at rest.'

'Right you are. We'll report our findings via the UHF,' Brandon said, then nodded to Joan. 'Let's head out.' He signalled to Geoffrey and the police officer nodded and put the four-wheel-drive back in motion, its bright spotlights lighting the way through the now dark paddock.

'Just as well it rained three or so hours ago. If the tracks were too muddy, we might have had trouble getting the ambulance out here,' Geoffrey said to Clover.

'This is the wet season now, right? Over Christmas and through until about February?' she asked, glancing in the side-mirror to check that the ambulance was still following them.

'You're correct, Clover. Hot days, a bit of a downpour and coolish nights.'

'And are overturned tractors the normal sort of accidents you might attend out here?'

'Not uncommon but not an everyday occurrence either. Brandon, however, is well versed with Outback medicine so you've nothing to worry about. I have the helicopter on standby and the State Emergency Services are probably about twenty minutes behind us because we'll need their help to right those tractors again.' Geoffrey glanced over at her for a second before returning his attention to the track before him. 'Just thought you might like to know all that because you do look a little anxious.'

'Me? Anxious? Oh, no. Just…interested and…intrigued.' This was so different from her life in Sydney. And so were the feelings that Brandon was stirring inside her. 'While I'm trained as an OB/GYN, I'm more than versed with emergency medicine and it's clear you have everything else under control.'

'Excellent.' Geoffrey guided the car over a cattle grid and pointed towards the group of tractor lights shining in the distance. 'There they are.' He nodded towards the UHF radio. 'Let Brandon and Joan know we're headed off track and to stay close.'

Grinning, Clover picked up the handset. 'I just press the button and talk?'

'Yep. Joan's radio will already be on the emergency frequency.'

She untangled the twisted cord and held the handset to her mouth.

'Uh…um… Brandon? We're going off track. Geoffrey says to stay close.'

'Copy that,' Brandon replied, and where Clover thought that might be the extent of his reply, he continued to talk. 'Been enjoying the drive?' he asked.

'Uh…yes.'

'Good. It's shockingly bumpy in the ambulance.'

'Oi!' they heard Joan protest, and Geoffrey laughed. He motioned for Clover to press the button.

'Stop upsetting my wife,' he told Brandon when Clover held the handset up to his mouth. The police officer was busy bush-bashing his way through the paddock, drawing closer to the lights in the distance.

'She's not your wife, she's my paramedic,' he joked

with Geoffrey as they drove through a paddock in the dark, heading towards a serious accident.

'You don't see me upsetting your colleague here,' Geoffrey countered.

'I doubt you'd be able to,' Brandon returned. 'Clover is…unflappable.'

Clover raised her eyebrows at that comment. He thought she was unflappable or was he teasing her again? Had he suggested she go with Geoffrey because the police vehicle had better suspension than the ambulance and therefore she'd be more comfortable? Unfortunately, she had no time to ponder things as Geoffrey was slowing the vehicle down.

Within minutes they were out of the cars, she and Brandon heading towards the tractors while Geoffrey busied himself setting up more lights so they could see what they were doing. Wes, the farm manager, greeted Brandon like an old friend.

'Tyson's not so bad, but Ryan's not too good. He keeps slipping in and out of consciousness but he hasn't stopped breathing.'

'You've done a good job keeping them stable.' Brandon clapped his mate on the shoulder before crouching down beside Ryan, whose legs appeared to be trapped beneath the cab of one of the overturned tractors. Clover had already headed towards Tyson and Joan was bringing over an emergency medical kit from the ambulance. After a brief glance at the tractors, Brandon had quickly summed up what had happened.

'As I suspected. Playing a game of "chicken" with the tractors?' he called to Tyson, his voice holding a strong thread of parental censure but it was clear he didn't really expect an answer.

'Chicken?' Clover asked Joan quietly as she pulled

on a pair of gloves and reached for the medical torch so she could check Tyson's pupils, but it was Tyson who answered her, dismay in his tone.

'We race the tractors towards each other and the first one to chicken out and swerve or jump off is the loser.'

'And judging by the state of the tractors, neither of you chickened out?' Clover asked as Joan wound the blood-pressure cuff around Tyson's arm.

'Is…is Ry going to be OK?' Tyson's voice quivered as he spoke.

Clover looked across at where Brandon was bending down next to Ryan's torso, the boy's legs buried beneath the tractor. 'Honestly? I don't know but we'll do everything we can to help him out.' While Clover spoke to Tyson, she continued to check his vital signs. 'Cognitive function is good. Pupils are equal and reacting to light. You've got a large scratch on your head where you've banged it but I don't think it'll need suturing. Let's get you cleaned up and then I'll know more.'

'Respiratory rate and blood pressure are both elevated but still within normal range,' Joan reported.

'Where exactly does it hurt, Tyson?' Clover asked.

'My right shoulder,' he stated, and Clover instantly felt his shoulder. Tyson yelped in pain.

'Feels dislocated. I'd like it X-rayed before it's relocated to check there's no fracture to the neck of humerus. IV line, ten milligrams of morphine for the pain, stabilise his shoulder, cervical collar, clean and bandage the head wound. I'll assess him before transfer to see if further analgesics are required.'

While she spoke, Clover continued to check Tyson's other arm and his leg bones, checking reflexes to make sure everything else was in order.

'You've been very lucky,' she told Tyson, before pulling off her gloves and reaching for another pair from Joan's medical kit. 'I'll go help Brandon,' she said and left Tyson in Joan's more than capable hands.

'What have we got?' she asked Brandon as she knelt down beside Ryan, who was breathing through a non-rebreather oxygen mask. Clover bent down even further to peer beneath the tractor's cab to try and see what was happening with Ryan's legs.

'He's roused once but wasn't able to articulate exactly where he felt pain. I've set up a drip and have administered a dose of morphine and Maxolon.'

As he spoke, he held out his hand towards Geoffrey, who was walking towards them, a bag of plasma in his hand and another portable stand. 'Thanks, mate,' he said to Geoffrey, then turned to continue with his set-up. 'The plasma drip will help replace the blood loss.'

Clover assisted him, the two working effortlessly together. 'Blood pressure is low so between the plasma and saline we'll boost his fluids, pupils are reacting to light but sluggish. Pulse is slower. He's holding but until we can get the tractor off him, there's not much we can do.'

'Once it's shifted, though, we'll have to move fast,' Clover added, looking behind her at the cab. 'There's a high risk of toxins building up in his blood due to crush syndrome. It's clear he's losing blood so we'll need to tie off the offending arteries and stabilise him as quickly as possible. I'll be ready to intubate and resuscitate if required.'

'Good.' Brandon watched her, noticing she was completely focused. 'Are you OK, Clover? Bit different from Sydney, hey?'

'It is, but I'm here to help and ready to do whatever is necessary to ensure Ryan pulls through with flying colours.' She smiled. 'As you've trained in emergency procedures and as this is *your* town, you take the lead and I'll be your lackey.'

'My lackey?' Brandon raised an interested eyebrow.

'For this emergency,' she clarified as they finished setting up the plasma drip. 'Once we have him stabilised, what happens next?'

'Geoffrey will organise for the helicopter to land somewhere close by.'

'Out here? In the paddock?'

'It's flat enough and that means we don't have to transport the boys back into Lewisville. They can go straight onto the chopper and be transferred to Broken Hill Base Hospital, where Ryan will no doubt undergo orthopaedic surgery, possibly microsurgery, depending on how bad his fractures are.'

Brandon looked up towards Geoffrey, who, with Wes's help, had finished setting up some bright spotlights, providing more than enough illumination for when they finally shifted the cab from Ryan's legs. 'How much longer for the SES?'

'Two minutes. They radioed in to say they can see us in the distance.'

'They could see us in outer space, mate. Good work on the lights.' He looked over at Joan. 'How's Tyson?'

'Blood pressure stabilising. Vital signs improving.'

'Good. Get him as stable as possible so Wes can monitor him because we'll need you over here once we lift this cab off Ryan's legs.'

'OK,' Joan answered.

'Ready for the chopper?' Geoffrey asked.

'Ready,' Brandon confirmed.

'I can hear those SES trucks in the distance,' Clover

remarked, and began checking Ryan's vital signs again, managing to rouse him once more but still not for long. 'His breathing is stable, pupils have no change from before. His blood pressure is still low. I wouldn't be surprised if the femoral artery's been damaged.'

'Agreed.'

'I'll get that intubation and resuscitation equipment ready.' Clover went to stand but Geoffrey was by her side in an instant.

'What do you need?' he asked, and she told him what supplies she'd require from the ambulance. 'You have him well trained,' she called to Joan, clearly impressed.

'I heard that,' Geoffrey retorted, and they all smiled. He returned a moment later with the equipment Clover required, then went to direct the SES trucks, which were now almost upon them. Together, she and Brandon continued to prepare, pleased when after five minutes of the drip and plasma doing their jobs Ryan's blood pressure was slowly beginning to rise.

'He's better stabilised now for what's about to happen. Ideally, I'd prefer to give him a spinal block but, given the circumstances, perhaps morphine, five milligrams, every five to ten minutes.'

'Agreed,' Clover said, even though she wasn't sure whether Brandon had been asking a question. She wanted him to know he could rely on her, that she was ready to work alongside him. Geoffrey and the SES captain came over, Brandon greeting him warmly.

'I'm Alistair.' He waved briefly at Clover. 'I'd heard we had a new doctor in town. Terrible circumstances for a first meeting.'

'True, but I'm pleased to meet you in any case. We appreciate the assistance you and your crew will be providing.' She smiled up at Alistair and Brandon watched as the SES captain became instantly enamoured with her.

Jealousy sliced through Brandon and he quickly pushed it away. He couldn't deny not only his attraction to Clover but that they made a great team.

'Have we got everything we need?' Clover asked, peering into the medical bag. 'Locking forceps? Sutures? Swabs? Bandages? Or do I need to get some stuff from the ambulance?'

'We need all those things. If you can get it organised, I'll take Ryan's vital signs again.' Brandon worked calmly and methodically alongside Clover.

This was the first time in a very long time that she'd attended an emergency where someone wasn't giving birth and, as such, she was having to draw on her long-term memory to recall exactly what the procedure was, which was why she was relying on Brandon to direct her in this particular matter.

'Chopper will be here in under five,' Geoffrey reported.

'Excellent,' Brandon responded, then called to Joan, 'How's Tyson?'

'His vital signs are improving. BP is now back to normal,' Joan added.

'Good.'

Alistair's tone blended with Brandon's as he gave instructions to his men. 'Right, lads, get those cables secure. Dunfield, you're on the winch. Peterson, get that flame retardant flowing. Jones, have you finished your assessment?' Alistair shifted around to the other side of the tractor's cab to have a look.

Clover headed to the ambulance, quite impressed with all the activity. When she returned with the supplies still in the sterile packaging, she set them out on a tray, eager to get the job done in order to save Ryan's life. Their patients were all that mattered now and both she and Brandon knew that once the tractor had been shifted, they'd need to work quickly to avoid Ryan bleeding out.

'Ready?' Alistair called a while later.

Brandon looked at Clover and their eyes locked. He held her gaze before nodding once questioningly. She immediately nodded back. 'Ready,' he confirmed.

As they had suspected, once the SES workers elevated the cab, righting the tractor, the need to work precisely yet swiftly was on them. As though they'd worked together all their lives, Clover and Brandon were able to find the ruptured femoral artery and clamp it off, while checking the fractured right femur, tibia and fibula for other possible problems.

'The left leg is fractured but just the tib and fib,' Clover confirmed. 'The fracture looks more like a jigsaw that will require careful piecing together,' she remarked, as they debrided the wound and stabilised the fractures as best they could.

Brandon temporarily sutured off the femoral artery before he packed and bandaged the leg, splinting it and readying Ryan for transfer to the helicopter, which had landed nearby. Geoffrey and one of the other SES workers had already transferred Tyson, who was now being monitored by Joan. There was the sound of a car approaching and Clover glanced over her shoulder to see Pamela pulling a car to a halt, then climbing out and helping another woman from the car, a woman who started sobbing as soon as she saw the boys.

'Your mum's here, Ryan,' Brandon told the boy, who

opened his eyes for a moment and mumbled something before closing his eyes again.

'Good response,' Clover said softly. 'Listening and acknowledging. Shows excellent cognitive function.'

After Ryan had been transferred, Brandon helped Clover into the helicopter as Joan climbed out, Susannah already secured in the front seat next to the pilot, a bag of clothes at her feet.

'I'll drive to Broken Hill straight away,' Pamela was telling her friend. 'Brandon will help you. Just...stay calm. The boys are going to be fine. Isn't that right, Doc?' she called.

'They'll pull through,' Brandon confirmed.

Clover looked from Brandon to the puffy-eyed woman in the front seat, who was wearing a set of headphones with a microphone attached. Clover put on her own headphones and started to strap herself in, ready for take-off. Brandon was thanking Geoffrey, Joan, Wes and the crew before the police officer bent his head, the chopper's blades starting to whirl around as he ensured the door was securely closed.

'Susannah,' Clover said into the microphone, 'can you hear me? It's Clover...er...Dr Farraday.'

'Uh...yes?' Susannah replied, and looked around behind her to where Clover was sitting. Clover waved as Geoffrey came around to ensure Susannah's door was securely closed before signalling to the pilot that he was ready for take-off.

Clover was aware of Brandon sitting down beside her and strapping himself in and donning a pair of headphones, but it was Susannah who mattered right at this moment. The mother of the two teenage boys was clearly distressed and Clover knew that when they arrived at the hospital Susannah would need to be calm and lucid for when the surgeons not only explained the procedures to her but required her to authorise the surgery.

'Your boys are doing very well. Tyson has been conscious the whole time, talking to us and helping us to understand what happened. At the moment, though, we've given him something for the pain to help his body begin the recovery process. I know what they did was wrong, playing with the tractors like that, but what I need you to focus on is that they're both all right. Ryan's injuries are a little more extensive than Tyson's but, given time, he'll pull through and will be back to causing mischief in no time.'

At these words Clover was rewarded with a small laugh from the mother. Susannah hiccupped a few more times but thankfully, for now, the tears seemed to have stopped.

Clover continued talking to Susannah, explaining some of the procedures and protocols that would happen when they landed at the hospital and what the surgeons would say to her. Susannah, while still distraught her sons would require surgical intervention, was at least able to accept that fact and asked Clover a few questions.

Brandon listened to what Clover was saying while monitoring the boys, ensuring their vital signs were stable. Clover's tone of voice was one of calm assurance and where Susannah had been an emotional wreck when she'd entered the helicopter, by the time they arrived at Broken Hill Base Hospital, she appeared far more in control and ready to be a parent to her boys. Clover was a complete natural, putting everyone at ease.

Brandon introduced Clover to the hospital staff and

they stayed with Susannah while the two teenagers headed off to Radiology.

'Will you stay with me when the surgeon comes to explain things?' Susannah asked Clover, almost clinging to her.

'Of course we will.' Clover turned to look at Brandon, who instantly nodded. He was in awe of the way she'd been able to calm Susannah, the way she supported the mother and the way both teenage boys, after returning from X-Ray, seemed to smile almost shyly whenever Clover paid them the slightest bit of attention. He'd never met anyone like her.

The woman with the long, luscious locks and big brown eyes had the most encompassing smile he'd ever seen. Was it her calm and empowering voice that set people at ease? Was it the words she used? Was it the way she carried herself? The natural way that Clover communicated with everyone took his breath away.

The woman before him was a calm and controlled doctor, who had handled the emergency with professionalism and grace. How she managed a clear mix of the two he had no idea but her ability to put anyone at ease, her soothing voice and natural charm was enough to make people promise her the moon, should she ask for it.

Brandon continued to watch her surreptitiously as she carried on charming those around her. Lynn had used her charms, had used her feminine wiles to lie and cheat her way into his heart. She'd told him she was a freelance journalist, travelling around, writing stories about the true Aussie Outback hero. She'd written an article on Ned Finnegan and how being mayor of an Outback community was different from being an inner-city politician, and when she'd decided to do a piece on the local doctors, she'd fixated on him.

Brandon had been taken with her clever words, her turn of phrase and the way she showed him she was definitely interested right from the start. She'd been in town for several months, the two of them becoming incredibly close, when he'd started to think about proposing. Lynn was everything he'd ever wanted in a lifelong partner and she'd appeared to love Lewisville, still travelling around, stopping at some of the outlying homesteads to do more research and gather more stories.

Turned out she'd gathered more than just stories, especially when he'd headed out to the Palmers' farm for an emergency case and discovered Lynn had been sleeping with one of the jackaroos.

When he'd confronted her, she hadn't denied it.

'It's too late, Brandon.' She'd spread her arms wide. 'Jamie and I are leaving tomorrow.'

'Were you going to tell me or just…disappear?' His hands had clenched into fists as he'd tried to control his emotions.

She'd shrugged. 'Disappear. It's cleaner, easier that way. Jumpin' Jamie's been offered a job at one of the theme parks in Queensland, riding horses and crackin' whips! Yee-ha!' She'd fanned her face and smiled seductively. 'Ooh, that man is hot! And things will be even hotter than here on the sunny Gold Coast. Beaches! Oh, how I've missed beaches!'

'But, Lynn…?' He hadn't been able to believe the woman he'd given his heart to was indeed a heartless, cheating, lying vixen. 'This can't be the real you. Where's the woman who loved watching the sun set? Or sitting quietly on the porch swing, enjoying the peace and quiet? Or joining in with the bush dances and being involved with the community?'

Lynn had spread her arms wide. 'Gone. This is the real me, Brandon. I thought for a moment there that I could have been something else…and then I met Jamie and realised that porch swings and quilting bees were *so* not who I am.'

'And Jamie? Is it serious with him?'

She'd laughed. 'What? No way. I'm not the settling-down kind of girl. He'll do…for a while.' Then she'd sauntered over to him and run her fingernail down his cheek. 'Until I find someone to replace him with.'

Brandon had stood his ground, disgust slowly re-placing the love he'd felt for her. 'Was any of it real?' he'd asked softly.

Lynn had taken a step back and met his eyes fair and square, whispering one simple word in his direc-tion. 'No.'

In the distance, someone coughed, bringing Brandon out of his reverie. He looked at Clover as she smiled at someone. He couldn't shake the thought that she was still hiding something. He was positive of it. Something deep and important, something that answered all the questions he had and yet somehow, when it was just the two of them, he found himself forgetting all those ques-tions, caught up in the moment, in her eyes, wanting desperately to touch her long, flowing hair.

'Is any of it real?' he whispered to himself, then shook his head, knowing that where personal matters of the heart were concerned, he'd be a fool to let him-self become involved with Clover.

CHAPTER SIX

THANKFULLY, they didn't have to wait around too long for the helicopter pilot to give them a ride back to Lewisville.

'What now?' Clover asked as they watched the chopper return to the sky and fly off into the night. Brandon pointed to the ambulance, which was garaged near the helipad.

'We can drive the ambulance back to town. Park it at the clinic for the night.'

'How far is Lewisville from here?'

'A ten-minute walk.'

'Oh, well, it's ridiculous to take the ambulance for such a short distance,' she remarked. 'It's a lovely night, a definite breeze in the air, so I vote we walk.'

'Sounds good.' Brandon shoved his hands into his pockets as they started walking back to town. He'd continued to watch Clover at the hospital, his intrigue increasing with every passing moment he spent with her. He'd noticed that she appeared genuine enough when she was with patients, really wanting to help them, but what about Outback life in general? Did she like it? Would she be like Lynn and say one thing but mean another? He decided to try digging a little. 'So…what do you think of Lewisville?'

Her smile was immediate. 'I love it. The community, the way everyone pulls together, the stars you can see in the sky.' She waved her hand upwards as though to prove it. 'It's like its own little world, so far away from the toxicity of the city.'

'You're not a city girl?'

Clover laughed without humour, then sighed. 'I'm not sure I know *what* sort of girl I am.'

'But you've lived in the city all your life?'

'Yes.' That was all she said and was silent for a moment before changing the subject. Right on cue, he thought as he listened to her talk about how pretty the town was at Christmastime. It was definitely clear that she really didn't like to talk about her life in Sydney and he was becoming more and more curious why.

What had happened to her? Why didn't she get along with her father? Did she have any siblings? Was she married but running away from her past? She didn't wear any rings but that didn't mean anything.

'I do like it here, though,' she continued, still talking about the town. 'And I especially can't wait for this billy-cart race. When do we start with all the hammering and sawing and stuff?'

'Clover, are you married?'

His question stunned her so much she stopped walking and stared at him. Although there were plenty of stars in the night sky, shining down with the help from the half-moon, there wasn't enough light for her to see Brandon's expression properly but she could tell from the tone of his voice that he was serious.

'No,' she replied after a pause. She started walking again. 'Where does the billy-cart construction take place? In the shed out the back of your mother's house?'

'Why don't you like talking about your life? Opening up? Sharing?'

'Why don't you?' she countered, still heading towards the town. Brandon spread his arms wide.

'In this town? You only need to ask the nearest resident to be told all my gossip.'

Clover shook her head. 'I don't listen to gossip.'

'Neither do I, which means we've both been gossiped about in the past. Right?'

'You could say that.' She thought of the media who would often surround her father wherever he went. He was used to it, though, encouraging it to a point. In fact, she'd often felt he had a better relationship with the media than he did with his own daughter. She shook her head, clearing away thoughts of her father.

They continued to walk on but Clover seemed more than happy not to question him further. 'You're really not going to ask.'

'About?'

'About my past.'

'I'm more than happy to listen if you want to talk. If not, I'm more than capable of making up my own mind about your personality and character from what I've observed.'

'And what's that?'

Clover's smile was instant. 'Fishing?'

'Well, when a beautiful woman is forming an opinion of me, naturally I'm going to want to know what she thinks. Curiosity is part of human nature.'

'OK, then. I think you're an amazing doctor, which was proved tonight with the way you treated Ryan and Tyson. You genuinely care for the community at large, pitching in and helping out wherever necessary, whether it be manning a roadside tent when Main Street is blocked off, hanging twinkle lights or judging a bake-off competition.'

'Hey, I thought you said you didn't listen to gossip.'

'It wasn't gossip. Your mother was showing me some of the awards she's won for her delicious goodies and happened to mention that sometimes you were one of the judges.'

Brandon preened a little. 'It's a tough job but some-one's got to do it.' Clover laughed, the sweet tinkling sound washing over him and warming his heart. 'Especially if Marissa Mandocicelli's entering.' He kissed his fingers. *'Delizioso!'*

'Did I mention how modest you are?' she added teas-ingly, and they both chuckled. 'You've already told me you don't like untruths, which means someone has lied to you in a big way. It's clear the way you're desperate to find out about me that you've been duped in the past, no doubt by a woman who broke your heart.'

'I thought she'd broken it,' he said as they turned the corner and began walking down the bitumen road on the outskirts of the town. 'Now I'm not so sure.'

'Really?'

'Clover, I almost kissed you again tonight.'

'Uh…um…right.' His blunt delivery caused her heart to flutter and she wasn't at all sure how to react to such forward statements. When she glanced at him, she could see he was smiling and wasn't sure whether that was good or bad.

'You're easily flustered. It's a nice, endearing quality, which I'm starting to realise is quite genuine.'

'You thought I was pretending?' When he didn't answer, she nodded knowingly. 'Because you've been hurt, you have to question everything. Everyone new to your life already starts off with three strikes against them until they can prove otherwise.'

He shrugged but didn't deny it. 'Call it an unfortunate byproduct of being lied to.'

'Did she cheat on you?'

'How…could you know that?'

'It was a guess but a calculated one as infidelity is one of the major causes for relationship breakdown.'

Brandon shrugged, deciding if he wanted to know more about Clover, perhaps if he opened up, she'd do the same. 'Lynn cheated, yes. I was getting ready to propose and she was getting ready to leave with another man. She said Lewisville wasn't for her, too boring, where nothing exciting ever really happened.'

'Where is she now?'

He shrugged. 'She was headed to Queensland from here, to the coast.'

'Was she a doctor?'

'No. A journalist.'

Clover couldn't help the shudder that passed through her but, thankfully, Brandon didn't seem to notice.

'You sound as though you know a lot about relationship breakdown. Any bad relationships in your past?'

Clover thought about this for a moment as they neared the town. 'Of the romantic variety?'

Brandon nodded.

'I can't say there have been any good ones.' She thought about the pointed look in her father's eyes when she'd confronted him about buying off her last boyfriend.

'Dad! You can't do this. You can't control my life in this way and pay them never to see me again. This is the second time you've done this. It's not fair.'

'Life isn't fair, Clover.' His tone had been disinterested as he'd perused a pile of spreadsheets. 'I offered them money. They took it. It's not my fault they didn't "love" you. I've done you a huge favour. Now at least you know they were only interested in you for your money and nothing else.'

Oswald had picked up the phone to make a call, glancing up at his daughter. 'It's part of being a Sampson. Everyone always wants something from you and everyone always has a price. Get used to it.'

He'd made his call, ignoring the way she'd stood there for another few minutes before she'd stormed to her room, weeping into her pillow when she'd realised he'd been right. It appeared everyone did have their price and as long as she was known to be a Sampson, people always would. It was during that long and lonely night that Clover had decided to change her name. After all, she'd been twenty-two years old, about to finish medical school, and if she didn't want people taking advantage of her for the rest of her life, then she'd do her best to hide her true identity. So she'd taken her mother's maiden name—Farraday—as her own, and she'd graduated from medical school as plain and simple Clover Farraday, as opposed to Clover Farraday-Sampson, heiress to the Sampson empire.

'What about your dad?' Brandon knew he was treading on unstable ground. 'You mentioned the two of you don't get along?'

She was silent for a minute and at first he thought she was going to ignore his question completely but finally she said softly, 'My father only knows I exist when I excel so as a child I tried to excel at everything in order to get his attention.' She shook her head, wondering what Oswald would make of his daughter up and leaving Sydney to spend three months in the Outback. Would he even care?

'After my mother passed away, things became worse. He threw himself into work and I was pushed even more into the background. I slowly became accustomed to being passed over, having him forget my birthdays, packing me off to boarding school so he didn't have to deal with me.'

'Clover…' Brandon frowned, his tone intense and sympathetic. 'I'm really sorry to hear that.'

Clover shrugged. 'I coped. Studying medicine helped a lot and, of course, I worked hard in order to get top marks in an attempt to impress him.'

'Did it work?'

'He scanned my grades then looked me directly in the eyes for a whole five seconds and said, "As expected," before moving on to the next item on his agenda.'

'Wow. That's harsh. What on earth does he do for a job? Is he a lawyer or something?'

'Or something,' Clover grumbled as they walked towards his mother's house, the town in darkness now as the twinkle lights had long since clicked off. They slowed their pace, both of them stopping at the steps leading up to the house. 'I don't want to talk about my past.' She sighed and looked around the quiet town. 'I just want to enjoy spending time in Lewisville over the next three months.'

'You're not missing the big city?'

Clover shook her head. 'Not at all. Sydney is just where I'm based.' She looked up at Brandon and shrugged one shoulder, her gaze holding his. 'I've yet to find where I belong.'

Brandon swallowed as he stared into her gorgeous eyes. Although it was dark, his eyes had long since adjusted to the lack of light and he could have sworn he saw the smallest hint of desperation in her face. Certainly he heard it in her voice.

'Aren't we all?' He placed a hand on the rail and gripped it tightly, trying to control the urge to pull her into his arms and wipe away all her uncertainty. The need to save, the need to help, the need to protect the woman before him was becoming too strong to fight—and she'd been back in Lewisville for less than one day.

The attraction he'd felt the first time they'd met had burst to life within minutes of their meeting. He'd thought it was ridiculous and as she'd only been passing through town he'd rationalised that it was OK for him to move fast. Now that she was here for another few months, he simply *had* to slow things down.

He'd rushed into his relationship with Lynn and he'd been burned. He *had* to learn from his past mistakes and, given that prior to tonight's emergency he'd been about to press his lips to Clover's, it would be best for both their sakes if they kept their relationship professional but friendly. Working together, being polite and, of course, constructing a billy-cart together.

'Anyway,' he said, and took a giant step back from his mother's house, 'we'd best get to bed.' His eyes widened at his words. 'Separately, I mean. You to yours.' He pointed to his mother's house. 'Me to mine.' He jerked a thumb over his shoulder to indicate towards his unit down the street.

Clover smiled. 'I knew what you meant. Clinic in about…' she checked her watch '…five hours.'

'Right.' He rubbed his hands together and then shoved them into his pockets. 'Lots of patients. Especially for you. First full day consulting and I think your clinic is already bursting at the seams.'

'Excellent news. While I'm in town, best to put my skills to use.'

They both stood there. Staring. Not moving. Barely breathing. Their gazes trained upon each other. Their fingers itching to reach out and touch. Their mouths going dry as they did their best to ignore the irrepressible tug of desire zinging through the air around them.

Clover was wondering just how much longer she could stand it and as she shifted her feet, wanting nothing more than to draw closer to him, Brandon took another step back, effectively putting more distance between them.

'Well…' He started walking slowly backwards down the street, his eyes still on her. 'See you later on this morning.'

Clover swallowed and nodded, forcing a polite smile. 'Absolutely.' Her erratic heart rate started to settle, the more distance he put between them. 'Bright and early.'

'At the clinic,' he confirmed.

'Big day.' She climbed up a few steps, still facing him, wanting to keep watching him for as long as possible. As she took another step, the sensor light came on and she blinked, startled. She held up a hand to block it so she could still see him, but while her eyes readjusted, she could hear his warm, sensual laughter floating over her.

'It's a little bright, isn't it?' he remarked, his tone now coming from down the street.

'Just a bit.' She returned his laughter. 'Good night, Brandon.'

'Good night, Clover.'

And as she walked towards the front door, she paused, watching his shadow retreat down the street until she could see him no more.

Heading inside, she tiptoed towards her bedroom, desperate not to wake Viola by tripping over something. In her room, she didn't immediately turn on the light. Instead, she headed to the window and peered out the lacy curtains to see if she could see him but was out of luck. No doubt he was already opening the door to his unit, going inside and forgetting all about her.

She hoped he wasn't and as she brushed her teeth and prepared for sleep, she wondered if she'd finally found the one man who was indeed right for her.

What would happen when she eventually told him about her father? About exactly whose daughter she was? About her family fortune? Would it make a difference? Would he be able to accept her for who she was rather than for what he could get from her? Would she also have his price? Was Brandon a man who could be bought? She desperately hoped not.

Brandon headed inside his unit but didn't switch on the light, moving easily around the place in the dark. He kicked off his shoes and lay back on his unmade bed. He'd tossed and turned last night, wondering what would happen when Clover returned to Lewisville, and now he had his answer. The fact that the attraction between them appeared to be still very much alive was something he'd just have to deal with.

Moving slow was of paramount importance. It was clear she was hiding something, not wanting to talk about her past or her childhood. All he knew about her was that she'd developed the maternity centre in the Blue Mountains and had applied the same model to a centre down in Tathra. Now she was here, helping him out with his clinic for the next three months. What would she be doing once her time here was finished?

Setting up another clinic somewhere else? Helping other people?

She was definitely a giving person, wanting to focus on other people rather than herself. Surely that was a good sign. Then again, Lynn had seemed to be the same way when she'd first arrived in town, wanting to write articles on the townsfolk, making them feel special and wanted.

Then, of course, it had transpired that she'd been playing them all, stringing them along until she'd secured her story. She'd pretended to enjoy the quilting bees, the little community events, the close relationship she'd shared with him before she'd ripped his heart out with her lies and deception.

Was Clover the same? Was she just saying she was looking for a place to belong to be polite? It hadn't seemed that way, especially with that slight hint of need and longing in her tone. Then again, she might be an even more accomplished actress than Lynn—but he hoped not. He really hoped not.

CHAPTER SEVEN

'THAT sounds like a great idea, Ned.' Brandon walked from his consulting room to the reception area with Ned Finnegan, the mayor of Lewisville, as the man continued to chatter about the Christmas street party and billy-cart events due to take place just before Christmas.

Clover had been in town now for two weeks and each day he was finding it more and more difficult to keep his distance, to look upon her as merely another colleague. To say she was brilliant with the patients was an understatement and along with his mother, Marissa and Ned's wife, May, the maternity centre programmes were up and running.

He'd already received feedback from the women of the community, each of them not only extolling the virtues of the support but also giving glowing reports about Clover.

'She's so natural and genuine with everyone,' one woman said.

'So giving. She really wants to help, to make sure we can cope,' another reported.

On a professional level Brandon was pleased to hear such reports, but on a personal level it only drew him closer to the woman he wasn't sure he should get involved with. To hear people saying she was natural and genuine should have promoted confidence in him but instead it only made him more cautious.

Everyone had taken to Lynn like a duck to water, eager to involve her in the community, and look what had happened there. She'd duped them all and left the town without a word of goodbye. Therefore it was impossible for him to let go so easily, to trust again so quickly, and with the way Clover played her cards close to her chest, caution was still his main theme.

'By the way,' Ned continued, raising his voice to combat the loud crying from little two-year-old Ryder in the waiting room. 'How are things going with your billy-cart? Construction should be completed sooner rather than later,' Ned went on, barely stopping to draw breath. 'I was so happy to hear you'd asked Clover to be your partner. A great way to involve her in the community. Anyway, as mayor, don't forget I still need to sight your final billy-cart design.'

Brandon nodded. He'd been dragging his heels where the billy-cart was concerned as he was hesitant to be alone with Clover. Talking, discussing, building. He'd asked her on a whim, wanting to do exactly as Ned had suggested and get her involved to see how she fared, but now, given the fact that his dreams about her were becoming more intense, he wasn't sure he'd made the right decision.

'I'll get them to you soon.'

'Tomorrow,' Ned said pointedly, raising his voice again to combat little Ryder's loud crying. The toddler's poor mother, Tan, was trying desperately to calm him down but the child refused to listen.

Just then, Clover came out of her consulting room, talking to her patient, a bright smile on her face. Brandon ignored the way his gut immediately tightened at the sight of her. She was his colleague and it was imperative he maintain a professional distance.

She was dressed in flat shoes, a dark pencil skirt, which came to mid-thigh, and a cream shirt with short capped sleeves. Her long, luscious brown hair was clipped back at the nape of her neck. She wore little make-up and a pair of simple gold studs in her ears. She was…classically stunning.

Today she was the demure professional. At the wedding she'd been the sexy temptress, causing him to have wild dreams about her…dreams that had only become more intense since she'd arrived in Lewisville. He was glad he no longer lived at home, more than happy to be sleeping in his little unit situated at the rear of the clinic.

To have to sleep under the same roof as Clover, to be in the next bedroom, to hear her moving around, sharing a bathroom…that would have made his attraction towards her even more difficult to fight.

Ned tapped him on the arm and Brandon instantly turned his attention back to the mayor, unable to believe he'd simply been standing there, staring at Clover. 'So don't forget. Designs by tomorrow.'

'Er…Ned…' Brandon began, but Ned was already talking to Joan, the clinic's receptionist-cum-paramedic.

'Hello,' Brandon heard Clover say, and he returned his attention to her, watching in astonishment as she sat down on the floor in the middle of the waiting room, giving little Ryder her full attention. Ryder, however, gave her none of his, still intent on having his temper tantrum.

'I can scream louder than you,' Clover remarked, and in the next instant she tipped her head back and let go with an extraordinarily loud scream.

Everyone in the waiting room stared in stunned disbelief, half of them covering their ears as she continued to yell. After ten seconds Ryder stopped and sat up from where he'd been lying on the floor at his mother's feet. Clover finished her yell then shrugged, not looking at anyone but the little boy who was staring at her in complete puzzlement as though to say, *Grown-ups aren't supposed to act like that!*

'Do you like my long hair?' she asked him, and unclipped the gorgeous locks, dragging a handful across her shoulder and shaking it in front of Ryder. Like a cat with a piece of string, the child was unable to resist and clamped his chubby hand around the glorious locks. He gave a good tug on it but Clover didn't seem to mind. Instead, she held out her hands to him. The toddler clearly forgot he'd been in the middle of a tantrum. 'Let's go into my room and play.'

Without another word and with his hand still securely around her hair, he leaned towards her and she picked him up, rising from the floor with poise and grace. As she walked towards her consulting room, she kept her attention focused on Ryder, talking softly to him. Ryder's bemused mother followed, shaking her head in disbelief.

However, before Clover closed her door, she glanced at Brandon then, without a word, angled her head sharply, beckoning him to follow her. It took half a second for Brandon's sluggish brain to receive the message and with a slight frown but an incredible amount of interest he headed for her room, closing the door behind him.

'I'll keep Master Ryder quiet while you examine him,' she remarked, her tone calm and controlled before she sat on the examination couch, Ryder on her lap. The toddler was staring at her as though still completely unsure how he was supposed to react to such a strange lady.

'I know how you feel, kid,' Brandon mumbled, before asking Tan why they'd come to the clinic.

'I was clearing up after lunch and he was playing in his room and then he just started screaming and clutching his head.'

'*How* did he clutch his head?' Brandon asked.

'I don't understand.' Tan looked at him, confused.

'Were his hands around his jaw? Around his ears? Over his eyes?'

'Uh...' Tan thought for a moment. 'His ears,' she announced with triumph.

'Right.' Brandon walked to Clover's desk, picked up her otoscope and slid a new plastic shield into place on the tip. He glanced at Clover, who was still somehow mesmerising Ryder with her long hair.

'We'll check his ears first,' he said, and leaned closer, highly aware of the summery scent surrounding Clover. Why did she have to smell so good? Being this close to her had the tantalising effect of heightening his awareness. His arm accidentally brushed hers and he actually pulled back at the contact, their gazes meshing and holding for a split second, as though both had felt that strange undercurrent that seemed to flow between them.

'Angle his head.' Brandon hadn't meant his words to come out so gruff but he didn't have time to worry about that. He needed to switch off his unbidden attraction to his colleague and focus on their little patient. Cradling the boy closer, Clover twisted her own body so Ryder was in the correct position for Brandon's examination.

'Ah,' he said a moment later, and pulled back, taking two huge steps away from the couch and almost bumping into Clover's desk, so desperate was he to put a bit of distance between them. 'He has a very small object in his ear. I'm not exactly sure what it is.'

'What?' Tan was astonished. 'But how? Why? You mean wax, right?'

'No. It's like a small toy or a pebble or something like that,' Brandon continued, and walked to the supply cupboard, pulling out a few different bits and pieces. Clover watched as he focused on the task at hand, obviously wanting to ignore that brief frisson that had passed between them. Perhaps that was the wisest course of action, especially when they were at work.

She'd been in Lewisville for two weeks now and to say they had been some of the best weeks of her life was an understatement. However, since her first eventful evening when Brandon had almost kissed her on the porch swing, things had cooled between them. She was still highly aware of him and she still found herself waking in the mornings, her dreams full of thoughts of the two of them together, but Brandon had definitely put on the brakes. She couldn't—and didn't—blame him. Someone had to be strong out of the two of them and she was glad it was him.

They were colleagues and it was better if they maintained a professional attitude towards each other, rather than cuddling close, dancing and kissing, as they'd done back at the wedding.

Her days had been filled with patients and clinics and getting programmes up and running at the maternity centre. The word that an OB/GYN was now working in Lewisville seemed to have been spread far and wide and she was not only seeing women from the district of Hueyton but beyond.

Working in the clinic and filling in for Ruby in a general practice capacity also gave Clover the opportunity to treat a wide variety of patients, such as little Ryder here. She watched as Brandon pulled out a pair of alligator forceps, a kidney dish and a mild anaesthetic spray.

Working with Brandon, being near him, seeing him every day at work, was internally thrilling, not only as she admired his clever hands or the way he would smile at a patient, instantly putting them at ease, but also in a practical way where the clinic was concerned. If a decision needed to be made, Brandon simply made it. There was no need to write a proposal, to submit letters to the hospital board for approval, to be bound by mounds of red tape as she'd been for so many years working at a larger institution.

It was glorious. *He* was glorious, and she'd come to admire him as a professional colleague…as well as a handsome man. He was still the last person she'd thought about before drifting off to sleep, dreaming of him…dancing with him…being held close, having him kiss her cheek, her eyes, her neck…her mouth.

Clover looked away, annoyed with herself for daydreaming again—and right in front of him, too. He was busy securing a head mirror in place to help him see more clearly into Ryder's ear canal and after pulling on a pair of gloves he appeared ready to begin. She swallowed, glancing at him again, desperate to control the telltale blush she could feel starting to spread across her cheeks.

'Tan…' Brandon's deep, rich tone washed over Clover, causing a delighted shiver to race down her spine. She swallowed, keeping her gaze firmly focused on entertaining the toddler. 'We're going to need to give Ryder a mild sedative as I don't think even Clover, with her hypnotising hair, is going to be able to keep Ryder still enough while I remove the object. He'll be awake the whole time,' he quickly reassured her. 'Just drowsy and not really knowing what's going on. The sedative might take a few hours to wear off so after you leave here, take him home and let him sleep.'

'Uh…oh. All right, then.' Tan stood by, nervously watching as the two doctors worked together. Clover sat Ryder up as Brandon sprayed midazolam into Ryder's nose, knowing it wouldn't take long for the medication to be absorbed and cause him to become drowsy.

'If you could just tilt him—' No sooner were the words out of Brandon's mouth than Clover had Ryder in the correct position with his head on the side, ear up. 'Er…thanks.' Brandon pulled the lamp attached to an articulating arm towards Ryder so he could see more clearly.

'He's ready,' Clover announced, ensuring she had a steady grip on the boy. It took the work of a moment for Brandon to reach in with the forceps and extract the offending article. He held it to the light and all of the adults peered closer to see what it was.

'It's a miniature car!'

'How on earth…?' Tan stared at it in astonishment. 'I have no idea where that came from.'

Clover smiled as Brandon dropped the car into the kidney dish and took another look in Ryder's ear to en-sure there was no damage. 'Kids pick things up from all sorts of places. Friends' houses, playgroups. It's quite easy so don't go beating yourself up about it. You acted promptly to his crying, brought him in here, and as Brandon is now packing everything up, we can clearly deduce that there will be no long-lasting effects to this incident.'

'The ear canal does looks fine,' Brandon added, con-firming Clover's words. 'A little red from having a foreign object shoved down it so I'll give you a prescription for antibiotics just to be on the safe side.'

'And he won't have any pain or anything?' Tan was looking at her son, rubbing her hand over his head as he lay dozing in Clover's arms.

'He'll be as right as rain by tonight,' Clover promised, smiling brightly at the caring mother. 'You're doing a wonderful job.'

Brandon watched as Tan smiled shyly at Clover's praise.

'Let me carry him out to the car for you.' Clover stood, ensured Tan had the prescription and waited while Brandon opened the consulting-room door for them.

'Thank you,' she said, and headed out with Tan.

Brandon watched them go, shaking his head slowly. What was it about Clover Farraday that seemed to mesmerise anyone she came into contact with? Even at the wedding he'd noticed the way men looked at her, at the way women seemed to respond naturally to her smile. When they'd been dancing, talking about the maternity centre, when he'd stood in the middle of the street and waved her goodbye, Brandon had felt a connection. He'd felt important, felt as though he and his opinions mattered. He'd seen the same sort of look cross Tan's face before she'd followed Clover out of the clinic.

Perhaps it was Clover's heartfelt words, or the way she looked directly at you, giving you her undivided attention, that caused the sensation. Either way, Brandon could tell she had a true gift when it came to the patients of the Goldmark Family Medical Practice and surely that was all that mattered, right?

It did leave him wondering whether the attraction, the connection he felt towards Clover, was merely the

result of her natural attention or whether he was once
again falling victim to a smooth-talking woman who
would break his heart with her lies and deception. Was
Clover for real? Could she honestly be trusted? Brandon
frowned as the thoughts continued to whirl around his
mind, finally deciding that it was up to him to find out.

By the end of most days, Clover had to admit she was
exhausted. She'd never been as happy in her life but
still she was very tired. The small community, even
though it covered a vast area, was extremely tight-knit
and everyone knew everyone, which meant everyone
knew everyone else's business. Gossip was rampant
and every patient who came into the clinic to see her
would spend an extra ten minutes just wanting to talk,
to share, to involve Clover in their lives.

After two weeks in Lewisville, she now knew that
Susie Moffat was the 'go-to' woman in the community
if she wanted any sort of knitting or crocheting pattern. Marissa Mandocicelli was a brilliant cook. May
Finnegan collected every recipe she could get her hands
on and Andie Davis was the best quilter in the district.

All of them held Viola, Brandon and Ruby in high
esteem and a few of the young women who came to see
her had once been runaway or difficult teens, having
stayed with Viola years ago and with her help and guidance had managed to turn their lives around.

'It must be so rewarding to see these women, who
were once hurt and conflicted, living happy and healthy
lives,' Clover remarked to Viola that evening as she
helped prepare the evening meal. After Clover's first
week there, Viola had been horrified to learn Clover
didn't cook much and had made it her mission to teach
Clover as much as she could.

'It's very rewarding.' Viola nodded, a bright light shining in her eyes. 'I expect you feel that same sort of feeling when you help one of your patients.'

'I guess so.' Clover's brow was puckered in a frown as she concentrated on her task. Viola looked down at the chopping board and praised Clover's efforts.

'Excellent chopping of the garnish. Nice and small. Now stir the sauce while I check the chicken in the oven,' Viola said as she removed the baking dish from the oven and took off the foil lid. 'See how the chicken looks? When it gets to this stage, you know it's time to add the sauce and then all those delicious flavours will infuse and…' Viola brought her fingers to her mouth and made a kissing noise.

The delicious aromas were starting to make Clover realise just how hungry she was and she wasn't surprised when her stomach grumbled. She'd come home from the clinic and been ordered by Viola to shower and freshen up. When that had been done, it had been time for her next cooking lesson. Clover poured the sauce over the chicken pieces before Viola put the foil back on and placed the dish back in the oven.

'It's just as well the maternity centre is up and running because I've been so worried about Brandon.'

'Brandon? Why?'

'These last four or five months it's as though he's been pushing himself too hard. Running on empty. I don't want him to work himself into an early grave.'

Clover swallowed over the sudden dryness of her throat at Viola's words. Even the fleeting thought of something happening to Brandon made her feel ill. 'We don't want that.'

'No.' Viola closed the oven and straightened up.

'Hopefully now I'm here, it'll take some of the pressure off.'

'You've taken a lot of pressure off him. Setting up the programmes and helping the women to know they're not alone has been a huge weight lifted from his shoulders, plus helping in the clinic while Ruby and Hamilton are away also helps.' Viola sighed. 'I just wish you could stay longer.'

'You mean after my three months?'

'Exactly. Even with Ruby and Hamilton back in Lewisville, the maternity centre will still require an OB/GYN to run it. What do you think about staying on?'

'That's a good question,' Brandon commented as he sauntered into the kitchen. He crossed to the bench and stole a piece of carrot from the dish, neatly shifting out of the way before his mother smacked his hand.

'Leave the dinner alone. Cheeky boy,' Viola chided, but Brandon only winked at his mother and munched on the carrot stick.

'Smells great.'

'Good. Clover's been learning how to cook.'

'You don't know how to cook?' Brandon was surprised by that and it only reiterated just how little he knew about his beautiful colleague.

Clover's answer was a shrug of her shoulders. 'Your mother's a great teacher.'

'Thank you, Clover, but you're avoiding the question. What are your plans once you leave Lewisville?'

Clover looked from Brandon to Viola and back again, realising she had the full attention of both Goldmarks. 'Well...before I left to come here, the CEO of the hospital I work at was eager for me to develop more maternity programmes so I'll be off to train staff at Walgett in upper New South Wales, where they're planning on opening a centre.'

'I see.' Brandon exhaled slowly. 'I guess the maternity centres really are your baby, given you were the one to develop the programmes in the first place.'

'Well, yes, but—'

'You're doing good work,' Viola added. 'We can't fault that, can we, Brandon?'

'But I do like—'

'Can't fault it.' Brandon nodded. 'It's good to know. Means I can try and advertise for another OB/GYN to come here once you leave.'

'It won't be easy. Not many specialists want to come to the Outback,' Viola agreed.

'Especially on a permanent basis.' Brandon took another carrot but this time Viola didn't even attempt to slap his hand. They both seemed despondent and Clover wanted to agree right then and there that she would love nothing better than to stay in Lewisville for the rest of her life and run the little maternity centre.

At both the Blue Mountains and Tathra clinics, she'd not only adjusted the programmes but she'd trained the staff, which was what she'd be doing in Walgett. Then after Walgett, there would probably be another clinic and more adjusting and training and…

Was that what she really wanted? There were a few other specialists at the Blue Mountain clinic who were more than capable of training the staff at Walgett. Here in Lewisville there was no other specialist but her. If she left and Brandon was unable to secure the services of another specialist, what would happen to the women of this community?

Plus there was also her father to consider. She might have been annoyed with him, desperate for him to realise she and Xavier were incompatible when she'd left to come here, but at the end of the day he *was* her father. She was an only child. She'd lost her mother and now the only real family she had left was her dad and despite their strange relationship, she wasn't sure she could move out here permanently without some sort of acknowledgement from him.

Xavier, well, hopefully if she did move to Lewisville permanently, it would slowly sink into his very thick skull that she wasn't going to marry him.

And that left Brandon. She swallowed as she looked at him, munching on another carrot as Viola finished off the dinner preparations. Would she be able to work alongside Brandon day in, day out and control the rising attraction she felt for him?

If she stayed, was it a possibility they might actually be able to figure out exactly what their relationship was? Would it be more than just colleagues? Was it worth the sacrifice of resigning from her job at St. Aloysius, giving up her connection to the working model of the maternity care centre and moving permanently here in the hope that it might happen?

Her heart rate increased at the thought of herself and Brandon together, laughing as they walked down the street holding hands, building a billy-cart together, helping their patients before going home to their own place in the evenings, content to simply *be* with each other.

Brandon's mobile phone rang, cutting into her thoughts, and he swallowed his mouthful before answering it. 'Brandon Goldmark,' he said into the phone, then a second later, 'Lacey? Calm down. Yes, yes. She's right here.' He held out the phone to Clover.

'Lacey Millar. Thinks she might be in labour.'

'Right.' Clover accepted the phone. 'Hi, Lacey. Have you been having some pain?'

Brandon marvelled at the way her tone was smooth and calm and completely in control. It was the same tone she'd used on the helicopter when she'd been talking to Suzanne, or when she'd been talking to Ryder's mother, or talking with any of her patients. Calm and in control.

'All right,' she was saying. 'I want you to lie down. Find a position that's the most comfortable and see if Damien can massage your back for you. Just concentrate on breathing nice and calmly. Brandon and I will come immediately so we'll be there in ten—'

'Fifteen,' Brandon quickly corrected her.

'Fifteen minutes,' she said. 'All right. Just relax. We'll see you soon. Bye.' Clover pressed the button to end the call and handed the phone back to Brandon, their fingers touching briefly in the exchange. She tried not to gasp as a wave of glorious warmth spread up her arm and exploded throughout the rest of her body.

'Uh…Viola?'

'I know. I'll dish up a plate of food for you both and put it in the fridge for whenever you get back.'

'Do you want to move Lacey to the maternity centre? Should I contact Joan?' Brandon asked, but Clover shook her head.

'Lacey's not in labour. This is a false alarm.'

'How can you tell?' he asked, completely perplexed.

'Because I'm clever.' She smiled. 'And because I've delivered well in excess of a hundred babies. My record was four in one day, all single babies from four different mothers,' she pointed out. 'I can tell by the way Lacey was breathing, by the tone of her voice.'

'Then why are we going to her place?'

'To reassure her. She may not go into labour for another few days—a week or two at best—and in the meantime the more sleep she can get, the more relaxed she is, the better it will all be when it comes to crunch time.'

'Fair enough.' He pulled his keys from his pocket. 'Shall we?'

Clover's smile increased. 'Just let me get my bag.' She headed into her room, noticing a lightness to her step, and she knew it had nothing to do with going to check on Lacey Millar and everything to do with spending one-on-one time with her handsome colleague.

CHAPTER EIGHT

DURING the fifteen-minute drive to the Millar house, which was situated just outside the main town of Lewisville, Brandon asked Clover about some of the baby deliveries she'd performed over the years. It was clear she was more than happy to talk about that side of her past and hopefully it would help her to relax a bit more and perhaps he could ask her more about her family and her life in Sydney.

He'd caught a glimpse of her face when he'd been talking about advertising for another specialist to come to Lewisville when her three months was up and he'd been surprised at the thoughtful look in her eyes. Was it possible she might actually decide to stay here in Lewisville? To continue running the maternity centre on a full-time basis?

On a professional level, he wanted that to happen more than anything simply because Clover was one of the best doctors he'd worked alongside. On a personal level, he had no idea how he'd be able to cope with fighting the constant attraction he felt for her.

Even here, within the close confines of the car, he was having to force himself to concentrate on driving rather than on the lovely lilt of her voice as she recounted a story of delivering a baby in a hotel restroom.

'The poor woman was mortified when she realised she hadn't *really* needed to go to the toilet. So there we both were, dressed up to the nines, in the ladies' restroom, her pushing and screaming abuse at her husband, who flatly refused to come in as it was *the ladies' room*, and me using whatever first-aid equipment the hotel had in order to bring bub safely into the world.'

'And the ambulance?'

'It arrived twenty minutes after the event.'

'Of course.'

Clover shrugged. 'There's a lot of traffic in Sydney. They do their best.'

'And I'll bet once mother, baby and father were on their way to the hospital, you simply washed your hands and returned to the hotel function?'

She smiled. 'No. Thanks to the delivery, I managed to wangle my way out of having to go back and sit in a ballroom full of people I don't know, listening to my father make a speech about how brilliant he is.'

'Why were you there in the first place?'

'Because he asked me to go…and, well, my dad doesn't ask me to do a lot of things with him, so when he does, I usually say yes.'

Brandon nodded. 'I think when you lose one parent, you really hang on to the other for dear life.'

'Yes. Exactly. Well, of course you'd understand. It's clear from the way both you and your mother talk about your dad that you were all very close.' Clover sighed. 'That's nice. Precious.'

Brandon slowed the car and turned off the dirt road onto a thin dirt driveway that led to the Millars' farmhouse. He didn't want this ride to end, especially as Clover hadn't clammed up at all. Perhaps now that she was getting to know him better, she'd be more forthcoming. He could only hope that was the case because he *really* was interested in *her*. Initially, he'd wanted to make sure she wasn't pulling the wool over his eyes, or the eyes of the community at large, but now he simply wanted to know more because she'd proved to be a person worth knowing.

Damien Millar was out on the front porch, running down to meet them the instant he spotted Brandon's vehicle. 'Thanks for coming. She's inside. I think she's resting. I tried rubbing her back, like you said, Clover, but in the end she said it made her even more uncomfortable.'

'Not to worry, Damien,' Clover replied as she carried her medical bag and followed the two men inside. 'At this stage, it's better to let Lacey call the shots.' She was led into the main bedroom, where she was astonished to find Lacey lying flat on her back with her legs going up the wall.

A smile sprang to her lips. 'Seriously? That's a comfortable position?' she asked on a laugh as she knelt down beside Lacey, her tone light and free.

'Is it wrong? Will it hurt the baby?'

'You're fine, Lacey, but I might get you to just shift a little and put your legs back on the floor so I can examine you.' She opened her bag and took out her portable sphygmomanometer, taking Lacey's blood pressure and declaring everything was nice and normal.

'The pains have stopped,' Lacey confessed. 'And now I feel guilty for asking you to come all the way out here. I was going to get Damien to call you and tell you not to bother but I really wanted you to come and just…'

'Reassure you? It's no trouble, Lacey. This is what I'm here for. To help you through this time, to guide you, to answer your questions, no matter how silly you might think they are.'

'Do I need to go to the maternity centre?'

'Not just yet. You've had what we call a false labour and right now everything is back to normal. You're fine to stay home, to do everything you usually do.'

'But it *is* starting to happen, right? I *am* going to go into labour soon?'

'Things are progressing but it might be as long as another two weeks before you actually go into labour, Lacey.' Clover brushed some hair out of the woman's forehead and again Brandon was struck by the way she *really* cared for her patients.

'But what if things go like this again and I get more contractions? Or my waters break?'

'Then you call me and I'll come running.'

'But I don't want to bother you or—'

'Shh,' she crooned. 'Lacey. I'm here for *you*. We'll work it out together. You, me, Damien, Brandon. We're all in this together. There's an old joke I remember my mother telling me. 'How do you eat an elephant?'

Lacey looked at her and shook her head.

'One bite at a time,' Clover answered. 'The point is to just relax. Try, as hard as it might be, to enjoy your time with just you and Damien because once this baby's born, things will be different for ever.'

Lacey nodded, clearly much calmer, and after helping her up from the floor they all had a soothing cup of herbal tea before Brandon and Clover took their leave, heading back to Lewisville, both content to listen and sing along to a Christmas CD.

'I've never sung along with someone else in the car before,' she remarked as he parked the car and the two of them alighted. Clover carried her medical bag with her as they walked to the foot of the steps outside Viola's house. It was exactly where they'd been standing on her first night in town after they'd returned from taking the teenagers to Broken Hill hospital. 'It was fun.'

'It *was* fun,' he agreed, and took her medical bag from her hands, putting it on the step out of the way. Tonight, watching her with Lacey, wondering what life would be like in Lewisville after Clover left, Brandon had realised one very important thing. Clover belonged here. In Lewisville. Working alongside him. It was a strange revelation and one that had completely stunned him. Now, though, he was unsure what to do next, how to proceed with this new-found information.

'Don't you sometimes wish life could be as fun as it was when you were a kid?'

'Not really. As previously stated…' she pointed to herself '…not a happy childhood.'

'Sorry. Momentarily forgot.' He thought for a second. 'OK, name one memory where you felt completely happy. I mean giddily happy. So happy with carefree freedom that you honestly thought you were going to burst. The crazy, silly, happy type of happy.'

He watched as a slow smile crossed Clover's face and after a brief pause she said, 'Dancing.'

'Dancing? Did your mother take you dancing?'

'No. I meant here.' She pointed down the road. 'At your sister's wedding. With you.'

Brandon was stunned, his heart pierced with surprise and sadness. 'Your one complete and utter moment of crazy, silly, happiness was when you were dancing at my sister's wedding?'

'With you.'

He looked more intently at her, wondering if she was pulling his leg, but from what she'd just told him about her life, it appeared she was indeed telling the truth. Poor Clover. To have been raised with such an uncaring and indifferent father. He found it difficult to imagine as his own dad had been so opposite.

Now, though, Brandon had the opportunity to provide her with a moment of happiness and, given what she'd shared, he was going to do just that. He stepped back and formally bowed before holding out his arms to her.

'May I have this dance?'

Clover frowned, a little confused. Had he just asked her to dance? 'Pardon?'

'Would you like to dance?'

'But there's no music.'

'Do you *need* music?'

Clover tilted her head to the side for a moment and considered the question. 'I guess not.' Her hair was heavy and tangled and she quickly pulled it from the band, letting it fall loose around her shoulders. If she was going to enjoy crazy, silly happiness with Brandon, dancing with him in the moonlight, then she was going to be comfortable.

Brandon had been about to speak but at her actions felt as though he'd just swallowed his tongue. Good heavens! Didn't the woman have any idea how alluring she was? He cleared his throat, standing in the street outside his mother's house, arms out wide, waiting for her. 'Well, then…surely you're not going to leave me standing here, are you?'

'No.' She raised her arms and slipped her hands into his. The moment they touched, Brandon started shuffling his feet, swaying from side to side. Clover couldn't help the giggle that bubbled up from deep inside.

'Something wrong, Dr Farraday?'

'No, there is not, Dr Goldmark. Except for the fact that I'm dancing in the middle of the road, in the Outback, with no music.'

'And you're having fun!'

'I'm having crazy, silly, happy fun,' she confirmed as he twirled them round. She laughed and looked up into his eyes. Even though it was dark, the moon in the sky was shining enough for her to see his face. There was no doubt about the attraction that existed between them and there was no doubt they were both feeling the same things but due to past hurts, past circumstances, neither were exactly sure how best to proceed.

They continued to move, shifting gently from side to side, Brandon's steps nowhere near as long as they'd been a few moments ago. He looked into her eyes, the warmth of his body close, his fresh scent winding its way through her senses, drawing her in, hypnotising her, making her desperate to take huge steps away from the secure walls she'd spent a long time erecting.

Was it time to slowly let them down? To let Brandon into her life? Would he hurt her? Would he accept her for who she was? Could she confess she'd come to Lewisville because she hadn't been able to stop thinking about him? Could she tell him who her father was? Could she trust him with the truth? Would it change the way he was presently looking at her? How *did* he feel about her? Perhaps she should just come right out and ask him…but in a roundabout way, of course.

'Brandon…'

'Clover.' He spoke her name as though it were the most perfect caress ever to leave his lips.

'Do you remember my first night here?'

'Yes.'

'When we were walking back from the helicopter and you were talking about Lynn, about how she'd hurt you?'

'Mmm-hmm.'

'I made a comment that she'd broken your heart and you said—'

'I thought she'd broken it,' he interrupted.

'But you weren't so sure. What does that mean?'

'Are you sure you want to know?'

'Yes.'

'It means I want to kiss you. It means that I've *wanted* to kiss you ever since your first night here. It means that if my mother hadn't interrupted us with an emergency, I may well have followed through on that urge and kissed you, Clover.' He looked up at the porch swing. 'Right up there.'

Her lips parted and she stared up at him in stunned disbelief.

'I haven't wanted to kiss any other woman since Lynn. You're the first.' He let go of her hand and tenderly reached out to scoop up a small handful of her hair.

'Just like I've always wanted to touch your hair, ever since my sister's wedding, to feel it slip through my fingers, so soft and silky.' He swallowed and she watched his Adam's apple slide up and down his throat. 'I'm not sure if you even realise just how alluring you are, driving me to distraction every time I see you.'

'Uh…um…' She bit her lip.

'And the way you bite your lip or tuck your hair behind your ear.' He did just that and tucked a lock behind one ear, then slid his hand around her waist, drawing her even closer.

'Oh.' Her gaze flicked between his mouth as he

spoke and his mesmerising blue eyes. She sighed, feeling much more than just crazy, silly, happy. She felt *free*. Completely and utterly free, and she couldn't ever remember feeling this way before.

'You…set me on fire when you say things like that.' Her breathing had increased and she slipped her tongue out to wet her suddenly dry lips. Brandon's gaze dipped to her mouth, following the action quite intently.

'Good.' He angled his head down, just a touch, bringing them a little closer than before.

'I don't know if it's good or bad or crazy-silly.'

'You forgot happy.'

Clover slid her hands from his shoulders down to rest on his chest, delighting in the firmness beneath his T-shirt, amazed at being able to touch him and fulfil one of the fantasies she'd often dreamed about. This really was crazy-silly, this powerful, magnetic attraction drawing them closer and closer together.

He was looking at her mouth now and she felt the fire inside ignite the next round of flames. Although she wanted nothing more than to kiss him, there was still something holding her back and she knew what it was. The plain and simple truth was that Brandon didn't like liars and here she was, standing in his arms, unable to find the words to tell him the truth of her situation. What if she told him who her father was and he rejected her? She wasn't sure she'd cope.

Biting her lip again, she eased slightly back and met his gaze. 'Brandon. My life is…not as straightforward as other people's lives.'

'Mmm-hmm.' Brandon nodded and she wondered if he was really listening.

'It's a little confusing at times and what with my father and—'

'Mmm?' he murmured again. 'I don't want to talk about your father, or anyone else for that matter. I want to dance with you in the moonlight, to forget the world, to stop the turning of the clock and just *be* in this moment.'

'But that's what I'm trying to— Oh, my!' She gasped as he brushed her hair to the side and dipped his head, pressing small butterfly kisses to her neck. Clover closed her eyes and tilted her head to the side, granting him access.

'But that's…the…point. My fath…' She was having a difficult time thinking, forming complete and coherent sentences, especially with the way he was now nuzzling her neck. The warm breath and the soft touch of his lips on her skin caused goose-bumps to spread like wildfire up and down her spine.

'What *is* the point?' he whispered near her ear, before pressing little kisses along her jaw.

'The point is…' She swallowed and parted her lips, her breathing almost out of control as he continued to make his way around towards her mouth. *Brandon is going to kiss you!* The words seemed to be screaming through her mind like an adolescent teenager high on excitement.

She'd dreamt of this moment over and over since the night of Ruby and Hamilton's wedding, which was the last time they'd danced together. Of course, she hadn't exactly pictured their first kiss to be quite like this, standing outside his mother's house, Christmas lights twinkling around them, making the street look like a magical fairyland and dancing with no music, but she wasn't about to quibble.

The fact of the matter was that Brandon was slowly and tenderly working his way towards her mouth, his eagerness and determination quite clear in their objective.

'I don't *know* what the point is,' she whispered, her words breathless, her mind unable to think clearly due to the havoc he was creating with her senses.

'Good, because I've been waiting to do this for far too long,' he returned, and before she could say anything else he'd covered her mouth with his, causing her to gasp with longing and delight.

The kiss was brief, testing, and he slowly pulled back—just a fraction—in order to try and gauge her reaction. Her eyes remained closed, her face upturned towards him, and as he gazed down at her lovely features, her straight nose, her parted lips, her dark lashes, he swallowed, unable to believe how incredibly perfect this woman was.

How could any man not cherish her? How could any man not be completely smitten by her and her incredible features? How could he stand here, with her leaning towards him and not plunder her mouth with all the fire, hunger and passion that was coursing through him at this very moment?

He shook his head, the movement barely perceptible but he knew the last thing she needed right now was to have the extent of his powerful need unleashed when instead she should be handled carefully and tenderly. She deserved it.

Slowly, he removed his hands from her waist and brought them to her face, sliding his fingers gently across her lower jaw, cupping her face and tilting her head upwards. As he continued to look at her, seeing the total trust, expectation and intrigue in her features, he knew what he felt for her wasn't a ploy or an innocent seduction. Didn't she have any idea just how powerfully she affected him?

Brandon lowered his head and pressed soft and tender kisses to first one closed eyelid then the other, secretly pleased when she gasped with surprised delight, her mouth opening a little wider. It was difficult for him to restrain himself when she behaved in such an adorable and innocent manner, but when his lips finally made contact with hers once more, he kept a tight leash on the hunger that now burned through him.

One, two, three more tiny, tantalising kisses before Clover leaned forward and pressed her open mouth to his, determined to deepen the kiss and have her fill of the man who was driving her to utter distraction. Didn't he have any idea how powerfully he affected her? She wanted him to know that whatever was happening between them was most definitely not one-sided.

'Clover?' Her name was a caress upon his lips. 'Is this what you want?'

'Shh,' she whispered, and urged his head down, the raging fire and burning desperation she'd been trying to deny since they'd first met bursting forth and overflowing.

She could tell he thought she was a tender little flower who no doubt needed to be treated with kid gloves, but he was wrong. She was a woman, a passionate woman, a woman who was more than happy to share in such an intimate, fiery moment with him and unleash her hunger for him.

The instant she deepened the kiss, he stilled, just for a split second as though his mind was working out what was happening, before hauling her as close as he possibly could, their bodies pressed firmly against each other as they gave way to the repressed sensations that both had pushed aside for what seemed like an eternity.

Never had he felt so drugged, so helpless, so desperate as he did holding Clover in his arms, his mouth moving over hers with such a sense of urgency, a sense she appeared to match in every way, shape and form.

Until this moment, with her summery scent winding its way about him, drugging his senses to where he couldn't focus on anything but her, he'd had no idea she'd felt the same irrepressible tug, the one that appeared to have been drawing them together since they'd first met. He'd tried to fight it and now, understanding her need as it mirrored his own, he realised he'd been a fool right from the start.

With Clover in his arms, her body against his, her mouth seeking, demanding and finding a response to the delight flowing between them, Brandon could well believe that *anything* in life was possible. He could also now admit that what he'd thought he'd felt for Lynn had been nothing compared to the wildfire blazing through him as he readily accepted everything the angel in his arms had to give, while giving to her in return.

Equality. Both had taken the plunge, had stepped out onto a quivering ledge of uncertainty and together had discovered a raging, mutual passion.

Clover was amazed at the intensity but pleased it wasn't one-sided. It didn't even seem to matter that her lungs felt as though they would burst if she didn't drag oxygen into them, simply because she couldn't bear the thought of not having Brandon's mouth on her own.

When he eased back slightly, his arms still firmly wrapped around her body, she was pleased to note his breathing was as erratic as hers.

He kissed her again and again, as though unable

to stop himself, needing to reassure himself that this was really happening. Slowly the pressure in her lungs began to ease as her breathing returned to normal. She spread butterfly kisses across his jaw, her lips tingling from his whiskers as he no doubt hadn't shaved since that morning.

At his throat, she continued to kiss his skin, pressing a soft kiss to his Adam's apple, her body still close as she stopped standing on tiptoe and rested her head against his chest.

Sighing with a happiness she'd never known she could feel, Clover was pleased to note his heart rate was as wild as her own. He began to sway again and she shuffled her feet beside his as they moved in unison.

'Do you hear that music?' he murmured. 'I've never heard it before but when I'm with you, it plays so clearly inside my head.'

Clover smiled against his chest. 'It's beautiful music.'

'Soft.'

'Intimate.'

'The perfect beat.'

'It matches our hearts.'

Brandon chuckled at her words and eased back a little, causing Clover to lift her head and look up into his face. 'That's a corny line.'

She shrugged a shoulder. 'What's wrong with being corny?'

He chuckled again and shook his head. 'Nothing. Nothing at all.' He brushed a soft kiss across her lips. 'This isn't normal, Clover.'

'I know.'

'I don't mean me kissing someone…or even me kissing you. I mean the kisses we just *shared*. That sort of thing doesn't—'

She reached up and kissed him, effectively shutting him up. 'Shh. I know.' And as he looked down into her upturned face, he realised she *did* know, that what had just transpired between them was something new, something different, something unique.

'You've never felt this way with anyone—' He found he couldn't even finish the sentence as the thought of Clover kissing any other man filled him with a possessive jealousy.

'No.' Her reply was instant.

'Do you…date much?'

She glanced away for a moment not really wanting to mention Xavier or the way he treated her like some sort of commodity. 'I'm a busy doctor, delivering babies at all hours of the day and night.'

'There's no one important in your life?' He shook his head, unable to believe how incredible she could make him feel. After Lynn, he'd thought he'd never experience such a powerful, possessive need ever again and yet she always seemed so evasive when he mentioned her life in Sydney. 'I feel like I know nothing about you, about your life in Sydney.'

'It's irrelevant because when I'm with you I feel more alive than ever before.'

From what she'd said about her father and her lonely childhood, he hoped it was the truth. Lynn had said something similar to him in the beginning and look how that had turned out. 'Really?'

She looked into his eyes, her words intent. 'One hundred per cent. The woman I am with you is not the woman I am with everyone else. Around you…I can be…' She shrugged one elegant shoulder. 'I can be *me*. The *real* me.'

'How are you with everyone else?'

She sighed. 'Meek. Oppressed. Sad.' She raked her fingers through his hair, loving the way she could touch him without having to figure out some sort of excuse to be close. 'Lewisville makes me happy.' She smiled shyly at him. '*You* make me happy, Brandon.'

He nodded slowly as he looked down into the chocolaty-brown depths of her eyes. 'What do you think we should do about this attraction?'

'We don't ignore it, that's for sure.'

Brandon exhaled and nodded. 'Agreed.' He smiled as he met her gaze. 'How could anyone possibly ignore you?'

'More easily than you would think.' Clover let out a deep sigh.

'You really haven't had a happy life, have you,' he stated rhetorically.

'As I've said before, it was a…different life from most.' When he started to ask her another question, Clover leaned up and pressed her mouth to his once more, effectively silencing him in the best way possible. She didn't want to talk about her past, about her life, because up until she'd first come to Lewisville her life had consisted of being in a holding pattern.

It was as though she'd been waiting for this, waiting for Brandon for the past thirty-one years, and when she was with him, feeling his arms holding her close, his mouth moving over hers as though they'd been designed for each other, it was all she could do not to sigh and wish upon a star that this could be her life for ever.

She knew she had to tell him about her father, about her Sydney life and the way Xavier didn't seem able to take 'no' for an answer, but this life here in Lewisville was so glorious she wanted it to last for a bit longer before the reality came crashing down on them.

'We have work tomorrow,' he murmured against her mouth as she slowly drew away.

'Patients who need us.'

'The price of responsibility.' He shook his head. 'Why is it our bodies require sleep?'

Clover smiled and brushed a kiss across his lips before easing out of the embrace but continued to hold on to his hand as she bent to pick up her bag. He walked with her, up the steps, and the porch security light came on, causing them both to squint. Brandon pressed one last kiss to her lips then with great reluctance let her go. 'Dream of me.'

'It would be difficult not to.' With a sigh she turned and headed into the house, ensuring the screen door didn't bang lest she should wake Viola, which was the last thing she wanted right now. How to explain to Viola that she was fast falling in love with her son was a conversation Clover wasn't ready to have…just yet.

She breezed through her night-time routine then snuggled into the pillows, hugging one close, pretending it was Brandon. Then with a goofy smile on her face she drifted off into one of the loveliest sleeps she had in such a very long time and it was all because Brandon had kissed her…*really* kissed her.

CHAPTER NINE

THAT morning, Clover almost danced her way through the clinic, feeling as though she was walking on feathers or pillows on air. At breakfast, Viola had laughed at her when she'd waltzed into the kitchen and placed a kiss on Viola's cheek.

'You've woken up in a good mood,' Viola said.

'The absolute best,' Clover admitted, accepting a glass of freshly squeezed orange juice. When she arrived at the clinic, Joan was astonished as Lewisville's OB/GYN danced in through the door, a big smile beaming on her face.

'Cup of tea?' Clover asked, and at Joan's bemused nod Clover headed to the kitchenette. Brandon wasn't in yet, which surprised her, but when he did arrive, rushing in ten minutes late, he found her still in the kitchenette. He stopped in the doorway and stared at her, their gazes holding, both of them uncertain for one split second, unsure what was supposed to happen next.

It didn't take Brandon long to decide and within a moment he crossed to her side and crushed her to him in a firm but powerful kiss.

'I overslept,' he told her as he drank her in. Her hair was pulled back into a perfect bun on top of her head, her cream-coloured shirt and pale green pencil-thin skirt highlighting her slim waist and gorgeous curves. 'You're a sight for sore eyes.'

Clover smiled at his words, unable to believe how shy she felt when he said such things. She simply wasn't used to compliments, especially from a man who was coming to mean so much to her. 'Tea?'

'I think I need coffee this morning. Have to get my mind back into gear, rather than allowing it to stay in Clover-land.'

A buzz of excitement rippled through her. 'Clover-land?'

He winked at her and smiled but didn't elaborate any further. As they made hot drinks, brushing up against each other and shamelessly flirting, she couldn't believe how happy he made her feel. 'From the look of the patient lists this morning, we should be done by about two o'clock, then we can get started on the billy-cart... uh, if that's all right with you.'

'I'd forgotten about the billy-cart.'

He raised an eyebrow. 'You do still want to do it, don't you?'

'Yes. Yes, of course.' Clover headed out of the kitchenette, two cups in her hand, but stopped for a moment and looked at him over her shoulder. 'See you later.' And then she did something she'd never done before. She returned his wink and swished her hips as she walked away. Her reward was an audible groan of agonised delight.

By three o'clock they were in his mother's shed, hammering and building, Clover more than happy to follow Brandon's instructions on what he needed her to do.

'You've really never built anything before?'

'Never.'

'Not even put together a piece of furniture? A book-shelf?'

Clover shook her head. 'No.'

'But you do have furniture in your…apartment? I presume you have an apartment in Sydney?' He shook his head. 'There is just so much I don't know about you.'

Clover smiled and touched a hand to his cheek. 'I have an apartment.' But she didn't add that it was on the prestigious North Shore and overlooked the Opera House and Sydney Harbour Bridge. 'It came furnished.'

When she'd decided to move out of her father's mansion, without asking, he'd organised her apartment with everything provided. She'd thought it might have been a small token of his affection, to reward her for becoming an obstetric consultant, but when she'd made the effort to thank him, he'd told her it was business, that he'd recently purchased the entire apartment complex and would receive a hefty tax break.

She pushed aside thoughts of her father and held up the hammer. 'What do I need to bash in next?'

Brandon tut-tutted. 'You don't *bash*, Clover, you gently tap the nail at first and then, once the tip is in the wood, you add a bit more oomph.'

'Oomph?' She smiled at the word. 'Is that the technical term? And why are you allowed to say the word "oomph" when I'm not allowed to say "bash"?'

Brandon laughed and hugged her close. 'I've never had this much fun building a billy-cart before.'

'Not even with your dad?'

'No. He was too big and hairy to kiss.'

Clover laughed at his words, slipping her hands around his waist and angling her head up so he could give her another one of the amazing kisses she was quickly become addicted to.

'You're much nicer,' he murmured against her mouth. 'Delicious. Addictive.' He punctuated his words with kisses and Clover sighed into him.

He closed his eyes and gave himself over to her glorious lips and the way she responded to him so ardently. Did it matter that she was still a little closed off with him? That each time he mentioned he didn't know her all that well, she'd offer him the slightest bit of information and then change the subject?

He could sense she was keeping something from him but right now, with her arms wrapped firmly around him, returning his kisses with such an ardent passion, he wasn't too sure he wanted to find out.

For the rest of the week they worked alongside each other at the clinic and maternity care centre, looking after their patients and providing top-of-the-line health care for the township and surrounding district. After work, enjoying the extended daylight hours, they'd hammer and build and laugh together out in the shed. Many other people were building their own billy-carts and on Friday night, their entry finally ready for tomorrow's big Christmas race, Clover and Brandon headed to the pub for a well-deserved drink.

'You've got paint on your cheek,' Brandon remarked as they sat down at a table, gently rubbing his thumb over the mark, his touch sweet and tender. Clover smiled as she sipped her ice-cold orange juice.

'How do I look in green paint?' she asked, leaning closer to his ear to deliver her words as the crowd behind them was starting to get a bit rowdy.

'Stunning,' he returned, his gaze devouring her. Throughout the week they'd tried to play down their new relationship, both of them still finding their feet, but that hadn't stopped the gossipers from doing what they did best.

'Mind if we join you?' Geoffrey asked, as he and Joan came to sit at the table. 'It's getting a tad crowded at the bar,' he remarked, jerking a thumb over his shoulder.

'Of course.' Clover and Brandon sat back in their chairs, smiling as though they shared an incredible secret. As they chatted to their friends, discussing an emergency plan for tomorrow's race should it be required, Brandon couldn't believe how content he felt with Clover by his side. The wariness he'd lived with since discovering Lynn's betrayal had all but vanished and he was glad he'd taken a chance with Clover as he was falling for her in a big way.

He'd learned over the past few days that Clover's favourite colour was green—hence their billy-cart was predominantly painted green, with two thin red racing stripes down the sides. 'To make it go faster,' Brandon had answered when Clover had queried it.

He'd learned she had a bit of a sweet tooth and would often take a smaller portion of the main meal if there was dessert being served afterwards. He'd learned she wasn't afraid to try something new when she'd joined the Lewisville quilters, even though she'd confessed to never having sewn before.

'Except for suturing wounds closed,' she'd added when he'd looked at her askance.

He'd learned she hadn't obtained her driver's licence until after her twenty-third birthday, saying she'd lived close to the medical school where she'd completed her training so hadn't really needed to drive.

But most of all he'd learned that she'd 'sort of dated' a younger colleague of her father's until a few months ago.

'We were a wrong fit right from the start,' she'd ventured as they'd sanded back the billy-cart before applying the first coat of paint. 'My father likes him and therefore approves but unlike my sanding, which is perfectly smooth, our time together was anything but that.'

'Then why date him in the first place?'

'Because my father approved.' She'd frowned. 'Sad but true.'

'You want his attention. I understand that.'

'I don't know if I'm ever going to get it.' She'd shaken her head and sighed. 'Since coming here, seeing a way of life that's so completely different from my own, I'm realising I need to stop looking for his approval. You've taught me that.'

'I have?'

'Sure. You accept me for who I am and you have no idea how…empowering that is.'

Brandon had felt a little uncomfortable with her words because he knew, in the beginning, he *hadn't*. He'd been hurt and bruised and highly sceptical but being here with her, getting to know her, having her finally open up and trust him a little bit more, had made him realise just how special she was.

'What about other boyfriends? You know, at high school?'

'All-girls' boarding school.'

'Oh. Medical school?'

Clover had nodded slowly. 'Two guys—not at the same time, I might add.'

Brandon had smiled. 'Good to know. What ended it?'

'My father. He didn't approve.'

'So you broke up with them?'

She'd shaken her head. 'No. They broke up with me *after* my father had had a little…chat with them.'

'Ah. So when he approved of this other guy, you thought—why not?'

'Exactly. It was a mistake.'

'So what did he say when you broke it off with his man of choice?'

Clover had shrugged again. 'I don't know. We didn't discuss it.' With that, he'd seen the shutters come down on her past as she'd vigorously continued to sand their billy-cart.

Now as they chatted and laughed with their friends, other people pulling up chairs so they ended up being quite a large group, Brandon watched as Clover joined in the good-natured teasing, smiling brightly, her eyes alive with happiness.

In all their conversations he'd never heard her mention any close friends or any times when she'd gone down to the pub with her work colleagues for a quick drink at the end of a shift. She had confessed to being a workaholic and he wondered if that was because she was always searching for the next best way to garner some attention from her father.

Medical school, obstetric specialisation, working at a prestigious private hospital, dating a man her father approved of…what else had she done to try and gain some attention from the man who should be showering her with love?

The strong possessive spark he'd felt throughout the week only intensified as he began to piece together a rough picture of her life before they'd met. She was highly intelligent, resourceful, caring and extremely pretty but it was the way she laughed, the way she would gently caress his arm, the way she felt against his body, the way her mouth fitted perfectly with his own that was drawing him in. She *was* the whole package—brains and beauty—and he knew he was close to being hooked.

When Saturday morning dawned bright and clear, Clover dressed in running shoes, long, sturdy denim jeans—as per Brandon's instructions—and was wearing a special red T-shirt that had 'Lewisville Billy-Cart Participant' printed on the front and a number on the back. It wasn't just any number…it was *her* number. She was just finishing a cup of coffee when Brandon came bounding in through the front door of his mother's house.

'You're up! Great. Ready for the best day of your life?'

'Ready,' she confirmed, and saluted. Brandon laughed and drew her close into his arms before giving her a good-morning kiss.

'I missed you,' he murmured near her ear.

'Likewise,' she responded, then kissed him again, before drawing back and pointing to the number on the back of her T-shirt. 'Look! I have a number.'

'Yep. I'm five and you're six.'

'I like six. *I'm* number six.' She giggled. 'I have a number.' Clover clapped her hands with great delight. 'I've never had a number before.'

'What does that mean?' Brandon poured himself a quick cup of coffee, knowing his mother was already out and about in the town, helping to set things up and keep things moving. He sipped his drink, smiling at the way a simple T-shirt had made Clover so happy.

'I means I'm finally a part of something big and great and awesome. I'm "in the know". I'm one of the cool kids for a change.'

'Cool kids?'

She waved his words away and stacked her empty cup in the dishwasher. 'You know what I mean.'

'I think I do. You're excited at joining in the fun.'

'Oh, no. I'm not just *joining in*. I *joined in* at Ruby's wedding. No. Today isn't about *joining in*.'

'It's not?'

'No. Today *I* am a *participant*.' She clapped her hands again and Brandon simply couldn't help himself and drew her to him once more, infected by her happiness. 'I helped *build* that billy-cart, even though I can't quite believe it.'

'I'm glad we're doing this together.'

'So am I and I love that we're the red team and we wear matching T-shirts—'

'With numbers on the back,' he quickly interjected.

'Exactly! While we race down the street at goodness only knows how fast, trying to balance and hold on and not fracture half the bones in our bodies. And I'm so excited!'

'Unlike the first test run the other day when you were terrified to get on and then squealed all the way from start to finish?' he asked rhetorically.

'I have never done *anything* like this before.' She leaned up and kissed him, sighing against his warm, comforting and protective arms. 'Thank you, Brandon.'

'For...?'

'Asking me to be your partner. For including me. For getting me a T-shirt that makes me feel like I truly belong for the first time in my life. You're amazing.' She kissed him again and this time, before she could draw back, he slid a hand around and up the centre of her back, urging her to stay closer as he deepened the kiss.

Outside, Ned Finnegan, dressed in a red top, red shorts, flip-flops and also wearing a Santa beard and wide-brimmed hat, was trying to call everyone to order using a bull-horn, and as it squeaked, Clover and Brandon drew apart, both of them blocking their ears against the sound.

'Time to go,' Brandon said, and Clover nodded eagerly, heading for the door. 'Wait a moment. You forgot this.'

When Clover turned to see what he was holding up, she couldn't help but laugh. In his hands Brandon held two red Santa hats but they weren't of the usual nightcap variety. No, these were red Akubra hats with a sprig of wattle on the band and Christmas tinsel around the broad rims.

'Don't forget your Santa hat, number six.'

Clover allowed him to place it on her head. 'It's perfect. Did you decorate them especially for us?' She flicked her long braid down her back, getting her hair well out of the way.

'I did,' Brandon replied, and once more found himself staring at her luscious lips. He took a step closer, his gaze never leaving her face as he angled his head down, twisting to angle it more so he didn't knock the hat from her head. Slowly, slowly, he continued in her direction, Clover licking her lips in delighted anticipation, then Ned gabbled something into the bull-horn, the only words Clover really able to process being 'To the starting line, please.'

Brandon pulled back and shoved his own hat onto his head. 'That's our cue.' Taking her hand in his, they left Viola's house and headed to the marshalling area, where a few of the younger kids were guarding their billy-cart.

Clover couldn't believe the number of people who had turned up for the race, everyone sporting something Christmassy, whether it was earrings, flashing brooches, reindeer ears or a Santa hat. Everyone was getting into the spirit of Christmas. The scent of sausages on a barbecue was starting to fill the air, with people swatting away flies with tassels of tinsel and drinking cool drinks. Stalls were set up along one side of the road.

'It really is a social calendar event,' she told him.

'Sure is. It's Christmas, plus it's also a fundraising event. All the money raised today goes to support the village in Tarparnii where I worked for six months. PMA is looking to set up another medical clinic there but first the sanitation and supply of fresh water needs to be addressed so I'll be heading over for a two-week vacation once Ruby and Hamilton return in February to help build the well.'

'You're going to *build* the well?'

'Well, not by myself but with other people helping, sure.' He slung and arm around her shoulders. 'I'm not just a pretty face, you know.'

Clover smiled. 'I know that but you really do give and give, not just money but practical support. This is what it's all about. Being a part of something, of a community, of *really* helping.'

She sighed with delight. Finally, she'd found someone who understood what she'd been wanting to do all along, to use her skills and knowledge to really make a difference somewhere. 'It's a lovely idea.' She shook her head in bemusement. 'Everyone here really does care.'

'You sound surprised.'

'I guess I'm not used to people simply helping others without wanting anything in return.'

Brandon stared at her. 'You really have had a different upbringing.'

Clover stood her ground, holding his gaze but still

feeling highly self-conscious when Brandon looked at her in such a way. She wanted him to see down into her soul, to see she was a good person, to see that she loved being in Lewisville. She wanted so desperately for him to accept her for who she was, rather than be like everyone else in her life who always saw her as the heiress to the Sampson fortune.

She knew her father and Xavier tolerated her desire to work as a doctor but they had always expected her to give up work after her marriage, to take her rightful place as patroness of many different organisations, holding fundraisers, attending lunches.

As Xavier had put it, 'Behaving like the heiress you are. One day your father will pass away and you'll inherit his shares in the Sampson Corporation. You need to be ready for that and you will be because I'll be right by your side, instructing you every step of the way.'

Clover didn't want that. She didn't want the label. She didn't want the fortune. She didn't want to give up her job. She didn't want to just throw money at people but instead help them in a hands-on way.

Brandon had done that when he'd gone to Tarparnii, working in a village that he and the rest of the Lewisville community had pledged to support. The people out here had their own problems and issues and often didn't have much money to spare but when they all pulled together, supporting and helping each other, a little bit could go a very long way and she admired that immensely.

As she continued to look into Brandon's gorgeous blue eyes, Ned gabbled something into his bull-horn that sounded as though the first race—the one for twelve-year-olds—was about to start.

'Let's go and watch,' she suggested, and he nodded,

the two of them making their way to the sidelines to
cheer on the competitors.

Clover saw Lacey Millar and her husband standing
on the opposite side of the road and waved, the couple
returning her greeting. Clover watched the smile on
Lacey's face, noting it didn't quite meet her eyes.

'Something's happening,' she murmured, giving
Lacey's abdomen a quick visual scan. Low and tight.

'Sorry? Did you say something?' Brandon asked,
dipping his head so his ear was closer to her mouth.

'It's fine. Nothing.' She waved his words away and
focused her attention on the race about to start, clapping and cheering along with everyone else.

There were a few cuts and scratches as people came
off their billy-carts but on the whole there were no serious broken bones or anything like that and soon it
was time for Clover and Brandon to take their places.

They changed their hats for proper racing helmets
and donned protective knee-pads, elbow-pads, shin-
pads, mouthguards and gloves. Safety first. It was almost eleven o'clock in the morning and the sun was
now starting to beat down on them, warm and strong.
It didn't matter because it was time for the real race,
not just a practice one, and Clover could feel her nervous tension beginning to rise.

'Are you feeling OK?' Brandon asked, having to yell
a little due to the helmets they were wearing. Clover
made the 'OK' signal with her thumb and forefinger.
'Hey, I have a surprise for you,' he said, and urged her
around to the rear of the cart, where he pulled off a sheet
of green paper to reveal their names.

'Ta-dah!' He held out his hands, indicating the surprise he had for her. Clover stared in delighted amazement. There they were, their names—Clover and

Brandon—intertwined with an ampersand in the middle, linking the names together. *Clover & Brandon*. She was deeply touched and lifted the visor of her helmet to gaze up into his eyes.

'Thank you. I *love* it.' I love you, she silently added, and breathed in the definitive knowledge to herself. She *loved* him. She *loved* Brandon. She could finally admit it to herself.

He smiled and nodded, wanting to remove the helmets and the rest of their protective gear and hold her close against his body, but it was time to start the race and so he winked at her before they took their places.

Clover's heart was beating wildly, not only from the lovely surprise he'd painted onto the back of their cart but because she'd just admitted to herself that she was in love with him. She hadn't wanted to think about her feelings too much but now she was forced to admit that she'd been in love with him for quite a while. What a time to discover she was in love!

She climbed into the billy-cart, her adrenaline beginning to pump as she shifted forward into position, ensuring she'd left enough room for Brandon to jump in after pushing them up to speed.

'Go get 'em, Clover and Brandon,' Viola cheered. Ned put the bull-horn to his mouth and began the countdown. It was still impossible to understand a word he was saying but as the actual starting signal was an air-horn, there was no chance they'd miss that. Brandon could only push for a certain distance, which was marked by a line further down the road, then he had to jump on behind Clover and see if they could make it to the finishing line first.

The green cart with red racing stripes was primed and ready to go and so when the air-horn sounded,

Clover found herself letting out a squeal of excitement as Brandon began to push. She didn't look at the other racers, instead focusing herself on the task at hand.

After what seemed like an age, Brandon jumped in behind her, his strong arms coming around her to assist with the steering as they sped down the street. Clover tried to lower her head, as they'd practised so often, imagining for one brief moment that she was a luge athlete at the winter Olympics.

As she curved her back, Brandon's chest pressed into it, his arms tightening on the steering rope, his legs alongside hers, so close and so confined and so intimately delightful. She didn't care whether they came first or last, being this close to the man of her heart made her feel like a winner.

Before she knew it, Brandon was angling the cart, both of them leaning to the side, but they must have leaned too far as in the next moment they tipped out of the cart, Clover landing on top of Brandon, their arms and legs sprawled and intertwined with each other's.

Brandon was shaking and Clover shifted, instantly concerned in case he'd hurt himself, but when she twisted around to look at his face she discovered he was laughing. A smile lit up her eyes and she grinned back at him, chuckling at what they'd just accomplished. She untangled her limbs from his and removed the helmet. 'That was completely awesome!'

'It was.' He sat up, removing his helmet and looking into her eyes. 'The most fun I've had in a long time. Ruby's always so competitive.'

Clover raised an eyebrow. 'And you're not?'

Brandon slowly shook his head. 'It doesn't matter if we come first or not, being with you, having fun with you, that's winning as far as I'm concerned.'

She smiled and touched a gloved hand tenderly to his cheek. 'That's one of the nicest thing anyone's ever said to me.'

Brandon leaned a little closer, his gaze centred on her mouth for a split second before he met her eyes once more. 'Then remind me to say lots of nice things to you in future.' His words were soft as he continued to lean towards her.

Clover closed her eyes, waiting in anticipation for his lips to meet hers. She didn't care where she was or what was happening in her life, she wanted Brandon to kiss her now more than anything. They'd survived the billy-cart race and Brandon was talking about a future…a future for them together?

Clover didn't want to get her hopes up as she'd been let down far too many times before. She pushed the thought from her mind and focused on his mouth, silently willing him to hurry up because she wasn't sure she could wait any longer for one of his spectacular kisses.

'And the winners are…the red team!' Ned announced through the bull-horn, which miraculously seemed to be working now. At the mention of their team and the round of applause that accompanied the announcement, Brandon jerked back and Clover looked around to discover all eyes were on them.

He helped her to her feet and they accepted the congratulations of their friends and family. Viola ran towards them, her arms held wide. She embraced them both together.

'That was so exciting. One of the best runs ever made. So fast—and although Parker and Damien were fast, too, you just pipped them at the post, so to speak. I can't believe you won!' Viola was filled with excitement and continued to chatter on, telling them how pleased his father would have been that Brandon had finally won a race after all these years.

'And we can display the trophy at the clinic so everyone can see it, especially as it belongs to both of you,' Viola continued, as Clover and Brandon removed their protective gear and cleared their poor billy-cart off the road. 'Or do we keep it at the new maternity care centre? It's a dilem—'

'Clover! Clover!' A loud cry came from Damien Millar, who was beckoning them both over to where Lacey was sitting on the ground with the sun beating down on her, holding her belly and panting. Damien was quickly pulling off all his protective gear and looking at his wife as though he wasn't sure what to do. 'Clover!' he shouted again, and Clover hurried to Lacey's side, kneeling down and pressing a hand to the other woman's abdomen.

'Is it happening?' Lacey asked as she gritted her teeth in pain. 'Or is it just Braxton-Hicks'?'

'It's happening.' She turned to look at Brandon. 'Looks as though we have our first birth at the maternity centre with or without equipment. This little one's coming and he's not waiting for anyone.'

'He's early,' Lacey stated. 'I can't go yet.'

'It looks as though Junior has other plans,' Clover countered.

CHAPTER TEN

GEOFFREY and Joan brought the ambulance stretcher over so they could transfer Lacey to the maternity centre. Quite a few people cheered them on as they moved through the crowd, wishing Lacey luck as they went. Clover was warmed by the caring community.

'Will it be OK, Clover?' Lacey asked, concern in her tone and worry etched on her brow. Damien was beside her, holding her hand. They entered the clinic and took Lacey through to a delivery room near the rear of the clinic.

'Everything will be fine,' Clover confirmed, her voice resonating pure calm and control.

'What do you need?' Geoffrey asked, after they'd transferred Lacey off the stretcher.

'I need Joan, Brandon, some cool air flowing through the centre and a bit of privacy,' she told him.

'Consider it done.' With that, Geoffrey wheeled the stretcher out of the room.

'*Very* well trained,' Clover couldn't help remark to Joan, the two women sharing a smile.

They all pulled on gowns to cover their clothing before Clover turned her focus to Lacey, who was lying back on the delivery bed, watching every move Clover made like a hawk.

'Now, Lacey. I need you to remember what we've talked about. We discussed what would happen if the baby came early and we know what to do. We're not going to panic.' Clover put her hand on Lacey's shoulder as the contraction eased. 'We're going to keep you comfortable and relaxed and let your body tell you what it wants to do.'

Clover's tone was soothing, caring and once again Brandon was struck by the way she could put people at ease, calm them down, which was exactly what Lacey needed right now.

'Remember, you're not in Broken Hill. Damien's here and Brandon, Joan and I will be caring for you both to the best of our abilities. This centre is all about providing for mother and babe, about making you feel as comfortable as possible.' While she spoke, concentrating on putting Lacey's mind at rest, Brandon and Joan rushed around like little worker ants, setting things up and getting ready.

'Now, it looks as though your waters have broken and—' As Clover started talking, Lacey began groaning again, her body tensing as the next contraction hit. 'That's it. Breathe through it. Squeeze the life out of Damien's hand if necessary. It's all right. He has another one.'

As the contraction began to subside, Clover took off Lacey's shoes and massaged her feet. 'There are pressure points here that help you to really let go of everything so just lie back and close your eyes. Conserving energy between contractions can really help.'

'Is there time for medication?' she asked.

'I'll do an exam in a minute once Joan's helped you into something a little more comfortable and practical for delivering a baby,' she answered.

Joan did exactly that, helping Lacey into a pale pink hospital gown. 'For now, though, we're going to use the new baby heart monitor and just see what sort of heart-beat the little fella is kicking out.'

Clover turned to look for the piece of equipment she needed and found Brandon holding it out for her. 'Thank you,' she said with a quick smile, then turned back to her patient.

Brandon couldn't get over how calm and in control she was. This was her speciality. She'd already deliv-ered hundreds of babies over the years, whereas, he had to confess, assisting with a delivery was not one of his favourite things to do as so much could go wrong, es-pecially out here in the Outback.

But now, thanks to Clover's brilliant idea, they had this little maternity centre where Lacey could have her baby closer to home with her husband by her side. She could stay on here for a few weeks, if she wanted and learn how to bath her baby, how to feed him, how to change his nappy and settle him down to sleep at night. She would be supported by the older women in the com-munity and Brandon knew his mother would be one of the first volunteers for the job.

Getting both mothers and babies into a routine before they went home would definitely set the young families of this community off to a good start.

'So how are you feeling?' Clover asked after she'd completed her exam.

'Like another contraction is coming,' Lacey replied, every muscle in her body tensing as the pain hit. Clover guided Lacey with her breathing then, and once the con-traction started to subside, Clover did another exam.

'You're fully dilated. Have you been having any sort of contractions over the past few days?'

'Yes,' Lacey admitted. 'I'd read up about Braxton-Hicks' contractions and thought it was just that.'

'Yes, they were, but those contractions let you know that things are starting to move.'

'I was going to call you and ask you if that's what was going on but I just didn't want him to come out now. He's four weeks early.'

'He's going to be fine…and fast by the look of things. Your contractions are just over two minutes apart. Chances are you've been in the early stages of labour since yesterday.'

'That's fast!'

'It is for a first baby but not to worry.'

'So…this is really it? I'm…in…labour?' Lacey was stunned.

Clover's smile was bright. 'You're in labour,' she confirmed. It wasn't the first time she'd had a conversation like this with a woman about to deliver. Nine times out of ten they'd turn up at the hospital concerned they might be in labour, but even after they'd started pushing, they'd found it difficult to accept that after nine or so months the labour was *actually happening*.

Clover held the foetal heart monitor to Lacey's abdomen and listened closely, her gaze meeting Brandon's as together they mentally counted the beats. Brandon nodded, as though silently confirming what Clover was thinking.

'What is it?' Damien asked, having witnessed the exchange between the two doctors.

'The beats aren't as fast as we'd like,' Clover said. Her tone was still calm and controlled but Brandon could tell she was mentally running through what she'd need in case of an emergency C-section. They may be in the new maternity centre, they may be delivering their first baby on the premises, but the humidi-cribs weren't due to arrive until after Christmas and as this little one was early, it meant they all needed to improvise.

'What…what does that mean?' Lacey asked.

'It means the baby could go into distress if we don't deliver him or her sooner rather than later,' Clover returned, as she checked Lacey's vitals, pleased everything was within normal parameters. Once that was done, she listened to the baby's heart rate again.

'It's a little lower than before.'

Lacey looked at her husband and squeezed his hand again. 'Something's wrong, Damien. Something's wrong with our baby.'

'It's all right, Lacey.' Clover could hear the panic beginning to rise in Lacey's tone. 'We can deal with this togeth—' But before she could finish her sentence Lacey let out a loud cry and started to push. 'Right. That's the first push so that's our cue.' She did another exam and could see the head was starting to crown.

'Joan, Brandon, I need you to prepare a makeshift humidi-crib and oxygen box.'

'Oxygen box?' Lacey asked, fear creeping into her tone.

'Precaution. I like to be set up for any eventuality. We have most things but for those we don't, we'll simply organise an alternative. Remember, Brandon's been working overseas in Tarparnii where, from what I've read in articles, women can sometimes have their babies on the side of the road. He knows how to improvise.'

Brandon was pleased to hear she had so much confidence in him, especially as obstetrics was her speciality. He could also tell she was trying not to startle Lacey too much but also wanted the new mother to know that, as professionals, they had everything under control. He left the room, intent on doing what Clover required.

'What we need you to do, Lacey,' Clover continued, 'is to concentrate on bringing this gorgeous little one into the world. I need you to keep breathing and listening to what I say. I might need you to push really hard or I might need you *not* to push—which is the most difficult thing to do in the world, especially when all your muscles are contracting and urging you to push. Just listen to my instructions and we'll take care of the rest.'

After the next contraction, when Lacey once more couldn't help but push, poor Damien's hand being squeezed so hard it was turning purple, Clover once more checked the baby's heart rate, disappointed to find it still decreasing. That wasn't good. She checked Lacey's blood pressure and found that it was well within normal limits. Something was affecting the baby, something bad, and Clover went over different scenarios in her mind.

'Good, Lacey. You're doing a fantastic job.'

'And the baby's heart rate?' Lacey asked. 'Why is it so slow? What do you think it is?'

Clover knew at a time like this that plain speaking was the best tack to take. 'Well, the most common cause of a decreased heart rate is that the cord is wrapped around the baby's neck. When the contractions start, that cord can become rather tight, but we'll sort it out. Just keep listening to my directions, OK? That's the most important thing at the moment.'

Lacey met Clover's eyes and nodded. 'I will,' she promised.

After several more contractions, with Lacey dutifully focusing on her breathing, Damien mopping the perspiration from her brow and offering her sips of water, Clover announced the baby's head was almost out.

'A few more nice big pushes. Come on, let's breathe together.' Clover counted down, breathing in time with Lacey.

She heard Brandon re-enter the room and glanced across at him for a split second, pleased when she received a thumbs-up and a big encouraging grin from him. It was exactly what she'd needed right at that point in time. She was concerned for the baby, well aware they were missing a lot of equipment but not wanting to alarm the mother too much.

Lacey gritted her teeth and pushed, yelling her frustration and pain into the room. 'Good. Well done,' Clover encouraged. 'One more big push and the head will be out. Then I'll be able to check the baby's neck. One more big one. Come on, Lacey. You can do it. Snatch a breath and *push*!'

Lacey followed Clover's instructions. 'Excellent. The head is out. Well done. Now comes the hard part. I need you not to push. Even if you feel like it. You must resist the urge to push. Damien? Help Lacey with her breathing.'

'On it,' Damien replied, completely focused on his wife.

'How are you doing, Brandon?' Clover asked, as she carefully felt the baby's neck for the cord. There it was. Wrapped firmly about the little one's neck. With deft fingers Clover managed to ease the cord over the baby's head.

'I want to push. *I want to push*,' Lacey demanded.

'Don't push,' Clover said firmly.

'Breathe. Breathe.' Joan came alongside Lacey and took her other hand. 'Breathe and squeeze all your pain into our hands,' she encouraged, with poor Damien groaning in agony as his wife once more squeezed his hand. 'That's it. Nice shallow breaths,' Joan encouraged.

'Almost there. Just a moment longer.' The cord was wrapped twice around the baby's neck and Clover gritted her teeth as she unlooped it the second time around, checking and double-checking that everything was now fine as the baby's shoulders started to rotate.

'Done. The cord is off.' There was a collective exhalation of breath at this news. 'Push when you're ready, Lacey.' But no sooner had Clover said the words than Lacey was pushing as though her life depended on it. The baby's shoulders appeared and a short while later the baby boy slid into Clover's waiting arms.

'It's a boy! It's a *boy*!' Damien whooped, and laughed. 'We have a son!'

'Is he all right?' Lacey asked, trying to raise her head. 'Is he breathing? How's his heart rate?'

'Just a moment,' Clover said as she and Brandon worked quickly to clamp the cord. 'Sorry, Damien. No time for you to do the honours,' she went on, as Brandon cut the cord and then took the baby, rubbing the little blue-tinged body to stimulate blood flow as well as remove the vermix.

'He's not breathing,' Brandon stated as Clover drew up an injection of Vitamin K to administer to Lacey to avoid post-partum haemorrhaging before the third stage of labour began.

'Clear the mouth and nose.'

She had hoped for the care centre to be completely set up before the first birth but with no humidi-crib, suction machine or oxygen boxes, they had to do their best. It was great to see she could rely on Brandon, that when it came to crunch time he was right in there, adapting and changing things around so they had exactly what they needed.

Somehow he'd managed to find a metal frame that looked as though it had come from the inside of a filing cabinet. Next, he'd wrapped the metal frame in plastic sandwich wrap to make a clear area for them to pump oxygen into so the baby could get what it needed. What a clever man.

'Doing it,' Brandon returned, as he carefully wiped the baby's mouth and nose out with a swab and a cotton bud.

Being an Outback GP often meant doing things either the old-fashioned way or adapting to the surroundings in order to get the job done. The baby still wasn't breathing and although he could do mouth-to-mouth resuscitation, he decided to try one more thing first, the old-fashioned way of getting a baby to breathe, the way that had been good enough for him and countless other babies throughout centuries. He lifted the little boy up by the feet, tipped him upside down and smacked his bottom.

There was a moment of complete and utter silence as everyone seemed to hold their breath, then…the most glorious sound, one of a soft, indignant cry, filled the air as Lacey's and Damien's little boy registered his protest.

Breathing a collective sigh of relief and happiness, everyone smiled. Brandon continued to care for the baby, ensuring the oxygen saturations were at the correct level as he placed him into the improvised oxygen tent, keeping him as warm as possible.

He looked over his shoulder at Clover, who was still attending to the weeping Lacey. Their gazes met and held, and together they shared a smile of relief, of success, of mutual admiration. After checking his little

boy out, Damien had headed outside and used Ned's
bull-horn to announce the news to the rest of the town.

'I have a son!'

Everyone in the delivery room smiled warmly at the
loud cheer that went up from outside and later, with
Lacey under Joan's watchful eye and as little baby
Orsonn was improving by leaps and bounds, enjoying his first feed and cuddle with his parents, Clover
removed her gown and stepped out onto the back veranda of the centre for a moment of peace.

'Mind if I join you?' Brandon's deep tones washed
over her and she turned, a smile already on her lips,
and held out her hand to him. 'First baby born in the
new maternity care centre. Orsonn Millar has himself
a place in the Lewisville history books.'

He went to her, sliding his arms around her waist
and holding her close, both of them content to just hold
each other. Clover couldn't believe how incredible, how
right, how perfect it felt to be exactly where she was.

Lifting her head, her heart hammering wildly against
her ribs, she looked into his gorgeous blue eyes, eyes
she would never tire of. 'Brandon?'

He frowned a little. 'Something wrong? You look
really worried.'

'Not worried. A bit apprehensive but that can't be
helped.'

'What is it? What's wrong?'

'Nothing's wrong,' she replied, her smile widen-
ing as she gently shook her head. 'Everything's right.
Everything is *so* right, *so* perfect. I had no idea life
could be like this.'

'I know.' After Lynn's betrayal, he'd wondered if
he'd ever be able to trust again and yet, standing here,
holding Clover in his arms, he felt wonderful. 'Come

on,' he said after a moment. 'Let's go get a nice cool drink. I think we deserve it.'

Her smile was bright as she nodded, and after checking on the newest addition to the Lewisville community, ensuring that mother and babe were fine and with Joan shooing them both away saying she'd keep an eye on things while they went and had a celebratory iced slushy, they left the maternity care centre and stepped out into the heat.

'Here you go,' Brandon said, as he placed Clover's red tinselled hat on her head. 'Don't want you getting burnt.' As they walked towards the cool-drink stand, they were both stopped along the way by several people, being congratulated and thanked for a job well done. Some people shook her hand, others—namely Viola—embraced Clover in an enormous hug.

'We're so lucky to have you here, Clover. Our first baby, born in the new care centre. It's all just perfect.'

After a while Clover lost sight of Brandon as she was still being asked all sorts of details by all sorts of people wanting to know how heavy little Orsonn was or how big his head was or how long he was. She presumed Brandon had made it to the drink stand but after she'd finished answering several questions and recounting the way Lacey had been amazing during the birth, Clover headed to the stall but found he wasn't there.

She searched the crowd for him, smiling and nodding to other people as they walked past, but still there was no sign of him. Perhaps he'd gone to the pub but after she'd checked, still unable to find him, she'd bumped into Geoffrey.

'Have you seen Brandon?'

'Yes. He's out the back of the pub, talking to some guy who's just passing by for the day.'

'Thanks.' Clover headed around the side of the pub down towards the small outdoor beer garden which was rarely used as most people preferred the air-conditioning inside the pub. As she rounded the corner, going up the two steps that led to the veranda covered deck, she heard Brandon's voice.

'Is that right? Wow. That's…a lot. I had no idea.' He had his back to her and she smiled, knowing it was just like him to make people passing through his town feel welcome—just as he'd done with her when they'd first met. He was such an incredible man, caring, giving, thoughtful. She couldn't see the man he was talking to as Brandon's gorgeously large shoulders were blocking her view.

'So this is where you're hiding,' she remarked, coming to stand beside him. It was only then she glanced across at the other man, ready to say hello, to be polite and shake hands and do her bit of welcoming a stranger to the amazing town of Lewisville—when she realised she already knew the stranger in question. 'Xavier!' Her jaw dropped open as she felt the blood drain from her body. 'Wh-what are you doing here?'

CHAPTER ELEVEN

SHE looked from Brandon to Xavier and back again, her mouth going dry as her heart hammered out a mortified rhythm.

'Clover. There you are.'

'Xavier, here, was just telling me all about your father's corporation. The *Sampson* Corporation, and how you're the sole heiress to the entire thing.'

Xavier nodded, clearly not realising what he'd just done. 'That's right. Our Clover is one special woman.'

'Oh, yes. *Our* Clover is certainly...*special*.'

Clover could hear the veiled pain hidden beneath Brandon's words. She met his gaze, unable to hide the truth. 'Brandon, I—'

'And all the time she's been in town, helping us out, joining in with all sorts of community events, we've all been none the wiser that we had a millionaire in our midst.'

Xavier chuckled. 'She does enjoy her little projects, helping others out with her doctoring skills. I have no idea why. There's no reason in the world why she should work but she does insist on it.'

'Maybe she likes playing games. Is that right, *Clover*? Do you enjoy tricking others?'

Clover sighed and shook her head sadly, seeing the

pain and anger in Brandon's eyes. He had every right to be angry and she knew now she should have made more of an effort to tell him the truth before something like this happened. She looked from Brandon to Xavier. 'How did you find me?'

Xavier tut-tutted. 'Darling, I'm a man of means and intelligence. I think I can track down my fiancée when she decides to wander off.'

'Fiancée?' Brandon kept his cool, his tone dry and filled with pain. 'Well, well, well. It's just one surprise after another. That's something else *our* Clover failed to mention.' He pierced Clover with a harsh look before turning his attention back to the city dweller, dressed in suit trousers, a crisp white shirt and university tie. 'Tell me, Xavier, how long have the two of you been engaged?'

'Let's see, I proposed in early July when we were in Port Douglas. The wedding's at the end of February and after her father's Christmas Eve party—which is spectacular, by the way—we'll be heading into major planning mode.' Xavier looked at Clover. 'My PAs have already arranged your dress fittings with the designer and drawn up the preliminary guest list. It's going to be the event of the year!'

Clover stared at Xavier as though he was completely insane. 'Wh—?' She stopped and shook her head, her hands clenched into fists by her sides. 'How da—?' She stopped again and gritted her teeth.

'Don't grind your teeth, Clover. I don't want a bride with a crooked smile.' Xavier laughed and nodded at Brandon. 'Am I right? I'm right, aren't I?'

'Ugh!' Clover had had enough and she was simply far too furious with Xavier to even begin to form coherent sentences. Throwing her arms in the air, she spun on her heel and stormed off, furious with Xavier and fearful of what Brandon was making of all of this. Tears stung at her eyes as she took the short cut around the rear of the buildings, hoping to make it back to Viola's place, where she could hibernate in her room until she calmed down.

'Clover?' She heard Brandon call her name just as she reached Viola's back door and she turned to face him. 'When were you going to tell me you were engaged? Or weren't you going to bother with that little detail?'

A fresh surge of anger exploded over her as she stared at him, then she shook her head and went inside.

'Avoiding the truth again?' Brandon followed her into the house, stopping in the laundry as she stood there, glaring at him, hands on her hips.

'I'm not avoiding the truth. I never have.'

'Yet you never thought to mention that you were engaged? Or is that just one of those minor details you've been concealing from me?' He shook his head. 'I knew it. I knew you were hiding things from me. I kept telling myself that you couldn't possibly be as perfect and glorious as you appeared to be. So calm and controlled all the time with that mesmerising hint of aloofness. I knew I was a fool to trust you and yet I let my guard down and once again fell for a woman who can't help but lie to me.'

'I have never lied to you,' Clover returned. Ordinarily, she avoided confrontation wherever possible but since coming to Lewisville she'd discovered a new Clover. Here she'd been valued, accepted and, as such, her personal confidence had grown. She didn't want Brandon to think she'd been lying to him when she hadn't.

'I applied for the job under my professional name—

Clover Farraday. Farraday was my mother's maiden name. My full name, if you care to know it, is Clover Beatrice Gertrude Hazel Farraday-Sampson, not that it should make any difference. And as far as not mentioning I was engaged, well, that's easy because I'm *not* engaged. I never *have* been engaged to Xavier. The ridiculous man simply refuses to take no for an answer.'

Clover turned and stormed down the corridor towards her room. Brandon followed, standing in the doorway.

'So you're saying that man didn't even propose?'

'What's that got to do with anything? Why can't you believe me?'

'And I suppose you're not the daughter of a multibillionaire who has so much money he could buy the entire country if he wanted to?'

'It's not my fault who my father is and as I've already told you, we don't exactly get along.' She shook her head and planted her hands on her hips.

'So are you really worth millions? Was coming here to Lewisville just your way of filling in time before your big society wedding?'

'I don't believe this.' She covered her face with her hands, knocking off her tinsel-covered hat.

'Neither do I because you're still avoiding the question,' he growled. 'Why didn't you tell me about your father? About who he is?'

'Because in the past, every time I've been interested in a man, my father has interfered by buying them off.'

'What? You mean he paid them money to *stop* dating you?'

'That's exactly what I mean. Everyone has their price, Brandon.' She spread her arms wide. 'Do you have any idea how it feels to have a person you thought you cared about, that you thought you could one day really come to love, take a better offer and ditch you—ditch you because of money?'

'Yes, as a matter of fact, I do know what it feels like. Lynn may not have ditched me for a fortune but she certainly ditched me because I wasn't good enough.'

'Then you know how worthless your life feels, how betraying, how belittling it is.'

'Yes.'

'And that's why I didn't tell you who my father was. That's why I don't tell anyone. That's why I changed my name.'

Brandon blinked once. 'You thought he'd buy me off?'

'Everyone has their price,' she reiterated, and she hadn't been able to bear the thought that he would leave her—just like the other men she'd cared about.

'Even after we came to mean something to each other, you still didn't trust me,' Brandon stated, and shook his head. Clover thought she might break down and sob right then and there at the look of disgust in his eyes. 'You know, every time I asked you about your life in Sydney, you'd give me a short answer and change the subject.'

She dropped her hands and shook her head. 'I don't like talking about my life for that exact reason and as I *have* told you, it was hardly a happy life.' She was getting hot under the collar now and raised her voice—something she'd never done before, especially during an argument.

'A life you still can't bring yourself to talk about.'

'It's my past. I can't change it.' She clenched her jaw so tightly her head really began to pound. 'Why is it so important?'

'Because it is,' Brandon yelled in exasperation.

Clover blinked once, twice, unable to believe he was yelling at her. She looked away, desperate to hold back the tears that were threatening to erupt. She clenched her hands and tried to swallow, needing to maintain control over her emotions. The last thing she wanted to do right now was to cry, to have Brandon think she was using tears, her feminine wiles, to get around him. He either could accept her for who she was or he couldn't. It really was that simple.

She pursed her lips and looked down at the floor then looked into his eyes. 'I love you, Brandon, and that *is* the truth.' She bit her lip as she waited for his response to her declaration but he just stood there, glaring at her. Finally, he shook his head.

'I don't know how I can trust anything you say. You want to know what my "price" is? My price is freedom—from you.' With that, he turned and walked from her room. A second later, the front screen door banged shut—just as he'd shut her out of his life.

As the band started to play and the guests began to arrive, Clover pasted on a smile. Not for her father and certainly not for Xavier. This Christmas Eve party was a great fundraiser for welfare agencies where the rich came to this party, giving lots of money without having to rub shoulders with the poor. Yet the last thing she felt like doing was smiling—for she really had nothing to smile about.

Since Brandon had stomped out of his mother's house three days ago, Clover had changed her clothes, packed her bags and allowed Xavier to take her back to Sydney. She'd barely spoken a word to him during the entire chopper ride to Sydney, not that it had both-ered Xavier, who had taken the opportunity to organise some more business. It was only when she'd finally been taken to her apartment that she'd allowed her emotions to have free rein.

Brandon hadn't believed in her. Brandon hadn't been able to accept her for who she was and it was that pain, that hurt, that had had her sobbing into her pillow for the past few nights.

On her first morning back in Sydney she'd sat on her balcony and watched the sunrise, annoyed with herself for failing to be moved by the beautiful sight, which had always managed to calm her down. It was then she realised that nothing mattered much any more simply because Brandon didn't love her.

Everything in life was just going through the motions and that was what she was doing tonight. Walking through her life as though it was a part in a play. She'd managed to arrange for one of her trusted OB/GYN colleagues to head to Lewisville over the Christmas period to fill in for her. After that, she'd sort out a more permanent replacement. There was no way Clover was leaving that town without obstetric support but neither was there any way she could go back and work alongside Brandon every day, knowing her heart would always be his when he didn't care for her. It would be too torturous.

She looked across the yard to where her father stood at the entrance to a large marquee, shaking hands with someone and having his photograph taken by a reporter. Since she'd arrived back in Sydney, they hadn't spoken. For some reason, that didn't bother her as much as it had in the past. Was it because she'd managed to find happiness in Lewisville? With Brandon? Even though it had been only for a short while, for one brief moment there, with her red number-six T-shirt on, she'd belonged.

'My PAs informed me this afternoon,' Xavier remarked as he came to stand beside her, 'that your engagement ring is finally perfect. I had to send it back twice because the diamond wasn't big enough. I'm having it sent over tonight as an early Christmas present for you. I think your father's scheduled a photo session for seven-thirty tomorrow morning.'

'Tomorrow's Christmas,' Clover pointed out, unable to believe Xavier was still persisting with this engagement.

'I know.'

'Xavier, what do you get if you marry me? I mean, what's your price?'

'My price! Honestly, Clover. Some days, you're incredibly vulgar.'

'Well…what is it? It has to be something. Everyone has a price.'

'Not me. I have plenty of money. That's one of the reasons your father gave his blessing to our engagement. The fact that he knows for sure I'm not a gold-digger.'

'But you are a snob and I'm going to say that your price is…prestige. You want prestige in being married into one of the wealthiest families in Australia. You want the Sampson name forever connected with your own.' She looked at his face and nodded. 'I'm right, too. I can see it in your eyes. That's the one thing my father's always been right about. Everyone has their price.' She turned to leave but stopped and levelled him with a direct look.

'And for the last time, we are *not* engaged, Xavier. I don't know how many times I have to say it but it may help you to know that I'm actually in love with another man and if I can ever get him to speak to me again, to give me the time of day once more, I will do whatever it takes to find a way to spend my life with him.'

As she turned and walked away, Clover realised that even *she* had a price.

Brandon stood in the lavishly lit gardens of the Sampson mansion, wondering how on earth he was supposed to find Clover in a throng of over a thousand people? He wasn't wearing a tuxedo, like every other man here, and with the way the women were dressed, in their latest designer clothes, dripping with jewels, he knew he stood out from the crowd.

The past three days—the three days since Clover had left Lewisville—had been the worst. Even when Lynn had left, he hadn't felt *this* bad. He snagged a drink from the tray of a passing waiter but even as he brought the glass to his lips, he decided he didn't want it after all. Nothing could quench his thirst any more. Nothing could fill his stomach. Nothing could help him sleep. Nothing could make him happy—and it was all because he'd been stupid enough to let Clover go.

Now it was Christmas Eve and over the past few days in Lewisville everything had been sparkly and bright and festive…and Clover had missed it. Far too often, he'd turned around to tell her something, to share a laugh, to hug her close, to kiss her…but she hadn't been there.

His life had been a shambles, cold, empty…pointless, which was why he'd strode from his bed earlier that morning, left a note for his mother and called in quite a few favours in order to get him to Sydney by tonight. It hadn't been easy but Clover was definitely worth it.

And now here he was, at her family mansion, and

all he wanted was to find her. He didn't care about her father or the money or whether or not she was engaged to Xavier. She belonged with him. She belonged with him *in* Lewisville and he refused to leave Sydney until he'd told her that. He had a price, she'd been right about that, but it wasn't the price she'd thought.

Where on earth could she be?

As he walked purposefully through the garden towards the large marquee that had been set up with a dance floor and an orchestra, he couldn't help comparing this type of fundraising event to the ones they held in Lewisville. So incredibly different.

Did Clover like all this stuff? The fancy twinkle lights, the trees in the garden that had been decorated with large baubles and tinsel, and the orchestral version of classic Christmas carols? Glasses of champagne clinked near him and bow-tied waiters carried silver trays of food through the throng of people.

It certainly was a different world here and he could well imagine lonely little Clover attending many of these parties as a child, wearing a pretty dress and looking perfect but never allowed to move from a chair lest she mess up her dress or ruin her hair. His heart bled for all those warm and wonderful times she'd missed with her mother. His family may not have been excessively wealthy, but they'd been rich with the blessings of familial love.

Brandon continued to scan the crowd, not finding her anywhere. Perhaps he should have called ahead, letting her know he was coming. He'd been too focused on actually getting to Sydney, calling in a favour from his friend who flew the emergency helicopter and then paying double for the taxi to get him here as fast as possible.

At the door to the mansion he'd been denied entry

as his name hadn't been on the guest list so he'd made a generous donation to tonight's charity and had reluctantly been permitted entry…and now he couldn't find her.

Raking a hand through his hair, he shook his head and decided to find a nice quiet corner where he could think through his next move. One thing was for sure, he wasn't leaving Sydney without talking to her.

As he made his way through the crowd, he spotted a small path leading down to a gazebo that overlooked a duck pond. With the hustle and bustle starting to ebb, he breathed a sigh of relief as he entered the gazebo.

'Brandon?'

He turned. 'Clover?'

And there she was. Sitting on a seat looking out at the duck pond.

'What are you doing here?'

'I've been looking for you.'

They spoke in unison as she stood and he took a step closer. His gaze travelled over her and even though there wasn't as much lighting here as there was behind them, he could well appreciate the exquisite red satin dress she wore, tied on one shoulder and leaving the other one bare. There was no need for a necklace as the bodice was adorned with sparkles of some sort. Her hair was secured in an elegant style that made her look regal and glorious.

Brandon was riveted to the spot, unable to take his eyes off her, and was fairly sure his jaw had hit the ground as he gaped at the stunning woman who had captured his heart.

'You look…amazing.'

'So do you.' With his jeans, running shoes and T-shirt that still fitted him to absolute perfection, he looked as gloriously handsome as he had the day they'd first met.

He laughed and shook his head as he pulled at his T-shirt. 'What? This ol' thing?'

Clover smiled and took a small step towards him. 'What are you doing here?' she asked again.

'I've come to grovel.'

'OK.'

He blinked once, surprised she was going to let him actually go through with it. Clover dug her nails into the palms of her hands, trying to stop the itching need to throw herself into his arms. She still couldn't believe he was actually there but now that he was, she wanted to hear what he had to say.

'I was an idiot.'

'Yes.'

'You really aren't going to make this easy, are you,' he stated.

'No.'

'Why?'

'Because you hurt me.'

'I know and I'm so sorry.' He raked a hand through his hair. 'I was just surprised to hear you were engaged—'

'*Not* engaged,' she said, pointing to herself.

'And I was hurt that you hadn't trusted me enough to tell me who your father really was.'

'It's not easy for me to open up because for far too long I've been ignored, shut out. My father, Xavier— they're the same. Neither of them listen to me. Neither of them ask me what it is *I* want to do with my life. That was different with you. You listened when I talked. You made me laugh, you made me feel as though I was a person of worth, not just a possession. You really do know me better than anyone else, Brandon. You know the *real* Clover because you didn't pressure me.'

'And yet when it came to crunch time, I *didn't* listen. That's why you left.'

'I've been ignored for most of my life.' Tears began to glisten in her eyes. 'I couldn't bear to stay in Lewisville and be ignored by *you*.'

'Oh, Clover.' With that, he covered the distance between them and gathered her into his arms. She buried her head into his shoulder and held him close, never wanting to let him go again. 'I can't ignore you because if I do, I'd be ignoring my own heart.' He eased back from her. 'You have it, you know. You've had my heart since my sister's wedding when I couldn't help but kiss you.'

'That was one of the happiest nights of my life.'

He smiled down into her upturned face, dabbing at the corner of her eyes with his thumbs, tenderly brushing away the few tears that had spilled over. 'Mine, too.' He caressed her cheek. 'I love you, Clover Beatrice Hazel Gertrude Farraday-Sampson. I love every single part of you and I always will.'

Clover bit her lip, unable to believe this was really happening, that Brandon was really here, holding her in his arms, telling her he loved her.

'Marry me?' He swallowed and she was astonished to see nervousness reflected in his eyes. Surely he knew how much she loved him? Surely he knew her answer would be yes to that heartfelt important question?

'Clover?' a male voice said from behind them, and both she and Brandon turned to find her father standing at the edge of the gazebo, looking at both of them. Brandon tightened his arms around Clover, indicating he wasn't about to let her go.

'What's going on?' Oswald asked as he looked from her to Brandon.

'Dad. I'd like you to meet my fiancé. My *real* fiancé,' she remarked, looking lovingly up at Brandon.

Brandon quickly held out one hand, the other still firmly around Clover's waist. Now that he'd found her, he wasn't letting her go. Oswald simply glanced at Brandon's hand as though it was covered with disease, before turning his attention once more to his daughter.

'You've done it again. Gone and got yourself mixed up with a hooligan. All right,' he sighed, and looked at Brandon. 'Name your price.'

Brandon shook his head and slid his ignored hand back around Clover's waist. 'I don't have one, sir. Not one money can buy.'

'That's what they all say, boy.'

'It's true,' Clover remarked. 'Brandon can't be bought.'

'If it isn't money, what is it you want?' Oswald asked, ignoring his daughter.

'Well, sir. I've given it a lot of thought.'

'I bet you have. What is it? New house? New car?'

'No sir. My price…' Brandon looked down into Clover's gorgeous face '…is to spend the rest of my days making your daughter as happy as possible.'

Oswald frowned for a moment. 'Seriously. Get to the point. I have a speech to make soon.'

'I am serious.' Brandon tucked a loose tendril of hair behind Clover's ear. 'I love her with all my heart and I'm going to marry her.' He bent his head and brushed a kiss over her lips before looking at her father once more. 'I'm sorry if that disappoints you and of course both of us would like you to come to the wedding, but if you feel you're incapable of doing that one small thing for your only daughter, then we respect your decision.' He returned his attention to his gorgeous fiancée.

'Clover doesn't need to vie for your attention any more, Mr Sampson, because I willingly give her mine.' He brushed the backs of his fingers across her cheek. 'I do love you so, my Clover. I really do need you to be with me for ever.'

'Oh, Brandon.' She stood on tiptoe and kissed him warmly, forgetting her father, forgetting the party, forgetting everything except the way he made her feel.

'This is ridiculous.' Oswald was about to say more but was cut short when an aide came to tell him it was time for the speeches. 'We'll discuss this later,' he warned his daughter.

'No, Dad. We won't.' She looked at him, releasing Brandon just for a moment before crossing to her father's side and pressing a small, sad kiss on his cheek. 'I don't *need* you in my life any more, Dad. I *want* you in it, of course, but my price—the price I'd pay to get what I want—is to leave Sydney, leave my job, leave my entire past here and go to Lewisville with Brandon, where I *know* I truly belong.'

Oswald stared at his daughter, seeing her perhaps for the first time, but he didn't say anything. Instead, he walked away, leaving Brandon and Clover to their peace and solitude, something both of them were more than happy about.

'Are you all right?' Brandon asked, once more drawing her into the circle of his arms.

'Yes. It was time.'

'So…I take it you're definitely going to marry me?'

Clover smiled. 'What gave you that idea?'

'Perhaps it was the way you introduced me as your fiancé. Or maybe it was the way you kissed me…' He brushed a tantalising kiss across her lips and Clover couldn't help but smile. 'Or maybe it was the way you—' He didn't get to finish his sentence as she effectively silenced him with a kiss.

'You talk too much,' she murmured against his mouth.

'Then allow me to rectify the situation,' he returned, then Brandon lowered his head and captured her mouth in the most wonderful of kisses, filled with the promises of an incredible life together.

Finally, he raised his head and looked down into her beautiful face, both of them slightly breathless but incredibly happy. 'Merry Christmas, my love.'

'Yes, it is going to be a *very* merry Christmas!'

EPILOGUE

'THE wedding was held in the middle of the main street of the sleepy Outback town of Lewisville, cordoned off especially for the festivities. The bride, as is traditional, wore white, but not a designer gown as you would expect for the heiress to the Sampson Corporation. Instead, the simple yet elegant dress was hand-stitched by the groom's mother, Mrs Viola Goldmark. Mrs Goldmark will be using this opportunity to launch her new career as a seamstress later this year.'

Viola laughed, as did Ruby, playfully hitting her husband's arm to get him to stop. 'Oh, Hamilton.'

'What are you laughing at?' Clover asked as she and Brandon came to sit down at their table. Clover kicked off her shoes and allowed Brandon to pull her onto his lap.

'Hamilton and his brothers keep writing tomorrow's newspaper headlines, describing the society wedding that never was.'

'We're positive there are journalists lurking around the outskirts of town, peering at us all through binoculars and telephoto lenses,' Bartholomew Goldmark added. The entire clan had returned to Lewisville for another wedding, all of them delighting at seeing Brandon so happily settled with Clover.

Naturally, Clover had been only too delighted to resume her position as OB/GYN to Lewisville and surrounding districts. The maternity care centre was now fully operational, with all the equipment having arrived the week after Christmas. Clover had now delivered three babies in the centre and Viola and Marissa Mandocicelli were running daily programmes for young mothers, helping them to cope.

'I wish there had been something like this when I'd had my children,' Marissa had told her. 'You're a genius, Clover.'

'Yes, she is,' Brandon had agreed.

When the band began to play again, Brandon urged Clover up off his knee before scooping her up into his arms and carrying her towards the makeshift dance floor. 'Care to dance, Mrs Goldmark?' he asked as she slid provocatively down his body.

'I thought you'd never ask, Mr Goldmark.' And barefoot and in his arms, Clover was more than happy, more than satisfied, more than content to dance with the man of her dreams. Amazingly enough, her father had actually relented and attended her wedding, walking her down the bitumen road of Main Street towards the man who would forever be her husband.

'It's not too late to change your mind,' her father had murmured out of the corner of his mouth.

'Be quiet, Dad, and just keep smiling,' had been her reply.

'Do you know your father offered me another bribe five minutes before the ceremony?' Brandon remarked, and Clover eased back to look at him, raising an eyebrow. 'He tripled his original offer and, of course, I refused.'

She smiled. 'I gathered that, otherwise we wouldn't

be standing here, dancing slowly and sensually together.'

'True…but it's what happened *after* I refused his final offer.'

'And what's that?'

'He shook my hand. The great and powerful Oz shook my hand.' Brandon held up the hand in question and Clover dutifully inspected it.

'Wow. That's big. It means…well, I think it means he might be coming to respect you.'

'So long as he respects *you*, I'll be happy.'

'My hero.'

'You'd better believe it, my love.'

'Pity he didn't choose to stay for the reception but he *did* come to the back of beyond to walk his only daughter down the aisle. That's the most attention I've had from him since…well, I can't remember when.'

'I'm happy you're happy.'

'I am.' Clover closed her eyes and once more leaned her cheek against her husband's chest. Content. Relaxed. Loved. She sighed, long and true.

'There's that sigh again,' he remarked.

'It's a sigh of complete and utter happiness because I've found you. I've finally found you. I can live in the town where I belong, practise medicine and start a new chapter in my life with you—my one true love.'

They continued to dance together, not caring whether the music was loud and rocking or slow and sensual. They were lost in their own little world and it was only when the MC said it was time for the traditional garter and bouquet toss that Brandon released his wife with great reluctance.

'To be continued,' he whispered in her ear, and she giggled.

'Promises, promises,' she replied, as they made their way towards the microphone.

'All right, time for all single women to gather in one crazy group, ready for the toss of the bridal bouquet,' Edward Goldmark announced. Clover smiled and took the microphone from Edward, her voice smooth and modulated.

'I caught Ruby's bouquet less than six months ago so perhaps this thing really works!' She laughed, then handed the microphone back to Edward and turned her back to the waiting women.

'On the count of three,' Brandon called, and together everyone joined in the countdown. On 'three', Clover pitched the bouquet over her head and turned to watch it fall into the waiting arms of Marissa, who had been a widow for over twenty years.

The woman yelped and squealed with delight. 'Yes,' she said with joy. 'Thank you, God. I will be getting married again soon.' And she turned, winking at Greg Filmore. To his credit, the sixty-year-old widower turned beetroot red but smiled at Marissa nonetheless.

'And now for the men,' Edward announced into the microphone, and laughed as Marissa nudged poor Greg into position. Brandon and Clover watched as the men, far more reluctant than the women, made their way into the centre of the dance floor, laughing as Hamilton and Benedict ensured their only single brother Bartholomew was in the mix.

'On three!' Edward said, and again the crowd counted down. Just before Brandon threw the garter, he focused his gaze on Bartholomew as though getting his bearings, then he turned his back to the crowd and threw the garter over head—his plan working to perfection as the garter landed in Bartholomew's half-heartedly open hand.

The crowd cheered, Marissa shrugged but still sidled up close to Greg, while the Goldmark men took great delight in teasing the only bachelor left among them.

'The garter toss doesn't lie,' Hamilton said, pointing to Brandon as though providing proof.

'Finally!' Honeysuckle remarked. 'A good woman is coming your way.'

'But I'm not interested in getting married,' Bartholomew protested, only to be laughed at again by his crazy family.

'Happens to the best of us,' Woody remarked, slapping Bart on the back.

'I wonder who she is?' Ruby asked.

'Whoever she is, she's a lucky woman,' Clover said, gazing into Brandon's eyes. 'To marry a member of the Goldmark family means to be embraced with pure happiness and love.'

'The bride has spoken!' Brandon declared, and everybody cheered!

* * * * *

REDEEMING
DR RICCARDI

BY
LEAH MARTYN

MILLS & BOON

First published in Great Britain 2012
by Mills & Boon, an imprint of Harlequin (UK) Limited.
Harlequin (UK) Limited, Eton House, 18-24 Paradise Road,
Richmond, Surrey TW9 1SR

© Leah Martyn 2012

ISBN: 978 0 263 89200 0

Harlequin (UK) policy is to use papers that are natural, renewable
and recyclable products and made from wood grown in sustainable
forests. The logging and manufacturing process conform to the
legal environmental regulations of the country of origin.

Printed and bound in Spain
by Blackprint CPI, Barcelona

Recent titles by Leah Martyn:

DAREDEVIL AND DR KATE
WEDDING IN DARLING DOWNS
OUTBACK DOCTOR, ENGLISH BRIDE

**These books are also available in eBook format
from www.millsandboon.co.uk**

For Zach, Hannah, Ava and Raphael.

'You are so beautiful.'

CHAPTER ONE

Valentine's Day had fallen on a Monday. And who on earth felt like partying on a Monday?

All the off-duty staff at the hospital apparently.

Nurse Manager Toni Morell's mouth lifted in a wry little twist, as she swung into the car park at the district hospital. For years now, Valentine's had been the day set aside for the annual fundraiser organised by the social committee and excuses for non-attendance were not allowed.

Toni just hoped she'd have enough energy at the end of her shift to get herself into party mode. It was her first day back from leave, and while her time in Sydney had been fun, it was nice to be back in the less hectic pace of the rural town of Forrestdale, where she'd now chosen to make her life.

As she gathered her bag from the passenger seat, her thoughts flew to the day ahead. Accident and Emergency had a new relieving senior registrar, Rafe Riccardi. Toni had spoken with him only briefly at the end of her shift before she'd taken off on holidays.

When they'd met, he'd been surrounded by board members and there had been no opportunity for a longer chat. But she recalled his handshake had been firm and he'd looked her in the eye. And she'd thought later

that he could be described as tall, dark and…not handsome exactly but there'd been something about him, a
presence that would be hard to ignore. Toni just hoped
he was proving a good fit for their team. Her tummy
swooped slightly. Staff changes at senior level always
came with a niggle of uncertainty. But it wasn't as
though Dr Riccardi was here for ever. He had a three-
month contract while he covered long-service leave for
their usual reg, Joe Lyons.

Toni's mind clicked into work mode as she made her
way along to the staffroom. She'd left home in plenty
of time, determined to get a jump start and catch up on
things generally.

But it seemed as though the entire shift had arrived
early as well and the place was buzzing. A love song
was pumping out from the local radio station, helium-
filled red hearts were floating against the ceiling and
by the look of it, gifts of flowers had already begun ar-
riving for some lucky recipients.

Toni wasn't expecting any flowers or chocolates. Not
even a card. She didn't have a special man in her life.
Hadn't for ages. But she could still dream. Dream that
someday she'd meet *the one*.

'Hi, stranger!' Liz Carey, Toni's senior counterpart
and close friend greeted her.

Toni's soft laughter rippled. 'It's only been a week.'

'Nice break, though?' Liz's hands spanned her coffee mug.

'Sydney's always fabulous. Spent lots of time on the
beach.'

'Mmm, I can see that,' Liz deadpanned. 'Love the
tan.'

'Oh, ha.' Toni took the comment as lightly as it
was meant. With her auburn hair and fair skin she had

about as much chance of acquiring a tan as representing Australia at the Nationals. 'How have things been here?'

'Fairly OK.'

'New reg?'

Liz shrugged. 'Earning his keep.'

'And?' Toni's voice rose a notch.

'And nothing,' Liz shook her head. 'He seems professional. Made it his business to do the rounds of the shifts early on. Had a coffee with us—well, he had a green tea. Said he wanted to get to know us all asap. Amy Chan's back, by the way.'

'Oh…' Toni's eyes softened. 'How is she?'

'Ask her yourself,' Liz said. 'Here she is.'

'Ames!' Toni dropped her bag on to a nearby table and swooped the younger woman into a hug. 'How are you?'

'I'm good, Toni.' Amy shook back her bob of shiny black hair and smiled.

'Really?'

'Really,' Amy affirmed softly.

'And Leo?'

'He's fine. And thanks from both of us for—well, everything.'

'Hey, no problem.' Toni waved the other's thanks away. As nurse manager, she regarded her team almost as family. 'And anything you need, little break here and there, just ask, all right?'

The young nurse nodded and then turned as Justin Lawrence, one of their junior resident doctors, stuck his head in and called, 'Amy, these just came for you.' He held up a ceramic pot of bright red gerberas swathed in scarlet ribbons.

'For me…?' Amy put a hand to her heart and blushed

prettily. 'They'll be from Leo.' She took off to collect her flowers as though her feet had wings.

'Leo's such a nice husband,' Liz said.

'Mmm.' Toni's gaze was faintly wistful. 'Red in the Chinese culture is the symbol for good luck, isn't it?'

'Something like that. Heaven knows, they could do with a bit.'

'Now, about the reg,' Toni persisted, tugging Liz aside. 'What are you not telling me?'

Liz rolled her eyes. 'You're like a dog with a damn great bone. It was a rotten week, stretched all of us. Riccardi was…tetchy.'

Toni frowned. 'With the staff?' She considered her team extremely well trained.

'With life in general, I think. There was an accident at that demolition job on Linton Road. A beam fell on a young apprentice. He…died.'

'Oh, lord.' Toni squeezed her eyes shut for a second. 'Was Riccardi called to the scene?'

Liz nodded. 'And that happened on Monday so it rather set the tone for the rest of the week.'

Toni looked thoughtful. Rotten days happened in A and E. That was the nature of the department. As a senior doctor, Riccardi should know how to hack it. And if he couldn't, why on earth had he taken the job? She was still holding the puzzling thought when the man himself strode in. *Oh, wow…* Toni's breath lodged and then came out slowly. He *was* as tall as she remembered. Taller, tougher, masculine to his fingertips. And his eyes, the shade of an early morning ocean, a kind of wintergreen, were tracking over her.

'Antonia.' He gave a formal little nod. 'Nice to see you back.'

And that, decided Toni, was where his effort to be polite stopped.

'Could someone turn that racket off?' he growled, making his way to the electric urn. He selected a tea bag from a canister and slammed it into a mug. 'Now,' he said levelly as he waited for his mug to fill with boiling water.

Ed, one of the junior nurses, obliged and the Beatles' version of *All you need is love* was strangled. 'It's Valentine's Day, Doc,' he protested with a laugh. 'You need to get in the zone.'

Riccardi's underbrowed look said, *Are you for real?*

'We'll all be going to the dance at the workers' club tonight.' Amy smiled, holding onto her little pot of flowers tightly. 'You must come, Dr Riccardi.'

The registrar snorted. 'I'd rather cut off my own feet.' He dangled his tea bag briefly and then discarded it in the bin. 'Without anaesthetic,' he added for good measure, before he strode out.

Liz sighed. 'Well, that went down well. Poor Amy. That was a bit unnecessary, wasn't it?'

'Yes.' Toni felt her temper fray. She'd seen Amy's expression falter; she'd bitten her lip and looked as though she hadn't known whether to laugh or cry. For heaven's sake, she was only trying to be friendly. She certainly hadn't deserved to cop the brunt of Riccardi's foul mood. Well, she wasn't having it! 'Lizzie, take handover, please? I need to sort this.'

Watching her friend take off out of the room, Liz muttered, 'Oh, you're for it, Riccardi.' When it came to standing up for her team, Toni was like a lioness defending her cubs.

'Dr Riccardi?' Toni raised her voice, moving along

the corridor with the speed of light. She caught up with the registrar outside his office. 'I'd like a word, please?'

'It's Rafe,' he said shortly. 'Is there a problem?'

'Yes.' Toni sucked in her breath. 'Your attitude.'

One dark eyebrow arched and her less than diplomatic statement hung in the air between them. 'You'd better come in, then.'

'No, thanks.' Toni shook her head. She didn't want to go into his office. She just wanted to state her case and get on with her day. 'I need time for a coffee before I start my shift.'

'I have coffee.' He flicked a hand towards his open office door.

Toni floundered for a second and then thought, Oh, what the heck. And followed him in.

He indicated the cafetière on the bench table near the window. 'Maureen still insists on providing fresh coffee every morning as she did for Joe, even though I've told her it's not necessary.'

Toni bit the edge of her lip through a reluctant smile. Maureen O'Dea had been Joe Lyons's secretary for ever and definitely wasn't about to be told to change her longstanding protocol. 'You don't drink coffee at all, then?'

'Not much. Help yourself,' he invited.

Toni did, drawing in the aroma of freshly brewed coffee as she poured. It was much nicer than the instant in the staffroom and she guessed she should be grateful for what was supposedly a small peace offering from Rafe Riccardi. But she wasn't about to be sidetracked from her mission.

'Have a seat,' he offered.

Nursing her mug of coffee, Toni slipped into the

chair, facing him across his desk. 'I don't want this to be confrontational.'

'OK.' He raised his mug and took a mouthful of his tea and studied her in silence for a second, then his mouth quirked. 'I won't bite. So, speak to me, Antonia.'

Toni took a deep breath and straightened her shoulders. 'I'm usually called Toni.'

'Pity.' His stormy green gaze tangled with hers. 'Antonia is a beautiful name.'

Well, it was the way *he* said it, low and expressive and newly awake, early-morning sexy. And it completely trashed her defences. She regrouped jerkily. She had to say what she'd come to say. 'Amy Chan is just getting over losing a baby at twenty weeks.'

A beat of silence.

'And I need to know this because…?' Riccardi leaned back in his chair and waited.

'Because your response when she invited you to the Valentine's party was offhand. In fact, it was bordering on rude. You embarrassed her and she's only just returned to work—she's still fragile. If we're to work successfully as a team, we need mutual respect and at least a show of good manners.'

Suddenly the silence was as thick as custard. Toni tightened her fingers around her coffee mug. Had she gone too far? As the senior medical officer for the department, Rafe Riccardi's toes were definitely not for treading on. 'I realise you're new to the place and getting to know everyone takes time…' She stopped and wished she could dive under the desk and hide from his penetrating green gaze. But there was no chance of that.

'Fine, then.' A contained little smile played around his mouth. 'You've made your point. I'll straighten things out with Amy and with the department in general.'

'And show your face at the Valentine dance?' Toni jumped in where a lesser person would have feared to tread.

His jaw tensed. 'You don't give up, do you? What's all the hype about St Valentine's Day anyway? It's for lovers, isn't it? Then let the lovers of the world get on with it.'

Toni dropped her gaze. This was the oddest kind of conversation to be having with a man she'd only known for five minutes. She took a mouthful of her coffee and tried to marshal her thoughts. 'I realise for some people Valentine's Day is a pain but for the others it's loaded with romance.'

He snorted.

'Well, it is!' Toni emphasised.

'It's commercialism at its worst.'

'OK.' Toni batted a hand in a kind of aggrieved acceptance. 'We've established you're not into it. But here at Forrestdale St Valentine's Day is always set aside for the big fundraiser of the year. This year's project is a state-of-the-art ultrasound. It will be mainly in use in Midwifery.' Toni paused. *If they'd had better scanning equipment for Amy...* But that wasn't the problem. As Amy's Ob, Hannah Gordon, had assured the couple, the baby had just been too early, not viable. Toni blinked a bit. 'Anyway, that's about it. Tonight's dinner-dance is about raising funds.'

'I'll give a donation,' Rafe said flatly. And he'd make it a hefty one. Anonymously, of course.

'Up to you.' Toni got to her feet. There'd been a glimmer of hope she could have talked him round. She may as well have saved her breath. She placed her mug back on the side table. 'I guess we'll catch up sooner rather than later, then. Mondays are usually a bit full on.'

And then she turned and he caught the full force of her smile. It was so warm, so natural, as if she did it a lot. Smiled, that was. He stood courteously as she left, his breath jamming in his throat.

Antonia Morell was one sassy lady. He sank back into his chair feeling a bit dazed. He'd actually enjoyed sparring with her. And that incredible auburn hair... The way she wore it, wild and untamed, had to say so much about her personality. Out of nowhere, he imagined her on a speedboat on Sydney Harbour, cutting through the spray, her hair windblown, crazy curls all over the place streaming out behind her. Or snugly tamed inside a snow beanie with just some bright tendrils poking out. Or softly shiny spread on a pillow...

Hell. He yanked his X-rated thoughts to a halt. Get a grip Riccardi. You're not on the prowl here, no matter how tempting the prize. You're on a timeline. Three months to be exact. So, just keep your head down and do your job and at the end of your contract you can show those boffins on the medical board you're fit and able to get back in the field.

Toni's thoughts were mixed as she made her way back to the nurses' station. Rafe Riccardi baffled her. Intrigued her. Self-contained. A bit of a loner. Could be nicer if he tried a bit harder. Oh, for heaven's sake. She made a little sound of dismissal. She wasn't giving him a school report.

One glance told her the department was already busy. Liz put down the phone and looked up, her well-shaped brows raised in query. 'Is he still in one piece?'

'Of course.' Toni began slotting pens into her top pocket. 'We got engaged.'

Liz smothered a squawk and then chuckled. 'We've missed you.'

'Yeah.' Toni shook back her halo of auburn curls. 'Now, who's doing what?'

'Justin's suturing in the small treatment room. Beryl Reilly took a dive down the post-office steps this morning. Kneecap nearly split in two.'

Toni grimaced. 'Poor old love.' Beryl, in her seventies, was one of their regulars at A and E. 'Why on earth was she out and about so early?'

'Posting coupons for some cruise or other. Today was the last day to enter apparently.'

'Oh, my lord,' Toni sighed. 'What would she do if she won? She'd never go on her own.'

Liz snickered. 'She'd probably hook up with one of the old guys from their indoor bowls team and take him along.'

'We shouldn't laugh.' Toni pressed a finger to her smiling lips. 'It's very sweet, really, the way they all look out for each other.'

'And Beryl probably has about as much chance of winning as we do of getting a raise.'

'OK, back to business,' Toni said firmly. 'Who's assisting Justin?'

'Harmony. Not that she wanted to,' Liz added caustically. 'She hates anything to do with blood.'

'Well, she's only newly graduated,' Toni reasoned. 'These days they're not exposed to much on the wards in their training. It's always a bit of shock when they strike the real thing. Where's Ed?'

'Doing an eye-wash. One of the council workers

copped a load of sand and grit when they were unloading turf for the new sports oval.'

Toni nodded. 'Amy OK?'

'I've assigned her to tidy the drugs cabinet with Mel. The night shift left a tip.'

'Well, they had two RTAs in quick succession, by the look of it.' Toni scanned the report. 'This one says Riccardi was the admitting MO.'

'So?'

'So that means he's been here since four o'clock this morning.' Toni made a small face. 'No wonder he was grouchy. The man's missing sleep.'

'It's his job.' Liz was not so forgiving. 'It's what he signed on for.'

'I wonder what he was doing before coming here?' Toni mused.

'Dunno. Don't tell me you're falling for him?'

'As if,' Toni responded with a little tsk. 'Perhaps we should cut him a bit of slack, though. Forrestdale might be a huge lifestyle change for him.'

'Well, there's usually a trigger for those kinds of decisions,' Liz pointed out pragmatically. 'But I'm for making love, not war, so we'll be nice to your reg.'

'He's not *my* reg,' Toni said in exasperation. 'Now, both Natalie and Samantha in?' she asked, referring to the department's assistants in nursing.

'By the grace of God. And Dr Tennant is circulating if we need her.'

'Excellent.' Toni clipped on her badge and checked it was straight. 'I'll ask her to pop in on our eye patient. He may need an antibiotic and a medical certificate for work.'

'Uh-oh,' Liz sighed as their phone lit up. 'Call from the ambulance base. Welcome to Monday!'

Toni took the details from Liz. 'Mine, I think, and I'll bleep the reg.'

They met at the ambulance bay and Toni relayed what details they had. 'Unrestrained two-year-old thrown against the dashboard when his mum had to brake suddenly. He appears to have been knocked out for a second but conscious now.'

'The child was in the front seat of the car?' Rafe asked in disbelief.

'Apparently.' Toni twitched a shoulder. 'We don't know the circumstances. It may not be the mother's fault.'

'Well, we certainly can't blame the child,' Rafe said grimly. 'Do we have names?'

'Child is Michael. Mum is Lisa.'

He received the information with a curt nod. He'd have a few words to say to *Lisa*. Having a child unrestrained in a moving vehicle was totally irresponsible.

The ambulance arrived and reversed into the receiving bay. One glance told Toni the mother was distraught. 'It's all my fault!' Lisa was all but wringing her hands. 'The childminder is only two streets away and I was running late so I just popped him in the front seat beside me—but he's learned how to undo the seat belt—' She broke off, rubbing tears away with the backs of her hands. She sent a frantic look at Rafe. 'Will I be in trouble? What will happen now?'

Despite his earlier silent disapproval at the mother's negligence, Rafe's heart melted at the sight of the little lad lying quietly under the blue blanket, his eyes wide and questioning.

His mouth tightened. There were extenuating circumstances and he didn't have the stomach for a confrontation anyway. Not today. And especially not with

Antonia watching his every reaction with those soulful brown eyes. He regrouped his thoughts.

'We'll take a look at Michael,' he said gruffly. 'Try not to worry. Children are remarkably resilient.'

'Can I stay with him?'

Toni jumped in, 'Of course you can.'

'Oh—thank you.' Lisa held tightly to her child's hand as he was whisked through into a cubicle.

'Lisa, if you could just stand back, please?' Toni eased the mother away from the side of the bed. 'Dr Riccardi will need room to examine Michael.'

Still visibly shaken, Lisa complied, wrapping her arms around her body almost as if she could hold herself together in some way. 'I'm here, baby,' she said brokenly. 'Mummy's just here...'

The child looked clean and well cared for, Toni noted, peeling the blanket back gently. 'Doctor?' She looked pointedly at Rafe.

'Thanks.' Rafe began his examination. 'Let's see how you're doing, little mate,' he said, his hands gentle, swift and sure as he tested the child's neurological responses. 'Looking good,' he murmured, as Michael's pupils appeared equal and responsive. Placing his pencil torch aside, he checked the little boy's limbs for any obvious deficits and then began a careful palpation of the child's tummy. Any hardening would indicate internal bleeding. But all seemed well. He replaced the blanket and turned to the mother.

'Was he sick at all, Lisa?'

'No.' She shook her head. 'He just seemed out of it for a second or two and then cried a bit...'

Rafe nodded. 'I'd like to run a scan to be on the safe side. And we'll need to keep your son for several hours, just to make sure there are no residual effects from the accident.'

'It really *was* an accident.' Lisa stood her ground bravely. 'This guy just shot out of his driveway without warning and I had to slam on my brakes. I realise I should have had Michael in the back in his safety seat.'

'But you didn't.' Rafe continued writing on the child's chart.

'I was going after a new job,' Lisa explained dispiritedly. 'But I've lost my interview time now.'

'There'll be other jobs.' Absorbed in Michael's chart, Rafe curled his lips into a silent no-further-comment moue. He handed the request form for the X-ray department to Toni. 'After Michael's scan could you see whether Kids could take him, please? He'll be more comfortable there. And ask Justin to check Lisa over and perhaps we could run to a coffee for her?'

Toni gave him a taut little smile. 'I'm sure we could.'

Rafe pulled back the curtain to make his exit and then wheeled back, the light from the window illuminating the hard line of his jaw with its rapidly darkening growth. 'I'd like to see the X-rays when they're back, please, Antonia?'

'Certainly, Doctor.' Toni's response was crisply calm but a niggle of uncertainty caught her unawares. She'd told Riccardi she was usually called *Toni*. Why couldn't he just do it? Perhaps it was as simple as his not liking shortened names. She frowned a bit. Whatever his reasons, it was already setting her apart and causing the oddest trickle of awareness along her spine.

CHAPTER TWO

BACK in his office, Rafe threw aside the medical journal he'd been reading.

It may as well have been written in a foreign language for all he'd taken in.

Antonia Morell. The cameo-like picture was still there in his head. Her complexion magnolia fair against the dazzling auburn hair; the quick, intelligent air about her. And the amazing smile that outlined the sweet curve of her mouth. Her mouth…

Disconcerted, he rubbed a hand across his cheekbones. The wild feelings of want were annoying him, disturbing him. He didn't need them. He just needed to get through the next few months, recoup his energy, regain his enthusiasm…

'Rafe…?' Toni popped her head around the door. He looked up and she saw at once she'd interrupted a very focused train of thought. 'Sorry…the door was open…'

'Come in, Antonia.' He voice was slightly rough. 'What's up?'

'You said you wanted to see Michael's CT scan.' Toni moved towards his desk, feeling as though she was walking in sand, ankle deep. 'He's up in Kids now. Amy asked to special him.'

Rafe's dark brows rose interrogatively. 'Is that wise?'

Toni bristled at his implied criticism. 'Are you saying I should be keeping her away from babies and toddlers?'

'No.' He glinted an impatient green glance at her. 'You mentioned she's a bit fragile at the moment, that's all.'

'It was her decision.' Toni placed the large envelope on the desk in front of him. 'In fact, she said she hoped we wouldn't think we had to keep walking on eggshells around her.'

'Well, that sounds positive.' Spinning off his chair, Rafe selected the first plate and slapped it on to the viewing screen. 'I'll need a word with Lisa,' he murmured almost absently. 'Ask her to pop in and see me when you have a minute.'

'Uh…' Toni hesitated. 'She's actually not in the hospital just now.'

'She's gone?' Rafe's dark head swooped back in question. 'She's left her boy here and just gone off somewhere? Where are the woman's priorities?' He put the next plate up and studied it. 'The whole trauma for this child is down to his mother's failure to carry out the basic safety rules for young children in cars.'

'You're putting the wrong spin on it,' Toni said heatedly and went on to explain, 'Lisa had a phone call. Apparently, she managed to reschedule her job interview. She's a sole parent, Rafe. She needs a full-time job not just the bits and pieces she presently has. You saw how upset she was about Michael's accident. She doesn't need you jumping all over her as well.'

'You're breaking my heart, Antonia,' he growled, clearly unimpressed with Toni's defence of the young mother.

'And which *heart* would that be, exactly?' she inquired tartly.

The corners of his mouth pulled down almost comically. 'I've really rained on your parade today, haven't I?'

Toni rolled her eyes heavenwards. Really, the man was impossible.

'This all looks good.' He drew her attention to the last of the X-rays. 'Michael has been fortunate.'

'He's sporting quite a lump on his forehead, though.' Toni positioned herself beside Rafe and looked at the screen.

'I'll write up some pain relief for him. That whack has possibly left the little guy with a headache. And let's keep the neuro obs going, please? I'm not letting him go until I'm quite sure he's stable.'

'All noted.' Toni swept out.

She made her way back to the nurses' station, the busyness of the morning enveloping her. But an hour later, she was on her way upstairs to the children's ward. Amy needed a break.

She popped her head in, turning to speak to Jennifer on the desk. 'Michael Yates, Jen?'

The senior nurse flapped a hand. 'Right down the end in the cot. The reg arrived a while ago to check him over. He's gorgeous, isn't he?'

'Michael?'

Jennifer rolled her eyes. 'Riccardi.'

Toni wasn't about to go there. She still hadn't made up her mind about anything to do with Rafe Riccardi. 'He probably is,' she flannelled instead. 'If you go for tall, dark, bloody-minded men.'

'Oh, my stars, Toni Morell!' A teasing smile curved Jen's mouth. 'You fancy him!'

Toni clicked her tongue exasperatedly and skipped away, drawing to an abrupt stop when she saw Rafe and

Amy, their heads together in obvious earnest conversation. She watched as Amy's dark little head came back and she laughed at something Rafe said. And then he touched the nurse briefly on the shoulder before exiting from the door at the far end of the ward.

'Well, ten out of ten,' Toni murmured, feeling a tiny flicker of satisfaction. Rafe had obviously taken their talk to heart and made the effort to smooth things over with Amy. He'd kept his word. And that, as far as Toni was concerned, had earned him a large tick of approval.

Oh, heck! Impatiently, she swept her hair up from the nape of her neck and let it fall back. Surely she wasn't actually beginning to *like* the man?

She walked briskly along the ward to Michael's cot. 'Everything OK?' she asked softly.

'Still a bit out of it, I think.' Amy was sitting by the cot, stroking the toddler's chubby little arm.

'That's understandable.' Toni ran her eye over the chart. Pain relief had been administered and the child was being kept hydrated. There was little more they could do now than to monitor Michael's neuro responses. If nothing untoward presented, Rafe would probably allow Lisa to take her son home. 'He'll probably drop off to sleep soon.' Toni bent and touched a finger to the baby-soft cheek. 'But, Amy, if for any reason you have to take him out of the cot, be sure to carry him, won't you? We don't want him falling.'

'I *have* nursed in Kids before, Toni,' Amy said with a wry little smile. 'I'll take great care of Michael.'

'Of course you will.' Toni made a face. 'Sorry. I'm a bit distracted this morning.'

Amy chuckled. 'The new reg would distract anyone.'

Toni held back a cryptic comment. Not Amy too.

'Mel is coming up to relieve you shortly. It's time for your break. Make sure you take it, please.'

There was a flurry around the station when Toni returned to Casualty. 'What's going on?'

'These amazing roses just arrived!' Harmony's blonde ponytail jiggled as her head tipped from side to side in excitement.

Toni's heart almost juddered to a stop. Surely he hadn't…? She looked helplessly at the blooms in the florist's basket, with the chirpy little red hearts dancing from the wicker handle. Oh, lord… There had to be dozens of roses, all colours, and the perfume was divine.

'They're old-fashioned garden roses,' Liz said knowledgeably. 'My granddad grows beauties like these. They must have cost a fortune.'

'Who are they for?' Toni hoped no one but her could hear the little catch in her voice.

'Apparently, they're for the whole staff of the A and E.' Liz held out the card. 'See?'

Oh, for heaven's sake. Toni stifled a groan. It seemed as though Riccardi was tearing around like a head stockman, mending fences all over the place.

'Someone must think we're pretty, damned hot,' Ed joked. 'The dream team!' He did a high five with Harmony.

'Could be from the Mayor,' Justin said. 'Remember, Joe operated on that infected ingrown toenail just before he left on leave?'

Liz snorted. 'Bit of an extravagant thank you for an ingrown toenail! Toni.' She turned to her friend. 'Any ideas?'

Plenty, Toni thought, her heart returning slowly to its rightful place. But none she could voice here. 'Perhaps, we'll never know.' She sidestepped the question deftly.

'But we should get them in water for a start.' She turned to one of their AINs. 'Job for you, Sam?'

'But there are heaps!' The youngster looked dismayed. 'What shall I do with them all?'

'We could send some up to Midwifery,' Toni suggested.

'No,' Liz dismissed. 'They always have plenty.'

'I'm about to take my break,' Ed said cheerfully. 'Why don't I bike some over to the aged-care home? Give the oldies a buzz?'

'*Seniors*, Ed,' Toni reminded him, and then gave one of her megawatt smiles. 'But I think that's a wonderful idea. Are we all agreed?'

There was a chorus of approval.

'The roses were from *him,* weren't they?' Liz demanded, when she and Toni had a minute on their own.

'Probably.' Toni had given up the fight to try to remain neutral.

'The atmosphere in the place has lightened a hundred per cent since the flowers arrived,' Liz said. 'What on earth did you say to him?'

'Probably far too much.' But he'd given back as much as he'd got. In fact, they'd matched strikes like a couple of jousting combatants. Toni smothered a reminiscent smile. She'd enjoyed it, jousting with Rafe Riccardi. She wondered if he'd felt the same…

'But it was such a nice gesture!' Liz shook her head in quiet amazement. 'You must have worked a small miracle on His Grumpiness.' She chuckled.

'I'm sure Rafe will be more sociable when he's caught up on sleep,' Toni responded, and wondered why she was going to bat for him. 'Are you coming to the dinner do?' She changed conversation lanes deftly.

'You bet. It's the first night out we've had in weeks.

Mum is babysitting Lulu and William, and Matt's promised to leave the studios early. Or I'll kill him,' Liz added calmly.

Toni smiled. Liz's husband worked as a producer at the local radio station. 'You're so lucky, Lizzie. Two sweet kids and a husband who comes home to you at night.'

Liz rolled her eyes. 'What about you? Are you bringing someone?'

'No.' Toni was definite. 'I aim to stay for the dinner and then take off.'

'Not staying for the slow dancing?' Liz waggled her brows suggestively.

'That's all right for young lovers and you old married folk,' Toni dismissed. 'If I want to get up close and personal with a bloke, I'd rather challenge him to a game of tennis.'

Liz flipped some files into an out-tray. 'You're such a romantic!'

Toni showed Liz the tip of her tongue. 'You'd be surprised what you can learn about someone's character in a sporting context—especially if they're losing. I believe the tickets have sold really well. Half the town seems to be going along.'

'Well, the raffle prizes are exceptional,' Liz said chattily. 'A couple of the motor dealers have combined and donated a new car. And the winery's putting up six cases of their finest. The council's come good as well and contributed a luxury weekend for two at the Gold Coast.'

'Then let's hope folk are feeling generous and buy zillions of tickets,' Toni endorsed. 'That way we might just make enough to get our scanner.'

'It's quiet at the moment.' Liz checked the depart-

ment with a practised eye. 'Mind if I take the early
lunch? I want to get a shampoo and blow-wave.'

'Go.' Toni flapped a hand. 'And thanks for jinxing
us. I bet every man and his dog will come trailing in
now.'

'Well, you'll cope with the men.' Liz chuckled. 'Just
send the dogs along to the vet. See you.' She grabbed
her bag and took off.

Toni leaned on the counter, allowing herself a few
moments of respite. Through the big plate-glass doors
at the entrance she could see the gardens the grounds-
man, Kenny, had such pride in. In Australia, February
was the hottest month on the calendar, yet he managed
to nurture the plants along and now there were riotous
splashes of colour everywhere.

Toni thought on. She was glad she lived in a country
town in so many ways. But what was Rafe doing here?
she wondered. And would they ever get close enough
for him to confide in her?

Beside Toni, the emergency phone rang, bringing
her back to reality with a snap. Replacing the receiver a
few seconds later, she took off at speed towards Rafe's
office. She hoped he was there.

He was, looking up in query as she popped her head
in.

'Possible arrest coming into Resus. ETA six minutes.'

He was on his feet immediately and they were moving swiftly to the resus area. 'Do we have a name?' he
asked.

'It's Carol McKay. She manages the dress shop in
town. Cardiac history. The paramedics have given an-
ginine with nil effect.'

'We'll have to wing it, then.' Rafe's voice was

clipped. 'And hope we come up with the right answers. What about family? Anyone to be notified?'

'She's a widow. Son works at the school. I'll chase it up.'

'Delegate to someone else,' Rafe was firm. 'I want you scrubbed and ready to catheterise. If our patient is overloaded, we don't have time to mess about. Harmony?' He rounded on the young RN. 'I want you involved here, please.'

Harmony's eyes went wide. 'Yes, Doctor.'

'And as soon as our patient hits the deck, I need the monitor leads on *pronto*.'

'If the patient arrests, you're number three, Harmony.' Toni was scrubbing furiously.

'Three?' Harmony looked agitatedly from one to the other.

'You'll write what drugs are being given on the whiteboard,' Toni said calmly. 'And help with the IV fluids where necessary. You'll be fine.' She sent out a brief encouraging smile to the nurse.

'Right.' Harmony seemed spurred on by Toni's confidence and began to get the intubation tray ready.

And then it was time for action.

The ambulance reversed into the bay, its doors already opening.

'Be good, team.' Rafe's words snapped out and Carol McKay was wheeled rapidly into Resus.

The paramedic relayed what treatment they'd given, adding, 'She's not looking great, Doc.'

Rafe wasted no time in supposition. They had a life to save here. His hands moved like lightning, securing a tourniquet and IV in seconds. 'Give me sixty of Lasix,' he barked. 'IDC in now, please, Toni. Let's make a dent in that fluid.'

Toni's hands were deft and sure. In seconds the indwelling catheter was in situ.

'Good work,' Rafe murmured, as the crippling fluid began draining away. 'OK, let's clamp at eight hundred mil. Sixty of Lasix, please.'

Harmony passed the dose. 'That's one-twenty so far, Doctor.'

'Adjust the oxygen to full now, please. Carol?' Rafe leaned closer to his patient. 'Can you hear me? You're in hospital. Did you forget to take your medication today?'

Carol's eyes fluttered open. 'Mmm,' she murmured. 'Sorry…'

'That's OK,' Rafe spoke gently. 'So long as we know, we can treat you. Try to relax now and breathe into the mask. How's the BP doing, Antonia?'

'One-sixty over a hundred. Pulse a hundred and ten, resps thirty.'

Rafe acknowledged her call with a swift nod. So far so good but his gut feeling was telling him they weren't out of the woods yet.

Toni began to sponge Carol's forehead. She still looked very unwell, very clammy… Alarm ripped through Toni and automatically she felt for a pulse. Nothing. She hit the arrest button. There was a flurry outside and Justin appeared.

'Will you intubate, please, Justin?' Rafe was professional and calm. 'And I need adrenaline ten here.'

Harmony slapped the prepared dose into his hand.

'And another ten. Any pulse?'

'No.' Toni felt her nerves pull tightly.

'Let's defib, then, please.'

'Charging.' Toni's teeth clenched on her lower lip.

'All clear.' Rafe discharged the paddles.

All gazes swung to the monitor.

'Damn all…' Rafe spat the words from between clenched teeth. 'Let's go again. Clear.'

This time the trace bleeped, faded and then staggered into a rhythm. 'Yes…' Rafe's relief was controlled. 'We've got her. Thanks, everyone.'

'You did really well today, Harmony.' Toni was fulsome in her praise for the younger woman.

'Oh—thanks, Toni.' Harmony gave a pleased smile.

They were putting the resus room back to rights, Carol McKay having been transferred to the hospital's small IC unit. 'I've had a few doubts about working in A and E,' she confessed, stuffing the used linen into a laundry bin.

'Well, it's not for everyone,' Toni agreed. 'Is there an area you'd prefer?'

Harmony bit her lip. 'It's difficult to know when I've only just begun my nursing. We were sheltered from quite a bit in our training. It's different when you're actually part of the team.'

'Well, never be afraid to ask,' Toni counselled. 'You're newly graduated. You're not expected to know everything. I think we're about finished in here.' She did a quick inventory. 'Anything you want to debrief about before we go?'

Harmony hesitated. 'Will we be transferring Carol on?'

'Not at this stage. Rafe is presently calling her cardiologist in Sydney. We'll know a bit more later.'

'I…guess she won't be able to open her shop for a while?'

'Not sure,' Toni said. 'She may have someone who could stand in for her. Carol has great stock. Have you bought anything there?'

'I actually bought a dress for the Valentine dance.' Harmony made a small face. 'Carol was having it altered it for me. I was supposed to pick it up after work today.'

Toni was sympathetic to the younger woman's obvious disappointment. 'Have you something else you could wear?'

'Nothing new.' Harmony shrugged dispiritedly. 'I so wanted this dress, Toni.' Her cheeks went pink. 'Justin's asked me to go with him.'

Dating a doctor. Toni gave an inward wry smile. She'd done a bit of that in her time. And it had been fun—until she'd met Dr Alex Nicol. He'd come as a relieving MO to St Vincent's in Sydney, where she'd been working in A and E. And she'd fallen for him, beguiled by his Geordie accent, his craggy looks, his sense of humour. He'd told her he was separated and getting divorced and she'd believed him. But then it turned out, he hadn't been truthful…

Toni stifled the unproductive trip into past. It was water under the Harbour bridge. Gone. Like Alex had gone back to England. To his wife.

'Hey, guys.' Amy popped her head in. 'Need a hand to clear up?'

'We're about done, thanks, Amy.' Toni jerked back to the present, refolding the blanket she'd been holding.

'What's up?' Amy had caught her air of introspection. 'Carol will be all right, won't she?'

'Should be,' Toni said. 'But with Carol away from her shop, Harmony has a bit of a dilemma about her dress for tonight.'

Amy was all attention. 'What's happened, Harms?'

Harmony explained her difficulty.

'I could lend you something.' Amy gave the junior a

quick assessing look. 'We're about the same size. And I got some amazing clothes recently when Leo and I were over in Singapore. Why don't we hook up after work and go back to mine? If you like something, it's yours. OK?'

'Are you kidding me?' Harmony's blue eyes widened in happy disbelief. 'That would so be totally awesome. I love your style, Amy!'

'Oh, thanks.' Harmony dimpled a smile. 'Deal, then?'

'Deal.'

Laughing, the two walked off together, heads turned towards each other, eagerly discussing the celebrations for the night ahead.

Toni smiled after them. It was good to see Amy so upbeat. Plus, professionally, she would be an excellent role model for Harmony.

Nice outcome. Somewhat thoughtfully, Toni made her way back to the station. There were good vibes all over the place. Had it all happened because of an armful of roses?

She wondered whether Rafe realised just what effect his gesture had achieved—if indeed the roses had been from him. But of course they had to have been…

And it was a bit daunting to think he'd been spurred into action because of something she'd said.

She wasn't about to ask him.

But he *had* to know that she knew.

So where did they go from here?

Toni puffed out a little breath to stem her consternation. Her heartbeat kicked up a notch. She hadn't expected this complication on her first day back. Correction. She hadn't expected it at all.

The afternoon ticked by. A few mild casualties trickled in that were handled competently by Justin and the nursing staff.

Liz had arrived back from the hairdresser, her hair sleek and shiny with little tendrils curling prettily from a loose knot.

'Hair looks great,' Toni said approvingly.

Liz sighed. 'Wish I'd had time for a spray tan.'

'Matt likes you just the way you are.' Toni tipped her head enquiringly. 'And the spark's still there, isn't it?'

Liz smiled mistily. 'Oh, yeah…'

'Well, then.' Toni glanced at the clock on the wall. It was almost the end of their working day. 'Lizzie, will you hand over, please? I need to see Rafe about a few things before end of shift.'

'Sure. See you tonight?'

'If you're there first, keep me a seat.'

Liz grinned wickedly. 'I'll keep two. You never know!'

Ten minutes later, Toni tapped on Rafe's door and waited. Her eyes went heavenwards at his growled response, '*It's open.*' Suddenly her heart felt as though it was beating in all the wrong places in her chest. Had this been a crazy idea? Well, it was too late now.

Angling herself through the door, she moved across to his desk. 'I pushed the boat out and got us an energy hit from the canteen.' She passed the disposable cup across to him. 'Hot chocolate for you, coffee for me.'

He eyed her a bit warily, seeming surprised and even a bit taken aback, and Toni wondered how long it had been since anyone had done a simple act of kindness for him. 'Thanks. How did you know I needed this?'

'Put it down to my powers of observation.' Toni slid into the same chair she'd occupied that morning.

Cradling her coffee between her hands, she asked, 'What's happening with Carol McKay?'

Rafe tilted his cup and took a mouthful of his hot chocolate. Seeming to enjoy it, he took another. 'I had a video hook-up with her cardiologist. He's of the opinion if there's no further deterioration in her condition, she can be safely managed here.'

'That should be less stressful for her anyway,' Toni replied. 'She can keep up with things at her business. Carol has quite a large customer base, most of whom have become her friends. They'll be concerned for her welfare.'

'Her son's with her now in ICU. I imagine he'll help her work out some kind of plan for the future.'

'I expect so. She won't want to lose trade if it's at all possible.'

'That's not likely, is it?'

'Probably not.' Toni sipped her coffee. 'It's the only decent dress shop in town so where else are the ladies going to go?'

'I have no idea, Antonia.' A tiny flicker of amusement appeared behind Rafe's eyes. 'Online perhaps?'

'Don't think so,' Toni drawled, a hint of laughter edging her voice. 'Online shopping hasn't hit Forrestdale to any great degree. As for the girls, they're more inclined to want to *touch* before they buy, rather than just visualise it on a screen.'

'Interesting.' He gave a guarded kind of smile that rapidly spun out to lighten his whole face. He had no idea what they were talking about but Toni smiled right back and their smiles dallied for a moment, then caught and held. And suddenly his office was full of something neither of them understood.

Toni drew back in her chair. Her body felt tingly with

electricity. Odd. And Rafe's laughing eyes were warming her from head to toe. Oh, boy, oh, boy… This could get complicated. And she needed *that* like a tax bill.

In a split second Rafe decided he didn't need whatever it was that was happening here. Were they flirting? Hell, this was a minefield. Silence permeated the atmosphere and in order to break it he swivelled his chair slightly so that he was looking through the window at the patchwork of distant gum trees, blue summer sky and high cloud. He took a deep breath to steady himself and then glanced pointedly at his watch. 'You'd better take off, hadn't you—if you're going out tonight?'

Toni looked startled. Was he dismissing her? It sure seemed like it. She swallowed the last mouthful of her coffee and rose to her feet. 'Why don't you take an early mark as well?' she said lightly. 'You look bushed.'

'Do I?' he replied blandly.

'Yes.' She'd already noticed the charcoal shadows beneath his eyes and the way he'd rolled back his shoulders out on the ward as if trying to stave off a bone-crunching weariness. 'Go home, Rafe.'

'Hey!' Rafe planted his feet and uncurled to his full height 'Who's the boss here?'

'You, Dr Riccardi,' Toni returned sweetly. 'But surely you know how to delegate? There's a competent late shift already on duty and I'm sure they'll call you in if anything unmanageable occurs.'

Rafe stifled a hoot of raw laughter. The only thing unmanageable was Antonia Morell. But she was right. He was whacked. 'OK, you win.' He gave in, dragging his hands through his hair and locking them at the back of his neck.

'I'll take off.'

'Have a good night, then. Although…' Toni paused

with her hand on the doorknob and shot him one of her smiles '…if you feel like it later, you could pop over to the dance and draw one of the raffle prizes for us.'

Rafe let out a breath of pure relief as he watched her neat little backside disappear out the door. But she'd left in her wake a whole chain of emotions that gnawed at his insides. He'd wanted this post in Forrestdale to be as straightforward as possible. No bumps in the road. No emotional involvement to leave behind. And now all that seemed turned on its head.

But only if he let it…

He whipped his medical case out of its locker. He needed to breathe in some fresh air, even swim fifty laps of the pool if that's what it took to get his head on straight again.

Had she really done that in there? A long breath jagged its way from Toni's lungs. Surely she hadn't batted her eyelashes at him, had she? But she'd certainly been *flirty*. Perhaps he hadn't noticed? But of course he had—he'd done it right back at her. Were they game-playing? Toni shook her head. She didn't do games. Ever. Then what on earth had got into her just now?

She fled to the staffroom. Hauling her bag out of the locker, she headed for the car park. Good grief! Why was she letting herself get tied in knots like this? And over a man again. A man who was here today and gone tomorrow—well, in three months' time. And she'd been down that road. Heck, she'd scrubbed the kitchen floor with one of his T-shirts!

As she slowed to accommodate the after-school traffic flow, Toni released a long calming breath. She needed something physical to unleash the frustration that was robbing her of plain common sense. She felt like thrashing someone at tennis but her club didn't meet until Thursday evening. Well, she'd just have to run. Run and run. And hope by the end of it she'd be restored to her usual level-headed thinking.

CHAPTER THREE

TONI pushed herself, running lap after lap around the track adjacent to the park. Then, deciding she'd had enough, she leaned forward, hands on the fence railings, warming down. She jogged home leisurely, deciding she'd left herself just enough time to get ready for the Valentine party.

Showered, she blotted her hair dry and then stepped into her favourite silk underwear. She'd bought new clothes on her recent trip to Sydney. Now she just had to decide what to wear. And these days she pleased herself.

After flicking through her choices, she decided to dress simply in a sleeveless silk dress with a crossover bodice. In a dusky blush pink, it had a short draped skirt that fell just above her knees. She puffed perfume into the air and walked through it, then reached for the dress and slid it over her head.

Her make-up was minimal as usual—a touch of tinted moisturiser on her cheeks, a flick of muted shadow on her lids and lipstick in a soft coral. She slipped her feet into high-heeled sandals, pushed a broad silver bangle on her arm and stood back to get the overall picture in the mirror. The dress was gorgeous, the faint shimmer in the material pearling the fairness of her skin and highlighting her hair.

She'd do.

Toni drove across to the club. She intended to have only one glass of wine to celebrate and then she'd stay with mineral water. Besides, the evening was too warm to drink alcohol. But that wouldn't stop most of the guests, she thought realistically.

She managed to park near the entrance of the club, which would be good for her early exit, she thought, sliding out of her car and activating the locking device on her keypad.

'Toni!' Hearing her name, Toni spun round to see Liz and Matt getting out of a taxi. She fluttered a wave and waited for them to catch up. 'You look terrific, Lizzie,' she said with a smile. Liz was wearing a bold red gown that floated to her ankles.

'Thanks, I think.' Liz looked doubtful. 'It's not too…?' She indicated the deep cleavage.

'It's gorgeous,' Toni reassured her. 'If you've got it, flaunt it!'

'That's what I told her.' Matt stuffed his wallet into his back pocket after paying off the cabbie. 'How are you, Tone?' He placed a peck on her cheek.

'I'm fine, thanks, Matt. It should be a good night.'

Chatting, they made their way inside to the club's function room.

'Doesn't everything look spectacular?' Toni gave a little cry of delight, casting her eyes around at the table settings with their crisp white cloths and tea-lights. The mandatory hearts and roses were everywhere, although Toni doubted the roses were real. Unlike the beauties they'd received at the hospital…

'Oh, here are some of our gang now,' Liz said as Amy and Harmony arrived with their respective partners.

'The girls look so pretty.' Toni smiled. Both were wearing soft, floaty florals.

'At their age, it would be a crime not to,' Liz responded dryly. 'This seems to be our table here.'

'I'll get some drinks,' Matt said. 'Toni, white wine?'

Toni nodded. 'Thanks, Matt.'

'You look amazing, by the way,' Liz said as they took their places at the big round table. 'Sydney?'

'My favourite dress shop in Rose Bay.'

'Shame Rafe's not coming.'

'Actually, he seemed pretty tired.'

'Still,' Liz contended, 'it would have been a good look for the department if he'd shown.'

Toni raised a shoulder stiffly. Well, she'd asked him and he wasn't here. But she was keeping that information strictly to herself.

The Valentine fundraiser would be a success, Toni decided as the evening wore on. Folk were in a happy and giving mood and tickets for their raffle were practically sold out. And the supper set out in buffet-style had been exceptional. And now people were beginning to drift on to the dance-floor.

Their table had emptied almost as soon as the dance music had begun. Left on her own, Toni took off towards the powder room, deciding she'd stay until they'd drawn the raffle and then she'd be away to her bed.

After refreshing her lipstick, Toni left the powder room. As she passed the bar on the way back to the table, she stopped and almost froze. Rafe was standing with his hip against the bar, elbow bent as he lifted a glass of orange juice to his mouth.

Toni took a step backwards as if to regain her equilibrium. Her breathing immediately felt tight and her stomach went into freefall as she admitted honestly, that physically Rafe Riccardi pushed every one of her buttons.

Steadying herself with a long breath, she went forward. 'Hi...'

Rafe spun round. 'Antonia—' In an almost jerky motion he lowered his arm and placed his glass on the bar top.

For a few seconds there was an awkward silence while they each took stock.

Sweet God, she was lovely, Rafe thought. Beautiful and warm and...sexy. And he wanted her, as he hadn't wanted a woman in ages. Maybe years.

He certainly scrubbed up well. Toni bit gently on the soft pad of her bottom lip. Her eyes flicked to the pale blue shirt that moulded his broad shoulders, followed the tailored line of his black trousers to his black leather shoes. She pressed her clutch-bag tightly against her chest.

'You managed to drag yourself here, then?' Oh, lord. Toni almost groaned. That hadn't come out right. But suddenly her tongue seemed to have a mind of its own.

Rafe gave a tight shrug. 'Bernie Maguire put the weights on me to draw one of the raffle prizes.'

'And you can't very well ignore the chairman of the board,' Toni agreed, oddly disappointed he hadn't felt the need to respond to *her* invitation. 'Our people are mostly at the table over here.' She indicated with her hand. 'Would you like to join us?'

'Thanks.' He picked up his glass. 'Can I get you something to drink while we're here?'

'I'm fine, thanks.' Toni shook her head. 'Have you eaten?'

'I had a steak at the pub.'

Toni flicked a tentative smile at him. 'There's dessert still going begging. Interested?'

'Might be. What's on offer?'

Well, not me. Toni's heart began to patter. Were they playing games again? 'There are three kinds of bread-and-butter pudding, for starters.'

His chuckle was a bit rusty. 'My grandmother used to make bread-and-butter pudding.'

'Not like this, she didn't.'

'Reckon?' Rafe turned his head a fraction and sent her a slow, lazy smile.

Toni blinked, feeling shock waves of its aftermath right down to her toes. His smile was like the sun coming out. Shame he didn't do it more often. They stopped at the table. 'I'm sitting here.' She put her clutch-bag down. 'Park your drink and let's find out, shall we?'

Rafe hesitated. 'I'm not taking someone's place, am I?'

'I'm not here with anyone.' Toni answered the question she assumed he was asking.

His mouth twitched. 'Lead on, then. I need to see these puddings.'

At the buffet they bypassed a luscious tropical fruit salad, sorbet and various kinds of cheesecakes. 'Now, here we have the bread and butter puddings,' Toni said, hamming it up with a graceful sweep of her hand. 'You could start with maple syrup and pecan, get a bit edgy and try the lemon curd and coconut and then give your tastebuds a real treat and finish with white chocolate and raspberry.'

Rafe clicked his tongue and sighed in mock-resignation. 'It's a hard call but someone has to do it. Going to join me?'

'Of course.' Toni's mouth fell into a soft pout. 'Can't

have you eating alone.' With their selections made, they went back to the table.

'So, where are you staying?' Toni asked conversationally.

'Joe and Cath kindly offered me the use of their annexe at the house.'

'What a good arrangement. It's a great space. They had it built for Joe's dad originally but he didn't stay long. Missed his mates in Sydney.'

'It's certainly very comfortable,' Rafe agreed. 'Close to the hospital. And the pool is a real bonus on these hot nights.'

'Yes, it would be,' Toni rejoined softly, her thoughts going into overdrive. She'd been invited to swim many times in the Lyons' pool. And at night especially it was magical, with the lights by the pool shining back through the tropical shrubbery and edging the white jasmine with soft radiance. And the air you breathed was heavy with woodsy scents. Cath and Joe had created a very private place. Special. She wondered if Rafe found it so.

The creamy dessert slid over her tongue.

Did he swim naked...?

As if he'd divined the pattern of her thoughts, he remarked, 'Joe said you swim at their place quite often. Don't feel you have to stop just because they're away.'

'I wouldn't want to invade your privacy.'

'You wouldn't be. Besides...' His spoon paused midway from his dessert bowl '...it's no fun swimming alone.'

Toni had no time to answer. Bernie Maguire materialised at the table. 'Good, you're both here,' he said. 'We'd like to get cracking if you don't mind and draw these raffles. The mayor will be drawing the main prize and, Rafe, if you'd draw the winners for the cases of wine? And Toni…' He looked down and gave her one of his big barracuda grins. 'Might be a nice touch if you could draw out the winner for the luxury weekend.'

'Me?' Toni's eyes went wide in alarm. 'Bernie, I don't think I should do it. There are more senior people at the hospital—'

'Nonsense.' Bernie clearly wasn't having that. 'It will be very appropriate having a good-looking couple from the hospital on stage. Very appropriate. Right, then.' He rubbed his hands together, indicating mission accomplished. 'I'll just go and get things rolling.'

'This is awful!' Toni glanced despairingly at Rafe. 'We…can't have people thinking we're a couple.'

Rafe shrugged. He could think of worse things. 'Don't worry about it. It's small-town politics. And folk will have found something more interesting to talk about tomorrow.'

Toni had her doubts about that but with Bernie's voice already booming from the stage, inviting everyone to return to their tables for the drawing of the raffle prizes, she got slowly to her feet. The sooner they got this over the better.

With the prizewinners announced, Rafe and Toni squeezed their way through the dancers already back on the floor. They joined Matt and Liz, who were already seated at the table. 'We're just taking a little breather,' Liz said, before introducing Rafe to her husband. She looked in sorrow at her pile of ticket stubs. 'You know, I really thought I was in with a chance to win that luxury weekend.'

'Sorry,' Toni said with dry irony. 'I couldn't seem to find your ticket when I stuck my hand in the barrel.'

The men laughed. 'I'll get another round of drinks in.' Matt got to his feet.

'I'll come with you,' Rafe said. 'But I'll stick to OJ. Antonia?'

'Oh...' Toni felt her cheeks warm. 'Mineral water, thanks.'

As the men walked companionably towards the bar, Liz turned to Toni, her raised brows speaking volumes. 'Antonia?'

Toni rolled her eyes.

Liz smirked. 'Scrubs up well, doesn't he?'

'Matt?' Toni responded innocently.'

'Oh, ha.' Liz made a small face. 'Riccardi, of course. And his voice—smooth as molasses. Do you think—you know?'She rocked her hand expressively. 'He might fancy you?'

Toni felt the nerves in her stomach clench. If the micro-currents already running between them were to be acknowledged, then perhaps she and Rafe Riccardi might just fancy each other. But she wasn't letting Liz get a whiff of that. No way. 'Get over yourself, Lizzy.'

'You looked pretty cosy together up on the stage.' Liz persisted with her banter.

'That was none of my doing. Bernie Maguire insisted. Anyway, enough of this crazy supposition,' Toni said. 'Here come the men with the drinks.'

The conversation between the two couples became general and light and then Matt asked, 'So, Rafe, where were you working before coming here to Forrestdale?' Always the journalist, he'd had begun to sniff out a story.

Rafe looked away, dropping his gaze to his glass, giving the orange juice his riveting attention. 'I've been overseas for the past year, working for Médecins Sans Frontières in Cambodia.'

Liz's arch look at Toni silently said, *So now we know.*

'I imagine the population are still suffering the effects from the reign of that dictator?' Matt considered himself well versed in world politics. 'How is it now?'

Rafe frowned. 'It's still one of the most heavily landmined countries in the world. One in every two hundred and fifty Cambodians has one or more amputations. But for all its tragic history, it's still a beautiful country.'

'Got to have had repercussions for the kids, though?' Matt pressed for more.

'They've lost a whole generation of their skills and professions. Of course it's effected the kids,' Rafe said tersely. 'As we speak, half the country's children are malnourished and one in seven will die before their fifth birthday, mostly from vaccine-preventable diseases.'

Toni felt her breathing falter. Rafe was clearly unsettled. The experience had obviously disturbed him deeply. And as a doctor it would be much worse dealing with so much heartache day after day. She hoped Matt would leave it alone now but of course he didn't.

'What about the basic necessities?' he asked. 'Drinking water? Sanitation?'

'Use your imagination,' Rafe growled.

'I produce a programme on local radio called *Conversations.*' Matt leaned forward eagerly. 'Your experiences working for MSF would make interesting listening. Would you feel like coming over to the studio some time and having a chat with our presenter?'

Rafe's mouth drew in. Probably not. Definitely not. But it wouldn't kill him to be diplomatic. Like him, Matt had a job to do. 'I'll think about it. There's no rush, is there?'

'Take your time.' Matt's shrug was open-handed. 'If, after a chat with Gillian, you don't feel comfortable with the concept, no worries.'

Toni saw Rafe relax—not much, just a slight shift of the muscles under his shirt, but enough to know he was back in control of his emotions. She watched as he drained his drink and rose to his feet.

'I'm going to split, guys. Enjoy the rest of the night.'

Toni's worried eyes followed his exit.

'So, now we know where's he's been.' This time Liz gave voice to her thoughts. 'I wonder if he intends going back?'

'Probably.' Matt's lips twisted into a thoughtful moue. 'Those guys in the front line tend to get addicted to the *cause*.' He bracketed the word in the air.

Toni bristled silently. Quite out of the blue she felt protective of Rafe's privacy. None of them here knew anything about his reasons for going to work for MSF. And she thought that Matt, whatever his best intentions, had ambushed him.

Suddenly, for reasons she couldn't explain, she felt out of sync with her friends. She dredged up an off-key smile and got to her feet. 'All that hard work drawing the raffle prizes has done me, guys. I think I'll call it a night as well.'

'I'll walk you out,' Matt said.'

'No need.' Toni waved away his offer. 'I'm parked close to the front entrance. See you tomorrow, Lizzy. And, Matt, thanks as always for the free publicity for our fundraiser.'

'Hey, any time.' Matt nodded his acknowledgment. 'I'll be sure to pass it along to our station manager. Drive safely.'

Toni fluttered a wave. ''Night.'

Toni's thoughts were unresolved as she drove home. She got that Matt was a facilitator for his programme. And that was fair enough but surely he could have laid off grilling Rafe the way he had?

Damn! Just when Rafe had seemed relaxed enough to start enjoying the evening too. And now he'd probably crawl back into shell and she'd have to start all over again to try to winkle him out so at least they could have some kind of decent working relationship.

She pulled into her carport, killed the engine and went inside. Tossing her clutch-bag on the hall table and kicking off her sandals, she went through to the kitchen. She was wound up. She crossed to the counter and looked through the window at the courtyard. The solar lights had come on, sending the baskets of ferns into feathery silhouettes.

The silvery light reminded her of the Lyons' pool at night. And reminded her that's what she needed right now—to dive into its cool depths and thresh the water until she'd driven off this foul mood of frustration. But she couldn't do that.

Rafe was in residence there.

Rafe heaved himself out of the pool. Standing naked in the moonlight, he shook the moisture from his hair and then bent and picked up his towel from the sun-lounger. Giving his body a cursory wipe, he slung the towel around his hips. He felt better now, his mind freed up from all those images that Matt's questions had dumped all over him.

Padding back along the path to the annexe, he pushed open the screen door and went inside. The place was air-conditioned but so far Rafe had refrained from switching it on. He preferred the weather as it came. And

in February it was stinking hot, the air almost brittle
with stillness, the pungent smell of ripening mangoes
everywhere. So intrinsic of everything Australian, he
couldn't get enough of it.

For now, anyway.

CHAPTER FOUR

Next morning.

IN THE clear light of day, Toni decided to put her concerns about Rafe Riccardi into perspective. But concern for his welfare still remained. Perhaps it all boiled down to being a nurse, she decided ruefully. You just couldn't help looking out for others—even adult males.

She took handover and wondered where on earth the rest of her team had suddenly disappeared to.

'Excuse me, Toni?' Samantha stopped at the nurses' station. 'That old guy is back again. What should I do with him?'

Toni looked up. 'You mean Denis?'

Sam nodded. 'The nurses said he only comes in for a chat so should I shoo him off?'

'No, don't do that.' Toni swung off the high swivel stool. 'The one time you do that could be the time he's actually ill. Anyway, we always get him a cup of tea, don't we?'

'I think so.' Samantha looked uncertain. 'I'll do that, shall I?'

'No, we'll have a chat to him first.' Toni glanced at the clock. 'Have you seen the rest of the team, Sam?'

'Uh…' The youngster bit her lip. 'Still in the staff-room, I think.'

'Still?' Toni's brows shot up. It was shaping up to be one of those days and she really didn't need it. She hated having to pull colleagues into line, especially when they'd all turned out last night to support the fundraiser. But rules were there for a purpose and they should know they couldn't come drifting in for their shift whenever they pleased.

Resolutely, she began to walk towards the casualty area where Denis O'Rourke was the only occupant among the rows of padded green chairs.

'Good morning, Denis.' Toni dropped into a chair beside the elderly man. 'How can we help you?'

Denis wheezed a bit. 'Wouldn't mind a cuppa, lovey.'

'Well, that can be arranged.' Toni smiled, lifting his wrist to check his pulse. A bit thready, she decided, and his skin felt hot. She made a tiny moue of concern. 'Are you not feeling well, Denis?'

'Feelin' a bit weak, like. Chest hurts when I breathe…' He tapered off and coughed into a hanky.

'Right.' Toni made a snap decision. 'Let's get a doctor to look at you, shall we? Samantha, here, will take you along to the examination room.'

Where was a doctor when you needed one? Toni cast a slightly exasperated look over the empty unit. Grace Tennant wasn't on duty until later but Justin should have shown his face by now.

'Can I help?'

Toni spun round. The tone of Rafe's voice clearly indicated he'd picked up on her frustration.

To cover her confusion, Toni bit out irritably, 'This place is a shambles this morning. You're in early,' she tacked on almost accusingly. 'Couldn't you sleep?'

'I slept,' he said calmly. And better than he had for a long time. Maybe his demons were beginning to leave him at last. God, he hoped so. He narrowed a look at Toni. 'You obviously didn't.'

She lifted a shoulder. 'Not much.' She'd spent half the night worrying about *him*. Which, looking at him, had been pathetic. Dressed in casual cargo pants and a cotton shirt left open at the neck, he looked upbeat and fresh. Whereas she felt far removed from her usual cheerful persona. 'It was hot,' she affirmed as her reason.

'It was,' he agreed. 'I had a swim before I turned in. You should have come round and joined me.'

And wouldn't that have been just dandy. Her chin snapped up. 'Could you see a patient, please? Justin doesn't seem to be anywhere in sight.'

'Sure. Fill me in.'

'Denis O'Rourke, seventies, regular in Casualty, wanders in for a chat, the odd ailment. We usually give him a bit of attention, a hot drink and send him off.'

Rafe listened attentively. 'So, what's different about your Denis O'Rourke today?'

Toni rolled her bottom lip between her teeth. 'I think he may be brewing something. But, then, maybe I'm wasting your time...'

'You're not wasting my time, Antonia. Trust your instincts. I know I do.'

Their eyes met for an intense moment before each looked away. Awareness, like an imminent thunderstorm, rocked the air between them. Toni breathed in and breathed out and they made their way to the cubicles together.

Rafe was thorough. And Toni felt a rush of gratitude

that he'd taken her concern for this lonely old man on board.

Slowly and carefully, Rafe began palpating his patient's stomach. 'That seems fine.' He repositioned the elderly man's worn flannelette shirt. 'Let's have a listen, now.'

Toni gently brought Denis to a sitting position and handed Rafe a stethoscope.

'Thanks,' he murmured. 'Denis, could you manage a cough for me, please? And again. You've a few rattles in there, mate.' Rafe hooked the stethoscope around his neck. 'How long have you been feeling ill?'

'Coupla days…' Denis wheezed. 'Felt real crook when I woke this morning.'

Rafe nodded. 'It's good you came in to see us, then. We'll arrange some treatment for you. Get you feeling fit again.' He went across to the basin to wash his hands, drying them quickly. 'I'd like a word, please, Antonia.'

They stepped outside the cubicle and Toni pulled the curtains closed. She looked questioningly at Rafe.

'Denis is exhibiting early signs of pneumonia,' the registrar said briskly. 'And he's quite seriously dehydrated.'

'So you'll admit him?'

'I'd like to. What's our bed situation?'

'Several for allocation. I've just checked.'

'Excellent.' Rafe pulled out his pen and took the chart Toni handed to him. 'I'd like Denis X-rayed for starters, both bases of lungs. And a sample of sputum, please. We'll see what that tells us.'

'I'll see to it all personally.' It was probably the only way she was going to get anything done today, Toni reflected, a bit tight-lipped.

'The sputum culture may take a while,' Rafe considered, 'so in the meantime we'll start Denis on a drugs regime. We may need to change it slightly when the lab results come back.'

Concern was etched on Toni's face. 'Denis is a great old chap, World War Two veteran. Bit of a loner. He will be all right, won't he, Rafe?'

'Let's hope so.' He began making a notation of the drugs he wanted used. 'We'll start with Amoxil four-hourly and bensyl six-hourly, both delivered IV.' Clicking his pen shut, he slid it back into his shirt pocket. 'Normal saline to get his fluids back up as a priority. What are his living arrangements like? Do you know?'

'I do, as a matter of fact,' Toni said. 'He was struggling home with his bit of shopping one day and I gave him a lift. He lives in a boarding house. Pretty basic accommodation. Breakfast is a bit of a scratch meal and the rest the residents have to make for themselves.'

'So his nutrition is probably way under what it should be.' Rafe leaned his back against the wall and folded his arms. 'Surely, the Veteran Affairs Department should be looking after his welfare?'

Toni shrugged. 'I doubt if he's ever contacted them. Anything to do with governments takes for ever anyway. He probably preferred to battle on himself.'

'Forrestdale has an excellent aged-care home, doesn't it? Couldn't a placement be found for him there?'

Toni huffed under her breath. 'Someone has to die before a vacancy becomes available there. The place needs extensions urgently. But it all takes money.'

'OK…' Rafe ran a hand across his cheekbones. 'Thanks for the heads up. I'll have a word with Bernie Maguire. He's a big wheel in the Rotary. He may be able to get some action happening. And after he dumped on us last night, he owes us—big time.' Rafe's mouth twitched.

'It wasn't that bad, I suppose,' Toni conceded, her smile a bit strained. It was what happened later when Matt had grilled him that had had her off balance. But she couldn't tell him that. She held up the chart. 'I'll get things under way with X-ray.'

'Thanks. And then perhaps come in for some of my coffee?'

'Sorry, can't.'

Rafe gaze became shuttered. 'Fine.'

Oh, lord—Toni almost ground her teeth. She hadn't meant to sound dismissive but she had more urgent priorities than sitting around, sipping coffee. 'I really have to chase up my nurses and get this place running like a casualty department,' she explained, turning as the electronic doors opened and several walking wounded shuffled in.

Rafe followed her gaze and gave a tight little nod. 'I'll find Justin and tell him to get his butt out here.'

'Thanks.' Toni gave a quick smile but it died on her face. Rafe had already turned and begun walking away.

Toni watched his long-limbed stride down the corridor. Had her acceptance of an invitation to coffee meant that much to him? A mountain of uncertainty engulfed her. She sucked in a deep breath and shook her head. Don't start feeling guilty about this, Toni.

Just don't.

With years of practice, she switched into professional mode, assembling her team and allotting jobs. 'Has anyone seen Liz?' she asked as they began to disperse.

Apparently no one had.

Perhaps she'd gone straight to the station, Toni

thought, making her own way there just as Liz sidled in from the opposite end. It was obvious she'd just arrived.

Toni clicked her tongue. 'What time do you call this, Sister Carey?'

'Sorry, I'm late.' Liz shoved her bag under the counter. 'Where do you need me?'

'Where do you want to be?' Toni quipped lightly.

'Dead…' Liz dropped her head into her hands. 'Oh, God, Toni…'

'Oh, my stars!' Toni's voice rippled with speculation. 'Are you hungover?'

'Bit—'

'A bit! Lizzy, you're green!'

Liz groaned. 'My head is spinning.'

'No wonder, you crazy woman.' Toni shook her head in disbelief.

'Don't remind me. But we hadn't been out for ages and the wine was chilled and so lovely…'

'So lovely you now have a king-sized hangover. How's Matt?'

'Creeping round like a wounded crow. Said he's been poisoned.'

Toni got a vivid mental picture and chuckled. 'I can't believe the pair of you! You're not safe out alone.'

Liz held a hand to her tummy. 'Isn't that the truth.'

'Have you taken anything?' Toni became professional.

Liz shook her head.

'Then dose yourself with some paracetamol and go and lie down. I'll call you if I need you.'

'Oh, thank you,' Liz said feelingly. 'I'll make up the time.'

'Don't be ridiculous. Oh, and, Lizzy?'

Liz turned, her eyes large in her pale face. 'Mmm?'

Toni grinned. 'Big drinks of water, OK?'

Liz fled.

Instinct told Toni it was shaping up to be a busy day. She'd just got back to the station after doing a quick tour of cubicles and checking their supplies of IV fluids were adequate when the emergency phone rang.

As she scribbled details, she was conscious of Rafe coming into the nurses' station. He leaned on the counter and waited.

'Workplace accident.' Toni replaced the phone. 'New-build about ten Ks out of town. Patient is a twenty-two-year-old male, Rhys Holland.'

Rafe's mouth tightened. 'What's the injury?'

'Nailgun misfired,' Toni said briskly. 'The nail has apparently gone right through his work boot into the top of his foot.'

Rafe made a dismissive growl in his throat. 'What's the problem with these guys and work tools—are they a bunch of cowboys?'

Toni's mouth drew in. She guessed he was thinking of the fatal workplace accident last week but she didn't appreciate his suggestion that the workers of their country town were less than efficient. 'Ambulance has gone out. They'll have to load the patient so ETA is about thirty minutes.'

'Right. For starters, could you tee up someone from the fire service to come in? We'll need that boot cut off. And I want someone who knows what they're doing.'

Toni bristled. As opposed to a *cowboy* apparently. 'I'll do my best,' she said shortly. 'But it's a voluntary service. It may take a while to locate someone *suitable*,' she emphasised.

'OK.' He gave a cool imitation of a smile, indicating he'd got her point. 'And alert Theatre, please? It sounds like a patch-up job for Keith Sutherland,' he added, referring to the hospital's general surgeon.'

And they'd need a blood specimen and cross-match immediately on arrival, Toni noted silently. Lord, she could do this in her sleep. She began dialling. At last she had joy and Dan Sessarago from the fire service was on his way.

Quickly, Toni assigned Amy to the nurses' station and then drew Harmony aside and filled her in about the incoming emergency. 'Would you like to be involved?' she asked, giving the young grad the option.

'I guess it's the only way I'm going to learn, isn't it?' Harmony looked less than enthusiastic.

'And gain confidence,' Toni agreed.

The nurses hurried towards the ambulance bay. Rafe was already waiting.

'Morning folks.' Erin Pascoe, one of the senior paramedics, sprang lightly from the rear of the vehicle.

Rafe's eyes narrowed. 'Any problems on the way in, Erin?'

'Nothing we couldn't handle. Rhys is not feeling too well, though. We've given Maxolon ten milligrams.'

Toni's gaze flew professionally over the young man. Rhys looked pale beneath his tan. His eyes were closed, clammy perspiration beading his forehead, each breath ending on a little moan.

'Let's move it, please.' Rafe's voice was clipped.

'Cube one is ready.' Toni's response was crisply calm and suddenly, professionally, they were working as a well-oiled team.

'On my count, then, guys.' Erin directed Rhys's transfer to the treatment couch.

'Right, let's get BP and temperature readings, please,' Rafe ordered.

'BP eighty-five on fifty,' Toni reported. 'Temperature thirty-five point five.'

'Thanks. Rhys, can you hear me?'

The young man's eyes fluttered open and closed. He licked his lips. 'Yeah…'

'Any tingling in your arms or legs?'

Rhys shook his head. 'Am I wrecked, Doc?'

'Of course you're not wrecked,' Rafe said bluntly. 'This is a hospital, sunshine. We're here to fix you up.' He turned to Toni. 'Let's get some fluids running, please.'

Toni quickly organised a cannula to run the saline drip. 'What drugs do you need?'

'Make it fifty of pethidine,' Rafe's mouth tightened. 'He's in a bit of pain here.'

Toni handed the keys of the drugs cabinet to Harmony. 'Take Mel with you to double-check. And quick as you can, please.'

'Dan Sessarago.' The fire officer poked his head into the treatment room. 'Let me know when you need me, Doc.'

Rafe's head came up. 'We'll need to stabilise the patient first, mate. Just hang on a tick, would you?'

A few minutes later the medication and saline drip were beginning to do their job. Toni breathed a sigh of relief. 'His colour's improving.' She gave Rafe a guarded smile.

'Mmm.' He seemed distracted. 'Time to get that boot off, I think.'

The fire officer performed the task with speedy expertise. Producing a sharp, thin blade, he sliced through the elastic-sided boot and peeled back the heel. Two forward cuts opened up the front section of the boot. 'If you could steady his leg here, Doc?'

Rafe obliged and all eyes watched as Dan finally eased the flapping pieces of leather away from Rhys's rapidly swelling foot.

'Well done, Dan. Thanks.' Rafe looked searchingly at the damaged foot after Toni had cut through their patient's thick socks with her scissors.

There was soft-tissue damage and an obvious bone fracture. 'What do you think, Harmony?'

'Oh!' Harmony's hand went to her throat. 'It looks very painful. I think I'd have passed out if it had happened to me.'

'Quite possibly.' Rafe's mouth twitched slightly. 'Now, do you think you could organise someone to get a portable X-ray unit down here, please? I don't want Rhys moved unnecessarily just yet.'

'Yes, Doctor.' Harmony flew.

'Thanks for including her.' Toni began gathering up the bits and pieces from the emergency and swept them into a bin.

Rafe lifted a shoulder as if shrugging off her thanks. 'As you've pointed out to me, Antonia, we're supposed to be a team, aren't we?'

A beat of silence.

Rafe saw her mouth tighten and heard the little staccato hiss of her breath and thought, *Now what?*

'I'll assign another nurse to prepare Rhys for Theatre,' Toni said briefly. 'I need to be elsewhere.'

Toni's expression was tightly controlled as she made her way back to the station. She hadn't appreciated Riccardi's retaliatory *dig* about them being a team. Let's face it, she acknowledged silently, the man just makes me feel unsettled. I need to get my head on straight. Oh, boy, do I ever. And if keeping out of his way for the moment is what it takes, then I'll do it.

'Toni?' Liz caught up with her.

'Feeling better?' Toni came to a halt.

Liz nodded. 'Sorry about all that. It won't happen again.'

'Don't beat yourself up, Lizzy'

'Thanks.' Liz looked relieved. 'Now, where do you need me?'

'There's an emergency in cube one.' Toni went on to give details. 'Riccardi wants the patient's foot X-rayed before they move him, so as soon as that's done, could you help Harmony with Rhys's theatre prep, please?'

'Fine, no worries.'

Liz's antennae began twitching. Why suddenly had *Rafe* become *Riccardi*? Had Toni had a run-in with him? Her friend looked a bit light-lipped. Not like herself at all.

She touched a light hand to Toni's shoulder. 'Hey, why don't you take a break and grab a coffee?'

'Mmm, maybe I will.'

Liz grinned. 'Ed's brought in sticky buns.'

Rafe slammed his car into gear and took off after work, just screeching to a stop in time to allow several people to walk over the zebra crossing. Hell's bells, where was his concentration?

Once home, he stripped off and swam length after length of the pool but that didn't assuage his disquiet. Consequently, he took his unsettled mood to bed with him and lay for ages, staring at the ceiling. But all he saw was Antonia's face. She was offside with him. And he didn't know why. He thumped the pillow in frustration. It was two steps forward and seven back with her, he thought darkly. And he hated it.

He had to clear the air with her. He didn't know how

but he would. If not tomorrow, then the next day. But it was almost at the end of her shift on Friday when he got the chance.

Toni had had no difficulty in avoiding Rafe for the rest of the week. She'd had a couple of management meetings elsewhere in the hospital that she'd had to attend and Liz, wanting to make up for her lapse, had offered to be here, there and everywhere. Toni had been more than happy to let her. It did help, of course, that Toni had swapped shifts with a colleague on Wednesday and worked a late shift.

It was now Friday afternoon and she was about to breathe a sigh of relief. She was so looking forward to her weekend. She'd chill out and relax.

And work out what to do about Rafe Riccardi.

A young woman carrying a toddler came into the casualty area almost at the end of her shift and Toni went across to her.

'Hi.' She sent out one of her smiles. 'I'm Toni, one of the nurses. How can we help you?'

'C-could I see a doctor?'

'Of course. I'll just need to get some details. Take a seat and I'll be right back.'

The woman gave her name as Joanne Carter. 'I need to ask about Zoe. She's vomiting everything...' Almost on cue, as though to hurry things along, Zoe began to whimper and pull her little legs up as if in pain.

'Oh, poor sweetheart.' Toni smoothed a twist of fair hair from the little one's forehead. 'Come with me, Joanne.' Toni got to her feet. 'Let's get Zoe more comfortable, shall we?'

Having settled mother and child in one of the treatment rooms, Toni went in search of a doctor. With a bit of luck Grace would be available. But Grace, it seemed, had taken an early mark and gone home.

'Rafe's still around,' Liz said helpfully. 'Want me to bleep him?'

'If you would, please, Lizzy.' Toni took a deep breath. 'Treatment one.'

Oh, lord. There was to be no escape. Her hand went to her heart, finding it over-beating like a trapped bird's. Having to confront Rafe shouldn't be having this effect on her. But there was no getting away from it. It was. She went back to the treatment room. 'Dr Riccardi is on his way, Joanne.'

Rafe strode in, sending a cursory nod to Toni.

'This is Joanne Carter, Doctor.' Toni drummed up a professional face. 'She's concerned about Zoe's vomiting.'

Rafe examined the child carefully. 'What have you been giving Zoe, Mrs Carter?'

'Not much—because she wouldn't take much. I tried her with her usual milk and a bit of custard—she usually loves that.'

'I'm guessing she threw it right back at you?'

The young mum looked baffled. 'Have I done something I shouldn't? This has never happened before. Zoe is so well usually but now...'

'Do you have a GP?' Rafe asked, thinking he might have been able to get an overview of the family's health.

Joanne shook her head. 'We've only just moved here. My husband was retrenched from his job in Sydney. The job search people sent us here so Brent could get work at the mine. He drives a truck.'

'And where are you living, Joanne?' Rafe gently straightened Zoe's little dress after listening to her tummy.

Joanne looked unhappy. 'At the caravan park. The facilities are pretty basic and the manager is the pits.'

Well, there wasn't much he could do about that, Rafe decided. As soon as the family's finances picked up, they could probably move to somewhere more suitable. Meanwhile, they had to get this little one treated. He took the chart from Toni's outstretched hand and backed up against the couch. 'For the present, I'd like you to keep Zoe off milk and milk products, Joanne. Instead, give her frequent amounts of clear fluids only.'

The young mum nodded. 'How small and how frequent?'

'Good questions.' Rafe's mouth turned up in a fleeting smile. 'Small amounts mean about twenty mils. Do you have a measure at home?'

'I'm not sure.' Joanne bit her lip. 'It's probably in one of the boxes but I haven't found it yet…'

'Not to worry. I'm sure we could spare one from the dispensary.' He shot a questioning glance at Toni.

She nodded, even forcing out a brief smile. 'Not a problem.

'Now, clear means not milk and not solids,' Rafe emphasised. 'Just fluid. I'll give you a note for the chemist. They'll have various mixtures you can add to water. They're especially formulated to replace all the water and chemicals Zoe may lose because of her continual vomiting.'

'I understand,' Joanne said quietly. 'What if she vomits it back, though?'

'OK, if that happens, try diluted lemonade. Say one part to four parts water. If you like, freeze it and make little ice cubes for her to suck. If Zoe can tolerate that, you should see a marked improvement quite soon.'

Joanne looked as though a huge weight had been

taken from her shoulders. 'So—how often should I give her the replacement fluids?'

Rafe considered. 'Let's go with every fifteen minutes to start with and then you can lengthen it to thirty minutes if she's keeping it down. If Zoe keeps vomiting, she'll begin dehydrating. In that case, bring her back here to Casualty immediately, day or night, and we'll treat her. All clear?' Rafe sent a rather winning smile at the young mother.

'Yes.' Joanne hesitated and then smiled back. 'Thank you so much, Doctor.' Getting to her feet, she scooped Zoe out of Toni's arms. 'I'll get this started straight away.'

'Good.' Rafe went ahead and pulled back the curtains. He hesitated, momentarily disturbed by a sudden train of thought, and turned back. 'Use bottled water for the time being, Joanne.'

'Oh—' Joanne bit the underside of her lip, looking disconcerted. 'I'll—um—get some on the way home.'

Toni ushered the young mother out. 'Take a seat back in the waiting area, Joanne. I'll just grab that measuring glass for you.'

Toni took off at speed and Rafe had to call her twice before she registered he was following her. She stopped and waited, only turning when he came abreast. 'Did you want something else?'

'I did.' Rafe planted his hands firmly on his hips. 'I'm about to email an urgent directive to all shifts of A and E. Would you see it's printed out and displayed where it'll be seen?'

Toni gave a twisted smile. 'And hopefully *read*?'

'Mmm, that too,' he agreed dryly.

Toni frowned a bit. 'I heard what you said to Joanne

about using bottled water. Do you think we're in for more cases of gastro?'

'Seeing that little kid so ill set off a few alarm bells.' His thoughts turned dark for a second. 'Where I was stationed in Cambodia, gastro was a constant source of concern but with our standard of living it's not so prevalent. All the more reason when we come across a case, to exercise vigilance, especially amongst the very young and the aged.'

'But surely if it's something to do with the water, we'd all be sick,' she suggested.

Rafe wasn't prepared to go any further with supposition. 'Just let's get the staff alerted to the possibility, and if any more cases present over the weekend, we'll take it from there and start investigating.'

Toni nodded. 'I'll let you get on, then.'

'Antonia…' Suddenly, Rafe felt every nerve in his body jerk to attention, his heart jostling for space inside his chest. But he had to do this now. 'Could we talk—properly?'

Toni stiffened and went very still, almost *feeling* the silence hanging between them like an unexploded bomb. She moistened her lips. 'Where?'

Spurred on by her acceptance, Rafe tried to think on his feet. 'Not here.'

'No.'

Well, at least they'd agreed on that. 'We're both off shift shortly. Come round for a swim.'

A beat of silence.

'Don't think so.' Toni heard her voice oddly calm and decisive.

'OK…' Rafe rubbed a hand across his forehead. Obviously too far, too fast. 'Somewhere you'd feel comfortable, then.'

Toni hesitated briefly. 'Perhaps the café in the main street? The Copper Kettle. It's a couple of doors down from the supermarket.'

'Fine.' His green eyes lit briefly. 'See you there in about twenty?'

'Make it twenty-five,' Toni countered. After all, a girl had to make herself presentable.

CHAPTER FIVE

TONI looked at her nurse's uniform of smoky blue shirt and navy trousers and made a face in the mirror, wishing that today of all days she'd brought a change of clothes to work. But she hadn't expected Rafe's invitation. Not for a second.

She'd have to make do with brushing her hair into some kind of order and refreshing her lip gloss.

She couldn't quite believe that in a few minutes she'd be meeting Rafe outside the hospital.

Suddenly her heartbeat reflected her slight panic. But she was glad he'd made the first move. They certainly could not have gone on in the kind of energy-sapping vacuum that had sprung up between them.

Sitting in one of the high-backed booths in the café, Rafe found his gaze hovering impatiently on the entrance. He tried to get a grip on his wayward thoughts. He prided himself on always being focused in the course of his working day but almost from the moment Antonia had turned that amazing smile on him, he'd found his thoughts wandering off at the most unexpected moments. Wild thoughts, he admitted, his gut turning over again. Thoughts of a man and a certain woman…

He sucked in a deep breath and looked around him,

for the first time noticing a group of girls sitting across
the aisle. They were obviously students. Rafe recog-
nised their blue and white checked uniforms as being
from the local high school. They were slurping drinks
out of old-fashioned soda glasses, their girlish chatter
constant. Perhaps this was their after-school Friday rit-
ual, he thought wryly, reflecting on his own high school
years in Sydney. They'd been good years. Happy years.

But then *life* had happened…

A subdued shriek from the girls' booth abruptly re-
focused his run into the past. Rafe gave them an en-
quiring under-brow glance. They were all busy with
their mobile phones.

'Luke's texted me!'

Obviously the owner of the shriek, Rafe decided, his
mouth tilting into something that was almost a smile.

'He wants to go out!'

'Oh, my God!' Another shriek from another of the
girls. 'You cow!'

Obviously, a compliment. Rafe felt his mouth twitch
again.

'It'll take me, like, *hours* to get ready! And I've a
zit on my chin!'

'The chemist's got concealer on special,' someone
said helpfully.

'I'm broke until I get my pay tomorrow!' Luke's date,
dramatically.

'I can lend you twenty bucks.' The helpful one again.

'Cool! Let's go, then.'

Decision made, they rose as one in a flurry of arms,
legs and backpacks. And female solidarity.

God, they learn it from the cradle, Rafe thought
broodingly. And then, as he watched the girls' giggly
progression towards the exit, he caught sight of Toni at

the entrance. Oh, hell. He struggled with an odd sense of unreality. With the afternoon sun streaming behind her and backlighting her, she looked like an angel.

Almost dazedly, he half rose, watching as the girls stood back for Toni to come in. 'Hi, Toni,' they chorused.

'Hi, girls.' Toni smiled, returning their finger waves as she slipped past them. She headed straight along the aisle to Rafe's booth. 'Sorry, I'm a bit later than I thought.'

'It's fine.' Rafe caught the tail end of her smile and they sat down together. 'I didn't mind the wait. I had free entertainment on tap.'

'The girls?' She laughed softly. 'They're gorgeous.'

'You know them?'

'Mmm.' Toni slid into the corner of the booth. 'I do the relationship talk at the high school.' She gave him a wide-eyed look. 'We cover health issues, *et cetera*.'

Rafe merely raised an eyebrow in acknowledgment. Young adults needed to be properly informed and in this day and age any health talk worthy of the name had to cover issues like safe sex. 'I'm sure you do it very well.' *Idiot.* Rafe groaned inwardly at his loaded comment.

'Oh, I do.' She smiled, activating the tiny dimple beside her mouth. She took up the menu. 'Now, what are we having? What about a pot of tea?'

Rafe scrubbed lean fingers across his cheekbones, trying to concentrate. 'Sounds good.'

'And a slice of chocolate cake?'

His lips twitched. 'What with bread and butter pudding the other night and now chocolate cake, I'm beginning to think you have a sweet tooth, Antonia.'

She shrugged. 'I do. But I exercise so it evens out.'

'I guess it does.' Rafe looked up as the waitress appeared at their table. He gave their order and then placed the menu carefully down on the table top. 'Thanks for coming, by the way.'

She raised an expressive eyebrow at him. 'What did you want to talk about?' As if she didn't know.

'I haven't seen you about much this week. Have you been avoiding me?'

Wow, that was direct. Toni felt a slick of embarrassment. 'Being nurse manager, I'm sometimes out of the department. You weren't inconvenienced, were you?'

'Professionally, no.' Rafe gave her a long, intense look. 'Personally...' he lifted a shoulder expressivel. '...I, uh, thought I might have offended you and you were keeping out of my way.'

'I was,' Toni heard herself say, and looking back at her motivations now, it all seemed a bit pathetic. And professionally it had been way out of line. 'My apologies.'

Rafe felt the wind taken right out of his sails. He hadn't expected her to be so upfront. But, then, how well did he know Antonia Morell? Not as well as he wanted to, that was certain. The admission unsettled him. He took a deep swallow. 'Was it something I said to make you upset in the first place?'

Toni expelled a sigh, recognising that this was a time when only the truth would do. 'Things got a bit ratty the day after the Valentine party. I hadn't slept well and my team and your resident were all over the place like recalcitrant children—'

'And I came in all upbeat and cheerful. I remember now. You were snippy.'

'I hadn't slept well,' she reiterated.

'Was there a reason—apart from the hot weather? You weren't drinking, as I recall.'

For heaven's sake! Toni almost rolled her eyes. What was this, an inquisition? She wasn't in the principal's office but it sure felt like it. *I was concerned about you!* She felt like letting him have it straight between the eyes. But that would be admitting she more than liked him. And she wasn't admitting that—not even to herself.

'It was just one of those things,' she said finally. 'I don't do late nights very well.'

She didn't do late nights? What kind of a ridiculous answer was that? Her job consisted of shift work, for God's sake. Rafe was still thinking about a response when their waitress arrived with their tea and cake.

'Oh, good,' Toni sidetracked quickly, thankful for the reprieve from his questions. 'Nice teacups instead of mugs. That's a change.' Taking up the pot, she began to pour. 'How do you take your tea?'

'Just black, thanks.'

'Oh, me too. Do you have the weekend off?'

A fleeting frown touched his eyes. 'Apart from a multi-trauma happening, I believe so.'

'So, any plans?' She passed his tea across the table. 'Are you hoping to see something of the district while you're here?'

'I'd like to.' Rafe was thoughtful. He knew when he'd been snowed. And the lady had done a brilliant job. But he wasn't without ammunition. 'Would you like to be my guide?'

Toni's mouth fell open. That invitation had come out of left field. It would mean spending the whole day with him. Was she up for it? When in doubt, don't. Her mother's invocation came back to her. But what was she, for heaven's sake? A woman or a wimp? He was new in town. It wouldn't hurt her to be friendly. 'OK…' she said slowly. 'This part of the country is steeped in history. There are a few interesting places we could visit. I'll have a bit of a think and have an itinerary planned for tomorrow.'

'Don't go overboard.' He flashed her a mocking kind of look. 'I'd prefer to keep things slow and easy.' His eyes gleamed with lazy intent.

Toni's heart hitched to a halt. 'I'll…bear that in mind.'

They made desultory conversation over their afternoon tea. Then Toni looked at her watch. 'I'm going to split. I need to do a quick swoop at the supermarket.' She gathered her bag and got to her feet. 'Thanks for the tea.'

'Thanks for the conversation—and the enlightenment.' Their eyes met and he could see the wariness in her gaze. 'See you tomorrow.'

Toni hovered. 'About ten suit you?'

'Ten o'clock is fine. I don't know where you live or I'd offer to pick you up.'

Then it might feel like a real date and Toni wasn't having that. 'Might be quicker and easier if I come round to you,' she said.

'Whatever makes you happy, Antonia,' he said sardonically.

She took a deep breath, about to flutter a little wave but thought better of it. Instead, she gripped the strap of her shoulder bag so hard her fingers almost turned blue. She offered a guarded kind of smile. 'Well—bye, then.'

He merely lifted a finger and nodded.

'Sleep well!'

Toni heard the laughter in his voice as he called after her. Her sense of triumph faltered. He hadn't believed her explanation for her tardiness. Hadn't believed her at all. Well, one to you, Doctor, she apportioned fairly. Grabbing a trolley, she shot into the supermarket and stood gaping. She'd completely forgotten what she'd come to buy.

Toni chose a soft, flirty sundress for her day out. She'd made herself eat museli and fruit for breakfast, despite her stomach leading her on a merry dance of its own. Stepping into flat-heeled sandals, she looked in the mirror, startled to see the slight flush in her cheeks. Well, she could tame that but there was nothing she could do about the light of expectancy in her eyes.

Oh, lord. She'd vowed to be practical and level-headed about this day out with Rafe. Instead, her image reflected a wide-eyed vulnerability. Get a grip, Toni, she warned silently. You've been round this track once before, remember?

But then again, Rafe wasn't a two-timing rat like Alex, was he…?

She turned away, collecting bits and pieces for her holdall, pausing as her eyes lit on the red and white bikini draped across the back of her bedroom chair. Without thinking twice, she picked up the brief garment and tossed it into her bag.

They might swim and they might not. But she'd be prepared. And the bikini might be brief but not that brief and it was comfortable and allowed her the freedom of feeling part of the water without being naked. Clipping on a big colourful sports watch, she made her way outside to the car port.

It took only a few minutes to get across town to the Lyons' place. Rafe's vehicle, a modest, black SUV, was already outside and waiting. Toni parked neatly behind it, took a few breaths to centre herself and got out of the car.

Weather-wise the morning was perfect, she decided. Sultry but perfect. For a moment she stopped, lifting her head and listening. Already the cicadas were up and about, whirring madly in the shrubbery, the air, when she breathed it in, was summery hot and sharp with the tang of lemon-scented tea trees.

And promise.

Rafe was waiting for her in the courtyard in front of the annexe. Had been for the past thirty minutes. He was sitting in one of the comfortable outdoor chairs, pretending to read a surfing magazine one of the Lyons kids had left behind.

It was useless. He couldn't concentrate. And his stomach was giving him gyp. He'd forced down a bacon sandwich that now felt like cement in his gut.

He was a lunatic. What had possessed him to think he was ready to start dating again?

But it wasn't really a date.

Yes, it was.

No, it wasn't…

He'd be cool. He'd be cool.

Relax, then.

He leaned back in his chair, one leg jiggling restlessly. He glanced at his watch and swore. Where the hell was she?

She came round the corner, her step silent across the lawn. She saw Rafe waiting. 'Morning,' she called across the short distance that separated them. 'You're ready, I see.'

Rafe jackknifed to his feet as if he'd been stung.

'You're late!' He squirmed inwardly. God, he'd barked at her.

Toni wasn't having that. 'I'm never late. Your watch must be fast.' And this was a ridiculous conversation. Another one. She lifted a hand and placed it against the lattice screen. And looked at him. He was dressed in baggy cargo shorts and a soft, pale blue polo shirt that showed up the deep tan of his arms and throat. She took a shallow breath, all her nerve-ends quivering. Mentally, she drew back, wanting them to get moving, get on their way, but her feet felt anchored. All she could do was to absorb the proud set of his head, the ripeness of his masculine bearing and the way he was looking at her mouth. Automatically, she moistened her lips. 'It's hot out there. You'll need a hat.'

'I have one in the car.' Sweet God. Rafe took a steadying breath. In her pretty dress, with her hair flowing, her glowing skin and that sweet, very sweet mouth, she wouldn't be out of place in a painting. Perhaps in a field, picking daisies. Or frolicking with lambs. Something stirred inside him. Something that hadn't been stirred in a long time. Something that had been breathed into life the moment Antonia Morell had smiled at him.

'Ready, then?' Toni removed the sunglasses from the top of her head and twirled them in her fingers.

'Yep.' Rafe broke out of the fanciful daydream. Touching his back pocket, he located his wallet. 'I'll… just shut the door.' He did, precisely and quickly, and then they were striding across the lawn and back to the path. At least Rafe was striding.

'Where's the fire?' Toni asked dryly.

'Sorry.' Rafe slowed, catching a drift of her flowery shampoo for his trouble. 'Force of habit.'

He released the catch on the double gates that led to

the footpath and waited for her to go through then followed her and shut the gates. He turned and stopped abruptly, eying her pewter-coloured sports car. He whistled under his breath. 'You drive a BMW?'

'A birthday present from my parents,' she said airily. 'They've a thing about road safety. I'm presuming you want us to go in your car?'

'I'd prefer to drive, if you wouldn't mind?'

Toni shrugged. 'I'll navigate. Hang on a tick. I'll just get my bag.'

Settling into the passenger seat of his car, Toni adjusted her seat belt and then, looking up, gave him a quick smile. 'How do you want to do this?'

'I'm sure you have a plan, Antonia.'

His reciprocal smile left a lingering warmth in his eyes and Toni felt her heart lurch. 'I thought perhaps we could follow a stretch of the old Cobb and Co. route,' she said, referring to Australia's first method of transportation.

'Back to the horse and coach days,' he reflected. 'Sounds good. Where to first, then?'

'About twenty Ks out to a township called Maeburn. They've re-created one of the coaches and have it on display. There's also a gorgeous church, St Anne's, supposed to be the oldest timber church in the state. Well worth a look, I think.'

Rafe needed no further encouragement. To spend time with her away from the hospital was going to be a heady experience. He couldn't wait.

In the close confines of his car Toni made herself relax. She guessed she was going to get to know a different Rafe Riccardi today. They'd sparred a bit already and she liked that. And he smelled nice, she decided. Soap and water nice. She flicked him a query. 'I'm supposed to be the navigator, so do you want me to keep up a running commentary or…?' She stopped and shrugged.

'Tell me a bit about Cobb and Co.,' he said, his eyes firmly on the road.

Surely, he was kidding. 'Didn't you learn Australian history at school?'

'Not much of it. We concentrated mostly on British history. When I left school, I could recite all the kings and queens of England but I couldn't tell you who our first PM was.'

'That's appalling, Rafe!'

'I agree,' he said with equanimity. 'But things have changed a bit now, I believe.'

'One would hope so.' She huffed a derogatory laugh. 'I'll bet you went to one of those exclusive boys' schools.'

He named it and she huffed again.

'I gather you were much more enlightened, then?' He teased.

'I went to a progressive, co-ed high school where we *did* learn Australian history,' she told him with a little curl of satisfaction.

'So, forgive my ignorance, then.' He laughed. 'And tell me about Cobb and Co.'

Toni was more than happy to launch into her spiel. 'Just stop me if I'm boring you, though,' she warned.

'You could *never* bore me, Antonia,' he said with a certainty that left her head spinning.

'OK…' She took a steadying breath. 'Cobb and Co. began in the 1850s in Victoria. Gold had just been dis-covered, so their prime purpose was to get folk from Melbourne to the diggings. As well as passengers, they carried the Royal Mail and a bit of freight.'

'And when did they come here to New South Wales?' Rafe wanted to know.

'Around the 1860s, apparently. And then Queensland after that. To travel, say, fifty miles, they had a team of forty horses. They had to change the teams regularly to give the horses a spell.'

Rafe was thoughtful. 'So, allowing for the vastness of our country, the company must have had a huge number of horses to cope with the distances they had to travel.'

'Thousands. And they had their own workshops where they built and maintained their coaches, and had hundreds of drivers and grooms. And you had to book days in advance, of course, to get a seat on the coach.'

'No going online, then.' He laughed. 'How long did the company operate?'

'Seventy-five years, they say. What a unique part of our history, though. Don't you agree?'

'Absolutely. But when you imagine some of those roads back then…'

'Makes you pleased we now have nice comfortable cars with upholstered seats,' she said with a laugh.

'Mmm. Thanks, that was great,' he said. 'Go on with your travelogue.'

'That's enough for now,' she countered. 'Tell me about you.'

'Ah…' Rafe felt his shoulders tense. He wasn't sure he wanted to go there. The whole idea of having this day out had been to get away from *himself.*

'Surely you're not modest, Dr Riccardi?' Toni sent him a teasing look.

No, he wanted to tell her. Just *private.* But obviously that wasn't going to satisfy the lady.

But before he could open his mouth she said chattily, 'Well, judging by the school you went to, you were obviously brought up in Sydney, right?'

'Right.' He forced a smile. 'Dover Heights, to be precise.'

'Oh, *very* nice. My family lives in Rose Bay,' Toni said. 'We must have been practically neighbours. Do you have siblings?'

'One brother, Ben. He's a freelance photo journalist. He travels the world.'

'I guess you'd have to be a certain kind of person to do that for a living,' Toni reflected. 'I'd prefer having roots, I think.'

Rafe kept his own counsel. This was way too deep and meaningful for the present fluid state of his life. 'What about you?' He changed tack skilfully. 'Any siblings?'

'Just me,' she said lightly.

His mouth crimped at the corners. 'Were you indulged?'

'I wouldn't have thought so. Mum and Dad are pretty grounded. Dad's an ENT consultant and Mum is a professional fundraiser for several charities.'

'Must be where you got your organisational ability,' Rafe suggested. 'Did you always want to be a nurse?'

She made a small face. 'I actually did a year and a half of medicine. As students, we were thrown out on to the wards pretty early. And when I saw the hands-on skills of the nurses, I figured that's where I wanted to be. I chucked medicine and enrolled in nursing.'

'Well, you excel at it,' he complimented her.

She blushed. 'Thanks. I like the feeling of being able to get things done for the patients, I suppose. What about you?' She turned a querying look on him. 'Are you from a medical background?'

'No.' He gave an amused chuckle. 'My dad's a bookie.'

'How interesting. What was it like growing up for you?'

He shrugged. 'It was good. Sometimes Ben and I pencilled for Dad at the races. That was an experience.'

'I can imagine…' Toni drifted off.

'My mother is an artist.'

Toni heard the pride in his voice. 'Fantastic. Does she exhibit?'

'She does and she actually has a small gallery in Rose Bay.'

'How incredible! I've probably walked past it a million times.'

'You should have walked *in*,' Rafe countered.

'Next time I'm down, I certainly will. And buy something,' she added on a laugh. Oh, lord, this was surely kismet. She and Rafe must have walked the same streets, swum at the same beaches. She might have passed him in the corridors of a Sydney hospital some time. But no. She'd have remembered that. Perhaps they had been destined to meet. But for what reason? She sobered. Time wasn't on their side. He was on the move. She wanted to put down roots. It was crazy to think they could ever be more than…friends.

Rafe flicked her a discerning look. 'You've gone very quiet, Antonia.'

For answer, she pointed to a sign up ahead. 'That's our turn-off for Maeburn. Just keep following the wagon-wheel logo directional signs. And I don't talk *all* the time,' she countered. 'Anyway, you've gone a bit quiet yourself.'

'Just thinking.'

'Care to tell me?'

Rafe felt his gut tighten. He couldn't possibly tell her that having her sitting next to him like this made his world feel right. And that if he didn't kiss her before the day was out, he'd go crazy. Instead, he managed a laugh of sorts. 'Maybe I'll tell you later.'

Very soon, they entered the township of Maeburn and Toni directed Rafe to a parking area from where they could walk to the various places of heritage interest. Rafe produced bottles of water from a cooler in the boot of the car and they began their tour.

The timber coach was painted a distinctive maroon with gold trim. It stood in a Perspex enclosure in the main street. Rafe and Toni joined the little knot of tourists viewing. 'It's smaller than I imagined,' Rafe said. 'That kind of dicky-seat at the rear was obviously intended for any overflow of passengers or freight.'

Toni pretended to shudder. 'Imagine being caught in a thunderstorm and having to sit out there. Or being pregnant and having to go over those rough roads.'

'Mmm.' Rafe took a long swallow of his water. 'Our forebears were certainly made of stern stuff.'

Toni looked thoughtful. 'I guess we all try to do our best with the circumstances we're faced with. Or I'd like to think we do.'

He gave a hard-edged laugh. 'That's far too weighty to discuss on such a nice day. Come on, Ms Morell.' He touched a hand to her shoulder. 'What else do you have to show me on this tour?'

'Let's do the church.' Toni could still feel the imprint of his fingers as they moved away. 'We cut through this little park at the end of the street,' she said in her role of official guide.

'And after we've seen the church, we'd better find somewhere to eat lunch.'

Toni sent him a teasing smile. 'I thought you might have packed us a picnic.'

'Not today.' His mouth folded in on a dry smile. 'But don't think I couldn't.'

She gave a throaty laugh. 'I'll hold you to that.'

Oh, I hope you will, Antonia, Rafe told himself fervently. *I hope you will.*

They took the path that ran between two beautiful old ghost gums, crested a gentle rise in the ground and stood looking across at St Anne's. The gracious old timber structure was set prettily among lawns and flower beds.

'Shall we go in?' Toni said.

Rafe hesitated. 'Are you sure it's open?'

'Of course it's open. It's only locked at night. And, amazingly, there's never been any kind of vandalism.'

'So the angels are guarding it, are they?' he responded, tongue in cheek.

Toni rolled her eyes. 'We'll go in through the side entrance.'

Rafe felt an odd kind of peace when they entered the old church. His gaze tracked to the stained-glass windows where the early afternoon sun streamed through, making dappled patterns on the light maple wood of the pews.

'Look up,' Toni whispered. 'The whole ceiling is pressed metal.'

'Impressive.' Rafe took in the dome-shaped ornate ceiling. 'When was the church built, do you know?'

'Nineteen-ten,' Toni replied without hesitation. 'Given its height, erecting that ceiling would have been quite a task for the builders back then. And here at the rear of the church is the choir loft.'

Rafe moved closer, to better appreciate the intricate

carving along the rails of the staircase leading up to the choir. 'It's very beautiful,' he murmured.

Toni nodded. 'Would you like to sit for a minute? It's nice to just *be,*' she added softly.

Rafe was like putty in her hands. He followed her into one of the pews and let the peace and tranquillity surround him. It had been a long time since he'd felt so relaxed, he thought, letting the burdens of the past slide away.

Toni was in her own little well of peace. This place never failed to do it for her and she'd been here many times. She glanced at Rafe, her gaze flicking all the way down his body and back again. He turned his head and they shared a smile, tremulous, hardly there. 'Thanks,' he said deeply. Toni gave a quick nod. She knew exactly what he meant.

No more words were needed.

As they left the church, Toni wondered how her hand had crept into his. But it had and he seemed determined to keep it there.

The day was beginning to take on a magic quality of its own, Rafe thought. He took a deep breath and asked lightly, 'Is that a barbecue I can smell?'

'One of the pubs does a special outdoor lunch on Saturdays,' Toni informed him with a grin. 'I can see you're interested.'

'Certainly. Aren't you?'

'Yes, thank you,' she answered sweetly. 'It's only a short stroll from here to the pub. Lunch is served in a beer garden kind of setting so the surroundings are nice and cool.'

'This is terrific,' Rafe said, as they made their way past a wall of tropical fern into the lattice-enclosed beer garden.

'And there's a free table,' Toni pointed out happily.

Rafe squeezed her hand. 'Grab it and I'll get us a drink. Light beer?' His dark brows rose in quick query.

'Perfect. Thanks.'

A little while later they touched glasses and sampled the icy-cold ale. Then set about collecting their food from the barbecue. Toni wasn't surprised when Rafe selected a prime T-bone steak while she herself preferred the chargrilled chicken. There were several kinds of salads on offer so, selections made and plates loaded, they made their way back to their table.

'Oh, yummy.' Toni made a show of licking her lips in anticipation. 'I'm starving.'

Rafe looked amused. 'Did you skip breakfast?'

'Uh-uh. Never do. Did you?'

He may as well have for all the good it had done. He lifted a shoulder in dismissal.

She tinkled a laugh. 'Were you uptight about coming out with me today?'

Hell. Was she a witch or something? 'I haven't been on anything resembling a date for a long time,' he admitted.

'So, this is a date, then?' Toni brought her head up, her look teasing.

'What else would you call it?' he growled, prodding a chunk of tomato with his fork.

Unabashed, Toni chuckled softly. 'I'd call it a date.'

They went on with their meal, talking inconsequentially, tuning in, tuning out, idle talk, getting-to-know-each-other kind of talk.

Toni didn't realise how engrossed they'd become in their conversation until a sharp, desperate plea broke the air of happy relaxation in the beer garden.

'Could someone help me?' A man thrust forward,

curving a path between the tables. 'Is there a doctor here? Or a nurse?'

'I'm a doctor.' Rafe was immediately on his feet. 'What's happened?'

The man took a hard breath to compose himself. 'We were on a hot-air balloon flight—struck turbulence— it's come down in the park. My daughter, Simone— she's hurt—it's bad—'

'Get my bag, Toni!' Rafe fished out his keys from the pocket of his shorts and tossed them across to her. 'It's in the boot. The park? You'll know where to come?'

'I'll know.' Toni ran.

'Geoff Mullins.' The man bit out the introduction as they ran from the beer garden and across the road to the park.

'Rafe Riccardi. How old is your daughter, Geoff?'

'Simone's eighteen today. The balloon ride was a birthday surprise. Wish now we'd never gone on the bloody thing—'

'Did you hit something on the way down?' Rafe was already formulating possible injuries in his mind.

'Tree. Bloody great branch broke off and got Simone under her ribs. Hell, Doc…' The father's voice broke. 'She's my little girl…'

Rafe wasted no time in commiserating. What could he say anyway until he'd seen the girl? Following Geoff's lead, he put on a fresh burst of speed as the crashed balloon came into sight, the basket lurching drunkenly on its side. A cluster of bewildered passengers was hovering nearby.

'Geoff! Oh, thank God!' A woman, obviously the mother, was cradling Simone on the ground. She looked a desperate plea at Rafe. 'Can you help?'

'I'm a doctor.' He dropped down beside the injured

girl. One swift, comprehensive glance told him they were in trouble of the worst kind. 'Hi, Simone,' he said gently. 'I'm Rafe.'

'Can't breathe,' she rasped. 'Hurts…sick…'

Rafe jerked up from his kneeling position. 'Has someone called an ambulance?' he yelled to the watching crowd.

A young man raised his hand. 'I called. There's one on the way from Forrestdale. Can I do anything?'

'Just keep a look out, mate, and direct them, if you would?'

'Can do.'

Rafe went back to his patient.

'Everything's blurry…' Screwing her eyes closed, Simone struggled to find air.

'My friend's gone to get my medical case, Simone. I'll be able to help you in a minute. Just hang in there. Good girl.'

'Here's your bag!' One hand on her chest, breathy from her run, Toni's experienced eye took in the emergency at a glance. Heard the girl's laboured breathing. She dropped beside Rafe. 'Pneumothorax?'

'Looks like it.' Rafe shot open his case and drew out his stethoscope. 'Simone, I need to listen to your chest.'

'Unn…' Simone mumbled, struggling harder for breath.

'Please…' The mother whispered. 'What's happening with my daughter?'

'Simone has a punctured lung, Mrs Mullins. That's why she's having so much trouble breathing. Now, we have an emergency here and we can't wait for the ambulance.'

On a groan of anguish Geoff Mullins took his daughter's hand and pressed it against his cheek. 'What are you gonna do, Doc?'

'I'm going to put a needle in. It'll help Simone to breathe more freely.'

'Oh, God…' The father's distress was painful to see. 'Will it hurt?'

Toni stepped in. 'It'll hurt but only for second.' Already she could see Rafe's fingers working their way down Simone's ribcage. He stopped.

'There?'

He nodded.

Toni swabbed the coolness of alcohol on the girl's skin and watched as the needle pierced her chest and broke through into her lung.

'You're OK, now Simone.' Rafe was taping the needle into place as he spoke. 'Just stay very still for me while I make sure it's secure.'

'Mmm…better,' Simone croaked.

'Don't try to talk,' Toni said gently. 'Once the ambulance gets here, we'll get you on some oxygen. In the meantime, folks, could we get Simone more comfortable?'

The parents, who'd been wearing warm clothing to compensate for the high altitude of the balloon flight, immediately whipped off their coats and helped Toni fold them under the injured girl's head.

'Better…' Simone raised the ghost of a smile. 'Thanks…'

'When you get to the hospital, they'll give you a proper chest tube and and X-ray,' Rafe said gently. 'You've been very brave, kiddo.'

'Thank you so much, both of you.' The mother drew shaky fingers across her eyes.

'Yeah—thanks,' Geoff added gruffly. 'Mighty job.'

Rafe shrugged. 'Just glad we were here. What about you and the rest of the passengers? Are you all right?'

'Bit shocked, I think,' Mrs Mullins said. 'The pilot's gone to call his base. He's upset, poor man.'

'Poor man! I'll sue his butt off,' Geoff growled. 'We could have all been killed.'

'Geoff, let it go,' his wife pleaded. 'It was an accident. The company will be insured. I'm sure we'll get compensation or whatever it is they do.'

'Ambulance is here!' someone shouted.

Rafe turned to Toni. 'I'll go with Simone to the hospital. Could you follow in my car?'

'Sure.' They exchanged a private kind of smile. 'Quite an eventful end to our day out!'

'It's not over yet, Antonia,' he countered, and his voice was soft, muted, almost a seductive caress that wound itself around her like the finest strands of silk as they stood in the sun-filled park on that Saturday afternoon.

CHAPTER SIX

KEITH SUTHERLAND was waiting for them in Resus. Looking at Rafe following along behind the ambulance trolley, he shook his head. 'What is it with you guys? Not content with emergencies coming to you, you go out and find them instead.'

'All the time,' Rafe said dryly. 'Keith, this is Simone Mullins, aged eighteen.' Rafe continued to give a brief handover. 'Her parents will be here directly.' He placed his hand gently on Simone's wrist. 'Dr Sutherland will take care of you now, Simone. I'll look in on you tomorrow to see how you're doing. Meantime, take it easy, all right?'

Simone's eyelids flickered and closed. ''Anks...' was all she could manage.

Toni was waiting in the car park.

Rafe piled into the driver's seat and they took off.

'How is she?' Toni asked.

'Exhausted. But she'll be fine.'

Toni sent him a quick look. 'Where are we going now?'

'Back to my place,' he said shortly. 'Let's try and salvage something from the rest of the day. Fancy a swim when we get there?'

'Yes…' Toni said on a long breath. 'Sounds wonderful.'

'Do you need to call in at home for your swimmers?'

'Not really,' Toni deadpanned. 'I thought we could swim in the nude.'

Rafe's jaw fell open. His heart gave a sideways skip. Was she serious?

'But maybe not.' She laughed softly. 'Had you going there, didn't I?'

He conceded a smile at that. Just a small one. 'Oh, you'll keep,' he said. But rather than a threat, he made it sound like a promise.

'I'm going to relish this swim.' Toni swung her bag, as they made their way along the path to the annexe.

Rafe opened the door and they went in.

'May I use your bedroom? Toni dragged a hand through her hair and eased it away from the back of her neck. 'I'll just slip into my bikini.'

She wore a bikini? Sweet God, what was she trying to do to him? Desire and very basic need slammed into him like a great breath of scorching wind.

'What?' Toni felt her throat dry. He was staring at her mouth as though it was beckoning him, bewitching him. In a nervous reaction she released her fingers, letting her bag fall in a crumpled heap to the floor.

Suddenly *everything* had changed between them.

Toni felt all her senses come to life, flaming into response as Rafe moved closer, moved into her personal space, so close she could feel his breath on her cheek.

The weight of a kiss that simply had to happen was only a whisper away.

Rafe took her face in his hands. He bent to her, his lips teasingly missing hers, moving instead slowly along her cheek, her jaw, her throat, savouring every part of her skin, the weight of his lips so close—daring her to respond.

How could she resist?

Her lips turned to his like petals to the sun and the wild, beautiful weight of his mouth was on hers. The cool control of his tongue was parting her lips, meeting the tip of hers and slowly coiling, tasting.

Toni sighed, feeling his hand guiding her, nestling in the small of her back. And she didn't let herself think whether this magical thing they were sharing had a future. She was just amazed that they should be kissing at all and that she'd so longed for it without even knowing why.

'I've never kissed anyone as amazing as you,' Rafe murmured much later, when they'd slowly, reluctantly drawn apart.

'Or not recently?' Toni teased softly, reluctant to accept his compliment. She didn't know why. 'You're pretty amazing yourself.'

'So, I take it we're both pretty amazing.' His eyes gleamed with humour.

Toni laughed shakily. This was dangerous ground. Scary.

She took a little step back from him. 'Are we going to have that swim, then?'

'We'd better, I think.' His mouth brushed hers again. And again. 'Otherwise I'm going to need a cold shower.'

They swam, stroking lazily up and down the pool. Then they floated. Blinking the droplets from her eyes, Toni looked up into the blueness of a summer sky—it was beautiful, vast. A feeling of pure gladness twisted inside her.

The beauty of the world, her world, was all around them. Rafe was barely an arm's length away and nothing had ever felt so right. Suddenly she wanted to share everything with him. The sky, the cool depths of the water, the musky perfume of the jasmine and the other more elusive smells that charged her senses.

'Rafe?' Scooping her hand into the water, she shot a spray of droplets on to his chest. 'Open your eyes.'

'They're open.'

'Look up. What do you see?' she asked, her voice hushed with expectancy.

'Blue sky,' he said without inflection. 'And more blue sky.'

'That's pathetic!' Toni showered him with water again. 'Where's your imagination, Riccardi!'

That was too much for Rafe. He made a lunge at her but she was too quick, stroking away from him. However, her stroke was no match for his long arms. He caught up to her quickly. Toni screamed her protest as he ducked her but she bobbed up in a second slicked with water, her hands clasped around his neck. Laughingly, they kissed playfully, once, twice.

Just when it changed into something else, Toni wasn't sure. Holding her gaze with an intensity that rocked her to the core, Rafe laid his open palm across her bare midriff. Then, bending his head, he kissed the soft swell of her breast above her bikini top.

'Rafe…' A jagged breath left Toni's mouth. Lifting her hands, she slid them down the wet sleekness of his naked back and he dragged in a huge breath and lifted his head.

'Out, I think, Antonia.' His voice was clogged and he shook the water from his hair. Towing her to the end of the pool, he hoisted her up the ladder.

'Coming?' Toni looked back over her shoulder.

'I need a minute.' His grin was rueful. 'Go, get your shower.'

Toni fled as if she'd been stung.

Stripping off her bikini, she threw herself into the shower, letting it run full pelt. She used Rafe's soap. Nice, she decided, lathering it and letting the bubbles run off her skin. She picked up his bottle of shampoo and let some nestle in the palm of her hand. It smelled nice too. As she shampooed her hair and rinsed it, her thoughts came to a dead end.

Were they playing games again? She bit the softness of her lower lip, turning off the water and reaching for a towel. Towels, she corrected. She'd need an extra one to dry her hair. She blinked a bit, seeing two pristine white towels hanging neatly on the rail. Obviously, he'd put them there. For her. He'd thought of the possibility of them swimming. Well, she had as well. Suddenly, she gave a shaky little laugh. Oh, Rafe… There was so much to love about him. *Like*, she amended quickly, and wrapping her body in one of the towels and her hair in the other, she tiptoed through to his bedroom.

As she dressed, she could hear the cicadas tick, tick, ticking outside in the shrubbery, feel the warm press of air, because he hadn't switched on the air-conditioning in the bedroom. The softest smile touched her mouth. I could make love with him right here, right now. And it would feel so perfect. But there was so much she didn't know about him. Would she ever get the chance?

She finished blotting her hair and, somewhat more composed, she made her way back outside to the courtyard. Rafe was still there. He was sitting forward on the chair, hands linked across his knees, looking across the pool to the enclosed tennis court beyond.

'Shower's free,' she said, taking the other chair beside him.

'Joe and Cath have a great set-up here,' he said quietly.

Toni sent him a sharp look. There'd been almost longing in his voice. 'I guess when you have to bring up five kids in a country town, you have to go all out to keep them entertained,' she said.

'I hope they enjoy Italy.'

'Oh, they will.' Toni was enthusiastic. 'My parents took me to France for a year when I was fifteen. It was magic. And Marcus, their eldest, is seventeen. He'll so enjoy the experience of living in another country, as will Rosie and Madeleine. Even the two little ones will have a ball.'

'You know the family well?'

'Mmm. Spent lots of time here. I helped Cath now and again with her fundraising for the school.'

Rafe looked thoughtful, lying back in his chair. 'How do you raise such a big family these days?'

Toni shrugged. 'Like Joe and Cath do, I guess. With plenty of imagination, a few ground rules and a good dose of love thrown in.'

She made it sound so easy. He expelled a hard breath and rubbed his hands back through his hair. 'I'll get that shower.' He hoisted himself to his feet. 'Make yourself at home.'

'Oh, I am.' Toni twinkled a smile up at him and wiggled her bare toes.

In the shower, Rafe lathered himself, letting the warm jet of water spray over his head and slick down over his shoulders to puddle round his feet.

He had to lighten up.

He'd think of Antonia. That should work. She continued to amaze him, startle him out of his prosaic routine of thinking, of acting. But he hadn't shaped up too badly today, he thought. Along with the lady herself, he decided they'd done pretty well for a first date. If that's what it was. Conversationally, there hadn't been any awkward pauses and they'd disclosed a little of their personal lives to one another.

And they'd kissed. He couldn't, *wouldn't* forget that.

Towelling himself dry, he pulled on washed-out jeans and a black T-shirt, and wandered outside to join Toni. He opened the door to the annexe and paused. She was still sitting there, looking as relaxed as a small, boneless cat. He noticed the afternoon sun was beginning to lose some of its heat and a breeze had begun to make snakelike ripples across the pool. 'Glass of wine?' he asked.

Toni looked back at him and smiled. 'Oh, yes, please. Could you bring it out? I don't feel like moving yet.'

Rafe merely raised an eyebrow. 'My pleasure,' he said. And it was, he told himself, all the way to the fridge and back again. It surely was.

Toni took her first sip of the wine. 'It's lovely.'

'I'm a bit out of the loop with choosing wine. This seems to have won a major award, though, so it should be all right.'

'It's gorgeous.' Toni relaxed back into the chair. It had been a very eventful day. But instead of feeling fatigued, she felt strangely exhilarated. And she didn't want it to end. She turned to Rafe. 'Would you like me to make us an early dinner or would you rather I took myself off?'

He reached across and took her hand, sliding his fingers through hers. 'Now, isn't that a loaded question, Antonia?' He gave her fingers a little more pressure. 'What do you think I'd want?'

His statement was enough to reignite the tension that had been lashing the air between them since their wild interaction in the pool. Toni's heartbeat revved. 'I think you'd like me to make dinner, Rafe. That's what I think.'

'And you'd be right.' He gave an off-key laugh and pressed her hand briefly to his mouth.

'Let's finish our drinks, then I'll get started.' Toni gently took back her hand. 'What do you have in by way of food? In other words, what possibilities do I have?'

He chuckled. 'If you're trying to catch me out, Ms Morell, I'm sorry to disappoint you. Cath left a heap of dry goods in the pantry and I did a shop for perishables on Thursday night.'

Toni smiled. 'So we're in business?'

'Yep.' He smiled back. 'We're in business.'

'OK, let's see what we have to work with here.' Toni did a quick inventory of the contents of the pantry and what she saw delighted her. 'There's canned tomatoes, spices and dried pasta. So if you have sweet potatoes in your crisper I can make us a feast.'

'I threw in all kinds of fruit and veg at the supermarket,' Rafe said. 'There's bound to be spuds of some kind.' He went to look. 'We're in luck.' He drew out two large sweet potatoes and laid them on the bench. 'What else do you need?'

'Parmesan cheese?'

'I have that.'

'Excellent. Then I'll just nip round to Cath's herb garden for some oregano and we're set.'

Watching indulgently as Toni prepared the meal, Rafe said, 'You really do know your way around the kitchen.'

Toni showed him the tip of her tongue. 'You thought I was just a spoilt little rich girl?'

He sobered. 'I've seen how brilliantly you run a busy casualty department, Antonia. I'd never think of you as that.'

She blushed a little at his compliment, turning to the stove to give the bubbling pasta a final twirl with her fork. 'Nearly there,' she said. 'And we'll need some large bowls.'

'I think I can manage that.' Rafe went to the wall cupboard, found the bowls and set them down on the table. 'We should have some authentic Italian music to accompany our meal.'

Toni turned from the stove. 'I'm surprised you don't have some.'

He shrugged. 'I only brought the basics with me to Forrestdale. The bulk of my stuff is at my parents' place.'

'Perhaps you could sing,' Toni deadpanned.

He chuckled. 'Perhaps I could—but I won't.'

They ate with obvious enjoyment. 'How did I do, then?' Toni sent him an arch little look.

'You did so well I might just keep you.' His gaze shimmered over her face and then roamed to register the gleam of lamplight in her hair and on the ridge of her collarbone. Hells bells, he could almost taste her... 'More wine?'

'No, one's my limit, thanks,' she said, feeling happy and fizzy inside. She wound pasta around her fork. 'So, why Doctors without Borders?'

His shoulders tensed slightly. He'd expected this question eventually. But how much or how little to tell her? 'Why not?' he prevaricated.

'It would seem an enormous decision to make,' Toni said practically. 'An interruption to your career path. So I'm guessing you had a pretty good reason.'

Oh, he'd had a good reason, all right. Rafe's mouth tightened fractionally. 'I went along to an MSF information evening. They were recruiting. What I saw inspired me. There's a saying about the needs being great but the labourers being few—or something like that. I signed on and after orientation, I was appointed to Seim Reap, a city in north-western Cambodia. Our hospital dealt mainly with children.'

So, treating desperately sick kids day in day out must surely have affected him, Toni thought. Was that the reason for the shadow behind his eyes sometimes? 'You've mentioned malnourishment. What other kinds of problems did you treat?'

'Dengue fever, malaria and school sores were high on the agenda. But pneumonia and diarrhoea are right up there as potential killers as well. We saw a lot of kids from the surrounding villages. The mothers used to make quite long journeys to bring them in. Sometimes they'd have to line up all day just to get seen.'

Toni shook her head. 'We don't have much to complain about here, then, do we?'

'We expect more. Demand more from our health system most probably. Whereas those folk were just grateful to be seen at all.'

Toni picked up the glass of water beside her plate and took a mouthful. She felt a wall of questions unanswered but how far could she go without invading his privacy? As far as he'd let her, she thought philosophically. She drummed up a smile. 'So, is it good to be home?'

Rafe considered his answer. Much about it was good, he had to admit. Meeting Antonia herself was good—better than good. And if he hadn't yet come to terms with the complex reasons why he'd gone in the first place, well, so be it…

'I'm on leave,' he said, neatly evading a direct answer. 'It's mandatory after a year.' It wasn't but he couldn't tell her about the PTSD. And that he'd been *ordered* to take leave.

That sounded like he was going back. Toni resumed eating. And if that didn't throw out warning flags to pull back before she went in boots and all again, nothing would.

But her heart wasn't listening.

By mutual, silent consent, they finished the meal talking about everything and nothing. 'Now I'm going to help you with the washing-up and then take my leave,' Toni said, getting up from the table.

'There's a perfectly good dishwasher,' Rafe countered. 'You're not here to skivvy for me.'

'Fine.' Toni got to her feet. 'I'll just grab my bag.' She walked along the hallway to his bedroom, collected her bag from the chair and came back.

'All set?' His attempt at a smile faded. 'I'll walk you out.' When they got to her car, he stopped and held her briefly. 'Thanks for today.'

'I had a lovely time,' she said softly. 'Did you?'

'Yes, it was a good day,' he answered shortly.

Toni blinked uncertainly. His response had sounded almost as detached, as if they'd done a great job weeding the garden. She hesitated, catching the flicker of something in his eyes under the streetlamp, and for a split second he swayed towards her. Not far enough to kiss her but…

'Well, goodnight,' he said.

Toni needed no second invitation. Using her keypad

to unlock the door, she slipped into the driver's seat and started the engine. In seconds, she was purring away.

Well, that was all a bit odd at the end, she mused as she drove. There'd been no little intimate farewell to acknowledge the very special day they'd had. Just—shut down. She sighed. The evening had all gone downhill after she'd asked him about his time with MSF. And he'd never really explained why he'd joined them in the first place. Well, let him keep his secrets. But whatever they were, they sure didn't make him happy.

Rafe thumped the control on the dishwasher to start the cycle. 'Idiot!' he muttered through clenched teeth. It had been the best day of his life for as long as he could remember. *The best day.* So, why had he let it end so crappily? Antonia must think he was the worst kind of jerk.

In a gesture of a man almost at the end of his tether, he raised his hands, ploughing his fingers through his hair and locking them at the back of his neck. He'd make it up to her. Just how, he didn't know yet.

Sunday morning.

Toni woke with a new purpose. She showered and dressed in shorts and a loose-fitting top and went to make breakfast. Life had to be lived, she'd decided. She wasn't going to over-analyse things where Rafe was concerned. She more than liked his company and she guessed he didn't find her too repulsive. They were adults. They could mix pleasure with working together. Surely that wasn't too difficult?

She took her breakfast outside to the pergola in her back garden. As she ate, she smiled at the busyness of the small-bird population. There were wagtails in abundance, switching their little tails from side to side as they snapped up insects from the lawn.

Seeing the birds so involved about their day, Toni thought of what to do with her own day. A few possibilities entered her head, one of which sent her indoors to the phone. Rafe picked up on the second ring.

'Riccardi.'

'Hi, it's me…'

'Hi, me.' His voice was suddenly eager. 'What can I do for you?'

'Ah—do you play tennis by any chance?'

'I can play a bit. We had a light plane strip next to the hospital in Seam Reip, which doubled as a court. Now and again we got the chance to down tools and enjoy a game or two. So, do you want to come over for a hit?'

'In a while.' She didn't want to appear too keen. 'I've a few things to do first.'

'And I want to run over to the hospital and check on Simone so can we say in an hour, then?'

'Suits me.'

'Fine. Look forward to it. And, Antonia?' He hesitated.

'Something else?'

'Just…thanks.'

Toni rolled her eyes at the inanimate instrument and hung up.

'The tennis net's in the garden shed,' Toni said when she arrived. 'I'll help you put it up. There are some racquets as well, although I have my own with me.'

'You play regularly, then?' Rafe asked as they made their way along the path.

'Thursday nights at the sports ground. You're welcome to come along any time. It's a friendly crowd.'

His mouth flickered in a controlled smile. 'Thanks for the invitation.'

Between them, they erected the net across the court and took their places at either end. Rafe looked on admiringly, watching as Toni executed a few light gym exercises. Turning away, he did his own warm-up of a few stretches against the steel-framed fence.

'Ready?' she called, sending him a sweetly innocent smile.

Rafe acknowledged her call with a lift of his hand. And then it was game on.

Shrugging off the loss of the first two games, Toni consoled herself that she was just getting her eye in. But Rafe was good, she allowed. Strong and purposeful.

At his end of the court, Rafe alternated his feet rhythmically on the spot and watched for Toni's first service. He could tell already she was a precise player, fast and deadly accurate. And those legs! Poetry in motion. Concentrate, Riccardi, he warned himself. This lady is no push-over.

Taking a moment to gather herself, Toni rocketed her first service in, the ball kicking up the chalk as it ripped past Rafe. Just out. He raised his racquet in acknowledgment, narrowing his eyes in concentration.

Game after game, they tested one another, both sweating with exertion, the score see-sawing until Toni had the advantage, the longed-for chance of clinching the game and set.

Pulling back, she struck the ball, a low grunt of satisfaction accompanying its speedy passage straight past him. Bemusedly, Rafe watched the ball's trajectory and shook his head. 'You aced me!'

'So I did.' Slightly breathless, laughing, Toni ran up to the net. 'Game and set to me, I think. Shake?'

'What about another set to prove your point?' Rafe enclosed her smaller hand in his. 'Don't I get the chance to break even?'

'Uh-uh.' Toni shook her head, puffing the tiny tendrils off her forehead. 'We'll have to make time for a rematch.'

'You'd better believe it,' he growled, marching her off the court and back to the annexe.

Laughing, Toni prodded him in the ribs. 'Not a sore loser, are you, Dr Riccardi?'

He gave a rueful grin. 'Just a tad humiliated. You really can play, can't you?'

'I made the finals of the state junior hard court titles when I was sixteen. And we have a court at home. Dad and I played a lot.'

A dry smile tugged his mouth. 'I guess I should be grateful I lost by only one point, then?'

Wrinkling her nose at him, Toni settled on one of the outdoor chairs in the courtyard. 'Any cool drinks on offer?'

'I'll get some juice.' Rafe went inside, returning with jug and glasses. 'This'll quench your thirst,' he said, pouring the liquid into the glasses. He handed one across to her.

'Oh, yes!' she said and licked her lips. 'That is so good. How is Simone?' Toni asked, as they drank slowly.

'Happier when she's allowed to have a shower.' He chuckled. 'Keith will let her home as soon as it's practical. She'll need to rest up, which is not making her too thrilled. She was supposed to go to her uni orientation day next week.'

'With care, she might be able to get there,' Toni said. 'Poor kid.'

'Thank heaven her parents were with her,' Rafe spoke with feeling.

'Thank heaven *you* were with her,' Toni countered.

A long beat of silence.

Rafe cleared his throat. 'Sorry I went weird on you last night.'

Toni's shoulders lifted in a shrug. 'It's OK.'

'No, it's not OK.' He shook his head. 'You gave up your Saturday to show me around the place. And it was magic.' His look softened. '*You* were magic.'

Toni blushed gently. 'I had fun too.' She paused. 'You seemed to withdraw a bit after I asked about the reasons you went to work for MSF. There has to be more than you're telling me. More than just going to a *talk*.' She stopped. 'I respect your privacy but sometimes it's just good to let it out…'

Rafe's breath came out on a sigh. 'I wanted to tell you…'

Toni held his gaze steadily. 'You've been hurt, haven't you?'

He tipped his head back and blew out a controlling breath. 'When I said I went to a talk, I should have said, we—my wife and I.'

'You're married!' Shocked into disbelief, Toni could only stare at him. Not this. She shook her head. Not again.

'*Was*,' he emphasised. 'We're divorced.'

Toni swallowed past the constriction in her throat. 'What happened?'

Another long beat of silence.

'We'd been married for six months. Going to work for one of the aid agencies was something we'd both always wanted to do. So we signed on.'

'She was a doctor too?'

'Yes.' His face was carefully expressionless. 'Gabrielle was training towards a specialty in paeds.'

Toni gave a sharp glance at the sudden tight set of his shoulders. 'So, working in a children's hospital would have fitted into her plans.'

'You'd have thought so. But a week after we'd signed, she told me she couldn't go.' He hesitated infinitesimally. 'Needless to say, I was stunned. I said I'd withdraw but she said I should go—in fact, I *needed* to go.'

'Was there no room for compromise?' Toni asked guardedly. 'I mean, could you both have gone for a shorter time?'

He shook his head. 'I asked what her reasons were for pulling out, I demanded them, in fact. It wasn't pretty. She finally broke down and told me she wanted out of the marriage. That she'd met someone else.'

Toni sat up straight. 'That's awful, Rafe! You must have been gutted.'

'Yep.' His mouth moved into a twist of a grim smile. 'The really obscene part was that it started on our wedding day. Or should I say started again.'

Toni made a sound of distress in her throat. What kind of a woman had he married, for heaven's sake?

'He was someone from her past. A lawyer. He'd been practising in the States. Their parents were best buddies,' he added bitterly. 'When he arrived back unexpectedly several days before the wedding, Gabrielle's mother invited him along. She didn't tell her daughter. But there he was, as large as life, when we walked down the aisle, grinning at her like a bloody banshee.'

Toni frowned a bit. She'd thought banshees wailed, not grinned, but that was beside the point. 'What happened then?'

His shoulders moved in a tight shrug. 'He, Michael,

monopolised her for the entire reception. She hardly talked to our other guests.'

'Did you not sense something was wrong?'

He snorted. 'You bet I did. I took him aside and told him to leave quietly or I'd help him out the door. Gabby and I had a short honeymoon and things seemed…all right. And then we were both busy in our jobs. I was doing my final part surgery so I was pushed, a bit jaded. I hadn't really noticed she'd been pulling away until she spelled it out.' He laughed, a harsh, angry sound. 'And that was that. I filed for divorce, deferred MSF and went to work for the Flying Doctors. When the divorce was through, I went to Cambodia. Gabrielle eventually married the banshee.'

Toni felt at a loss for words but finally came up with, 'I can imagine how angry you must have felt.'

'Oh, yes, I felt angry. And *conned*.'

'I know how that feels.' Toni gave a hard-edged laugh. Briefly, she told him about her affair with Alex.

A soft oath left his mouth. 'How could he have done that to you?'

Toni brought her head up. 'I don't still have feelings for him, if that's what you're thinking. It just galls me sometimes to realise I gave so much to the relationship and it was all built on sand. But it's history now, as they say.' She got to her feet. 'My laundry's not going to do itself, so I'm going to run. Thanks for the drink and the game of tennis.'

Rafe rose as well. Without thinking, he reached out and his arms went around her. 'I wish you didn't have to go…' This time it was his eyes that were filled with longing.

Toni steeled herself. It would so easy to just forget everything and go to bed with him. But at the moment that was a bridge too far. 'That's not a good idea, Rafe. You need to heal.'

His mouth turned down. 'Maybe I am healed.'

And maybe he was using her as a lifeline. She wasn't about to leave herself open for that. Not again. She gently pulled away. 'See you tomorrow.'

CHAPTER SEVEN

TONI'S heart was all but leaping against her chest wall as she drove to work next morning. She'd spent half the night trying to get Rafe out of her head but he wouldn't go. She just hoped he hadn't had second thoughts about confiding in her. But if he turned all awkward with her, well, she wasn't having it. Not for a second.

But she need not have worried. Rafe was brisk and professional, whisking her into his office the moment she'd arrived in the department. 'We have a problem,' he said, pointing her to a chair and dropping into his own. Having gained Toni's attention, he went on, 'Three more toddlers have presented with vomiting and diarrhoea, one had to be admitted. All from the caravan park.'

Toni went still. 'That's very serious. We'll obviously have to move fast before we have a full-scale epidemic on our hands.' Or a tragedy, she added silently, a sick feeling beginning to shred the nerves in her stomach.

'I've already been on to Bernie Maguire,' Rafe said. 'He's had someone making discreet enquiries on general conditions at the caravan park.' His mouth drew in. 'It's not looking good.'

'Joanne Carter mentioned the manager was the pits, do you recall?'

Rafe nodded. 'At this stage we can only assume the

infection is coming from the water. But it's tank water,' he emphasised. 'Apparently, the manager, Tyler Bendix, decided the council water rates were too high and cutting into his profits, so he installed tanks. God alone knows where the water has come from.'

'That's appalling, Rafe. Let's get cracking and get over there, demand he give us a sample of water for testing—'

'Steady on, Antonia.' He raised a staying hand. 'We have to follow protocol.'

'Meanwhile toddlers are falling ill all over the place!' Toni was outraged. 'It's not good enough, Rafe!'

'I know that.' He was patient. 'As acting health officer for the place, I'm about to go over to the council offices now. They have ultimate jurisdiction for the regulations at the caravan park so it'll have to be someone from their community health team who has the authority to get the sample.'

Toni half rose. 'I'll come with you.'

'Good.' Rafe swung to his feet. 'I'd hoped you'd want to.'

As they drove uptown to the council offices, Rafe asked, 'You seem to know everyone in the place. Do you know this Mary Gilchrist we have to see?'

'Mmm. She's been an alderman for a couple of years, former nurse. She'll know how to get things moving.'

Mary Gilchrist came out of her office to greet them. She was in her early fifties, her blonde-grey hair smartly styled into a sharp bob, her manner professional but friendly. 'Toni, hello.' Her smile was warm.

Toni returned her greeting. 'Mary, this is Dr Rafe Riccardi. He's acting health officer while Dr Lyons is away.'

'Dr Riccardi.' Mary held out her hand. 'I believe this a matter of some urgency you've come about?'

'It is, Mrs Gilchrist,'Rafe said. 'We'd appreciate your help.'

Mary ushered them into her office. When they were seated, Rafe gave brief, succinct facts as they knew them.

'So, you see, we really need to sort this before things get out of hand,' Toni added earnestly.

'Oh, indeed,' Mary agreed. 'As you probably know, all health matters pertaining to caravan parks come under the council's banner, so let's see what further information we can find out about Mr Bendix, shall we?' She began running information through on her computer screen. 'Ah! According to what we have here, this gentleman doesn't actually own the park. He's the appointed manager of a company called Gretel Holdings.'

'So...' Rafe exchanged a quick look with Toni. 'Tyler Bendix has taken it upon himself to make these changes.'

'Logically, we could assume that,' Mary was guarded. 'I'll get one of our officers over there smartly to take a sample of the tank water. But I'm afraid it'll have to go to Sydney for testing. It's a rather involved process.'

'Immunomagnetic separation,' Rafe supplied quietly.

Mary raised a well-defined brow. 'You know about it, Doctor?'

He gave a tight smile. 'I've been working in Cambodia.'

'Ah.' Mary's little nod, acknowledged the significance of his words. 'Then you'd be well acquainted with what we may be up against.'

'To save time and negate the possibility of more children going down, we could do a very preliminary analysis here,' Rafe offered.

Toni spun him a wide-eyed searching look. 'The slide-under-the-microscope technique?'

He shrugged. 'How's your science?'

'A-plus. I have enough to know what to look for,' she said shortly.

Slightly bemused, Mary Gilchrist looked from one to the other. 'As long as you feel capable of getting some answers…?'

'The test may be elementary,' Rafe allowed, 'but it will certainly tell us if there are bugs in the water. We had scare after scare when I was working overseas. Initially we did our own very basic sampling so we could act to minimise the risks to people's health. A proper breakdown will have to be left to the lab, of course,' he allowed.

'Naturally. But let's get the ball rolling, shall we?' Mary picked up the phone. 'You'll have your sample within the hour.'

'Thanks, Mary.' Rafe stuck out his hand. 'Ask your officer to deliver it to me personally, would you, please? My office is on the ground floor. We'll get back to you as soon as we have anything to report.'

But an hour passed and then another and there was still no water sample. And another young child had been admitted with the same severe symptoms.

Toni was worried. To stave off wild alarm, she couldn't tell any of her staff, not even Liz.

'You're like a cat on the proverbial tin roof,' Liz remarked. 'What's up?'

Toni flapped a hand. 'Internal matter. I'll put you in the picture as soon as I can, Lizzie.'

'I've hardly seen you all morning.' Liz's brows rose interrogatively. 'Nice weekend?'

'Mmm, lovely,' Toni responded absently. And then, because she just had to tell someone, she blurted out, 'Rafe wanted to see something of the district so I acted as his guide. We went over to Maeburn.'

'Wow! You dark filly!'

'We had a swim at his place too. And a game of tennis.'

'Wow, again!' Liz's gaze narrowed. 'I thought you looked a bit dreamy earlier.'

Toni scoffed. 'I've never looked dreamy in my life!'

'Well...' Liz thought for a minute. 'Expectant, then.'

'Oh, lord, Lizzie! Don't use that word around me. Please!'

'My stars!' Liz's blue eyes gleamed. 'You slept with him!'

'I did not! And when you've quite finished writing this ridiculous script of my life, perhaps you'd check if Friday's bloods have come back.'

'Antonia, could you—?' Rafe popped his head in at the station. Seeing Liz, he stopped abruptly. 'Could you give me a minute, please?'

'Certainly.' Toni looked a warning at Liz before departing. All she heard in return was Liz's throaty chuckle.

Rafe stopped when they were out of earshot. 'The water sample's here,' he said. 'Finally.'

'What was the hold-up? I was beginning to wonder.'

His jaw tightened. 'Our man Bendix wouldn't allow the council officer onto the premises. He had to get a court order.'

'That just proves he's as guilty as sin,' Toni asserted

with the air of a kitten about to turn into a tiger. 'Where do you want to do this testing?'

'We'll use the facilities in X-Ray,' Rafe said. 'We'll do it now while the techs are on a break.'

'It's all a bit clandestine, isn't it?' Toni said grimly.

'Can't be helped. We don't want the dogs barking before we've something tangible to go on.'

It took only seconds to set up their respective microscopes and slides. And only a few seconds more to own their worse fears were now realities.

'Sweet God…' Rafe muttered, his gaze narrowing into the lens. 'If this water's ever seen the inside of a filtering plant, I'll shout all the shifts' free booze for a month.'

'Oh, Rafe…this is sickening.' Toni homed in on her own sample. 'This has to be seething with pollutants.'

'And breeding lovely bugs like cryptosporidium and giardia,' he growled. 'And heaven knows what else.'

Toni's stomach felt hollowed out at the implications. 'Giardia can take months to be eradicated from the system, can't it?'

'Try *years,*' Refe affirmed grimly.

Toni met his gaze fearfully. 'What about the families who have left the park and who might have consumed some of the water? They'll need to be contacted urgently.'

'We'll have to find them first.' Rafe's expression became tight. 'But from what I gathered from Bernie, the tanks were installed very recently. So with a bit of luck we may have caught it in time. But it'll have to be a matter for the police now. So let's not hang about here. Mary will be waiting for our findings.'

'Then do it now, Rafe.' Toni practically pushed him out the door. 'I'll clear up here.'

He was just putting the phone down when she caught up with him in his office. 'What's happening?' She slid into a chair and faced him across his desk.

'The council is organising crates of bottled water to be trucked over to the park as we speak. The residents will have to keep using that until things can be sorted.'

'And the park manager?'

'It's out of our hands. Mary's informed the police. They'll do a door-knock around the park residents and tell them what's going on. If the law's been broken, the police are the ones with the authority to lay charges.'

'Good.' Toni nodded her satisfaction. 'And, hey, well done, you!'

Rafe smiled a little crookedly. 'Well done, us, I think.'

There was a heightened buzz in the staffroom next morning as the early shift caught up about what had happened at the caravan park. This time Rafe sat among them, relaxed over his mug of green tea.

'So, what's happened about this Bendix guy?' Ed wanted to know.

Rafe's mouth turned down. 'He's done a runner.'

'No!' Liz was outraged. 'How come?'

'As soon as the council people came with authority to collect a water sample, he guessed the game was up and he scarpered.'

'Will they find him?' Amy asked, wide-eyed at the drama.

'Let's hope so. According to Bernie Maguire, the police put out an APB pretty quickly.'

Harmony looked blank. 'What's an APB?'

'All-points bulletin,' Ed, who was a devotee of police

TV shows, said knowledgeably. 'And if he's driving that clapped-out yellow wagon, they'll spot him a mile off.'

Toni, who had remained silent, absorbing with something like pleasure Rafe's relaxed interaction with the team, asked, 'So, what's the water situation now at the park? Do we know?'

Rafe 's gaze went to her mouth and lingered. 'The town water was reconnected last night. The park residents are safe again.'

'Oh, man,' Ed said, serious for once. 'Lucky you spotted it, Doc.'

'Right place at the right time.' Rafe shrugged off the compliment.

'Now, while we're all here…'Liz gained everyone's attention with a ting-ting on the side of her empty coffee mug. 'My granddad, Tom Marchant, turns eighty on Saturday. He's invited half the district out to his place so if any of you feel like a day out in the bush, you're most welcome to come along.'

'Old Tom is eighty?' Ed marvelled. 'He doesn't look it. He's as fit as.'

'That's what he'd have us believe,' Liz said dryly. 'Anyway, Granddad's place is called Blue Hills and it's about twenty Ks out of town on North Road. The creek's there and it's safe for the kids to swim or paddle and Tom'll have his ponies around to give them rides.'

'Well, I for one would love to come,' Mel, single mum of two, who lived in a flat in town, said quietly. 'My boys would relish getting out in the bush.'

'I'll have to pass.' Amy looked crestfallen. 'I swapped shifts with Dayle Burton. She's got a wedding on.'

'Not to worry, Ames. I'll keep you some birthday cake,' Liz promised.

'Speaking of food, what can we bring?' someone else asked.

'Just yourselves,' Liz said firmly. 'We're doing a barbecue. And, Rafe...' she tilted an arch smile at the senior registrar '...might be a nice chance for you to see a bit *more* of our district.'

'Thanks, Liz.' Rafe gave a slight bow of his head in acknowledgment. 'I'd appreciate that. I'll do my best to be there. Antonia has already given me a tour of Maeburn. It was amazing.'

A few curious eyes swung in Toni's direction and she flashed Liz a *thanks-for-nothing* look. And then smiled with mock-sweetness. 'What time do you want us, Lizzie?'

Liz gave an open-handed shrug. 'Wander out whenever and stay as long as you like.'

The week sped by. Conscious of speculative looks her way, Toni kept her interaction with Rafe to a minimum. She'd become quite good at that, she decided, and then wondered why she cared if the staff knew about her and Rafe. What was there to know anyway? she rationalised. He was keeping out of her way as well. Were they both being ridiculous? Probably.

Buoyed up by this train of thought, she sped along to his office at the end of her shift on Friday afternoon. She knocked and popped her head in. 'Got a minute?'

He waved her in. 'I won't keep you,' Toni said, placing her hands across the back of a chair.

He sent her a lazy smile. 'I'm happy to be *kept*.'

She rolled her eyes. 'I'm just wondering if you're still coming out to Tom Marchant's do tomorrow?'

Rafe pulled himself upright. 'I thought perhaps we could go together.'

Toni's heart jolted under her ribs. 'You realise we'd probably be an *item* by midday?'

'Let's give 'em their money's worth, then.' He flashed her a grin. 'Tell me where you live and I'll pick you up.'

Toni bit her lip. 'Are you sure about this, Rafe?'

'Aren't you?' he flung back.

Toni felt her need to spend time with him widen to a river. 'I'd love it,' she said simply.

On Saturday morning, Toni was ready early. Her spirits felt light. She was spending the day with Rafe. Smiling, she did a little twirl in front of the mirror. She felt cool and chic in white cotton pants and a white shirt with a pinstripe of lime green. A floppy sun hat was already in her bag.

She spun from the mirror when a rap sounded on her front door. It seemed Rafe was early too. She almost skipped to let him in.

'All set?' His grin was infectious Toni found as she grinned back at him.

She beckoned him in. 'I'll just get my bag.'

'Wait,' he said softly. He leaned forward, putting his hands to her elbows, smoothing them up inside the sleeves of her shirt to enclose her upper arms. 'Good morning…'

A jagged breath left Toni's mouth. She felt her skin prickle and then contract. Lifting her hands to the back of his neck, she gusted a tiny sound of release and drew his face down to hers.

And when they kissed, she felt renewed all over again. Brand new and sparkling.

'Antonia…you're beautiful…' Pulling back, Rafe buried his face in her throat, his hands sliding beneath her shirt to roam restlessly across her back and then to

her midriff, half circling her ribcage, smoothing upwards until his thumbs stroked the soft underswell of
her breasts.

They kissed again and with a passion she hardly
knew she possessed she kissed him back, opening her
mouth on his, inviting him into all her secret places,
tasting him all over again.

'We could skip the party...'

Rafe's meaning was clear and Toni felt a fluttering inside, her mind zeroing in on the fact that they
were alone and there was no one here to disturb them.
Whatever they chose to do...

'I want to be with you, Antonia...' His hands stroked
up her arms before he gathered her in again, holding
her to him so that she felt the imprint of him from thigh
to breast.

'Rafe...' She drew in a small breath, feeling his
hands on her lower back, tilting her closer still and the
sweet sting of anticipation slithered up her spine.

'Just say the word.' His voice was muffled against
her hair.

Toni took a breath so deep it almost hurt. Could
she? Dare she? Winding her arms around his neck, she
closed her eyes picturing him as her lover, dreaming of
his body claiming hers completely, fully.

Honestly.

And when he took her mouth again, the feeling of
oneness was so intense, so tangible she almost gave
the answer he wanted to hear. But a little voice in her
head kept insisting that once they'd taken that step,
there was no going back. Nothing would be simple between them again.

Nothing.

Wordlessly, she stepped away from him. Wrapping

her arms around her midriff, she shook her head slowly. 'It's not that I don't want you too. But I can't take this lightly, Rafe.'

'Are you saying I am?'

She looked at him squarely. 'No, I'm not saying that. But there's a thousand reasons why we shouldn't go rushing into things.'

He made a sound of dissension in his throat and turned away.

'You're vulnerable, Rafe.'

Toni's bald statement had him turning back and tilting his head towards her. 'Perhaps it's you who's vulnerable, Antonia.'

She threw up her hands. 'All right! Perhaps we both are. We trusted people and they let us down. It would be so easy to let things get complicated between us.'

His throat moved convulsively as he swallowed. He speared his hands into the back pockets of his cargos. 'You're probably right,' he conceded, a note of apology in his voice. 'I appreciate what we have. Don't look like that,' he said soothingly, 'or everyone will think we've had a row.'

She managed a token smile. 'We can't have that and spoil their matchmaking.'

He gave a click of annoyance. 'I'd almost forgotten how lethal hospital gossip can be.' His mouth kicked up in a crooked smile. 'Friends again?'

'Of course.'

'Go, get your stuff, then, and we'll make tracks.'

'Hang on a tick.' Toni reached into her pocket for a tissue. 'You're wearing a trace of my lipstick. There,' she blotted his mouth expertly. 'Not even Liz would suspect anything.'

* * *

'So, tell me about granddad Tom,' Rafe said as they began their journey to Blue Hills.

Toni relaxed. This was safe ground. 'He was born and bred here, one of the most respected seniors in the district. Tom's an amazing old chap, one of nature's gentlemen, as my mother would say. He and his late wife Jeannie were champion equestrians in their younger days. That's probably why he's kept his interest in the ponies.

'For years he and Jeannie conducted a riding school for differently abled children. They even had several little cottages built on their farm so the parents could stay and make it a kind of holiday. And they never accepted any payment. Just asked the parents to do their own catering.'

'That's remarkable.' Rafe was clearly impressed. 'Kindness in any form can't be measured, can it?'

'I'm so glad you feel like that.'

'Why wouldn't I?' He jerked a shoulder self-deprecatingly.

Toni chose to ignore that question. 'He's Liz's paternal grandfather, by the way. You might have noticed Marchant's Engineering in town? That's Liz's dad Cliff's business. He runs it with her two brothers, Jason and Todd.'

'Sounds like you and Liz go back a way?'

'Liz came to Sydney to do her nurse training. We had our placements together at the Royal North Shore. We clicked almost at once. Became best friends. I was one of her bridesmaids.'

Rafe's mouth tilted. 'One?'

Toni chuckled. 'She had six. Country weddings are inclined to get a bit out of hand, because you daren't leave anyone off the invitation list.' She paused. 'When

I'd decided to get out of Sydney, Liz said there was a senior job going here, so I applied and, as luck would have it, I got it.'

'Nothing to do with your outstanding qualifications, I suppose,' Rafe said wryly. 'You seem to have made yourself very much at home here.'

Toni shrugged. 'I enjoy my job. The people are friendly. What's not to like?'

'You don't miss the buzz of the city?'

'Sometimes. But then I can take a break and head back to Sydney. A few days there refreshes me and then I'm more than happy to come back to a more laid-back existence. What about you?'

'I'm enjoying the slower pace here. The hospital is well supported by the board. And not having to scrounge for drugs when you need them is a real bonus.'

'Has working in Cambodia changed you for ever, do you think?'

Oh, boy. That was a loaded question. Rafe's hands tightened on the steering-wheel. 'I'd have to be made of wood if it hadn't.'

Obviously, some deep and meaningful stuff had gone down there, Toni thought soberly. Stuff he'd maybe rather forget. 'I gather you're not going to take up Matt's offer of a spot on his talk programme, then?'

'No.' His mouth flattened. 'I called him. He was cool about it. I went down that road with a journalist in Seim Reap. She was working for television. She assured she'd be objective and unobtrusive but before I knew it she was dragging stuff out of me about my involvement as a doctor in such a ravaged country. How difficult was it not to let my emotions become involved? Bloody difficult, I should have said, and left it at that. Instead I found myself speechless and shedding tears on camera.' He glanced at Toni, his smile bleak. 'It was heaven-sent footage for the journalist. She was out of there in seconds. She'd got what she wanted.'

'And you were left trying to pick up the pieces,' she surmised softly.

'Something like that.'

'Oh, Rafe… Is that why you took leave?' she asked, hardly daring to breathe.

'I was *told* to take leave.'

Toni bit her lips together. So, he'd been sent home and she wondered why on earth he would even consider going back to a world that seemingly had left him feeling…broken. 'It was a stress issue, then?' she asked carefully.

'So they said. I'm dealing with it. And I'm on *leave*,' he emphasised. 'They haven't booted me out.'

A long beat of silence.

'Rafe, I'm so sorry,' she murmured.

'About what?'

'I was hard on you…judgmental. I had you pegged as an arrogant—'

He gave a throaty laugh. 'Pig.'

'I feel awful now. I was so rude.'

'On the contrary, Antonia.' He found her hand and pressed her knuckles to his lips. 'You were just what I needed.' His eyes turned soft as he glanced at her. 'Still need.'

They lapsed into silence and Toni thought they'd probably given each other a lot to think about. Quite a lot.

'Oh, look,' she said, pointing at the windscreen. 'There's Tom's place up ahead and they've put balloons out to welcome us! I'll bet that was Lizzie's idea.'

Rafe felt his spirits lift. He was glad he'd come. Very glad.

Already, party guests had arrived in droves. There was an air of celebration, of sheer joy at being there to honour Tom Marchant on his eightieth birthday.

'There's Tom.' Toni touched Rafe's arm. 'Come and meet him.'

Toni made the introductions. 'G'day, young fella.' Tom's handshake was firm. 'Liz tells me you've been overseas, working for one of the aid agencies.'

'That's right.' Rafe didn't elaborate.

Tom's blue eyes under his Akubra hat were shrewd and wise. 'So, it must feel good to be back on Aussie soil again, hmm?'

Rafe looked from the slight rise where they were standing down towards the tree-lined creek and then raised his eyes to the ring of blue hills. His nostrils were filled with the scent of the surrounding bush of eucalypts and wild honeysuckle. The clicking of cicadas was ever-present, yet there was a hush that enveloped him, a feeling like no other. His chest lifted in a long breath. 'Yes, it's good to be back. But, hey, today is about you, Mr Marchant. Congratulations on reaching such a milestone.'

Tom gave a wry grin. 'Eighty isn't a bad innings. And it's Tom, son.' Turning, he reached out an arm and gave Toni a hug. 'How are you, sweetheart?'

'I'm good, thanks, Tom. And happy birthday from me as well.' She gave him a peck on the cheek. 'Thanks for inviting us.'

Tom waved a hand in dismissal. 'This do was all the kids' idea but I guess it's not bad to be remembered on your birthday.'

'What can we do to help?' Rafe asked.

'Just enjoy yourselves,' Tom said. 'But if you must help, young Liz will have a job for you, no doubt.'

They left Tom to greet some of his other guests and made their way towards the house. 'I'll give Ed a hand with the pony rides.' Rafe pointed to where Ed was fast becoming embroiled in kids, bridles and circling ponies.

'Oh, lord.' Toni chuckled. 'Ed is such a *helper.* You'd better rescue him before he maims himself. I'll see what Liz needs. Catch you later?' She smiled up at him.

'If I come out of this alive.' He jogged off.

Toni found Liz in the kitchen. 'Hi, honey, I'm here,' she sing-songed and popped her head around the door.

'Oh, praise be.' Liz indicated a mountain of scones and Australian bush bread, better known as damper. 'All this has to be either slathered with honey or jam and cream. Get stuck in, please, Toni. We're supposed to be serving morning tea in fifteen minutes.'

Toni rolled her eyes. 'Where's your mum? She usually handles this side of things, doesn't she?'

'Still on her way. The bakery was late getting Granddad's birthday cake decorated. Mum's had to hang about. Personally, I think they just plain forgot! Did you bring Rafe?' Liz hopped conversational channels quickly.

'I didn't bring him,' Toni countered. 'We came along together. He's presently helping Ed with the pony rides.'

Liz tutted. 'Todd was supposed to be in charge. Where's he got to?'

Toni laughed softly. 'Actually, he seemed pretty tied up with Mel and her boys.'

'Really? Liz perked up. 'Do we scent a romance in the making?'

'You'd approve, then?'

'Oh, yes. Mel is a real gem and as for Todd—it's

about time he got his bachelor butt off the shelf. What about Rafe, though? Will he be safe around the ponies?'

Toni was swiping honey on to the slices of damper. 'His uncle bred racehorses. He told me he learned to ride as a kid.'

Liz gave an arch look. 'So, you've become quite close, then?'

'Yes,' Toni said simply and without embarrassment.

'Oh, Tone…' Liz flashed her friend a sharp look. 'Don't get hurt again, will you?'

'I've my eyes wide open, Lizzie.'

Liz shook her head, cautioning, 'He'll go back, you know?'

Toni spread a crisp tea towel over the food. 'He may not.' And if she honest with herself, she was hanging onto that for all she was worth.

CHAPTER EIGHT

'It's been a great day, hasn't it?' Toni said. Most of the party guests had left and she and Rafe had gone for a walk to the creek. Now they sat under the fringe of a lacy willow that grew along the bank. 'Glad you came?'

'Mmm,' he said lazily, stretching out his legs and making himself comfortable against the trunk of the tree. The day had had a healing quality about it that he couldn't explain. But he was storing up every moment. Holding onto the thought, he closed his eyes, listening to the murmur of the creek mingling with the dozing hum of the cicadas.

Toni snuggled in against him. She would treasure these moments all the days of her life. She felt so in tune with him she could not imagine a time when that could change. Some things were just meant to be.

So engrossed were they with their own thoughts they had no idea of the drama unfolding in the barn, until their names were being called and echoed. And called and echoed.

'That's Liz!' Toni sprang upright. 'I told her we were coming down here. Something must have happened!'

They emerged from under the willow and exploded into a run back up towards the house. Liz came running to meet them.

'It's Granddad! He's fallen, trying to get feed out of the bin for the ponies. It's tipped forward and knocked him off the ladder onto the cement floor—' She stopped and put a hand to her heart. 'I think it's bad…'

'He's in the barn?' Rafe rapped.

'Mmm.' Liz swallowed. 'Dad's with him…'

'Don't move him.' Rafe was firm. 'I'll get my bag.'

'Oh, Lizzie, I'm so sorry.' Toni grabbed her friend's arm. 'Let's get back to Tom.'

'I think he's broken something, Tone.' Liz's composure began slipping. 'Oh, God, we all love him to bits… but the silly old coot climbing ladders at his age—'

'Take it easy, Liz,' Toni counselled. 'You have to think like a nurse here and not as Tom's granddaughter. For starters, we'll need some blankets and a pillow. And what about Tom's medical history? Do you know if he's taking any medication?'

'Oh, God, I don't…' Liz's voice cracked and she clamped her lips hard, struggling with her tumbled emotions.

'You're around Tom a lot, Lizzie. For heaven's sake, think!'

'Sorry—I don't know.' Liz's mouth wobbled.

'Well, do you know who his GP is?'

'Reid McAndrew. Tom's been his patient for years.'

'Then get on to him and see what you can find out,' Toni said urgently.

Liz shook her head. 'It's Saturday—he could be anywhere!'

'He'll have an answering service. They'll tell you where to find him. And if all else fails, ring his wife. She's listed under her business name, Andrea Charles. Can you remember that?'

Liz repeated the name. 'But if I can't get onto anyone, Rafe will know what to do, won't he?' she asked desperately.

'It will be a lot easier if he has some history. But he'll do his best for Tom, you know that. Have you rung for an ambulance?'

'Mmm—Mum was doing that. Dad's a mess…'

Toni bit her lips together, dragging her professionalism up from her toes. She had to be doubly strong for Liz, who seemed to have lost it completely. 'Now, you go for the blankets and make the phone calls and I'll go to Tom.' They were at the barn door. 'Rafe will find us. He won't be far behind.'

Rafe was running as though his life depended on it. Worst-case scenario could be a severe break. The resultant blood loss could prove fatal, especially to someone of Tom's advanced age. He hoped not. For all their sakes.

It was definitely a fractured neck of femur. Toni saw at once the irregularity of Tom's right leg. It was fractionally shorter than the other and sitting painfully out of joint. She looked up thankfully as Rafe burst in through the barn door and joined her at Tom's side.

'Silly old buzzard…' Cliff Marchant kept repeating. 'I'd have got the damned pony feed for him but, no, he's got to be independent…'

'Cliff, I know you're upset,' Rafe said firmly, 'but railing against your dad won't help. Now…' he turned to Toni '…what do we know?'

Toni relayed what had been set in train. 'And I've checked his pulse. It's weak and thready. His oxygen sats would have to be low as well.'

'We can't do much about that until the ambulance

gets here,' Rafe said. 'Just let's hope we have a bit more joy about Tom's history when Liz gets back.'

Tom began muttering incoherently, his restive movements alerting Rafe.

'It's OK, Tom. You've had a fall, mate. We're getting help for you.'

Gently, Toni brushed the fine silver hair back from the elderly man's forehead. 'Will you give him some pain relief?'

'I'll give him a jab of morphine.' Rafe shot open his case. 'Plus Maxolon to combat any nausea. But I'd be a lot happier if I knew some history.'

'Oh—' Toni shot up from her kneeling position. 'Here's Lizzie now!'

Liz took a moment to get her breath. 'I got Dr McAndrew on his mobile. He…said he's prescribed digoxin for Tom.'

The medication was used to strengthen the action of the heart. Rafe's gaze narrowed in conjecture. With that kind of history perhaps the elderly man had become giddy. It would explain his fall. 'Right. At least that gives us something to go on. Well done, Liz.'

Liz dropped to her grandfather's side and took his hand. 'He's never said anything about his health. We all thought he was as fit as. But he's not…' Her voice cracked.

'Lizzie, I need your help here,' Toni said bracingly. 'Let's make use of these blankets and get Tom more comfortable.'

'I can do that.' Liz seemed grateful to be doing something.

'And, Cliff, might be an idea if you'd keep a look out

for the ambulance,' Rafe said. 'Direct them over here to the barn, OK?'

'Uh—yes.' Cliff scrambled upright. 'I'll tell them to back up as close as they can.' He looked at his daughter. 'What's your mum doing, love?'

'She's phoning the boys to let them know. And she'll pack a bag for Granddad for hospital.' Liz took a steadying breath. 'Dad, he'll be all right. Rafe's here and he's a fine doctor. We couldn't have anyone better to look after Granddad.'

'Yeah. Thanks, Doc…' Cliff seemed to pull himself together and then began making his way outside.

Within seconds of the ambulance's arrival Rafe began issuing orders. 'Let's get our patient on oxygen. Antonia, will you monitor Tom, please?' He turned to the paramedic. 'Mr Marchant needs fluids, mate. We'll run Haemaccel, stat.'

'Right you are, Doc. I'll hook up the heart monitor as well.'

'Excellent, thanks.' Rafe's hands moved skilfully to secure a line to receive the IV fluids. 'How're the oxygen sats, Toni?'

'Low. Eighty-nine per cent.'

Rafe scrubbed a hand across his cheekbones. He wasn't surprised. But he was placing his bets on the heart monitor telling him more. Seconds later his prognosis was confirmed. Tom was showing every sign of being in atrial fibrillation. And although that didn't mean his condition was life-threatening, he was certainly very ill.

He'd make a more in-depth investigation when they'd got Tom to Resus. If a digoxin boost was indicated, it could be introduced very carefully through an IV. He sent a swift look towards Liz. 'Mobile reception OK from here? I need to get onto the hospital.'

'Should be.' Liz bit her lip. 'He'll need surgery, won't he?'

'I'm afraid he will, Liz,' Rafe said gently. 'But Tom's a tough cookie…' Rafe left the sentence unfinished, stepping away he hit a number on speed dial. 'Amy? Rafe. I'm bringing in Tom Marchant. Probable NOF repair. Could you alert Keith, please?'

'There we might have a problem.' Amy was calm. 'Keith's already in Theatre. Young biker came off at speed with resultant pelvic injury.'

'OK…' Rafe expelled a hard breath. 'Do we have enough staff available to assist in Theatre Two?'

'On call as needed,' Amy said. 'And Grace is available to gas.'

'Excellent. I'll scrub, then. I'll need all orthorpaedic trays sterilised and ready, please, Amy. Could you organise all that, asap?'

'I'll get onto it now.'

'Thanks. Our ETA is around thirty minutes.' Rafe closed off his mobile to find Toni standing silently by his side.

'Are you sure about this?' she asked quietly.

'I'm accredited to perform surgery, Antonia.'

'I'm not questioning your ability.' Her eyes clouded. 'It's just…'

His jaw tightened. 'You're doubting my physical stamina?'

'You've been through a lot recently—' She stopped and clamped her lips together.

'I wouldn't do this if I thought I'd be compromising Tom's outcome. This is *my* decision, Antonia.'

In other words, butt out. Toni gave the semblance of a nod. 'Will you travel with Tom?'

'Yes. And they're about ready for me. Sorry to do this to you again.' He tossed her his keys. 'Could you drive my car back to town, please? Just leave it in the doctors' car park and the keys at the nurses' station. I'll pick them up when I'm through. And, Toni?'

She tilted her chin at him. 'Yes?'

'I'll be a while. *Don't hang about.*'

Of course she'd hang about. Toni's fingers tightened on his keys. She'd want to be there for Liz and her family. As for anything else? Well, that was her business.

It was almost eight o'clock that evening. Toni sat with Liz in the staffroom. Liz had shooed her parents off and they'd gone to get a bite to eat. She looked bleakly into her third cup of coffee. 'Life can change in a minute, can't it?'

Toni huffed dryly. 'Make that a second. One or two words can change a life for ever.' Words like *I'm married. You have cancer. The baby's not viable.*

Oh, good grief. Toni suppressed a shiver. I'm getting morbid. She rose to her feet. 'Another coffee?'

'God, no. I'm all coffeed out.' Liz sighed. 'How much longer?'

Toni glanced at her watch. 'We should hear any time now.'

No sooner had she'd spoken than Rafe pushed through the louvred doors into the staffroom. Toni felt her stomach twist at his grave demeanour. Had something gone wrong with Tom's surgery?

'How is he, Rafe?' Liz was on her feet. 'I asked Theatre to ring here when—'

'I decided to let you know myself,' Rafe broke in.

'And?'

Rafe finally smiled. 'Everything went well, Liz. Tom's in Recovery.'

'Oh…' Liz's voice cracked. 'Thank you so much, Rafe. Thank you…'

Rafe lifted a blocking hand. 'You should be able to see your granddad in a half-hour or so.'

'That'll just give me time to collect Mum and Dad from the coffee shop.' Liz was already gathering up her bag. She sprinted for the door and then turned back. 'Toni…thanks for…well, you know…'

Toni waggled a finger wave. 'You're welcome, Lizzie. Take care.' She stood, and sent a level glance at Rafe. 'Cup of tea? Won't take a minute.'

Rafe shook his head. 'Why are you still here, Antonia?'

Seeing his closed expression, Toni felt wrong-footed. 'I'm here for Liz and her parents.'

'It's been hours. They wouldn't have expected that. And I'd specifically asked you not to hang about.'

'*Ordered*, more like,' she countered sharply. 'What's your problem, Rafe?'

'I don't have one,' he said grittily. 'But apparently you do. With me.'

'With you?' Toni's voice rose interrogatively. 'What do you mean, *with you*?'

'I don't need a minder, Antonia.'

Toni's heartbeat surged to a sickening rhythm. Was that what he thought she was doing there? 'Get over yourself, Rafe.'

His brows twitched into a frown. 'What's that supposed to mean?'

'I didn't *need* to be here,' she said. 'But I stayed. For Liz, of course, but mostly for you. I foolishly thought

you might have appreciated a bit of professional support
after the op, a bit of down time to just…talk.'

Rafe stared at her in silence for a moment, his jaw
clenched. 'In other words, you were keeping a watching
brief on my professionalism. Maybe you even had me
breaking down in the middle of surgery so you could
say, *I told you so*?'

'Nothing was further from my mind.' Two spots of
colour glazed Toni's cheeks. 'I don't know what kinds
of problems are still bugging you, Rafe but don't presume to disrespect my reasons for being here. Don't
disrespect *me*.'

In one fluid movement she threw his keys on to the
table, her breath coming hard and fast. 'You're not the
man I thought you were!' Hauling her shoulder bag off
the back of the chair, she gave him one last disdainful
glare and stormed out.

'Antonia! Toni, wait…!'

Toni's response to Rafe's urgent plea was to walk
even faster until she was out of the building. Her
thoughts were in turmoil. How could he have mis-
judged her actions so badly? She'd wanted to wait with
Liz. That's what friends did. And if that meant she was
around for Rafe as well, that wasn't a crime, was it? But
he'd gone and accused her of having a hidden agenda.
And instead of feeling supported by her presence, he'd
interpreted her motives as those of almost spying on
him.

Did he feel vulnerable because of what he'd con-
fided to her about his past? Both professionally and
personally?

Whatever, it was clear he didn't trust her as a colleague, a friend, and as for anything deeper—forget it.

Anger and pain fought for equal room in her heart. Words again. Words said in anger. Words that could injure a heart, kill a hope.

Destroy a budding love affair.

Her throat tightened as she made her way along the street to the taxi rank and climbed into the first waiting cab.

'Where to, love?' the cabbie asked.

Bleakly Toni gave him her address. Sinking back into the cushioned seat, she thanked heaven for the safety of home.

Rafe felt like ramming his fist through the wall. Had he learned nothing from the past? It seemed he couldn't even differentiate between the amazing level of trust that Antonia had offered and the two-faced version from Gabrielle. Antonia was worth a hundred of her. A thousand! She'd done nothing, other than offer her support, listened to the story of his heartbreak, trusted him with her own. And he'd lashed her to pieces with his rant.

Was he so afraid of getting close to a woman again that he'd struck out the way he had? Get her before she got him? Was that it? He shook his head. He was like a fighter who couldn't let down his guard for fear of being hurt. Well, now he'd been the one doing the hurting. He'd hurt Antonia irrevocably. She was gone.

Moving across to the window, he reached out like a blind man towards the sill, gripping it with both hands, staring out at the night. God, whoever said *sorry* was the hardest word had had it right. But somehow he'd have to find a way to say it.

But whether or not she'd listen was another matter entirely.

* * *

Well, another one bites the dust, Toni thought bitterly as she opened her front door and went inside. She stopped and looked around her. It seemed an eternity since she'd been here with Rafe this morning. This morning when everything between them had seemed so promising, so wonderfully new and…safe. For the first time in a long time she'd begun to trust again. Now everything was ashes.

Something in her heart scrunched tight. It hurt so much that he didn't trust her. More than hurt. It felt as though he'd cut out her heart and left nothing behind.

Despondently, she stripped off her clothes and stepped under the shower, telling herself she was a survivor. She'd damned well better be. Dressed in a pair of silk sleep shorts and a vest top, she felt marginally better. Going to the kitchen, she peered into the fridge but found nothing to interest her. The freezer was a better option and she took out a tub of chocolate-chip ice cream.

A few spoonfuls of ice cream later she sighed and replaced the tub in the freezer. Perhaps she'd make some peppermint tea but, then, perhaps she wouldn't.

When her doorbell rang, she stood stock still, her heart going into freefall. If that was Rafe—and it would be—she couldn't deal with him now. Just go away, she pleaded silently. But it seemed her caller wasn't going anywhere.

Her hands trembled slightly as she smoothed them down the sides of her shorts. She was hardly dressed for company but he'd seen her in a bikini so what she was wearing was modest by comparison. 'OK, OK,' she muttered, heading off along the hallway to the front door. She swung the door open and they stood there looking at one another.

Toni felt goose-bumps break out all over her, felt the atmosphere between them tightening like the strings of a violin. He'd obviously been home and changed. His hair was ruffled, still damp from the shower. And she was so pleased to see him it almost hurt. Lifting her chin, she said with as much coolness as she could manage, 'Are you going to stand there glaring at me or would you like to come in?'

For a second Rafe's wintergreen gaze seem to lose its colour, glaze over and go still. Giving an almost imperceptible inclination of his head, he said, 'I'd like to come in, if it's all right…?'

Toni stood aside, allowed him through, and then closed the door behind him. She led the way to the lounge. And then turned and faced him.

Rafe felt his heart spin out of rhythm. Yet her response was more, much more forgiving than he'd expected, indeed deserved. He shifted from one foot to the other, his hands jammed into the back pockets of his cargos. 'I'd like to apologise for my appalling behaviour earlier. I've hurt you and I'm deeply sorry.'

'And so you should be…' Toni's teeth caught her bottom lip. 'I…thought we'd come such a long way, Rafe. In every way that counted…'

He was silent for a long moment and then he let his breath out in a ragged sigh. 'And then I dismantled everything in a few seconds flat.'

'You have issues with trust and I can understand that after what happened with your ex-wife. But I'm not *her*, Rafe. I never will be. You have to let me in.' Toni paused, swallowing back the well of emotion that rose in her chest. 'That's if you want to…'

'Oh, God, yes.' Rafe allowed himself no more time to ponder, to hesitate, to start weighing up the pros and cons. Everything he wanted, needed was here. With this woman. This woman of the generous spirit, the forgiving heart. The lover he wanted for his own.

'Oh, Rafe...' Toni took a deep-throated swallow as he reached out and gathered her in.

'Don't say anything,' he murmured. 'Just let me hold you.'

Toni wasn't sure when the wordless comfort changed or even if it did. Perhaps it just grew and took on a life of its own, drawing them into one volatile storm of emotions.

She shivered when Rafe's hands began to smooth her back and shoulders, moving until his fingers were bracketing her head and his hands were holding her with infinite gentleness, while he kissed her with deep tenderness, deep giving.

Making a little sound in her throat, she curled against him and when his kiss deepened she welcomed it, oh, how she welcomed it, opening her mouth to his, wanting it all.

Suddenly, out of nowhere, she felt an enormous sense of freedom, a sense of rightness she'd never felt before. And when his ragged declaration came, *'You're everything I want,'* she felt so physical, so alive.

Rafe felt the shudder that ran through her as she arched up against him with a little cry. He told himself to take it slowly but that was never going to be the way of it. The soft waistband of her shorts came away to allow him the access he craved. With the utmost care for her, he traced the bowl of her pelvis and lower... 'Let's not do this here, Toni,' he breathed hoarsely. 'Come to bed with me—if that's what you want too?'

'Yes.' One word. That's all it needed for Rafe to lift her right off her feet in celebration and then to gently lower her until her feet touched the floor again. Then, slowly and deliberately, stopping to kiss along the way, they finally made it to the bedroom.

Their lovemaking was slow, dreamlike, hushed sounds of delight, of ecstasy as they pleasured one another. Then there was no going back. And all of it—everything else in the entire world—became meaningless against the flood tide of their shared release.

They slept for a while and then made love again and around midnight they had a crazy, fun-filled shower together. After that they raided Toni's fridge and cooked eggs and bacon and drank big mugs of tea.

And talked.

'In my whole life I've never been so happy,' Toni said.

Rafe leaned across and took her hand, running his thumb along the tips of her fingers. 'You make me feel brand new.'

She smiled indulgently. 'That's the name of a song.'

'Is it?' His mouth turned down comically. 'I thought I was being original.'

His look changed and became serious. 'I still can't believe how forgiving you've been, Antonia.'

'Why?' She lifted a shoulder dismissively. 'I'm a fairly straightforward kind of person. If things are muddled, I like to deal with them—not let them fester. And we've sorted things now, haven't we?'

He sent her a guarded smile. 'I guess we have.' He should tell her about the PTSD but now wasn't the time. He'd get round to it. She'd probably guessed most of it anyway.

'Mind you, if you hadn't come round tonight, I might have given you a wide berth at work next week.'

'I would have hated that,' he said honestly.

'Mmm, me too.' Toni blocked a yawn. 'So, are we going back to bed?'

'Ah…' Rafe sought for an excuse that sounded plausible. But he couldn't risk the possibility of the nightmares recurring and frightening the daylights out of her. He hadn't had one for a while now, but if they were going to happen, they usually happened in the early hours. He needed to be gone. 'I'll take off, I think. Bit to think about.'

'I see…' Although clearly she didn't. 'But you're OK with us—aren't you?'

'Oh, yes! Don't ever doubt that. I want to be up early as well, check in on Tom.'

Toni sent him one of her bewitching smiles. 'And if you stayed, there's a possibility—just a slight one—you might be *delayed?*'

'More a probability.' Rafe jumped at the flimsy excuse.

Their farewell was long and tender. 'Will I see you tomorrow—I mean today?' Toni asked as they stood achingly close to each other.

'Have a sleep in,' Rafe urged, 'and then come round to me for a swim. I'll dazzle you with something for lunch.'

She gave a throaty chuckle. 'Something from the deli, I'll bet.'

'It's a great deli,' he protested. 'And I'll be selective.' He pressed his forehead to hers. 'Everything about this seems right, doesn't it?'

'Oh, yes…' Toni was dazzled with the newness of it.

Instead of taking his leave, Rafe held her more tightly, amazed at the way their bodies called to one another, how every dip and curve in her willowy suppleness found a home in his.

'Go now,' she whispered, and gave him a little push towards the door. 'You need your sleep too.'

He reached out a finger, his touch feather-like along her jaw, her throat into the soft hollow of her collarbone. 'I think this is boots and all for me, Antonia.'

'Me too,' she whispered, her voice hardly there.

CHAPTER NINE

Monday morning.

TONI came in to work early but it seemed Liz had beaten her to it. They were the only ones in the staffroom. 'Well, isn't this a treat?' Toni smiled, dropping her bag and taking a mug from the dishwasher. 'Having the place to ourselves for two minutes, I mean.'

'Mmm,' Liz said automatically, mug of coffee at her side, her chin resting on her upturned hand.

'Gorgeous morning outside.' Toni gave a theatrical sigh. 'Just the kind of day to take off and play hooky.'

Liz's head shot up. That didn't sound like their conscientious nurse manager. 'Well, well.' Her eyes opened to questioning wideness. 'Who's looking all chirpy and loved up this morning? What *did* you get up to on the weekend, Ms Morell?'

Toni gave a Mona Lisa smile, for once not responding to her friend's mild teasing. Picking up her coffee, she sat opposite Liz at the table. 'How's Tom?'

'I've just popped up to see him. Poor old love...' Liz stopped, her voice becoming husky. 'He looks a bit fragile, actually.'

'Still confused from the effect of the anaesthetic,

probably,' Toni commiserated. 'But that'll reverse in a day or so, Lizzy.'

'Yes, I know all that but it's awful seeing someone so vital as Granddad…cut down.'

Toni gave a tut. 'Lizzy, he'll recover quite quickly, according to Rafe. He's very pleased with him. In fact, he's hoping to have Tom up in a day or two and beginning some physio on a rollator.'

'That soon!' Liz brightened. 'Then Rafe must be very confident about Tom's recovery. He's going to need several weeks' rehab, though, isn't he?'

'Of course. That's standard.'

'I doubt Dad will want him living on his own again.'

'Well, plenty of time to think about that,' Toni said. 'Just be glad Tom is still with us.'

'Thanks to Rafe.' Liz's hands spanned her mug. 'Did you both have a nice day at the farm on Saturday?'

And later. Toni gave an inward smile. That information was not for sharing. 'Yes, it was wonderful. Have you got everything squared away at Blue Hills?'

'Mostly.' Liz rocked a hand. 'Dad and the boys will take it in turns to go out each day and check on the animals. Other than that, we just have to keep Tom happy and get him on his feet again.'

'That's the way,' Toni said bracingly. 'Let me know if I can do anything.' She stood, taking her coffee. 'That sounds like the fairy footsteps of the team so I'll take handover and then I have to consult with Rafe about a couple of things. Are you up to allocating jobs or would you rather have a quiet day?'

'I'm fine.' Liz flapped a hand. 'I'd rather keep busy.' Her mouth pleated at the corners. 'Go and have your tryst. Oops!' Liz gave an exaggerated pout and placed the tips of her fingers over her lips.

Toni flashed her a wry grin. 'Early days, Lizzy.'

'Of course.' Liz nodded. 'I think it's lovely, by the way.'

Rafe couldn't believe how energised he felt, especially for a Monday morning. And he couldn't stop grinning like an idiot. Heck, he felt like a teenager in love for the first time. That thought brought him up short. As did the swift knock on his door.

'Oh…' Toni popped her head in. 'I wondered if you were in.'

'As you see.' He held out his arms and she ran straight into them. 'Good morning…' His smile was tender.

Toni's mouth curved. 'Good *night* as well. You OK?'

'Better than OK.'

Their kiss started gently but in a second they were on fire for each other. Rafe growled deep in his throat and lifted his head. 'That's what I call beginning the day on a high. You smell like roses.'

'Do I?' She cupped his face with both hands. 'And you smell like summer.'

He grimaced. 'Not sweaty summer?'

'No.' She laughed softly. 'Nice summer. Soap and water summer.'

Rafe stepped back, parking himself on the edge of his desk and folding his arms. 'Actually, I was about to come and find you. I wanted to pass on some good news. Bernie Maguire called me. The Rotary club has purchased acreage a little way out of town. They're calling tenders to build a retirement village. The plans he outlined sound just what our seniors need and it will include a nursing facility for those who need a bit of extra care.'

'Oh, that's amazing!' Toni pressed her hands together under her chin. 'Is it going to be self-contained units?'

'More like one-bedroomed cottages, from what Bernie said. They're hoping some of the seniors will want to do a bit of gardening, keep a small pet if they'd like to.'

'So, folk like Denis will have somewhere nice to live and be as independent as they want to be.'

Rafe grinned. 'Bernie's pretending he thought of the idea himself, of course. But if it gets the job done…'

'Well done, you.'

'And you,' he insisted. 'You inspire me, Antonia. You really do.'

Toni blushed. 'Perhaps we inspire each other. Now, I have a casualty department to run, Doctor…'

He slid off the desk. 'Now *I* need a hug before you go.'

Four weeks later, Tom Marchant was released from hospital.

Rafe, Toni and Liz watched as Liz's parents shepherded Tom into their car. He was going to stay with them for the time being.

'Granddad would far rather be going home to Blue Hills,' Liz lamented.

'I'm sure he would.' Rafe was sympathetic. 'But even you can see he can't be on his own at the moment, Liz.'

'But later on, in the future?' She looked hopefully at the registrar.

Rafe lifted a shoulder. 'If he keeps up his physio and his general health remains good, he'll possibly be able to go back.'

'Come on, Lizzy,' Toni cajoled. 'Tom is gutsy. He'll dig in and do whatever it takes to get back into life.'

Liz looked wry. 'I'm being a pain, whereas you two have been so good to Tom while he's been in.'

Rafe snorted. 'A few games of chess hardly took up much of my time. And Tom is great company. Knows a lot too.' He looked at his watch. 'Now, if you ladies will excuse me, I have an informal meeting with the board. Dig me out if you need to.'

'So, how is it going with you and Rafe?' Liz asked as they walked back to the station.

'Things are fine.' Toni didn't mention that so far they'd not spent an entire night together. Obviously Rafe had his reasons for not staying and she hadn't pushed him.

'Fine?' Liz sent her a puzzled look. 'That seems seriously underwhelming, if I may say so. Are you sure everything's OK?'

Toni's nerves tightened. She would love to have her friend's down-to-earth opinion but there was no way she could share that kind of intimate information. Instead, she gave a warning little eye roll. 'Lizzie…'

'OK.' Liz lifted her hands in retraction. 'I'll mind my own. Just have to keep reminding myself you're all grown up. And you're a savvy chick as well.'

Toni chuckled. 'When were we ever *chicks?*'

'Dunno,' Liz responded blithely. 'But we must have been. Once.'

It was almost at the end of the shift when Rafe stuck his head round the cubicle curtain. 'Antonia, can you get someone else to finish up in here? MVA out on North Road. Ambulance has gone out but they need a doctor at the scene. I'd like you along as well, please.'

'Give me a minute.' Toni apologised to her patient and assigned Amy to take over. Hurrying to the staffroom, she collected a couple of high-visibility vests, designating 'Doctor' and 'Nurse' on the backs, and ran to find Rafe.

He was taking delivery of a trauma kit from Liz, and looked up as Toni joined them at the station. 'All set?'

She nodded. 'Liz, would you hand over, please? Don't know when we'll be back.'

'Absolutely.' Liz waved them away. 'Mind how you go.'

'What do we know?' Toni asked the inevitable question as they headed out of town.

'Two vehicles involved. A fully loaded refrigerated truck coming into town sideswiped a Land Rover going in the opposite direction. Driver of the truck dead at the wheel.' Rafe's jaw clenched and unclenched. 'The weight of the truck has forced the car off the road and it's run downhill and crashed into a belt of scrub.'

'Oh, my lord…' Toni whispered. 'Who's in the car, do we know?'

'Family.'

'So, possibly children?'

Rafe didn't answer.

All emergency services were in attendance when they got to the accident scene. Erin hurried to meet them. 'Not a mark on the truck driver,' she said grimly. 'Possible heart attack. Fortunately, his truck hit an embankment and stopped, otherwise who knows what other damage could have been caused?'

'Who's in the car?' Rafe snapped, pulling on his vest.

'Family. Not sure of the dynamics yet. It seems all the doors on the Land Rover are jammed from the impact. Just lucky it didn't roll. The fire lads have to cut the scrub back from the car first so we can get to them.' Even as Erin spoke, the ripping sound of chainsaws could be heard echoing up from the valley below.

'Stuart and Chris are standing by there,' she said, referring to the other two senior paramedics. 'Brandon
is staying with the fatality until the police sort things.'

'Right,' Rafe said tersely. 'Let's get down there,
Toni.' He turned to Erin. 'Could you bring both ambu-
lances as close as you can, please? Sounds like we're
going to need all the help we can get.'

'And be extra-careful, Erin,' Toni warned. 'That hill
is very steep.'

'We've managed to make enough room to get the
back doors marginally open, Doc,' Stuart said as Rafe
and Toni reached the crashed small car. 'Mum and Dad
are in the front and two little kids in the back. Dad's
out of it but seems unhurt elsewhere. Mum's trapped
and drifting a bit.' He lowered his voice. 'Frantic about
the kids in the back. We can't get the door open properly to make any assessment. We need someone small
to get in there.'

'I'll go,' Toni said sharply. Already she could hear
the pitiful little keening sounds of distress coming from
the back seat. Ducking her head, she began to wiggle
her way through the half-open door and crawl inside.

'We have to do better than this!' Rafe spoke to one
of the firemen. 'I need to get in there, mate. Get the
damned doors off!'

'Fair go, Doc.' The fireman said stoically. 'We're
doing our best.'

Rafe swore impatiently. 'Toni, what's happening?'

'Two little boys,' Toni reported. As she spoke, her
hands were running over one of them, checking his
body. 'First one seems OK. I'm checking the other one
now.' What she observed sent Toni's clinical instincts
into overdrive. The child's chest was heaving but his
breath sounds were laboured. Too laboured. They had

a problem here. A big one. 'We need to treat this child, Rafe—fast!'

'Right, back doors are off!' The firemen lurched under the heavy weight and dragged the crushed metal out of the way.

Rafe wasted no time. Bending his head, he edged inside the car.

'It's a throat injury,' Toni said urgently. 'He was holding a toy aeroplane. See, the tip of the wing's caught him. It's still in his seat belt.'

'Let's take a look.' Rafe peered down at the injured little boy. 'He's cyanosed. Throat's swelling.'

'And his resps are high,' Toni said. 'Can we move him?'

'No time.' Rafe let his breath go in a stream. He'd have to act fast and intubate immediately to protect the child's airway, otherwise he'd be faced with having to perform a laryngotomy. And the circumstances were far from ideal for that. He stuck his head back out of the door. 'Can someone get the uninjured child out, please? And I need the trauma kit. Now!'

'Please, help my little boy…' The mother's plea came brokenly from the front seat.

For a second Rafe's face contorted and then he seemed to gather himself. 'I'm going to need you to help me here, Toni.'

'I understand. Tell me what you want.'

Rafe's mouth tightened. What he wanted was a sterile theatre and time on his side. And leg room.

Behind them there was a flurry of activity and the trauma kit was shoved onto the now vacant space on the back seat.

Rafe began unzipping sections, gathering equipment.

'Give this little guy hundred per cent oxygen, please, Toni, while I set up.'

Toni quickly had everything in position, holding the mask over the boy's face, giving him every breath of oxygen he could take, the steady rhythmic hiss of the bag drowned out by the din of the cutting tools working to free the parents in the front.

'More oxygen. He's still too light,' Rafe said. 'No way he'll tolerate a tube. That's better. Can you apply some cricoid pressure, please.'

Toni automatically complied. Using her thumb, she squeezed pressure on the cricoid cartilage. The action would stop any possibility of reflux from the child's stomach into his airway. 'Airway secured,' she reported quietly.

With quick precision, Rafe found a vein, inserted the cannula and injected the anaesthetic, just enough to knock his small patient out so he could be intubated without further distress.

The muscle relaxant took effect almost instantaneously. 'He's out,' Toni said.

'OK...gentle manoeuvre here,' Rafe murmured. Without moving the child's neck, he simply lifted his jaw forward, slipping the laryngoscope into his mouth and then sliding the tube in. 'Cricoid pressure off,' he directed, quickly attaching the tube to the oxygen supply. Snatching up the stethoscope, he listened to the little boy's lungs for breath sounds as he bagged him.

'He's looking better already.' Toni's voice was hushed in relief.

Rafe nodded. 'I want him on a spinal board and out of here. Erin, will you go with him?' He turned to the paramedic, who was leaning over from the front seat, the parents having been removed. 'He'll need careful monitoring.'

'I'll watch him every second.' Erin looked slightly in awe. 'That's some skill you have there, Doctor. You just saved that child's life.'

Rafe grunted a non-reply. 'Over to you,' he said instead. 'I'll look at the parents now.'

Toni stood closely beside Rafe as they watched the second ambulance take off slowly up the hill to the road. Suddenly Rafe turned his back on the sight and sank to the ground, his head drooping almost to his knees.

'Rafe?' Immediately, Toni dropped beside him. She touched his shoulders, finding them taut and stiff. 'Are you OK?'

He brought his head up and looked at her bleakly. 'Why do we do this job?'

Toni shrugged. 'Are we deranged, do you think?'

He gave a hollow laugh. 'It's quite possible. You were brilliant, Toni.'

'Just part of the team,' she said modestly.

'You should really think about becoming a doctor.'

She made a face. 'I like doing what I do. I'll leave the heavy lifting to clever chaps like you.'

He rolled back his shoulders and lay on the grass, putting out a hand and tugging her down beside him.

'Thank goodness that little family will be all right.' Toni smiled at him as his arm went under her head and she tucked in beside him. The father had suffered concussion but otherwise seemed unhurt, and although the children's mother had some deep cuts and was obviously very shocked, she too would recover well. 'They'll keep the whole family in, won't they?'

'Keith will sort them. Did we get the names of the boys?'

'Nicholas and Harry. Harry caused the drama.'

'Young Harry, hmm?' Rafe turned his head and kissed her gently. 'Coming home with me?'

At last. Toni's chest lifted in a long sigh. 'Yes, please.'

It was the early hours when Rafe woke. Toni's rhythmic breathing, the fluttering of her lashes on her cheek told him she was sound asleep. Her hair in all its silken glory rippled over the pillow. He knew if he bent and kissed her, her skin would be baby-soft and warm. He watched almost spellbound as she turned over and curled up, resisting the urge to run the tip of his finger along the fine-boned outline of her spine. Instead, he got quietly out of bed and padded to the window to look out over the garden and the soft beginning of a brand-new day.

But it was still too early to be up and he didn't want to wake her. Slipping back under the sheet, he closed his eyes. He needn't have worried after all. His sleep had been undisturbed.

Rafe's harsh cry woke Toni with a start.

She jerked upright, her heart pounding. 'Rafe...' Her hand went to his shoulder. He was tangled in the bed-clothes, between sleep and wakefulness and caught in the grip of some awful nightmare. His muffled pleas of desperation tore at Toni's heart. 'Rafe, wake up,' she urged softly. 'It's OK... It's OK... Hush...'

His moan became a shuddering breath. 'It's all right.' Toni bent over him, cradling his dark head against her, murmuring reassurances over and over. Finally, he went still and she sensed he'd woken fully but it was a long time until he moved. His eyes flicked open and he looked at her. 'So now you know,' he said bitterly.

Toni's arms tightened around him as it all fell into place—the reasons why he never stayed the entire night with her. The nightmares were obviously a symptom of post-traumatic stress. And he'd been trying to hide it from her.

She looked down at him. He'd covered his eyes with his forearm. 'Do you want to talk?'

He shook his head. 'Not now,' he said tersely.

'Then when, Rafe?' Toni was determined not to let this go.

For answer, he shook his head and said nothing.

Toni felt suddenly alienated. This was hardly adult behaviour from him and she deserved better. *They* deserved better. She made a snap decision. 'I'll go home, then. I need to shower and get ready for work.'

'You could do that here.'

No, she couldn't. Couldn't pretend things were normal when he obviously still had a load of baggage to deal with. *Baggage* he refused to share with her.

'I think it's best if I go. You obviously need your space.'

'Sorry.' He removed his forearm and spun to face her, an almost feverish sheen in his eyes.

A tiny frown lingered for a second on her forehead. 'For what?'

He worked his fingers across his eyes. 'This debacle…'

'It's not your fault, Rafe.' And if he couldn't get past that, how were they to go on? She slid out of bed. 'I'll… see you at work later.'

Toni arrived at work with her mind spinning, her thoughts so tangled, it felt like they'd run into a brick wall and bounced back to engulf her. She had to talk to Rafe. Correction, *he* had to open up and talk to her. He hadn't managed to do it up to now and time was running out for that to happen. In only a matter of weeks his tenure here would be over.

She had a management meeting first thing and, leaving Liz to take handover, Toni took herself off to the second floor, where the nurse managers were scheduled to meet. She greeted her contemporaries and, grabbing a coffee, took her place in the circle.

Larissa Grant, the DON, looked around the group and said, 'We're all busy people, so if no one has any urgent business, we'll keep today's meeting short.'

There were murmurs of relief and the meeting wound up in record time. Toni sped back to Casualty.

'Thank goodness you're back,' Liz said. 'All hell's broken loose in here.'

'What do we have, Lizzie?'

The senior nurse grimaced. 'The high-school bus ran off the road and hit a tree. Fortunately, the driver had only begun his pick-up from the outlying farms so there weren't many kids on board.'

'Usual driver?'

''Mmm. Gordon Aspinall. He's very reliable so it could be a problem with the bus.'

'Well, that's for the police,' Toni dismissed. 'What casualties do we have?'

'Well, Gordon himself, who needs to be checked over, and two students. One sixteen-year-old female with a knee injury and the other is a fourteen-year-old, Damon Spiteri. He hit his forehead on the metal bar of the seat in front of him. Justin is presently suturing him. He was pretty bloody and a bit shocked so Justin took him first.'

'OK…' Toni blew out a resigned breath. She hadn't needed another road accident coming on top of yesterday's. But, then, neither did the victims. 'Is Rafe in, do you know?'

'Just arrived, I think. I'll page him.'

'Thanks. Meanwhile, I'll pop my head in on the girl. Do we have her name?'

'Kristal Holmes. And you'll need all your PR skills. Her mother's just arrived and is on the warpath. Apparently, Kristal was due to audition for some cheerleading dance thing. I reckon nothing less than Gordon being sent to jail will convince Mrs Holmes we're doing our job.'

'Oh, bliss,' Toni sighed. 'Nothing like being the meat in the sandwich. I'll see if I can sort things.'

Liz gave a wry smile. 'You're good at that.'

Except where it counted most. Toni walked quickly towards the cubicles. Swishing back the curtain, she could see at a glance it was going to be one of *those* encounters. 'Mrs Holmes?' she queried the thin blonde woman who was hovering impatiently.

'Yes. And about time my daughter was looked at.'

Toni turned to the teenager on the treatment couch. 'Hi, Kristal. I'm Toni. Can you tell me where you're hurt?'

'It's my knee.' Blocking a tear with the tips of her fingers, the youngster tried to sit up.

'Stay there, honey.' Toni squeezed her shoulder. 'The doctor will be with you shortly.'

'That Gordon Aspinall should be jailed for what he's done.' The mother's tone was bordering on warlike. 'Kristal was selected to audition for the cheerleading squad for one of the big Sydney football teams next

week. She's got an agent and everything—and now
look at her...'

All heads turned as one as the curtains swished back
and Rafe strode in. Judging by his tight-lipped expression, Toni guessed Liz had already briefed him. 'This
is Dr Riccardi,' she jumped in diplomatically. 'Doctor,
this is Mrs Holmes and her daughter, Kristal, who was
brought in as a result of an accident with the school
bus this morning.'

Acknowledging Toni's information with a curt nod,
Rafe hitched himself against a corner of the treatment
couch and asked, 'Where are you hurt, Kristal?'

'She's hurt her knee!' With an exasperated sigh, Mrs
Holmes sent her gaze heavenwards. 'How many more
times do we have to explain before you do something?'

'Mrs Holmes.' Rafe folded his arms, his lean jaw set
as he swivelled to address the woman. 'I'd appreciate it
if you'd let Kristal speak for herself, otherwise I may
have to ask you to leave.'

'You can't do that!' The mother was clearly outraged.
'My daughter is underage. I have to be here.'

Rafe's jaw tightened. After the soul-destroying
start to his morning, his tolerance was on a short fuse.
'Perhaps you'd sit quietly, then, while I examine my
patient.'

With a little sniff the mother took a couple of steps
back and perched on the edge of a chair Toni held for
her.

'Now, Kristal.' Rafe turned to his young patient and
asked gently, 'Like to tell me what happened?'

The teenager blinked fast and swallowed. 'I was
thrown off the seat when the bus hit the tree. I landed
really hard on my right knee. It was all a bit scary but

Mr Aspinall looked after us and called our parents and the ambulance and kept us all calm…'

'That's good…' Rafe nodded slowly. He wasn't about to hurry the youngster, since it was essential she debrief in her own time. Poor kid. He guessed she'd not been able to get a word in edgeways since her mother had come on the scene. 'And did you feel the pain right away?'

'Mmm. My knee felt all wobbly.'

'Right. Antonia, if you'd give me a hand, please, we'll get Kristal more comfortable.'

'Just relax, sweetie.' Toni smiled, easing off the girl's trainers. Today she was dressed in her sports strip of shorts and polo shirt so access to her knee was made simple.

'OK, let's see what we have.' Rafe worked the knee slightly and Kristal gasped. His eyes narrowed. 'Would this be an old sports injury, by any chance?'

'I'm not sure. Sometimes it feels…not sore exactly…'

'But a bit uncomfortable?'

Kristal clenched her bottom lip and nodded.

'Has she broken anything?' Mrs Holmes's tone still had an accusing edge.

'No, I'm sure she hasn't,' Rafe responded with studied calm. 'Kristal, you've obviously partly dislocated your patella. Your kneecap. We'll give you some pain relief and pop it back in for you.'

'OK…' The youngster managed a shaky smile.

'So, how is high school going?' Rafe chatted for a minute while the pain relief took effect.

'It's good. I'm captain of the netball team. I take dance lessons as well.'

Rafe listened, making an appropriate comment here and there as he worked her patella gently, ensuring it was relocated. 'There you are. All done. We'll get a support bandage on that for you now. Any problems, come straight back to Casualty. In the meantime, no undue stress on your knee. So, sorry, kiddo, it looks like your audition will have to wait for another time.'

'This is outrageous!' The girl's mother flew to her feet. 'This was Kristal's chance to get into the big time. To be noticed. Maybe get on TV.' She took a step towards Rafe. 'That Gordon Aspinall should be brought to account. He's obviously been drinking and I hope you're going to blood-test him, Doctor. You mark my words, it'll be over the limit. You—'

'Do you have a medical degree, Mrs Holmes?' Rafe cut in, his voice lethally cool.

Her jaw dropped. 'Of course I don't.'

'Well, I do. So I'll be the one to decide what treatment, if any, is appropriate for Mr Aspinall. Is that clear?'

Blotchy patches of red stood out on the woman's cheeks. Suddenly her aggression collapsed like a pack of cards and she burst into tears.

'Mum, don't...' Kristal looked on in distress. 'It's OK.'

'It's not OK...' Mrs Holmes hiccuped a sob. 'I wanted this so much for you, Kristal.'

Enough! Tight-lipped, Rafe walked out.

'Mrs Holmes, sit down again, please.' Toni strove to restore calm. 'I know how disappointed you must be for Kristal.'

'Yes...'

'Of course you are.' Toni passed the box of tissues to her.

'Thank you, Sister. You've been very kind.' The

mother's voice was muffled as she mopped up. 'You never know what's round the corner, do you?'

'No, you certainly don't.' Toni's agreement was heartfelt. 'Back in a tick.' She touched a hand to Mrs Holmes's shoulder and stepped out of the cubicle to find Rafe pacing restlessly.

He stared at her for a long moment, his jaw clenched, before he asked directly, 'Could you delegate someone else to finish up in there, please? I'd like you with me when I examine the bus driver.'

Toni frowned. 'Do you need me as a witness?'

'After that performance in there?' His tone echoed disgust. 'You bet I do.'

Toni called Mel, who was passing, and handed over Kristal's care. Turning back to Rafe, she said tersely, 'Gordon Aspinall is in cube three. And for goodness' sake don't jump all over him.'

'You think I came on too strongly with Mrs Holmes?'

Toni's shoulder lifted in a tight shrug. 'She'd try the patience of a saint but you could have been kinder,' she added, her comment sharp and to the point.

Rafe's mouth pulled tight. Toni's frustration and disappointment with him were palpable. He rubbed at the back of his neck. Dammit. Judging by the way things had gone pear-shaped between them this morning, he'd have done better to have pulled rank and taken himself off for the day. He drew in a long breath and let it go. 'Fill me in a bit, then, would you, please?'

'Gordon is as steady as they come. Well liked in the town. I can't imagine he'd be drinking. And he'd never risk the kids' lives with an unsafe bus.'

'What age group?'

Toni considered. 'Early sixties, possibly.'

Rafe's mouth drew in. This could all be more complicated than anyone thought. Various possibilities for the accident passed through his mind and, unfortunately for Gordon, he couldn't discount any of them.

'I'll just check Mel has everything she needs.' Toni broke into his thoughts abruptly. 'Do you want to go ahead with Gordon and I'll be with you presently?'

'Uh—yes.' He managed a tight smile. 'Thanks for the heads up.'

'You're welcome to my help any time, Rafe. You should know that by now.'

Rafe's jaw clenched and unclenched. He couldn't doubt her sincerity. His heart twisted as he watched his lover hurry away. He wanted, needed to sort things with her but his mind was in overload. Feeling as though a giant steel hand had taken hold of his guts, he forced his mind into neutral and went in search of his patient.

Pulling back the curtains on cubicle three, he strode in. 'Gordon Aspinall?'

'Yes.' The driver jerked to attention.

Poor coot. Rafe's keen gaze ran over the man's dejected body language. 'I'm Rafe Riccardi.' He offered his hand briefly and then turned aside to drag up another chair and sit opposite his patient. 'I'm covering for Dr Lyons while he's on leave,' he explained.

'I was hoping I could've seen Joe,' Gordon said awkwardly. 'We're both in the Rotary, like…'

'Sorry about that.' Reaching one hand back behind him, Rafe took Gordon's chart from the rack, perusing it swiftly. 'I understand you had a mishap with the school bus this morning?'

'Bit more than a mishap,' Gordon responded gruffly. 'Couple of the youngsters were injured.' His shoulders slumped. 'Mrs Holmes wants me charged.'

Rafe gave a bark of unamused laughter. 'Well, that's

not for anyone but the police to decide. Have they been to talk to you yet?'

Gordon shook his head. 'Still at the accident scene, I reckon.'

'So, Gordon…' Rafe tossed the chart aside and leaned back in his chair '…how's your general health?'

'I feel OK most of the time. Not one to be taking sick days.'

'And what about this morning? Did you feel at any time you weren't in control of the bus? For instance, could you have blacked out for a second or two?'

Gordon pursed his lips thoughtfully. 'Might've got confused for a couple of seconds, I suppose.'

'In what way?'

'Hard to explain.'

'Take your time,' Rafe said gently. 'I'm not going anywhere.'

Gordon's pale blue eyes regarded the senior doctor steadily. 'There was a bit of wash-out on the side of the road. I tried to steer away from it but my hands wouldn't co-operate—felt kind of weak. So I went for the brakes but…my feet couldn't give me enough pressure. And then the bus just left the road and there was nothing I could do. It happened in a flash.'

'And there's no chance of mechanical failure?'

'The bus had a full service recently.' Gordon paused, clearly waiting for Rafe to start giving him some answers.

Instead, Rafe swung up from his chair, glancing up as Toni came in quietly. He raised an eyebrow. 'Everything OK?'

She guessed he was asking whether Mrs Holmes had been placated. 'For the moment.' Toni wasn't about to let him off the hook just yet. She did think he'd been harsh with Kristal's mother. And arrogant.

Rafe lifted a shoulder indifferently. There were more important matters to be dealt with than whether he'd offended the Holmes woman. He turned his attention back to his patient. 'Gordon, I'm going to give you a general examination. I'll also be checking for any whip-lash injury and any deficits in your hands and feet. Is that OK with you?'

'I suppose you gotta do what you gotta do.' Gordon sent a slightly trapped look at Toni.

'Just relax, Gordon.' Toni deliberately tried to infuse some lightness into the situation. 'We'll try to make it as easy as we can for you.'

Rafe reached for a stethoscope. 'Antonia, would you be good enough to record my findings, please?'

'Certainly, Doctor.' Toni took up the patient chart, unclipped her pen and waited.

Rafe's examination was painstaking, but he wasn't satisfied. 'OK, Gordon, you can hop down from the couch now.' His eyes narrowed as Gordon lowered his feet to the floor.

'And that's it, is it, Doc?' Gordon looked relieved.

'Not quite. I want you to walk for me, please. Just across to the far wall and back. Keep going until I ask you to stop.'

Gordon's eyes clouded. 'I haven't touched a drop of alcohol—'

'Just routine,' Rafe said easily. 'Will you walk now, please?' As Gordon walked, Rafe looked thoughtful, his mouth compressing as he watched. 'That's fine.' He held up his hand for Gordon to stop. 'Just one more thing and then we'll let you go. We'll need to take a blood sample from you.'

A few minutes later it was all done and Gordon was winding down his sleeve. 'When will I know something, Doc?'

'I'll have a chat with your GP first.' Rafe scribbled a notation on the chart and then watched as Toni labelled the blood and placed it aside for testing.

'We may need you back as early as this afternoon for a CT scan.'

All three turned as Liz popped her head in. 'The sergeant's just arrived to have a word with Gordon. Shall I ask him to wait?'

'No need. We're done here for the moment,' Rafe said. 'Use my office.'

Moving with quiet efficiency, Toni began putting the treatment room back to rights. 'You suspect the onset of Parkinson's, don't you?'

Rafe stroked a finger across his chin. 'It's looking that way. Several things are pointing to Gordon's co-ordination beginning to deteriorate.'

'So, why the blood test?' Toni stuffed the used linen into a receptacle. 'That won't help you make a diagnosis for Parkinson's. And it was obvious Gordon hadn't been drinking.'

Dark humour flickered in Rafe eyes and pulled at the corner of his mouth. 'Ever heard of covering our butts?' With a precise movement he thrust the chart at her and turned towards the doorway.

'Ra—fe…' His name died on her lips. He'd already gone.

CHAPTER TEN

TONI registered his departure with something like disbelief. How could he just walk out as though they had nothing to discuss? That they had nothing more than colleague status between them?

The fact that he so easily could, left her fuming. But what a fool she'd been, letting her personal life overlap into her professional life. Her mouth tightened. She'd done it again.

Disgust with herself hardened her resolve. She'd just have to tough it out. She'd done it before, after all. Giving the cubicle a cursory glance to make sure it was restored to order, she went back to the station.

Liz looked up from her paperwork. 'What's happening with Gordon?'

Toni forced her mind to focus. 'More investigation. The reg is getting some history from his GP.'

The reg? Liz twitched an eyebrow. So formal. What on earth was going on with those two? 'Delegate and let's get a cuppa,' she said abruptly.

Toni looked dubious. 'I suppose we could…'

'You're the boss, Toni. Of course we could,' Liz sighed dramatically. 'I'm giving us permission.'

They took their tea and helped themselves to a couple of home-made muffins from a batch someone had brought in then made their way outside to the garden. 'This is more like it,' Liz said with satisfaction as they parked themselves at the outdoor table under a huge old elm. 'And we're only two minutes away if we're needed. We should do this more often, don't you agree?'

Toni took a mouthful of her tea. 'You're about as transparent as a pane of glass, Lizzie. But you're right. I needed to get out of that place, if only briefly.'

For once Liz followed her instincts and kept silent, focusing on the garden sprinkler dancing silver in the sun.

After a while, Toni asked, 'Really and truly, Liz, why do we bother with men?'

'Because for most of the time we need them,' Liz responded mildly. 'And although they would rather take rat poison than admit it, *they* need us.'

More silence.

'Is everything OK with you and Rafe?' Liz asked.

Toni spanned her hands around her tea mug and looked into its depths. 'We've hit a bit of a rough patch.' More like a yawning chasm, she rephrased silently.

'You know if you want to talk…?' Liz offered.

Toni made a strangled sound in her throat. 'I wouldn't know where to start, Lizzie. But thanks…'

Damn Rafe Riccardi! Liz bit savagely into her muffin. If he'd hurt Toni, she, Elizabeth Carey, would personally have his guts for hair ribbons! 'You're owed plenty of leave,' she said. 'Why don't you just go home? Take the rest of the day off?'

'No, that's not me,' Toni refuted quietly. 'It's like running away. And I'm not doing that. Oh, Lizzie…' she shook her head '…I just want to thump some sense into him.'

Liz snorted inelegantly. 'I'd like a dollar for the number of times I've wanted to do exactly that to Matt.'

'You don't fight much, do you?' Toni's eyes widened in surprise.

Liz shrugged. 'Not now. But we did in our early days. Once I even packed a bag, took the kids and went home to Mum.'

'Oh, my stars! How long were you away?'

'About an hour. Matt came storming over with flowers. And not from the supermarket either.' She grinned reminiscently. 'The make-up sex was wild.'

Despite her problems, Toni laughed. 'Lizzie, you're priceless.'

'And so are you, my friend.' Suddenly serious, Liz leaned over and tapped Toni on the forearm. 'Don't ever forget that. Now, here's what we're going to do,' she said purposefully. 'If you won't go home, then let me deputise for the rest of the shift. Go and busy yourself elsewhere in the hospital. Have a wander through Kids. I believe young Harry is still in. Read him a story. Have a giggle. I'll deal with His Nibs if he asks.'

Toni felt her insides pinch. 'You won't say anything?'

'Would I?' Liz sent her a wounded look. 'I can be the soul of discretion when it's needed.'

'I know,' Toni said, cheering up. 'That's why you're my trusted deputy.'

For the umpteenth time Rafe roamed through the department and back to his office. Antonia was keeping clear, that much was obvious. He balled his hands into fists of frustration. He couldn't believe how badly he was handling things with her. He knew she only wanted to help and it was purely his own stiff-necked pride that was keeping him from letting her. Perhaps it was the fact he didn't do trust very well—or not since Gabby…

But then why couldn't he get it into his head that Antonia was the antithesis of her, as Toni herself had already pointed out? With nothing resolved, he finished his shift and went home.

But when he went to bed, he could still smell her on his pillow—something so subtle it was barely there, but he couldn't breathe in enough of it. Face it. He growled a huff of self-derision. This is the closest you're going to get to her, mate, if you don't start taking control of your life.

Life had to go on, Toni resolved as she took handover next morning. She had to believe she and Rafe had a future. Somehow.

Casualty was busy, for which Toni was grateful. But with Justin and Grace well able to deal with any medical emergencies, Toni had no need to call Rafe. Nevertheless, she couldn't avoid him as he did his usual rounds but she exchanged only a brief good morning, almost *feeling* the weight of his gaze on her back as she hurried away.

If he'd looked taken aback, tough. She was all out of olive branches.

At the station Toni went through the charts from the morning. There'd been several walking wounded whose notes had to be sent on to their GPs...

'Toni, could I have a private word, please?'

Toni's gaze came up to see Harmony hovering nervously. 'Of course.' She got to her feet. 'My office?'

The young nurse nodded and followed as Toni led the way.

'Let's sit over here.' Toni indicated the informal cane setting near the window. When they were seated, she smiled. 'How can I help?'

Harmony rested her folded hands on the lacquered table top. 'I want to give in my notice.'

'You're leaving us?' Toni's brows twitched in query. 'Are you not happy here, Harmony?'

Harmony sent her boss a very straight look. 'I'm not enjoying being a nurse, Toni. It's not the staff here,' she was quick to add. 'You've all been lovely to me. It's just…' She stopped and bit her lip. 'I can't do it any more. I hate the smells and the noises the machines make.' She swallowed and grimaced. 'And the blood…'

Toni nodded. 'I understand. But there are other forms of nursing not necessarily in a hospital setting. Have you thought about that?'

'Not really. I mean, I like the patients—or most of them—and I like looking after people, but the clinical side of nursing is not for me.'

'That has to be your decision,' Toni said calmly. It was obvious Harmony had made up her mind. 'Have you any idea about what you'd really like to do?'

'I'm joining one of the airlines as cabin crew.' Harmony's cute dimple showed as she smiled. 'At least I will be as soon as I've undergone a medical and I need a couple of referees.' She paused. 'I wondered whether you would be one—if that's all right?' she tacked on quickly.

'No problem.' Toni flapped a hand. 'I'd be glad to, Harmony. But we'll be sorry to see you go. You really had the makings of a fine nurse. But I understand that it's not for everyone. Your patient skills were excellent and that will stand you in good stead as a flight attendant.'

'That's what attracted me to the job,' Harmony said seriously. 'And the interviewing panel commented on my people skills so I feel I'm making the right choice for me.'

Toni gave a wry smile. 'I dare say the corporate uniform is a lot smarter too. When do you want to finish?'

Harmony looked uncertain. 'I know it's mandatory to give two weeks' notice—'

'I'm sure we could waive that, if you need to get on with your own plans. You'll be based in Sydney, I take it?'

'Yes and I'm so looking forward to getting back.'

Toni left her chair and picked up the calendar from her deck. 'What say we make your finishing date a week from today?'

Harmony nodded enthusiastically. 'Thanks so much, Toni. Uh—about the references—do you think I could ask Dr Riccardi for one as well?'

Toni's gaze became shuttered. Just the mention of his name made every nerve in her body pinch and knot. 'I—' She stopped short when a cursory knock sounded on her door and Rafe himself poked his head in.

'Oh, sorry. I didn't mean to interrupt.'

'You're not.' Toni sent him a cool look. 'Harmony is leaving us. She was just wondering whether you would provide a character reference for her.'

'Of course.' Rafe's green gaze went from one to the other before he came in and parked himself against the window frame and crossed his feet at the ankles. 'Don't feel you're cut out for nursing, then, Harmony?' he asked lightly.

She dimpled up at the registrar. 'No. I'm joining an airline as cabin crew.'

Rafe gave a slight shrug. 'Good for you. Better than trying to struggle on in a situation when you're not happy.'

Toni felt her nerve ends, already raw, grate further. Was there a subtle message for her somewhere in there?

There was a beat of silence before Rafe continued, 'I guess you'll just need my phone number for the HR people, then, Harmony? That's the way it works nowadays, isn't it?'

'Thank you, yes.' Harmony blushed slightly. 'I can tell the others that I'm leaving, then?' She looked at Toni for confirmation.

'Feel free.' Toni dredged up a warm smile. 'And we must have a farewell party for you. I'll ask Ed to organise something.'

'That'd be cool.' Harmony sounded youthfully eager. 'You'll come along won't you, Dr Riccardi?'

'Wouldn't miss it, Harmony.' Rafe extended his hand. 'Good luck. I hope everything goes well for you.'

With Harmony gone, so was their buffer and Rafe and Toni stood facing one another.

'Was there something you wanted?' Toni finally asked.

Of course there was something he damned well wanted. Rafe's mouth curled. 'You're determined to make this difficult, aren't you?'

Toni took a breath, stung by his accusation. She wanted to yell at him but instead she went for a nonchalant shrug. 'You're doing a fine job of that yourself.'

'OK…' Rafe sighed and rubbed a hand through his hair. If he didn't get this sorted, he'd go crazy. 'Could we talk?'

A swirl of emotions had Toni gripping the back of the cane chair. *Talk.* Such a tiny word. The result of which could either mean a new beginning for their relationship. Or letting it go for ever. 'That's probably an excellent idea.'

Rafe held himself very still. 'Where and when, then? You choose.'

'My place,' Toni said coolly. 'There's just one proviso, Rafe.'

'What?' His head tilted at an angle that was almost arrogant until his eyes began taking in her bravely held little chin, the soft curve of her cheek, the sweet, very sweet fullness of her mouth. 'What…?' His voice descended into soft appeal.

'That we actually talk.' Her mouth trembled infinitesimally. 'That means it's a two-way conversation with an outcome. Is that clear?'

'Exceptionally.' Something like respect showed in Rafe's face. 'What time?'

'Eight o'clock.' Toni would have asked him for a meal but she knew neither of them would be able to eat it.

Rafe walked to the door and turned. 'I'll be there.'

As eight o'clock approached, Toni felt a lurching sensation in the pit of her stomach. And when the doorbell rang just after eight, she nearly jumped out of her skin.

She opened the door and let Rafe in. 'Thanks for coming,' she said quietly.

His brow rose briefly. He wasn't aware he'd had a choice. But he tamped down any desire to start the evening argumentatively.

'Would you mind coming through to the kitchen?' Toni asked. 'I'm making a cake for the hospital's street stall on Friday. I'd like to keep an eye on it.'

'Fine with me.' In the kitchen, he edgily accepted her offer of a glass of wine. 'Cake smells good.'

Very aware of him so close to her, Toni steadied her hand and carefully poured the wine. 'It's a chocolate mud cake,' she said. 'Well, it's a packet one but they're pretty good these days so no one will guess.' Handing him his glass of wine, she thought here they went again with another of those ridiculous conversations they were so good at.

They sat facing one another across the kitchen table, a heavy silence descending on them with the intensity of a fog rolling in from the ocean in winter.

'I don't want to start drawing up battle lines, Antonia.' Rafe stroked the stem of his glass with his thumb, his dark head bent over the golden liquid. 'I'd hope we could just...talk.'

Toni dragged in a deep breath. 'That's all I've ever wanted to do.' When it seemed as though nothing more was forthcoming from him, she said with a flash of spirit, 'If you want out of this relationship, Rafe, then tell me. Let's end it cleanly.'

End it? Rafe felt a cramp in his chest. Is that what *she* wanted? The words went round and round in his head, thumping intolerably like a physical pain. 'For God's sake!' he rasped. 'I don't want to end it!'

'Oh. I thought...' Drawing back sharply, Toni looked into his anguished face.

'There's stuff I should have told you about.' Lifting a hand, he scrubbed the tips of fingers across his forehead. 'Stuff you had a right to know.'

Toni took a careful mouthful of her wine. 'Why did you feel you had to hide the fact you were have nightmares from me?'

'I didn't want to alarm you.'

'And we both know there's not a shred of credibility in that statement,' she threw at him. 'I've worked in Emergency for years. I hardly think a nightmare is going to alarm me.'

'OK.' He flicked a hand impatiently. 'Put it down to male ego or self-preservation. Or both.'

Toni softened. 'Has it been diagnosed as PTSD?'

He nodded.

'And what have they told you?'

'That the nightmares will probably stop of their own accord.'

Toni frowned. 'That's a bit open-ended, isn't it? Have you spoken to anyone since you've been back?'

He lifted a shoulder. 'I had a few sessions with a shrink. It helped. And I hadn't had a nightmare for weeks.'

'Well, that's positive, isn't it?' She sent him a guarded smile. And now he was out of the environment that had caused his stress in the first place, surely the chances of the nightmares recurring would diminish accordingly. 'Have you been given some strategies to enhance your well-being?'

He looked up, his jaw working. 'Swimming has been a great help.'

Well, of course it would be, Toni thought. Exercise in general was a proven method to enhance endorphins and reduce stress. She hesitated and then asked, 'Do you think the emergency with Harry brought stuff back into your subconscious?'

'It's possible. But I can't avoid treating children, Antonia.' His look was almost hostile.

'I'm not suggesting you do.' Toni willed herself to stay detached. 'Has my knowing made you feel uncomfortable?'

'It doesn't make me feel great.'

'Why is that? Do you think it makes you less of a person, less of a *man,* because you've experienced post-traumatic stress?'

He finished his wine in a couple of gulps. She was probably right but there was no way he wanted to go there.

'Couldn't it prove the opposite?' In an impatient gesture she shook her cascading hair back over her shoulders. 'That you're a compassionate human being, a dedicated doctor? Rafe, you have to know that any… condition that's not visible is isolating for the person concerned. It doesn't make you *odd,* for heaven's sake!'

He grunted a non-reply.

'I think you've done brilliantly.'

He sighed, managing a small smile. 'Really?'

'Yes.' She held out her hand and he took it, lacing their fingers. 'And you need to be realistic. This is a glitch. It's not as though you've lost an arm and your ability to practise medicine.'

He smiled crookedly. 'I like your logic, Antonia.'

'So, just keep tossing your baggage to me and we'll handle it together. Deal?'

Rafe felt the crippling weight of indecision fall away. He should have been upfront with her weeks ago. Trusted her. He'd do better from now on. Hell, he'd better. He didn't think she'd offer him too many more chances. 'Deal,' he said.

The days were rushing by with a speed that was leaving Toni almost breathless. Harmony was long gone and had been replaced by a nice young RN, David Kerwin, who was three years post-grad and who seemed to be fitting into their team very well.

And Rafe's term was drawing to a close. Only a few weeks to go now. And with every day that passed, Toni's good sense was struggling to retain ascendancy over her impatience about the future. She wasn't aware Rafe had made any plans. Well, if he had, he hadn't told her. And she'd thought they'd got over all those hurdles of not communicating.

She wanted a future with him but she wasn't about to push. Perhaps she could gently instigate a discussion about it, she thought. Maybe tonight. She looked at her watch and gave a half-smile. Why wait until night? They were both due a break. They could grab a few bits and pieces from the canteen and go across to the park. Relaxed under one of the beautiful old gum trees, the mellow hint of autumn in the air, who knew? Rafe might just start talking about the future...their future.

Together.

Leaving her office, she went back to the station. 'I'm taking the early lunch, Lizzie.'

Liz looked up from the computer. 'Go for it,' she said absently. 'Oh, we should probably have a think about a send-off for Rafe. Time's running out. Have you two made any plans?'

'Not yet.' Toni tried to look unconcerned. 'Still up in the air a bit. It'll sort itself out.'

'Of course it will.' She sent Toni a provocative, Liz-like grin. 'Wouldn't hurt to give him a nudge, you know.'

Toni flicked a smile in return. 'You read my mind.' Holding the thought, she went along to Rafe's office, tapped and poked her head in. He looked up from his computer and beckoned her in.

'Just finishing an email,' he said. 'Won't be a second.'

Toni went to stand behind him, her hands automatically smoothing across the breadth of his shoulders. Bending, she smudged a kiss on his nape, only to feel him make a restive movement before he hit 'Send' and then swung round on his chair to face her. 'I was just coming to find you. We need to talk.'

'Snap.' Tony smiled. 'I was on the same wavelength. I thought we could have lunch in the park.'

'Uh—can't, sorry.' Abruptly, he swung off his chair and went to stand against the window, facing her, his hands pressed down on the sill. 'A lot has happened over the last twelve hours, Antonia.'

Toni felt an immediate lick of unease. His demeanour showed…*excitement*. And somehow it didn't seem the kind she could share. She swallowed unevenly. 'Better tell me, then.'

'Last night I had a call from Ari Cohen, my former boss in Siem Reap. They have an outbreak of whooping cough among the children. The need to do a mass inoculation is critically urgent. He's asked me to go over and help.'

Toni felt all the strength drain from her legs. So this was yet another hurdle they had to negotiate. Would it ever end? She drew in all her powers of self-protection. 'Surely they have trained people to do that. Why you?'

'Because I'm already accredited to work there. They have recruits coming on line but they have to be brought up to speed. And this is an emergency.'

'And you're going.'

'Yes.' A muscle pulled in his jaw. 'If the inoculation programme isn't carried out, it'll be a catastrophe.'

But why did he think it was down to him to take all the responsibility? Why? Toni fought for calm. 'Won't you need medical clearance?'

'Keith took care of that this morning.'

'Did you tell him about the nightmares?'

'They've stopped.'

Well, she only had his word for that. It wasn't as

though they spent every night together. 'Aren't you risking your complete recovery by going back into that environment? Don't they care?'

His dark brows shot together. 'Of course they care! In fact, Ari stressed the point.' Rafe hesitated as if searching for the right words. 'Antonia, this is something I need to do.'

'And what about us?' Toni demanded, her eyes flashing. To hell with him and what he *needed* to do. 'Did you even think to talk about this with me before you just decided to go?'

'I'm talking to you now!' Rafe's voice rose. 'Antonia, this couldn't wait. Surely, as a health professional, you can understand that?'

Well, she could and she couldn't. 'You know I play straight, Rafe. You know that! If the situation had been reversed, I would have come to you first, before I decided anything. So what do I actually mean to you? It seems to me I've been nothing more than a convenient bedmate!'

Rafe recoiled as if she'd slapped him. 'That remark is not worthy of you, Toni. Not worthy of us, of what we've shared. I care deeply about you. You have to know that. And I *will* be back.'

'The hell you will.' Her voice hardened. 'Once you get back there, it will consume you again.' Toni's throat felt like sandpaper as she swallowed. But she hadn't finished. 'What about your commitments to the hospital here? Are you walking out on them as well?'

'They're covered.' His mouth snapped shut, his tightly clamped lips a harsh line across his face. 'And Joe will be back in a couple of weeks.'

She looked at him, her eyes unguarded. 'When do you go?'

'I'm driving to Sydney this afternoon, flying out tomorrow morning. You've—uh—left some of your things at the annexe…' His throat jerked as he swallowed. 'I'll leave the key in the usual place so you can collect them whenever…'

'When you've gone.'

'Antonia, please believe me, none of this is meant to hurt you.' He moved to hold her but she waved him away, although she hoped he wouldn't guess what it cost her to pull away from the reassurance of those warm, strong arms.

'It's too late, Rafe.'

'It needn't be.'

Oh, but it was and they both knew it. 'Just…stay well…' Blindly, she began making her way across to the door.

'Toni!' Rafe leapt after her as though he could actually halt her desperation. 'Don't leave like this.'

Hand on the doorknob, she turned. She gave a sad little shake of her head. 'I'm not the one leaving, Rafe. *You* are.'

Safely outside his office, Toni almost ran back to the nurses' station, the drum-heavy thud in her heart almost suffocating her. In just a few minutes Rafe had turned her life on its head. And he'd had the hide to say he cared!

'Oh, lord!' Liz jumped up from her chair. 'Toni, what's wrong?'

Toni threw caution to the winds. It would be all over the hospital shortly. 'He's leaving, Lizzie. Going back to Cambodia.'

Liz swore quietly and pithily. 'You look in shock.' Liz quickly guided Toni into an empty cubicle. 'Sit down,' she ordered, pulling the screen for privacy. 'I'll get you a glass of water.'

'Now, tell me what happened,' Liz coaxed a little while later. 'If you want to,' she added diplomatically.

Toni filled her friend in as best she could. 'He says he'll be back,' she ended with a mirthless little huff.

'And you don't believe him?'

'Would you?' Toni shook her head. 'Once he's there it's obvious it will take over his life again.'

Liz bit her lip. So Matt's prediction had been right. But she couldn't stick another knife into Toni and remind her of that. 'You could be wrong, you know,' she said instead.

'Yeah…' Toni felt her heart shrink even further. 'If you believe in fairy-tales.'

'Go home, Toni.' Liz's tone brooked no argument. 'You don't need to be here.'

Toni nodded listlessly. 'I think I will.'

Rafe fell back into his chair as if his strings had been cut. God, what a disaster. He hadn't expected Toni's reaction. He'd wanted her onside about his decision. Surely she should have been able to understand he needed to do this. Apart from the medical emergency, he had to, if ever he was to be truly whole again. He pressed his fingers across his eyes as if staving off pain. 'How could she think I didn't love her?' he rasped under his breath. Hell, I'm doing this for her as well as myself. I'm doing it for *us*.

When his phone rang, he reached out groggily and picked it up. 'Yes, Maureen.'

'I've confirmed your flight to Bangkok, Rafe.'

'Could I have the flight number please?' He scribbled down the information. 'And the connecting flight to Seim Reap?'

'I was able to do that as well.'

'Good. What's the arrival time for that? Thanks, got all that. I'll email MSF and pass on the details.'

'Safe trip, then…'

'Maureen, thanks for everything.' Rafe took a steadying breath. 'You've been great.' Replacing the receiver, he got slowly to his feet.

Now he had to tell the team.

CHAPTER ELEVEN

IN HER office, Toni finished writing up the shift ros-
ters for another month. Logging off the computer, she
looked into space.

It seemed half a lifetime since Rafe had left but in
reality it was only a matter of weeks. And despite her
best efforts to block him out, to restart her life, her
thoughts, especially at night, would push past the block
she'd striven to make Rafe-proof. The heady feeling of
completeness she'd felt with him would ambush her
out of nowhere.

Maybe he'd loved her in his way, she thought now.
But he walked to a different drummer. And she couldn't
walk with him. *But why couldn't she? Why?* The sudden thought almost her made her dizzy. A reed of hope
as slender as a gossamer strand sprang in her heart as
the thought took hold.

She'd been so self-involved, she owned with something like shame. So...insular. Rafe had wanted to do
something good, something worthwhile with his medical skills. Why couldn't she have understood that? She
thought back to the day when he'd tried to explain his
reasons for going. But instead of listening, she'd taken
the high moral ground.

And walked out on him.

She closed her eyes. She wanted to turn back the clock. Spin the hands into reverse. But she couldn't do that. But there was something she could do—she could go to him…

'OK…' She exhaled a deep breath. First things first.

Aware of the accelerated beat of her heart, she picked up the phone to call the DON.

'Loretta, I need to take some leave. Well, whatever's owing to me and as soon as you can arrange it, please. A family matter I have to deal with,' Toni said, forgiving herself the white lie. 'No, I'll hold.' Her fingers tightened on the phone as she waited. 'Today?' Toni felt her heart go into freefall. 'Thank you so much, Loretta. Thank you…'

Toni had barely put the phone down when Liz burst in. Without ceremony, she spun out a chair and sat facing Toni across the desk. 'I've just got off the phone with Loretta,' she said. 'Apparently I'm to be acting NUM for the next three weeks. Care to tell me what's going on?'

'I think you can guess, Lizzie. I'm going to Rafe.'

Liz blinked her uncertainty. 'Have you heard from him?'

Toni shook her head.

'So, you're just going over there…' Liz made a vague rocking movement with her hand. 'Shouldn't you try to call him first?'

'I need to see him.'

Liz sucked down on her bottom lip in consternation. 'I worry for you, Toni. Have you thought about what you're doing?'

'No, Lizzie, I haven't. It was a snap decision. But I'm slowly going nuts just hanging about in limbo. I love him. I have to find out of he loves me.'

'OK…' Liz expelled a deep breath. 'I can see you've made up your mind.' She looked at her watch. 'The shift's only got an hour to run. Why don't you take off? Whizz up town and see the travel agent and get your flights booked.'

'Would you mind?' Toni was already getting to her feet.

'Of course I don't mind,' Liz said, whirling upright as well. 'Anyway, I'm the boss as of ten minutes ago. So, Ms Morell, you have my permission to take an early mark. And if you need help of any kind, call me,' Liz insisted. 'Matt has contacts all over the place.'

The two friends hugged briefly. 'Thanks, Lizzie…' Toni clamped her lips to stop them trembling. It was really happening. She was going to Rafe.

She only hoped he'd still want her. As much as she wanted him.

Toni had read her travel guide from cover to cover on her flight from Sydney to Bangkok. And on the connecting flight to Seim Reap, her excitement grew until it was almost combustible. But there was trepidation as well. Perhaps she should have let Rafe know of her impending arrival…

Because she'd wanted somewhere lovely for her and Rafe to be together, she'd booked at one of Seim Reap's upmarket hotels, surprised and delighted with her suite. Now, she just had to let him know she was here.

She couldn't waste any more time in conjecture. Hoping he still had his cellphone and that it worked here, she dialled his number and waited, prepared for it to go to voicemail, but it was picked up almost immediately.

'Dr Riccardi.'

'Rafe…? It's me…' She swallowed the huskiness of nerves.

'Antonia?' His voice was laced with amazement. 'Where are you?'

'I'm here in Seim Reap. Could we catch up—I mean, if you want to…?'

He was noncommittal. 'Where are you staying?'

She told him the name of the boutique hotel.

'I'll be right over.'

'But aren't you at the hospital?'

'I'm off duty.'

'Oh.' Her composure slipped every which way. In a matter of minutes she could be in his arms. Or not. He hadn't sounded exactly thrilled. 'I'm in an outdoor lounge near the pool—'

'Fine. Don't move.'

As if she could. Toni felt her legs turn to jelly as she turned from the railing and took a chair at one of the tables, facing the entrance that was delineated by an archway of tropical ferns and twining deep purple bougainvilleas.

And steeled herself for the most important meeting of her life.

Rafe's heart was clamouring as he took to the street, making his way through the endless bustle to Antonia's hotel. After the way they'd parted, he couldn't believe she was here. Surely she'd come to reconcile. Surely. Why else? But old habits died hard so he'd make no assumptions. Play it cool. But his heart was far from playing it cool. Instead it thumped against his chest wall like a native drum as he crossed the bridge over the lotus pond and entered the hotel's walled garden.

Toni's breathing almost hitched to a halt when she

saw him weaving his way through the pre-lunch crowd that was beginning to gather. He was wearing chinos and a pale blue cotton shirt. And looked so familiar her heart ached just at seeing him. She stood to greet him, wanting to throw herself into his arms. But her guide book on protocol had decreed that overt displays of affection were considered disrespectful. Instead, she waited.

Seeing her standing there, in her long cotton skirt and simple button-down blouse, Rafe took a breath so deep it hurt, causing his heart to knock harder against his ribs. He wanted to vault over the tables and run to her, gather her up. But that kind of behaviour would be frowned on here. Instead, he held himself in check. After all, she mightn't want to be *gathered* up, he reminded himself in a swift reality check. After the way they'd parted, nothing was certain here. Nothing.

'Hi...' Toni felt heat high on cheekbones as he stood in front of her.

Rafe moved a hand to brush her cheek but pulled it back before it could connect. Instead, he took both her hands and held them loosely. He looked down at her.

'I'm real,' she said on a jagged laugh.

'I know...' His eyes burned like emeralds. 'When did you arrive?'

'Couple of hours ago. The hotel's a bit posh,' she said, as if she needed to explain. 'But the travel agent said it was safe because I was on my own...'

'It's a good place. Our World Health people always stay here when they visit.'

She nodded. And this was yet another of these ridiculous conversations they seemed destined to have. 'Shall we sit down?'

'Ah...' He looked around, letting her hands go and

planting them on his hips. 'It's nearly lunchtime. Would you like a drink?'

'That'd be nice.'

'Lager? It goes well with Asian food.'

She managed a fleeting smile. 'Fine.'

Rafe returned with the glasses of icy cold beer.

Toni picked up her glass. 'What should we drink to?'

Determined to keep things low-key until he knew where he stood—where they stood—he said, 'Let's drink to a happy holiday for you. How long are you staying?'

'Five days. It was a package offer.' And I wasn't sure how long I'd need to set things right between us, Toni added silently.

'You can see a lot in five days,' Rafe said helpfully. 'Angkor Wat is a must see for any tourist. I'm sure the hotel will arrange a guide for you.'

She'd read about the amazing temple complex in her guide book and had been hoping Rafe would visit it with her. But, of course, if he was working… 'You've been there?'

'Many times. It's heart-stopping. The guide will explain the significance of every Hindu and Buddhist god. Both religions receive tribute there. And you won't have seen anything like the giant kapok trees. And the markets are fantastic.'

Toni felt her eyes glaze. This was going right over her head. Rafe was sounding like a tourist guide himself. She hated it but she was at a loss to know what to say to feel close with him again. 'You look well,' she managed at last.

'I *am* well.' He hitched a shoulder impatiently. Hell, had she come to check up on his health? Was that it?

Suddenly the atmosphere between them was crackling with instability.

'And the inoculation programme?' Toni ploughed on.

He blinked. 'Sorry?'

'The inoculation programme.'

He gave a tight shrug. 'We've managed to contain the spread of the disease. Unfortunately, we lost a few of the children but that was inevitable.'

And he seemed calm about it. Philosophical. Professional. Toni felt lost in a sea of confusion. He had his life back on track. He belonged here. And she felt alienated, foolish. For once her instincts had let her down. She had to make her escape. Be anywhere but here. With him. 'I shouldn't have come here…' she whispered through a throat so tight it hurt.

Rafe took such a deep breath his chest heaved. The pain in her words grabbed at his gut. He still felt stunned seeing her after all this time. And thrown right out of his comfort zone. 'Then why exactly did you come, Antonia?'

She gave a bitter laugh. 'Well, silly me, I missed you. And I thought there might still be a chance for us. But I see I was wrong. You're obviously in your element here. You've moved on.' She half rose. 'And I think it's time I do as well.'

'Toni, wait! Don't go making assumptions. I'm a bit stunned that you've come all this way…' Stunned? He was poleaxed. 'Don't go. Please…' His voice was rough, halfway between a whisper and a groan. He looked around wildly. 'We need to go somewhere and talk.'

'I have a room…' Her voice shook.

'Give me the number and go up. I'll book on the same floor.' His gaze shimmered over her. 'And then I'll come to you. It'll be better that way.'

Protocol again. Toni bit her lip. 'You don't have any luggage.'

'It won't be a problem. They know me here. I'll tell them my luggage is on its way. And it would be. He knew that for certain.

Toni felt a wild mix of emotions tumble around inside her as she waited for Rafe. She walked out onto her balcony, turned round and walked back inside. Oh, lord, it was like waiting for a first date to arrive.

When the soft knock came on her door, she took a deep breath and went to let him in. 'Hello.' Her voice was a breath of sound. 'Have you checked in?'

'Yes.' He reached out, moving his hands very gently beneath the silky fall of her hair, encircling her nape.

Toni felt herself trembling, vibrations moving through her body as his mouth trailed down from her temple, across her cheek, finally taking and closing in on her mouth.

With an urgent need throbbing down low in her body she sank into his arms and they were kissing like they'd never kissed before.

'Oh, Rafe…'. Toni finally eased away, blinking the sudden tears from her eyes. 'I'm so sorry about the way we parted. I walked out on you.'

'You don't need to apologise,' he said softly. 'I'm not without fault. I went at everything like a bull at a gate.'

'But I was so…judgmental. I should have understood you had important work to do here.'

'And I should have been more upfront from the beginning.' He heaved in a long breath and let it go. 'I love you, Antonia. And that's what I should have spelled out before I left.'

Toni's heart beat faster at the sincerity of his declaration and the words she'd so longed to hear. 'And I would have told you right back.'

His green eyes glinted. 'So, say it now.'

'I…love you, Rafe. Oh, I do.' It felt such a relief to be able to say it that she laughed.

He smiled down into her happy face. 'We're sorted, then?'

'I think we are, aren't we?'

The curve of her bottom felt good snuggled into his palms and he nodded. 'So, how are we going to spend these five days of your holiday?'

'Well…' She fiddled with the button on his shirt front. 'Perhaps I could just fit in around your duty hours at the hospital. You're not working every minute, are you?'

'I'm not working at all,' he said. 'I finished yesterday. My work here is done. I was coming home. To you.'

'Oh…' She snuggled closer. 'Then we were both on the same mission.'

'It seems like it,' he said softly, touching a hand to her hair, lingering over its softness. 'And just so we have things straight, and I don't care what it takes, I'm never letting you go again.'

Joy, clear and pure, streamed through her. 'And that goes for me as well. I'm not letting *you* go, either, Rafe Riccardi.' She frowned a bit. 'I can't believe the needless unhappiness we've put each other through—'

'Hush,' he said, placing his finger on her lips. 'No looking back. This is our whole new beginning.'

'Then where better to start it than here in this beautiful place? Come and look,' she invited, gently disengaging from his arms and holding out her hand. 'This is what's called a spa suite,' she said almost shyly. 'The bath is almost big as a car.'

'Never mind the bath.' Desire was roaring through him like a storm. He had his brave, beautiful Antonia back. He wanted just to hold her, love her as she deserved to be loved. He tipped up her chin before urgently caressing her mouth. 'Does this place have a bed?'

'What a silly question.' Very slowly, she began to unbutton his shirt, all the while staring up into his tautened face. With his shirt hanging open, she began moving her hands in caressing little semi-circles over the tanned skin of his chest. 'Shall we try it out?'

His gaze deepened and darkened. 'I think it would be very remiss of us not to.'

Next morning.

Rafe and Toni were enjoying breakfast on the poolside deck at the hotel. 'This fruit is truly fabulous,' she said, as the red papaya melted against her tongue.

'And so was last night.' His look was tender. 'You continue to amaze me, Antonia.'

She wrinkled her nose at him but her smile was tender in return. 'What are we doing today?'

He dug into his blueberry pancake with obvious pleasure. 'Any preference?'

'I want to get some presents to take home.'

'So, the markets? What else?'

She hesitated, not sure how he would react to her request. 'I'd like to see your hospital.'

He brought his head up slowly. It was the last thing he'd thought she'd want to do. 'Are you sure? I mean, you're on holidays.'

She flicked a hand in dismissal. 'I need to see for myself the kind of work you've done here, Rafe. It's all part of who you are. It would mean a lot to me.'

'No problem. We can do that. You can meet Ari. I've told him all about you.'

Toni looked taken aback. 'What did you tell him?'

Rafe hitched a shoulder in a shrug. 'Just that you were the most beautiful woman in the world and that I'd stuffed things up with you. And that as soon as my work was done, I was going home to Australia to win you back.'

'Oh, my God...' She took his outstretched hand across the table. 'I don't know what to say.'

'What do you think about marriage?' He expelled the words as though they might have burned him.

Toni blinked. *Wow*, this was right out of left field. 'In general or to you?'

His grip on her hand tightened. 'Don't split hairs, Ms Morell. To me, of course.'

She smiled mistily. 'I think it would be lovely. But what about you? Is it something you want to do again?'

'With my history, you mean?'

'It has to be the right decision for you,' Toni insisted.

'OK...' Rafe knew there were still words to be said, answers to be given. Hearts to be bared and made whole again. 'What I had with Gabrielle was nothing like a marriage should have been. I know that now. But with you...' He stopped and looked at her. 'So different.' He shook his head as if it still amazed him. 'You light up my life.'

'I think that's a song.'

He smiled. 'And there I was thinking I was getting better at expressing my feelings.'

'I think you do wonderfully well.' She looked into his eyes, seeing the sheen of tenderness. 'You make me feel so loved, Rafe.'

'I always will,' he promised. 'Uh—I have something

for you.' He reached into his shirt pocket and pulled out a tiny silk bag. 'I was going to give you this when I got back home—that's if you still wanted—well, I'd like you to have it now…with my love.'

Heart overflowing, Toni took the scrap of silk and opened the drawstring at the top. 'It's a ring…'

'Well, fancy that,' he mocked, but gently. 'I had it made especially.'

'It's beautiful.' Toni looked down at the exquisitely fashioned ring. It was wide, with a lotus flower edged with tiny diamonds in the centre on a band of white gold studded with sapphires. 'Oh, Rafe…I love it…'

He gave an audible sigh of relief. 'That's one hurdle over.' He held out his hand for the ring and slipped it on her finger. His gaze held hers steadily. 'Will you marry me, Antonia?'

She nodded, too close to the edge to speak.

Grinning, Raph cupped a hand to his ear. 'Sorry, I didn't quite get that.'

Toni batted the happy tears away, her new ring sparkling as it caught the morning sun. 'Yes, I'll marry you, Rafe.' She managed a watery smile. 'I can't believe we're doing this over breakfast in a public place. I can't even kiss you.'

He took her hand as if reaffirming their commitment. 'We'll make up for it later. Where do you want to get married?'

Toni looked dreamily at her ring. 'I've always thought St Anne's would be pretty special. And it's where we first…connected, if you recall?'

He nodded. 'St Anne's it is then.'

'Have you booked your flight home?' Toni asked.

'Not yet. And now that you're here, we could fly home together.'

'And in the immediate future...' She paused. 'Where is *home* going to be for us?'

'Ah...' He took her hand again. 'I need to talk to you about that.'

Toni felt an odd glitch in her breathing. That sounded a bit ominous. What if he wanted to go on working in the developing world? Could she work by his side, live his dream with him? There was only one answer. Of course she could. They were matching parts of the same whole. He was her *one*. 'Better talk to me, then,' she said carefully.

'You realise Joe is back at Forrestdale?'

'Of course. They had a wonderful time in Italy.'

'But it seems the trip has left them with a taste for adventure. He and the family want to move on.'

'They do?' Toni was startled. 'He's not said anything—neither has Cath. How do you know all this?'

Rafe's mouth drew in. 'We've been in touch. Joe's been offered a senior post at the Randwick in Sydney. But the board at Forrestdale won't release him until they have a replacement.'

Toni looked wide-eyed as everything began falling into place. 'Are you thinking of applying, by any chance?'

'I am. But ultimately it has to be a joint decision for us.'

Toni could hardly believe the joy she felt. 'I think it would be amazing to begin our lives together in Forrestdale, amongst our friends.'

Rafe's green gaze lit. 'So, I'll go ahead and speak to Bernie?'

She nodded happily.

'I might not get it, of course,' he warned.

Toni made a not-too-polite huff of disbelief. 'Bernie will boast he headhunted you.'

Rafe chuckled. 'It feels good to be going back home together, doesn't it.'

'Magic.' She looked dreamy and then sobered. 'Is working at Forrestdale going to be enough for you, Rafe? I mean, career-wise'

'Are you asking if I want to keep working for MSF?'

'I suppose... But I want you to know that if you do, even occasionally, I'll go with you.'

'Thank you for that.' His eyes squeezed shut and when he opened them they were lit with purpose. 'I feel rewarded in countless ways that I've been able to use my medical training to help the less fortunate. And I'll never forget it. But that part of my life is over now. I need to put down roots. With you.'

Toni felt she was overdosing on sheer happiness. 'We'll have to get a home in Forrestdale, then.'

'Well—we kind of have one,' he said vaguely. 'Joe and Cath want to sell. I put in an offer. But I wouldn't have done anything definite without your approval,' he added hurriedly.

Toni's eyes opened wide in amazement. 'But I'd love to live in that beautiful home. We could have an amazing life there. Raise our family there.' Her gaze faltered. 'You'd like children, wouldn't you, Rafe?'

Looking at her, so sweet and sexy in her cheesecloth shirt open all the way down and the snug little vest top underneath showing just a peep of cleavage, Rafe knew a certainty he wouldn't have believed a year ago. He felt as though he had the world in his hands. He'd never felt so...grounded. Loving Antonia had changed his life. And with her as their mother, their children would be amazingly loved and bright and beautiful. 'I'd love us to have kids,' he said throatily. 'All this is meant to be, Antonia. I've never been so sure of anything in my life. I promise to be true to you and make you happy.'

'Then right back at you, Riccardi.' She smiled, her gaze as clear and soft as the air around them. Reaching for the delicate porcelain teapot, she began to pour. 'Now, I wouldn't want to rush my future husband, but don't you have a phone call to make?'

* * * * *

A sneaky peek at next month...

Medical Romance™

CAPTIVATING MEDICAL DRAMA—WITH HEART

My wish list for next month's titles...

In stores from 2nd November 2012:

☐ Maybe This Christmas...? – Alison Roberts

& A Doctor, A Fling & A Wedding Ring – Fiona McArthur

☐ Dr Chandler's Sleeping Beauty – Melanie Milburne

& Her Christmas Eve Diamond – Scarlet Wilson

☐ Newborn Baby For Christmas – Fiona Lowe

& The War Hero's Locked-Away Heart – Louisa George

Available at WHSmith, Tesco, Asda, Eason, Amazon and Apple

Just can't wait?

Visit us Online

You can buy our books online a month before they hit the shops! **www.millsandboon.co.uk**

1012/03

Special Offers

Every month we put together collections and longer reads written by your favourite authors.

Here are some of next month's highlights— and don't miss our fabulous discount online!

On sale 19th October

On sale 2nd November

On sale 2nd November

Save 20% on all Special Releases